D0242954

The Standard Life of a Temporary Pantyhose Salesman

Aldo Busi was born in Montichiari, Italy, in 1948. He has translated Goethe, John Ashbery, Christine Stead and J. R. Ackerly into Italian, as well as *Alice in Wonderland*.

Aldo Busi is the author of *Seminar on Youth* and *The Standard Life of a Temporary Pantyhose Salesman*. English translations of his other works, *La Dolfina Bizantina* and *Sodomie in Corpo II*, are forthcoming.

by the same author

Seminar on Youth

ff

ALDO BUSI

The Standard Life of a Temporary Pantyhose Salesman

Translated by Raymond Rosenthal

faber and faber

LONDON · BOSTON

First published in Italian as
Vita standard di un venditore provvisorio di collant
in 1985 by Editore S.p.A., Milan
First published in translation in the USA in 1988
by Farrar, Straus and Giroux, Inc.
and simultaneously in Canada
by Collins Publishers, Toronto
First published in Great Britain in 1989
by Faber and Faber Limited
3 Queen Square London WC1N 3AU
This paperback edition first published in 1990
Reprinted in 1990

Printed in England by Clays Ltd, St Ives plc

A CIP record for this book is available
from the British Library

ISBN 0-571-14162-5

To Giorgina Washington

Contents

Book One

Book Two

Book Three

In less than five minutes I shall have thrown my pen into the fire, and the little drop of thick ink which is left remaining at the bottom of my ink-horn, after it—I have but half a score of things to do in the time—I have a thing to name—a thing to lament—a thing to hope—a thing to promise, and a thing to threaten—I have a thing to suppose—a thing to declare—a thing to conceal—a thing to choose, and a thing to pray for—

—*The Life and Opinions of Tristram Shandy, Gentleman.*

BY LAURENCE STERNE

BOOK ONE

Monday.

Giuditta drags along a rag doll and stares straight ahead. Angelo drives at a crawl, turning his head toward her. The little girl is not fazed. She walks barefoot in her small blue bathing suit and the dusty road is as sinuous as a dried-up brook. Giuditta advances like a betrayed but proud bather over the tar's burning coal. Angelo smiles at her, in vain. If only he could take her with him to the lake, watch her in the water, dry her, comb her, set her before the ice-cream counter. Giuditta disappears down the slope; voices rise calling her. The doll is speared on a yucca thorn. Could this be the end reserved for "he-whores"?

One of the central themes of Angelo's cogitations, even when at the wheel, is the impossibility of lightning revenge, of revenging oneself "immediately." To plan revenge usually means seeing it fray between one's fingers by dint of perfecting the weave.

Now, one of the most intense moments, the most exalting of his improper past, one of those which justify the existence of existence, is tied to the memory of a revenge which, fortuitously, or due to the enemy's indigestion, was accomplished simultaneously, or almost, with a desire for vengeance which had just preceded it.

It happened at the so-called Grotte di Catullo at Sirmione last year, in the summer of '82, when he decided to take the thermal nose-and-throat cure paid for by his health insurance. Having finished his inhalations, he climbed up to the Grotte, supposedly an archaeological site: everything peaks, little or nothing hollowed out by excavations. He entered by climbing over the iron gate and descended a jagged stairway, coasting along the eastern side of the peninsular point. Arrived at the kiosk, he jumped over a wire fence amid a growth of black-eyed Susans dirtied with coffee grounds and small sugar packets, and he was on the rocky beach.

He likes to think about it when he drives, he becomes more easily distracted in his enjoyment and is sure he won't have any accidents.

That time he was starting to walk along the slabs covered with a slimy patina and his feet under control followed one another toward the water, when he saw a hand open like a fan. The gesture of greeting and the smile were definitely directed at him.

It was the man whom for four days Angelo had seen there without seeing him, never any exchange of words or looks. A guy about thirty like himself, good athletic physique, the somewhat reserved and absent air of one who tries to pretend that he happens to be there by mistake, chestnut-colored hair, long at the nape of the neck, white or red shorts, long, sturdy legs. He always turned his back.

Now, for Angelo, Sirmione had always been a place of dutiful business and not initiation. One goes to the Grotte with one's head full of pneuma and it doesn't even seem that there ever was a first time or a first encounter. And the conversations: detailed and always the same and formulated in the same way. It is the repository of a pleasant boredom which excludes unexpected or exciting things. A kind of sunbathing harem for fading odalisques and eunuchs perfidious for convention's sake and contemplative by vocation. He very much liked to go there to see himself age in the faces of the others still remaining young. Everybody thought the same thing. Everybody caught in the rituals of habit and nobody ever suddenly for one moment asking himself: what the hell am I coming here for? One answer: to see the devil let his horns grow limp and leave behind chips of goat hoof and tufts of tail hair. In order to change one's spots and lose the hopeless illusion of vice. It is exactly because of the lassitude of the hellos and the museumlike chatter that Angelo, feeling onstage in this terrarium of memoryless amphibians, never did anything to bring to the footlights some dormant expectations, some letch. The sexual backdrop is skimmed over at the height of surreal winks, the flesh so far down at the bottom of the shopping list that one never gets to it. He—perhaps the only one to break the sacrality of ritual with his terroristic causticness, or, if he is in a vein of martyrdom, with the other "inner" polemic on how to affirm oneself homo-socially, that is, with bazookas—saw only sexless angels around himself and in himself. There the law of courtship and conquest reigned; and he was much more excited by a quick blandishment than by a mannered collision between prey and hunter. Pursuit is fatiguing, like exchanging season's greetings, vows, faithfulness, or looking forward to debility, or even facing each other for too many minutes. No, he was an observer, like a lizard on a beam.

Here too, certainly, it would have been lovely to desire and be clearly desired and go on to that ineffable "point" of sex without planning to shut the door in the face of the world or turning pumpkins into carriages. Take only a few steps to meet, know how to remain immobile face to face for the time necessary and concentrate in a shared mental state, if possible, then move away with one step to the side and proceed, starting again to walk straight ahead.

Now, seeing this smile of friendly complicity and the cordially waving hand, Angelo had thought to find in it the signal of a route traveled halfway against all expectations, and he plunged toward the remaining goal, toward this completely unknown man who was calling him. And the surroundings: the midday light fulminating from the sky against sea rocks, olive trees, the scales of steel hulls in the water, and in there, in this immobile aquarium where nothing ever lifts the blood, the direct smile of someone you like.

Angelo, step by step, careful not to slip, realized that during those four days all he had done was follow out of the corner of his eye this aloof, disdainful figure of a man, even when he thought he was looking at the shape of the Manerba promontory down there on the shore, or the Hovercraft darting away.

He approached him without looking at him, continuing to imagine him as, without effort, everything about him soberly rose in his memory, which had registered the fleshy mouth, the long and slightly asymmetrical nose, the hairless chest, the fan-shaped ears protruding over the smoothed-back hair, and the red or white colors of shorts worn on alternate days.

Angelo found it difficult to hide his general unhappiness, which vertiginously twisted together in a sensation of euphoria several unexpectedly sharpened senses. Even on the tips of his fingers he felt a notion of the future, of that very same evening. "Oh" the man said laconically "I took you for someone else."

Angelo's eyes linger on those beautiful lips now seen in the flesh: they discover teeth yellowed just a little by tartar. Another justification and the narrow pass of the crown is driven into the gums, leaving between tooth and tooth interstices, through which issue sibilant sounds of smugness, sparkles of second thoughts, the dismissiveness of "I'm sorry." He is fascinated by this row of teeth which incinerates him word by word, and reminds him of a school outing to the Risorgimento Ossuary at Solferino–San Martino, the neutrality of the skulls, which no longer expect a great deal from the end of the world.

Swallowing and lost by now, he had said, "Oh, you too look a lot like a childhood friend of mine. He's in jail, in Hong Kong or Bangkok, I don't know which. I knew you couldn't be him."

"That'll do. Things like this happen." And he falls silent. For him the encounter is over; in fact, it's lasted too long.

Angelo stands there, embarrassed, partly bowed over those serrated grafts of bony death and features fished up out of a school satchel, a man reduced to a small pile of shoved-down desires, which from blithe and bright are dulled in a pap of fury and humiliation in which he merges, turbid, and fetid to himself. Angelo says in a breath:

"Well, if I'm not that friend of yours, so much the better. It's an excuse to get to know each other now."

It is incredible how, always, he has this unfortunate ability to formulate perfect sentences not marred by exhausted or excessive irony, when perhaps something mumbled, uncertain, arousing sympathy or compassion or liberating laughter, would be more profitable.

The other says curtly: "But I don't want to know you. Tell me, didn't it ever happen to you that you mistook a person? So get a move on, right? How am I supposed to tell you? That's it."

"You're the one who bothered me. I didn't."

"Enough. I'm through talking" and he turns to the other side, toward a man and a woman, at whom he smiles, vexed, as if to say, "They *all* pick on me."

Angelo had stood there, his gaze at water level, and did not know which way to turn. He didn't know whether he should say hello or goodbye or just stay there like that, swollen with unwanted breath. If only he had had quicker reflexes, and more courage: jump on him and beat him up. He had called him and now he was telling him he did not feel like talking or getting to know him *because he wasn't he.*

He returned to his rock; he no longer felt like swimming. He would have gone in only if he could have drowned right away. He felt choked up by that humiliation mixed with attraction which now, confused, acquired from the rejection an overflowing sharpness that shook his lungs. It was stimulating to be rejected, to be mistaken for *another*—one might as well admit it. It forced one to go beyond the ritual, the brain jumped off the usual tracks of a renunciation that doesn't cost anything. The sudden hatred, mixed with desire and now shattered into paltry self-justification, stunned in an unusual manner, summed up life.

That afternoon he had spent some time playing with ideas on what to do, without ever turning his head again toward the site of the insult, or even elsewhere. The colors plunged down in victimized languor, cowardly punishments to be delivered within the mind's enclosure. Beneath closed lids—while he seemed to be working on his tan—he saw the skeleton of death: tore off his scalp with his own teeth, stripped the flesh from the skull, spat out the gray matter to the frogs. If only he could tear him limb from limb! He pulled on his pants very slowly, somebody asked for some mundane explanation of why he was leaving so early, and once out of everyone's sight, he began to run beyond the wire fence.

He thought he had always been so polite and fraternal whenever he said "No." He knew he wasn't being honest.

That same evening he received a telephone call from Galeazzo, a policeman in Naples, an invitation. His course of treatment, however, was not yet finished. But he decided that after his inhalations he would return to the Grotte, see him again, even be compelled to macerate in that inconclusive hatred for one week more. He called Lometto—his own car had engine trouble again—and got Lometto to accompany him to the railroad station in Verona, missed the 12:39 a.m. train, the next was at 2:37. Lometto had left. He stayed there, roaming around the station amid crises of abstinence, giggles of cocaine addicts, the "let's love each other" of drunken bums; a girl was lifting up her skirt and had nothing underneath, a French transsexual with hair styled like a sansculotte and his pimp, dazed with sleepiness: for years now he no longer felt any attraction for that railroad fauna. Then four guys of the railroad police surround him, ask him for his ticket, his papers—

everything was in order. But one of these nocturnal idlers, so odiously well educated, wanted to know why he was going to Naples.

"You won't believe me, but I'm going to stick it up the ass of one of your colleagues" he said smoothly and without detaching his stare of fixed cordiality from that of the southern youngster, whose fingers were cracking their joints to give themselves a governmental air.

"Follow us."

They wasted an hour of his time in a cubicle, one standing by the door, his pistol half cocked, two with their hands on their hips, the fourth rummaging through his tote bag. The transsexual made an infernal racket and kept squeaking in French "In Italy it's always like this! Once a day! Every day!" One of them asked him to translate, since Angelo had advised the imbecile to calm down, and defended Italy.

"I charge twenty thousand an hour as an interpreter" Angelo answered. "Or at least twenty thousand courtesies."

"So you're going to put it up the ass of one of our colleagues."

"I insist on being addressed properly or I won't answer."

"So you're going to put it up the ass of one of our colleagues, eh? A faggot?"

"And not only are you to address me as 'sir'; as soon as I get out of here, I'll go to police headquarters to make a complaint and right after that to the newspapers. You either take me in or leave me alone."

"Did you hear that? What a pleasant fellow, our 'sir' . . ."

"I am a pleasant fellow, I know. And also that colleague of yours in Naples is pleasant. You don't push it up the ass of people who aren't. That business of the 'affront' is nothing but an excuse invented by the southern fraternity."

Attack was the best spell. To cast a spell on them in order not to get a good beating in places where the bruises don't show. Usually it was the meek ones who came out of it battered, because they didn't know how to play the game.

"Do you know, you big faggot, that we can haul you in for insulting an officer? Or keep you as long as we want? Or . . ."

"Keep your hands to yourself! Point one: call me 'sir' and it would be a good idea for you to hurry and call the police barracks in my town, so you can check out my rap sheet and I won't miss the train. Point two: to take it up one's ass is not a crime, and if it were I would travel with a machine gun. If anything, it is by now a pastime accessible to everyone, even the police. Point three: I know another colleague of yours—and I took down his license number—who one evening here in Verona forced me with his pistol to my head to give him a blow job. And he might turn out to be one of your commanding officers, with wife and kids . . ."

Angelo loved to listen to himself; panic created aurally irresistible concatenations of self-evident spells. They politely accompanied him to the train; one of them told him to get in touch when he returned, "to have coffee together."

He was ashamed of having such an immaculate police record; he had nothing he could boast of. In recompense, he could punctually take all the trains he wished. And he was also ashamed of those so frustratingly furnished and worn-out buffooneries, his "letters to the editor," stuff that probably did not have the slightest effect even in the barracks. He had no previous convictions, not because he was so shrewd like a lot of people, but because he was conformistically law-abiding in his reprisals. In fine, anyone looking at him must see a cleric's face, and that always pleased everyone. On the train he was surprised at how his cold-bloodedness was traversed by a warm current of reformistic cowardice, the desire to rebel by belonging. But this was the price of getting away from the cliché of differentness, of scandal, of a not very noble and hysterical old-style exclusion. He preferred to invent a new hysteria for himself. In Naples he was forced to face up to an unpleasant sequel: Galeazzo had anal condylomas—Angelo translated it for him: cockscombs. He hadn't seen Galeazzo for two years and the southern situation had become even more frazzled and fistulated. His answer was that he too had been grazed by the doubt that "something was wrong" but, being in the police, he was afraid that if he went to be operated on, central headquarters would find out. Angelo realized that his friend felt himself to be at the center of interest of the Secret Service, venereal section, and that it was impossible to convince him otherwise. In a fraction of a second, Angelo took a survey of the Southern Assistance Program and asked to be taken to the telephone exchange. If the need for an epic was so deeply rooted also when it came to cockscombs, if the only things the South had left were its fears and its cock-dramatics, there was nothing Angelo could do about it. When he came out of the telephone booth, he waved the scalpel of a sudden commitment: he must leave for Holland the very next day, as soon as he got back, because of the pantyhose. Galeazzo objected: But why? He hadn't even rested after his trip, and what about Amalfi? And Capri? On the steps of the train the civilian's farewell contritely skimmed over "the electric scalpel, it's nothing" while the uniform's laudatory goodbye continued to cruise "down Capri's Via Krupp."

In the compartment Angelo had felt ill at ease about Jürgen Oelberg, his friend who was always so avid for new illnesses. Jürgen had not yet added cockscomb to his collection and he, who had been right on the brink of managing to catch it, had run away, like any ordinary mortal still contaminated by the categories of *illness* and *cure*. But Angelo was fed up to his gills with clinical analyses and rubber gloves. It was just as well to resign oneself to dying of health and not say a word about it to Jürgen.

The moment he was home he was unable to resist for another instant the impending inhalation.

The man with the white or red shorts was having a light snack, together with that man and that woman, who were just as haughty, without reason, since both were covered with freckles and freckles entail the loss of all regality on lakes which aren't Scandinavian. It seemed to Angelo that three minutes and not three days had passed since he had suffered that insult. He must try to think of something else. At Portese an old innkeeper-fisherman had complained that the catch was becoming increasingly meager because "the lake is on an incline" due to dumping. Below Riva he saw a wedge, as if under a table leg, and water overflowing in all directions of the imaginary geographical vulva. But the first to be overwhelmed and sucked in by this "incline" were still those three, placid and masticating, with their backs turned.

It was at that instant that he saw the yacht, which certainly had been there for hours, pop out from nowhere and cautiously approach the surfacing rocks.

Angelo was very attentive to the signs of social opulence and genetic misery which simultaneously intertwine in the same family. In his opinion one of the things that were most appalling (but splendidly destructive: and here nothing like *nature* could intervene with a more candidly vindictive and subversive hand) was an economic empire founded by a couple of *dynamic* and *capable* persons with leadership aptitude who, as their sole heir, had generated a seriously handicapped or mentally impaired being. In this multifaceted misfortune he saw the drama of a capitalistic quest for immortality gone bad at the root, rendered here and now ridiculous and absurd, although the shattered dream does not because of this bow moment by moment to the irreparable evidence of the chromosomal hoax.

The couple's overall economic and future power could continue to be exalted and multiply on other pretexts: to insure a future for the unfortunate offspring, subjected in the meantime to inhuman reeducational tortures to reaffirm in the betrayed parents the illusion of a future after the future. Very often the monsters, impotent, pretended to cooperate, pretended to understand, pretended to wish not to be what they are. And now from that yacht with its exaggerated tonnage for lacustrine navigation, a tender is lowered by a servant and three figures in bathing suits row up to the nearest rock. Evidently none of the three wants to get wet; the woman holds a wicker basket in her hand and is the first to set her feet in the water, and she now proceeds ahead of the other two. The lady, in her well-preserved late fifties, her hair an artificial white, has soon found shelter from the high sun beneath the olive trees, but the little girl behind her has started to splash about and the husband has stopped alongside his daughter and begun to wave his index finger at her. But the little girl wants no part of learning how to swim. She shrieks like an animal caught in a trap: short screams which even in the midst of the summer hubbub have raised the interest of the bystanders.

Angelo came a bit closer because those sounds of fury mixed with fright seemed to echo out of him, from him, him who thought of nothing but hatred.

He saw two extremely pale, tiny eyes flit in the smooth forehead of the female mongoloid whom the father tried in vain to convince that she should relax with her armpits in the crooks of his elbows. The tiny hands cling with all their might to his arms and the hair on his chest, while he repeats the order without ever altering the tone of his voice, and adds German and affectionate words—"silly little girl"—"I'm your daddy"—to the lifted index finger whenever he manages to free a hand. The little girl screams and swallows water and suddenly, despite the terrified glance darting from pupils with their idiotic brilliance, her mouth gapes wide in a smile which has the hallucinated sweetness of someone trying to please.

Another German has risen from a rock and started to shout, gesticulating with one hand: "Leave her alone, stop it, nasty swine, do you want her to drown?"—certainly acquaintances, one of them shouting from anonymity at someone famous, an improvised newspaper-reading knight. The child's father did not react, ignored it. The woman under the olive trees, a subscriber to misfortune, leafed through *Bild am Sonntag* and showed no interest whatsoever, not even about opening the wicker basket. Perhaps she was used to all this, perhaps she was ashamed. From the poop the servant-sailor shouted threatening words at the German who had meddled with the attitude of someone who knows what it's all about.

Now from quite close by Angelo watched the expressions of that child (a young girl?): how at times she attempted an impossible abandon, how at others she opened wide her gray eyes, how she turned up the corners of that small slit of a mouth in a disarming smile of desperate trust, how she threw back her head with its long hair—with corkscrew curls, oh God—as if she were resting it on the block. She was the fat mongoloid of a steel and real estate empire, and everyone knew it.

The heiress was then left free to squawk and wallow like a graceless duck in the shallow water, until she reached the shore and ran up under the olive tree. Her mother barely raised her head from the cheap magazine and bestowed on her a public caress. Now the child was being dried off by her father with a bathrobe taken from the tender. The mother nibbled on a green apple. The offspring's corkscrew curls had gone limp and become a cruel, comical headdress. The old guy had started to pull a comb through it carefully, perhaps pressing the teeth too hard against the scalp. "*Mutti! Mutti!*" squeaked the mongoloid, and with her head quickly thrown back from the comb, she rubbed against the shoulder of the woman, who now rummaged in the basket and took a serious, lunar bite from the second apple, staring at her husband.

Angelo continued to stay there, not very far away, entranced. The little girl was good-natured, she furtively caressed her mother's knee, and without a word took the hand of the old man with the gray sideburns. Then the child's eyes meet Angelo's, she smiles at him in an open and loving way, he feels his blood stirred by white-hot emotion, sentimental as only that of an arid nihilist can be. There was so much generosity in that slightly coquettish look, so much unbreakable familiarity with the world, the reliance of one who has no other choice but that of not having any, and no longer any trace of the anguish of a short while back, the animal fear of the water. Sorrow did not fester in rancor. The little girl looked at him as if she were opening her eyes for the first time and seeing someone. The little girl was already a young woman. She seemed not to have any memory, memory of remote insults or sufferings coming one after the other, her hands were full of the convex caresses of her first menstruation. For the first person who might appear. For him. Then she forgot Angelo, began to eat with appetite, and when he again turned his head over there, to that spot which still had not been erased by the oblique furies of his thirst for vengeance bent on its own impossible dream of realization, he saw that the man with the white or red shorts and his two friends were looking in his direction, or just beyond, at the girl, and that all three had revealed the total foundation for their superiority and were now laughing a thin and vulgar laugh. Angelo did not care whether they laughed about him or the child or both of them. He felt sick, hatred rushed back to his brain in a devastating flare. Then it was as though everything, outside, projected the mirror of his thought: the man with the white or red shorts got up and, alone, walked to the water, dove in and began to swim with long strokes out from shore.

There are always a lot of motorboats passing in front of that stretch of beach. They make waves that are very high for a swimmer and, since there are also currents, nobody trusts himself to go any farther out than fifteen or twenty meters. There's always a propeller suddenly hurling toward you. The swimming is done lengthwise. And that is what Angelo is doing, savoring the acrid pleasure of meeting up with him in a few meters and continuing on, winning out over himself.

Then everything happened a trifle spectacularly, as in all tragedies that respect the Aristotelian unities, deprived of the rankling sedimentation of time dripped out in years and not instants: too sudden, no matter what one may say, and discounted, because this improvisation, this "present" lasts for innumerable acts, and just as many intermissions with always that pair of fixed pictures of the world's history from its origins onward. The head which goes underwater, the stroke which slows down, the hand which rises vertically and the long and violent wave of a motorboat which toots its horn, like a bell behind the flats of the usual rigmarole's eternity, and leaves. Certainly the wave, and a fatal indigestion due to a light snack. The first glug-glug between those nasty teeth, the certainty of being able to handle this that must now seize him . . . it's only forty meters and besides you can touch with your feet, but that bottom always becomes more elusive with every passing moment and the dilated pupil must perceive the bottom as always a little more definitive than that precise instant in which something universally inevitable is repeated in its detail and creates the event's horrified surprise, a few meters' depth of water or earth, which until then only concerned others. The certainty of not being like the others and of being able to handle this which every time sinks a bit deeper and surfaces a bit more choked. And Angelo, who has understood everything, is the only one, the only one interested now in contemplating those beautiful long locks which flit electrically through the water and sink. Other swimmers here and there, each on his own, all of them in any case at least twenty meters away. The only possible interlocutor for a mouth-to-mouth is he, the outcast. And he has stopped swimming and, for fear of not being caught by the terrorized eye of the freckled man by now at the end of his strength, he has stood up on the very rock the other will never again be able to reach, and Angelo would like to stare at him at least once, if only he were able to. There is no shadow of a doubt, no hesitation to discompose his deferent immobility before that offensive body which gulps in silence. And it is also a posthumous homage to Epaminonda from Mantua, who always told him that he had a sucker's heart, ready to be moved even by sons of bitches. How proud she would be of him, now, for his eye for an eye, tooth for a tooth.

He would like those wide-open bloodshot eyes and teeth to close with the image of his own eyes, cold and mocking, fixed forever in the retina. To enter as the last and first image in the "other world." To recover his own identity at the moment of the enemy's death, no longer be mistaken for someone else or for what one is not or what others wish one to be.

The woman and her companion get up and move to the water, incredulous in their pinkish, scorched skins. They shout something which shakes the torpor of the bodies lying under the sun. Limbs rise and enter the water hesitantly, the probable nuisance of being publicly summoned to a heroic deed, where one does not wish for preference. But Angelo feels good and, listening to the approaching bustle behind him, is comforted by the unnegotiable watery distance that separates the drowned man from his rescuers. The rocks under the water are laminated with a thin slime and sharp mollusks, and it is impossible to run. Oh, the Band-Aids and bandages that give expression to the dramatic talent of the woman in the kiosk! It would be more convenient for everyone if Angelo were to call from there the outboard skiff which now passes with its head in the clouds a few meters from where what by now is already a cadaver was seen popping up for the last time.

At the kiosk, around the body covered with purple and black bruises, a large crowd has gathered holding Popsicles and ice-cream sandwiches. The ice-cream vendor makes the mascara of her eyelashes playact Greekly. "Do you have change?" she declaims across the two small tables set side by side. She gives change the way other women, betrayed, set fire to home and children.

Angelo thinks that death would not be a sufficient revenge, that the best is yet to come, if it does come, for the living. Looks heavy with anguish graze him: all because of him, *who was the closest*, someone else has risked taking on the burden of a hero's gesture. Nobody dares ask for explanations, the moment is too powerful even for the most untrammeled hypocrites. Angelo meets every gaze, routs all words on the tips of tongues.

Nobody, outside the body stretched over the small tables, while a little fellow gives mouth-to-mouth respiration and presses his two hands on his chest, nobody knows how things really went. That's why Angelo stays there, and does not move away from the hostile circle: so that someone might give him the opportunity to announce the news that this was a revenge seized on the wing of an unknowing propeller, of a salami sandwich somewhat heavy on the stomach, and not the gesture of a pusillanimous person. Who knows whether the reddish woman and that washed-out friend of hers will, by attacking him, serve as his straight men. Both, stunned, glare at him with disgust. Angelo emanates an unflinching indifference that costs him very little. He has even taken off his sunglasses.

There, he has begun to breathe again weakly, gushes water; the eyes of his woman friend seem to brim with mucus; the crowd is kept back. It is always thought that in such cases it uses up too much air. The vendor draws and redraws a barrier all around, cursing and handing out bags of popcorn. Angelo's heart spurts with delirious throbs. Indifference is a debilitating pang. He would be satisfied if someone lent him an opening for just one remark.

The man raises his eyelids, moves his head slightly. It will take centuries for the ambulance-motorboat to cover the stretch all the way to the port of Desenzano and from there he will be taken to the hospital.

There is time. The endings of tragedies are banal, the important thing is that the right sentence be said, seeing that the daggers are made of tinfoil and only the sentence which rings down the curtain is lethal. Time therefore for the remark to be granted him but not before that breath which has mortally resumed breathing has carried to the brain all the oxygen and nitrogen necessary for awareness. Angelo takes a few steps forward, theoretically enters the resuscitated man's field of vision, intercepts his look of cringing horror, the humiliated look of those summoned back to life, of someone who from now on through a brief future will be better and will recognize his fellow man, unknown or mistaken, as he recognizes himself.

"He almost drowned!" the freckled woman now shrieks, hurling herself with unsheathed claws at Angelo. They stop her. Angelo is seized by a slight alphabetic vertigo because the remarks he excogitated during that slowed-down stretch of time are such and so many that the possibility of choice now intoxicates and annihilates him. The best is almost a commonplace, something that will reach everyone clearly and comprehensively, popular, at the expense of those more artistic but more ambiguous and not so direct: "it would have been no loss to humanity." And this is the remark he does not utter, but without paying any attention to the woman, shrugging his shoulders, he flashes it in a zigzag at the eyes of the man gasping on the Formica. Something plumpish and warm falls like a dead weight into the hand hanging at his side.

"*Komm hier*" scolds a female voice, appropriating those comforting fingers in his hand.

"It's all right, signora. What's your name?" Angelo asks in German, regaining control and staring lovingly at the mongoloid.

"*Renate, sehr gut sehr gut*" the little girl says in a wisp of a voice.

"Come, Soraya, why do you tell lies? Let's go" says the mother, pushing her gently by the shoulders.

The dry and once again twisted corkscrew curls chime forward reluctantly.

Then the young girl turned around and, unable to smile in any other way, whispered in German, narrowing her eyes:

"Bye-bye, little brother, little brother. Very good. Very good."

Had she too felt avenged?

• • •

How much more exciting it would be to think now that this was a premonitory sign of the misfortune that struck Giorgina Washington? But Angelo, on his way to the lake, does not grant himself romantic releases. It is only twelve-thirty, his meals have become increasingly hasty and desolate. Discussions about money with his old mother, the straitjacket of a cohabitation that becomes ever more constrictive. And twenty thousand dollars locked up in a safe-deposit box, unusable. Dollars which during that last two months have besides everything else grown twenty percent greener. Mysteries of international finance! Dry up harvests over there in order to regreen here, destroy in one place in order to bring forth flowers in another. Bludgeon seals up there in order to finance the unearthing of Troy down here. This is what is commonly called "life," with a sigh. A fortune segregated in a bank, and he almost completely broke. Put on a new roof, install a boiler—and farewell to three of his honestly earned six thousand dollars. The Nile—another thousand five hundred.

The old dented white Volkswagen, year of registration 1972, runs as best it can down the semi-deserted road.

He no longer gets phone calls from clients.

And also this morning not a sign from Lometto. Not that Angelo expects him to explain what really happened. One would need a deus ex machina to resolve this stalled situation. It is the anguish of half-wakefulness, the nightmare sweats that blend with resolute moods to drop it all, withdraw those dollars and disappear. Drop the threadbare revenge and hand over the tape and release him from that condition of consuming torment. Poor Lometto, after all, a great gesture of magnanimity toward an enemy whom Angelo cannot really bring himself to consider an enemy. Poor, my foot. A gesture which would cost him such circumspection in his moves and hiding places as to end in persecution mania, and he himself would be giving a definitive helping hand to Lometto's revenge without the latter moving a finger.

No, there is nothing left for him but to spend his afternoons at "the Terrazzine" and for the nth time take a turn around that immobile world, where nothing ever turned or ever will turn. Where the faces are incontinent dishes flat with the usual little highlighted pond disguised as luxurious Atlantis. Last night on television he saw a horror movie, with two Methuselahesque Hollywood muses. Now the title of that movie opportunely provides a sequence to his tormenting questions, which for more than two months have been the cause of insomnia and tension. The vulgarity of giving a title to the obfuscated screen of his thoughts has in itself a soothing effect. Being able to put to oneself a well-devised question in terms of synthesis and choice of words is already half the answer one is seeking. And cursing the big bug which refuses to remain in neutral at the stop signs, slamming the door after picking up the gift tote of the Automobile Club containing bathing suit, book, and towel, he inhales that image of the lake which pierces him like a spear dipped in phenolic acid. The pink and white oleanders with their scent of bitter almonds impart a nuance of cyanide to the sentence that he repeats, pushing aside the branches along the path:

"What Ever Happened to Giorgina Washington?"

It is because of the escarpment descending in ledges to the shore that this stretch of the coast is called the Terrazzine.

Going down the path on the far left of the parking lot there are birch trees, wild figs, clumps of violets and brambles, more bags of garbage than torn underpants hanging from the thorns burnt off in the spring. This is where the families come, hordes of Longobards who eat incessantly, rarely get wet, and, getting ready for dinner, while building fires with brush, watch the promenading of some emaciated, aging, effeminate little faggots. Who will want to remain isolated and lie down for five minutes behind a willow tree or a cluster of reeds, and then begin again to cruise among fathers, uncles, brothers-in-law, nephews, cousins, fathers-in-law, sons-in-law of all kinds intimidated by the swaying loins of the little faggots. Farther ahead are the "founders" of the beach, those who have given it its name, old glories who began to take over the place at the time of the Republic of Salò, protected by Fascist big shots and their comrades stationed in the small city almost right across the way, who often visited this place to discharge at bargain prices the tensions of the advancing defeat. It is said nowadays that the weather during that April and May 1944 was the same as now, August 1983, because the seasons too have changed. The heat in those days was already prevalent in March. Now, instead, etc.

Aside from Organista's silences and the quarter-soprano grunts of Magra dei Veleni—who, during the winters standing among the buttons and tassels and elastics of his notions store, has devoted himself to bel canto and learned all the female arias from Puccini to Verdi to

Ponchielli—it is all these joyous shouts and these thunderous welcomes ("Whore! Whore!") that cause so many motorboats and curious people on catamarans and surfboards to converge offshore there: they hear the voices but don't see anyone through the curtain of reeds in which narrow rows open leading to the water. The catamarans every so often accost Amanda, doing the dead man's float to show his metallic red tanga, and ask what's happening back there.

"Witless sisters" he answers with a haughty grimace, and they know as much as before. Amanda is willing to stand guard, but then he suddenly disappears, swallowed up by the abrupt turn of a motorboat which has a solitary helmsman. Or like that time last year invited to climb up the rope ladder onto the launch *La Spia d'Italia* rented by the draftees and released, after only eight hours of cruising, at Riva del Garda, tenderly deposited on the pier—sodden drunk, a hundred kilometers from the Terrazzine, and without underpants but with a tricolor kerchief wound like a turban on his head, he had come back at four o'clock in the morning raped at a hitchhiking average of once every three kilometers. Legends. Amanda is about five feet tall, he has a small, slightly horsey British face, blondish kinky hair, large blue eyes, a thin little nose, a vaguely rabbity mouth, small and pretty ears, new teeth every six months. With the tanga his thighs look a bit longer, his little body is very well made and without hair. One pair of pantyhose would be enough to dress him from head to foot, balaclava included.

The Terrazzine is a strip of gravel, three by twenty-five. It is no-man's-land—that is, theirs.

Larousse, the crossword-puzzle addict, works in a canning factory and has the night shift, and so he is never absent if the weather is good. He has given stomach cramps to everyone with industrially produced egg-and-vegetable salad. This year he showed up with flowing, flaming red curls and Angelo burst out laughing right in his face.

"It's not a dye, you know, it's a chemical product I use for tripe Parmesan!"

He and Pinuccia already broke up last season. They were together for seven years. Then, the inevitable crisis. Pinuccia continues to come there, undisturbed: in the space of a week their reciprocal indifference was so evident that the story of their mad passion seemed a fable.

Larousse still has a gripe against Pinuccia for financial reasons.

"If I had only known! The hell I would have put the apartment in his name! I picked him up out of the shit, he was covered with lice when I met him. And he up there in the Cambodia bushes, taking it in the fanny with me here waiting for him with the Cokes."

Pinuccia's looks are not even human enough for anyone to make a distinction out of gallantry or eccentricity between him and a canopy of dangling boughs. His face is rectangular, sloping from right to left, all nose and chin, long teeth, with a mushy gaze and thin hair on throbbing temples. He works in a sugar factory; he has diabetes. And one begins to understand something about this relationship when, having overcome the diffuse mist of effeminacy exhaling from that naked, straw-colored body, one lingers for a moment on his crotch and surroundings and rapidly turns one's gaze to that of his lover, he too stretched out naked under the sun, but with his knees pulled up and his legs bent and splayed, so that the buttocks stick out, evidentially. When soft, Pinuccia has a tool not inferior to twenty-five centimeters; Larousse, with his bullying, muscular pirate's manner, has an asshole like pokeweed, color magenta, slightly crinkled, the rusty nozzle of a watering can, so many circular, concentric crossword puzzles impaled on years of quizzes with the same prize: the insulin which Pinuccia's overworked pancreas, in making love, stuffed into him, tearing it from his brain.

Here nobody hesitates to leave the group, smack in the middle of an apocalyptic conversation about AIDS, and follow someone who has appeared over there in the water, dragging along a rubber boat with one hand and with the other picking on the herpes sore at the corner of his lips; or to follow some suit of clothes up the path leading to the parking lot formed by the two arms of packed dirt separated by a stretch of oleander. Beyond the highway begins the slope that leads to Cambodia—here too millions of steps have often with bare feet shaped paths that seemed to have been there since always. In the copse and the underbrush that precedes it as you go up, there are pursuits in Indian file, orderly pursuits without encounters. In this segregated intimacy there is no room for shelter. Beneath rustling steps the paths always say: "Farther, farther." It is the ritual of moving away.

This year the beach is but a small, leafless token among the reeds for the very latest generation, sixteen-year-olds with thin chains around the waist or ankles, a couple of professional transvestites, a slim little girl with a bold, challenging look who lifts weights and follows them everywhere like a bodyguard. Farther ahead there is a villa with a peristyle: the columns of cancerous tufa erode beyond the iron enclosure that surrounds the site, the small gate that gives access to the elevated dock is adorned by two Littorian fasces in wrought iron. Flaking shutters are always the same, locked but as if the slats, swollen by rain and weariness, had given up to fall one on top of the other once and for all. The weeds in the garden have welcomed various seeds carried by wind and insects; lilies with a real lily scent, snapdragons, a few sunflowers. There are no apparent electric lines to the villa, and when it was built one certainly could not talk about underground cables as today. Whoever lives there must consume tremendous quantities of wax. But the subject, just touched upon by Magra dei Veleni, immediately jumped on by Organista, has been dropped by the others. This is not the time for more ghosts.

Angelo has always stopped this side of the villa, as a rule he does not go beyond the transvestites' mini-clearing and he has never actually realized that, circling around the containing bulwark of the '30s mansion, the beach continues in small sandy kerchiefs all the way to the camping ground, and that beyond the pier there are even uninhabited boathouses. He never sits down in one particular place, also because this year he has good reason for having mental blanks, continuous and sudden. People talk to him and he doesn't answer, because he is running down that labyrinth of intentions, hypotheses, spidery facts that flicker around Giorgina Washington and her death and do not leave a trace behind—of how it happened. And his behavior is taken for haughtiness; but it is because he does not hear himself ask "You were saying?" suddenly to someone who has said nothing and not to him.

Sometimes he brings along his translation work and corrects and polishes his latest job. This month too he has skipped the fixed rate agreed upon with his mother and she has begun to curse her own stupidity, that if she had only known she certainly would not have put the house in his name. It's war.

When he's alone and must leave the folder with the typed sheets unguarded, he does not go for a swim, he waits until someone arrives whom he knows and will remain in the vicinity of his stuff all during his swim. Not that Angelo is distrustful; nothing has ever disappeared there. It's just that if by chance something were to happen to the completed, polished section of the translation, he would not have the heart to begin all over something already so perfectly sweated out against publisher and author: he would rather turn the pen against himself, that is, write something of his own, the extreme punishment, instead of translating. Oh, bless pantyhose and the one who invented them. What lovely times! And because of the "Dawn Syndrome," the sun has set on everything.

If he has not brought with him any twenty-one by twenty-nine point seven worries, he leaves his pants there with money and everything and strolls about in his bathing suit through the reeds and bushes. When he runs into some couple or a trio which gives signs of life with one hand and with the other smooths down its hair, he walks straight ahead saying "Excuse me!" The most sublime thought is a nullity compared to the most cretinous word.

No unfulfilled curiosity makes him regret not turning his head and spying. God, how he detested voyeurs, those emaciated old men who at an age for prayers decide to go into the maquis and now come here to torment compact young men with their horny irises. Fathers or grandfathers stripped of all sexual illusion regarding their old women at home, those who have decided now to come out into the open from behind the tree bark, tomcat catafalques with the sly arthritics, nothing to lose and everything not to gain. They believe they're entitled to enjoy starting right now, actively spying from the hopper of an evening's consolation which by this time is permanently unoccupied. To enjoy: within the limits granted by their having a strong stomach, carving out a libido for themselves between a hair setting and a white cotton outfit. The ones watched are Italian, therefore elegant. Bereft of all lucid mating urge. Be careful you don't get me dirty. No, for goodness' sake! not on the grass. Afraid of muddying their shoes. Stern or vacant gaze of the watched dandies, balancing on their unwindable laundry line stretched from ear to ear, the terror that the *primordial stain down there* might show up on a breast pocket, the trouser cuff, flap of the fly. Angelo walked straight ahead without regrets, even when he met up with blue jeans: definitely designer and with a crease. People who are afraid to *get dirty* should be condemned to stay among themselves, to make each other die of tomato-paste pathos or gravy phlegm. But if you have such an intolerant attitude, they all asked him, what are you doing here? And nobody to whom to tell all about Giorgina Washington.

• • •

Lido di Lonato is about a kilometer away from here and on the map it coincides with the middle of Lake Garda's western side.

Down there are the swamps of summer-resort normality which send messages all the way here on wind surfboards, local newspapers, catamarans, motorboats that drag along water-skiers, transistor radio and jukebox music, news from "No swimming" signs which have been uprooted or, if attached to the poplars, turned to face the trunks.

Sometimes the news is tragic and always appears in pairs: two girls dead in one week because bitten by rats—one at the breast normally deceased because of leptospirosis, the other who did not have the time to die of the same cause, deceased due to cardiac arrest at the very instant in which she saw the beast open its tiny teeth over her throat; *two* Germans hospitalized for viral hepatitis type B, they too struck down; two pizzas and two beers, twenty-two thousand eight hundred lire. At any event, that world really seems "down there," a season in hell, and nobody regrets it, openly. Indeed, it is not by chance that the "old glories," the coddled Fascist fairies who caught the drips in the whorehouse toilets, have chosen this place and no other: they always know the best emplacement for everything. This is a zone of sweet currents and the water is spring water, healthy, and will always be so, and here the rats stay away during the day. A silent pact of daily partition of the territory has been established between rats and habitués, and the arrangement works well. One can't occupy a sewer and then complain about the rats, as down there. Here one can almost feel the pack rat's tiny eyes behind the blackthorn shrubs or imagine them red, as by magnetic force instant by instant they release the sun's splendor until they make it plunge into a sunset: but not one of them has ever shown up off schedule. It is not from here that the plague, which already has run its course elsewhere, unbeknown to everyone, will be unleashed.

Today, steeped in thought, Angelo walks toward the villa. Something carries him along and does not let him lift his head, and if he does so it is sideways, toward the wide-lozenged metal fence which contains chunks of bolstering rocks.

In the wavy movement of the wall along which he is walking absentmindedly he again sees the white corridor gone down hundreds of times to make sure that the small, almond-eyed prodigy in her incubator has not become the victim of a euthanasia thwarting his disobedience with a financial feint. And those plastic tubes stuck in her nostrils to suck up presages of a pointless clamber; at the peak of survival there is death, decisively. Angelo, back from Egypt, could have sworn that the idea of poisoning had come precisely from him, because of his depressions which were quick both in appearing and disappearing. And while they lasted quite a few things came to mind. It seemed that cyanide was the most expeditious of them all. Wasn't it after that Jasmine Belart business at the border, with all those torn and unpackaged pantyhose, the forbidden drug, that Angelo—that year it hadn't been necessary for him to go to the barber and have his head shaved to zero—had asked him for the second time how one could get hold of a capsule of cyanide? Lometto had said "If that's all, it depends on how much you're ready to spend. Put the house in my name" because he had understood very well that Angelo wanted the capsule for himself and not his mother. There was no way one could wrest a gift from Lometto even in extremis.

When he was a child, Angelo cracked peach and apricot pits because his mother wanted the *almonds* to flavor the stuffing. The pungent odor. Giorgina Washington reduced with one injection to a piece of wild marzipan? And not a word if he doesn't want to have a charge of murder or accessory to murder turned against him. In fact he must pretend that nothing happened, and disappear, like a vulgar, silenced blackmailer. But his had been a blackmail for life and not death. It hadn't worked. Those dollars were filth. But, belonging to Lometto, that money did not stink more than so much and, since the pact had been broken, he could consider them completely his. But under the ground there is one life less and he does not feel up to dancing on top of it. Returning them would also be a sin, seeing that Lometto, looking at him for the last time with feigned indifference through the car window outside the airport, had not given the slightest consideration to the condition Angelo set for the return of the dollars—only the dollars, the tapes never.

Angelo lifts a hand to his temple, the wrong temple: he should not sit like this, under the blazing sun, his blood pressure is low and he feels faint, and last week he got—again got—gastroenteritis.

Stock-still, waiting for that prickly swarming that obscures everything to pass, he reopens his eyes, sees the tufa column, the small, decomposed statues of fairy-tale characters among the weeds: the

Dwarfs, Snow White, Red Riding Hood, the Wolf, the Mad Hatter. All fairy tales that Giorgina did not have the time to know, and it is not true that in many ways she would have understood them only in her own way. We all do that.

Angelo raises his head toward the fenced-in dock, his subdued lips whisper another title:

"How did this end begin?"

It began in July 1979.

Angelo, in his room at the university apartments on Via Verdi, waits with trepidation for this Mantuan industrialist with the unforgettable and chromatic name. Nicola, a salesman of lingerie and related apparel from Orzinuovi, needs an interpreter for a short trip to Germany. Then we'll see, one pantyhose leads to another. The appointment was for two o'clock, now it's already a quarter past three. Two hours ago he rushed to mail the last letter. It was number 38; the addressee: a native of Italy.

Every ten minutes Angelo goes to the kitchen balcony, kicks Gino's crate of peaches—Pasqua, his sister, is again at Borgo Roma, in the maternity ward—looks down to the end of the street, torn up by construction sites and filled with traffic barriers, then he returns to his room, stretches out on the bench and does twelve push-ups. Then he moves to his desk and resignedly reads a page of German philology. He has no talent for it, he has done too little Latin and no Greek. This is the only exam for which he's been studying for six months. He needs money. He's already gathering the material for his thesis. He can't afford to be dropped from the course, after taking twenty-one exams in two and a half years. He hasn't paid a lira of tuition up until now and has collected his pre-salary, with which he paid room and board for the whole year at subsidized rates. The discrepancy between it and the real price is right there before his eyes from morning till night: those boys over there on the scaffolding slaving away every month to pay a thirty percent tax on their wages. The monthly checks which the fifty-year-old virgin used to send him at the beginning are distant memories. In accordance with instructions, he was supposed to study without further preoccupations. He had followed it to the letter. That bonanza had lasted three months, too long actually, considering that such nuptials would require something else. And what a business with that woman exhausted at seeing the affectations of an entire life put into question. By now she must be out of the clinic for quite some time, and he will probably be summoned to be the scape-kid—certainly not the ram: he had left her as he had found her—between one kiss of the hand and the next by chief physicians and analysts. The clinic was private and exclusive, a paradise in the Black Forest. To transfer against payment of a thousand marks per day the poisons of a sick or even only disturbed mind (it always depends on the daily rate the mind is able to pay) to a distant fetish-body incapable of reacting: the customary tribal ritual by which in order to save someone who can afford it, someone who *cannot* is sacrificed. He had been *transferred* and the dissatisfied virgin had thus been able to *recover* and be happily released after a short stop in surgery, a matter of five minutes. It just goes to show you how a tiny cut, properly executed by a masked team in the right place, can make a wealthy depressed woman cough up a lot of money. And then that same clinic put her in touch after five months elapsed with that other private Swiss clinic, so as to restore the recidivist virgin's integrity. No one knows whether Professor Schmidt or Mueller or Gottlieb had been informed that that woman had undergone two electroshock treatments during the war and that he, Angelo, in those days, was still a vagrant possibility in the balls of his father, who was jumping from a prisoner's convoy headed for Germany and then returned on foot to Brescia from the Brenner pass . . .

His room is the largest in the apartment and he has it to himself; there are students packed in two rooms smaller than his. Angelo, by preference, was unable to cohabit. And so, in view of his twenty-nine years and with the complicity of the most tender Adele, the housekeeper (whom he lectures on how to bring up children in case they turn out to be different—she listens, red in the face, the broom handle indenting one cheek as she gulps down all that knowledge), he has been given special consideration. He has declared his parents' cumulative pension, the family certificate states that the three of them are together: they never were, to tell the truth, but there is a bed for him at his brother's, where the old couple went to live, and so the result is that, never having asked for a change of residence, not having a steady occupation, he is taking the bread out of the mouths of two low-income pensioners. He's already gone to Paris three times as a salesman of ready-to-wear clothing and in order to economize on the hotel he bought a sleeping bag, and every time, for the duration of the "Salon," he slept in the service elevator, for which he had the key. A service elevator has all imaginable comforts for the night—that is, lighting. On the floor he had completed the preparation for two minor exams. In the morning, automatic alarm with the first summons of the elevator by the man in charge of the warehouse. Then he went a few times to Austria for a wooden-clog company. Then no more, it was like going to Samos with pots. The year before, he went to the area around Trent with Abdul to pick apples, but not for long. Since he had started to sing and with him all those in his group—distinguished post-'68s, because all *ex's* have settled down in the offices of the Red Cross, the Department of Agricultural Development, etc.—the foreman came running, a '77 rookie who, on hearing songs on the order of "Old Mountain Boot," "Our Lovely Colors Will Be Back," etc., said "What's all this racket? We're not paying you to sing here." And Angelo had shouted so that everyone could hear him "What do you mean? Didn't you tell us we were getting union pay, four thousand an hour? But why don't you get things straight, *Kapo*, it's five thousand two hundred and you won't even let us sing? What do you think, we pick with our mouths too!" "You got a smart tongue in your head, haven't you?" he answered. "And you're not to call me *Kapo*, get it? Move move pick pick!" And Angelo at the top of his lungs: "We'll have night classes for the handicapped so we'll learn how to pick them with our feet too, okay?" And singing on the truck "There's our bossy with his pretty white trousers" he bade farewell to that work contracted with the Region in support of *youth* employment. In that affair of apples and employment paradises and trees of knowledge, it was always the snake that got the worst of it.

In Valsugana, three months ago, he stuck it out for three days picking cherries. Cherries are the fruit of poor, greedy and timid childhood: one can't just pick them, period, he hadn't been able to resist. He had to check his dysentery with a tiny piece of raw opium, exactly as happened to him in New York two years before. Bless Africans and Jehovah's Witnesses, for they never lack anything.

Now it's five past four.

Angelo, thanks to the first real period of material and psychic prosperity in his life, could spend his days reading—*studying*, as it is called in academic jargon. At the end of his reading session he had to attend small receptions among initiated women, none of whom knew anything about the work of minors on the scaffoldings of building sites, ladies in crisis, bejeweled and garishly dressed, who amiably spent time with him conversing about the "Socialist novel" or politely inquired about the well-being of one or the other. These receptions, which he sometimes attended cum laude, had come thick and fast like electric shocks from a defective socket. In the end, after so much gossipy delight, there would be a somewhat more formal reception, from claret one would go on to other things and he would be issued a certificate on parchment by Veuve Clicquot. The joy of being able to devote one's time to doing nothing, adorn it with activity and commitment, filled him with self-esteem, and always more rarely he happened to find himself at the mercy of a hundred badly paid awful jobs supposed to keep you going when you're young. Privilege was, rightfully, rewarded: in a near future one could put in front of the Otium the title Doctor, and offer to those exploited in factories and on construction sites a higher reason in which to fiscally believe.

But his high-fashion savings are almost finished, and it is already five o'clock and nobody has come.

The prospect of presenting himself as a candidate together with Abdul and Valeriano and the Jehovah's Witness at the Central Markets to load and unload fruit and vegetables and sanitation refuse at dawn every day (with the risk of having Gino underfoot there too), and besides everything else consider this a piece of luck "with unemployment all over the place," frightened him a bit. Hadn't this water—this rain along the groove of your back—stopped once and for all? When a few days earlier Nicola at Montichiari had told him about a certain customer list to be evaluated (a portfolio: this word had pleasantly tickled his eardrums), all of them German and Dutch and Belgian and French, which had belonged to his recently deceased relative, and all of whom he intended to contact, Angelo had leafed through the fat ring binder and made a quick calculation: at least three thousand names. Also Nicola, despite his easygoing and non-commercial eyes, had immediately become aware of the extravagance of the undertaking, and had limited himself to extrapolating only a couple of them—that is, the only ones he knew by hearsay. One had to get in touch with these two for the time being; he didn't know a word of German, nor did this *supplier*, this pantyhose industrialist. In short, everything seemed rather confused to Angelo, he did not understand what the business relationship between the two was, the interests involved, and he didn't care either. He had given Nicola the address in Verona and a telephone number—that of the beloved Adele, who would send one of her two gigantic foals at a gallop with the message written in beautiful Art Nouveau script on a scrap of butcher's wrapping paper. One could no longer rely on vocal transmission: both of them, when standing before his reputation and himself, pawed the ground and became tongue-tied and you knew less than before. Nicola had telephoned to say that he would come the day before to find out how to get there and confirm the appointment with the industrialist. Sure enough, yesterday he was here. He had been vague in talking about this Lometto and that possible trip of a couple of days. Angelo had been much less so in tossing off a figure which seemed to him insane and which he didn't even earn in Paris: fifty thousand lire a day plus expenses. Nicola had said in a neutral tone "Fine." Angelo had instantly understood that he had asked for too little, but it was too late. Nicola had stopped for a few hours to talk about women and cars, and his motorboat. Two hours, and a century. Angelo had monastically lent an ear.

"Come on, you really don't know what a turbine is? Starboard? But is it true that you're an assholer? You can't fool me, you know."

Half past five.

The room is tidier than usual, even though weights and dumbbells lie like sculptures strewn between bed and desk. On the desk several stamped envelopes numbered in one corner, all addressed to a certain Italo. Every now and then he shuffled them like a pack of cards, closed his eyes and pulled one out. He remembers that the first one mailed was number 14 and that number 1 had come after number 8. He had even played numbers to be drawn in Rome on the State Lottery, even though the girl at the Lotto office had told him it would be easier to hit a trio than a pair and that in gambling as well as love the more something seems false, the more it seems true, and vice versa. Only a single number had come up—the 1. It was also the number of the letter which, looking back, contained all the other tens of letters, the last one included. He had smiled at the hunchbacked girl brimming with goodwill toward the docile superstitions of unfortunates ready to conform. But he would persevere in the only way he knew to appear true: to be it. At times, however, he wonders whether he hasn't chosen only the most convenient aspect of his folly . . . The shutter is halfway down. Infernal heat . . . Ciuditta would come to meet him holding the small seat to be attached to the handlebars in her small arms and saying "Anjo, Anjo, bikey, bikey." The marble floor magnetizes the dehydrated dust of the burnt country paths in back. The toot of a horn. He runs to the balcony overlooking the street.

"Here we are, hey" says Nicola, opening his arms wide as soon as he reaches the small gate, exultant. "I couldn't find the street."

"Well, you know how it is."

Slowly the other door of the car opens, a curse rises all the way to the balcony, to all the balconies of the adjacent dwellings. Across the way the taxi driver's devout wife looks out. Then, a clearly scanned roar:

"Shit! Via Verdi! Via Verdi my cunt!"

The wife pulls back, closes the casement window and down comes the shutter with a thud. A mass of sweating flesh restrained by white-and-bluish shorts unloads from the seat onto the scorching asphalt. The face is a battleground of rivulets in which the small pale eyes, each on its own as after great tension, struggle to regain a single direction. The man is a bowling ball of fat with extremities that drag themselves to the small gate in absurd black shoes with India-rubber soles. He looks around incredulous at being here, at having arrived, lifts his greasy, dripping head.

"We're here, we're here, I tell you this is it, I tell you it's right after this corner. The fuck we're here! It's since three o'clock that we're running around like geese, three o'clock! And Via Puscini, and Via Schobert, and Via Schooman, and this cunt of a Via Verdi, nothing, but nothing, nothing, absolutely nothing. Shit!"

Nicola smiles under his sparse mustache and goes "Hee-hee-hee!" and the other one is busy trying to coax up the zipper of his shorts. Angelo hears them twitter as they climb the stairs. He's never before met an industrialist with black winter shoes in a hundred degrees in the shade. Nor in an undershirt and shorts either. And not this fat. But not so hilariously furious either.

"Oh, at last, here we are. How do you do, Lometto Celestino."

"How do you do. And so you couldn't find the street. All these one-way streets, all this construction going on" he says, turning to Nicola as he goes into the kitchen and moves the chairs around the table. "But how come? You were here yesterday."

Angelo repeats his veiled reproach. But by this time he no longer expected them and had already resigned himself to stay put until midnight. He knows all about such waits, such missed appointments. From a certain point on, the effort to put through something that before ran all by itself was so great that perhaps it was better to accept defeat.

"Don't get me started, otherwise I don't know where it will end up, I really don't know. 'Leave it to me, I know how to get there,' he kept saying" Lometto blathers, wiping his forehead and drying his hand on his shorts. "Can I take off my shoes? They fucking hurt so much! Hey! You wouldn't have a basin with a bit of cold water? Three hours, threeee!"

"Come on now, maybe an hour."

"An hour, goddamnit an hour! Anybody who honked passed us."

"No, I haven't got a basin. But in the tub . . ." Angelo suggests, getting up again and at the threshold running into the goblin emanating from Lometto's feet, which is beginning to thicken the stagnant air of the furnacelike kitchen.

In his bare feet Lometto follows him into the bathroom.

"Forget the tub. I don't want to be a ballbreaker. I don't want to impose. In the bidet."

And so here they are, the three of them, in the small bathroom, discussing this trip "to the Krauts." ("Oh, it's just around the corner, you get in the car, you turn right, and that's it" Lometto minimizes, rubbing his big toe.) Sitting on the rim of the tub, Lometto lets the water run in the bidet and heaves sighs of relief. Nicola wedges between tub and sink, Angelo leaning squeezed against the windowsill with one leg on the toilet bowl. Lometto splashes carefreely about in the ceramic shell, immediately flooding the entire floor. He's utterly at ease, as if in an Olympic swimming pool in his own house. He didn't want to impose.

"Do you have a towel or something?" he asks, not questioningly after twenty minutes of absolute aggressive bliss. From his undershirt pour out in waves shapeless rolls of flesh compressed by his bent position, with certain ovoidal movements independent of the rest, as though some of them were Frisbeeing off on their own, spreading in the tub like lifesavers or leaping in flight out the window.

Now the oblivious pachyderm has pulled down his zipper and splashes handfuls of water on his face, his back and underbelly. He might as well have taken a bath. Angelo contritely gazes at the flood that he will have to drain so as not to become too prominent in the behind-the-back complaints of his roommates, whom he is always ready to reproach at the slightest sign of untidiness. He does not want Adele to waste time in the bathroom and kitchen, where the "raw recruits" can also do some work. He has given her a lecture "on excremental recycling in the love of married couples" and she said—it was mealtime and she had to leave right away—that as soon as she had a moment she'd wax the floor of his room.

Every time he butts in about the business of the trip and the customers, Nicola is immediately told to shut up by Lometto, who begins his sentences with: "But no, it's not like that. Let me tell you what you're supposed to do, damnit!"

Then he asks for a comb. Angelo picks one up at random, he doesn't own one. Then he asks for slippers and another towel. As soon as he finally flops in the mock-leather armchair in the bedroom and stretches out his legs on the small coffee table between the radio and the pile of newspapers, Lometto says, clucking: "Do you have some mineral water and mint?"

"No, I'm sorry. I have . . ."

"Some grapefruit juice?"

You got to have some nerve to ask a student for such things. Lometto does not seem a bit discomposed as he coarsely dribbles out his impudent requests. And neither does Angelo when he turns them down, even though his instinct for hospitality would prompt him to rush out into the street to the fruit vendor. He simply thinks: go take a crap. And Gino too! Green apricots, baskets of artichokes, carrots, potatoes, spinach, even cauliflower! And not even one three-piece grapefruit tray.

"I have some lemons. There's ice. It's thirst-quenching. If you want."

"Oh yes, it's very excellent!"

"For me too, okay?"

Angelo goes into the kitchen and prepares the drinks for those two. He's no longer thirsty. Crabs and big bucks stick to the balls. This trip is going to be torture, he can feel it. And he repeats while squeezing: three strands, six strands, nylon six, nylon six/six.

He arrives with the glasses, which are lightly fogged because of the sugar, and Lometto empties his in one gulp. He holds out his glass again, with tacit and watery imploration. When he wants something that is not coming to him, he hams, plays the big baby. In doing this, he exploits even the unmetabolized element of fat: the excess fat. He tries to arouse tenderness. Probably he's the one who put out the rumor that "fat man means good man."

"I could drink a whole pail of it."

Angelo looks at Nicola, who tries to keep from laughing. He goes back to the kitchen, his wrist hurts from so much squeezing. Luckily he has only four bags of lemons.

"Is he always like this?" he asks, coming back into the room and looking at Nicola. Nicola blushes. Angelo thinks: if he asks me for another glass I'll throw him out, this skinful of shit who comes here and thinks he can con me.

"Fine, fine, it's agreed then" says Lometto, slightly intimidated by the sibilant touch of impatience in Angelo's voice. "Sunday at twelve o'clock. Fifty thou, you sure you want that much?"

"It's fifty percent less than I usually make" Angelo had his answer ready.

Now he looks around, continually rubbing his nose, itching from Lometto's penetrant foot whiff: on the table the rinds of fifteen lemons, the empty sugar tin; the ice was already gone by the third glass. And a wake of water from bath to kitchen to the hallway and to his room.

The first thing he sees beyond the wall of the villa is a small crater of ashes and burnt-out embers, perhaps somebody bivouacked there last night, and then two calves, arched knees, tiny black bathing trunks, a navel and, just above, the tip of a red beard sticking up, always higher. It's a guy with eyes of a sorrowful gray, very long ocher hair, fleshy lips which protrude from beneath the mustache smoothed down to the sides. There are two other guys, one of whom has a chestnut-colored beard just as long, and a third has a beard which is curly and not uniform, black. They resemble the nasty Boers in the movies.

There is an exchange of looks between Angelo and the ocher-red beardo. So intense that Angelo has to shift his eyes, which fall on a scorched rat carcass among the spent embers. Only the muzzle and head are intact, the rest of the body seems emptied out. The tail is long, stiff, charred.

The trio lie stretched out on the cement jetty which rises up along the boathouse, closed by a rusted metal rolling door; there is a channel for the keels of boats or motorboats or even, considering its dilapidated condition, canoes. Angelo sits down on the other parallel jetty, about three meters away. He watches the trio in his particular way—trying to steal sufficient visual material out of the corner of his eye in order to recycle it at leisure in his inner pupils more than bestowing real attention to the immediate image of the yellow beard with carmine lips. Of average height, the body here and there has yielded to the pressure, one would say, of beer: on the hips, on the rounding belly. But chest and shoulders are well built, and so is the face, the part not covered by that saffroned thicket: an aquiline nose, and again the mouth, displayed, with the upper dental arch more protuberant than the lower, the lip forever kissing air. At a common signal the trio rise, a soccer ball with black and white hexagons appears—passes, little headers, resounding "hooplas!"

It seems to him that he is very distant geographically, that he is using binoculars to probe this man who squints in his direction whenever Angelo, dissatisfied by the results produced by the whites of his eyes, shifts his pupil by a micron.

The ball bounces against the wall, the trio enter the water with circumspection, pursue each other for a short stretch, the ball leaps up and comes to rest next to his tote bag.

Angelo extracts the green folder containing the typed pages and begins to read, to correct typing errors here and there. He smiles: he wrote "homophiliac" instead of "hemophiliac." He continues even after the trio have climbed back onshore and begun drying themselves. The soccer ball is on his side. So he now turns his back completely: the ball lies there right in front of him. He pictures the bearded man with carmine lips as he pulls the towel through his legs and lingers between the buttocks, the droplets of water shattering in the hairs, wraps his beard in the cloth and wrings it. Angelo has one of those bellicose experiences harking back to when he did not have to ask for anyone's permission: an erection. This bothers him, it is the sign of a complication. He closes his eyes over a railroad sentence: "beginning today *crash* discounts also for families of three" . . . he inserts it in his beard, wraps it up, then nozzles it into the dimple on the chin, there: he is touching the first of the infinite lips of sex.

When his vertigo encounters the balustrade of a visual valley bottom, Angelo opens his eyes a slit and glides over a back encased in a tank top bent over the soccer ball.

"Writer?" asks red beard, rising and stuffing the ball into an army duffel bag. The other two stand there nearby, ready to leave.

"No, translator. And you?" answers and asks Angelo in a cordial but dry voice. He hates subdued voices, those that would always like you to hear that they are governed by a certain wonder or complacent timidity.

"I work in photography. Are you coming here tomorrow?"

"Yes. If the weather's good."

"See you tomorrow then. My name's Armando, what's yours?"

Armando, by now at the end of the wall, turns around and waves.

Angelo goes back to correcting but then jumps up and runs after the trio, who, however, are already at the top of the escarpment. He suddenly remembered that this evening he must leave for Arezzo and that from there he goes to Monte San Savino, where the day after an American translator will be waiting for him to help him translate some colloquial expressions he does not understand.

"Will you be here tomorrow?" he asks a fellow with a well-parted flesh-blond toupee, perfectly even teeth and translucent skin.

"If it's sunny, yes" he answers, flattered by that point-blank question.

"If you see that boy with the beard, the redhead, would you tell him that I didn't come because I was tied up?"

"Who? Armando? I'll tell him" and he sucks in his two coy little cheeks.

"You know him?"

"Yes, he's the fellow at the pizzeria in Manerba" he adds, popping the mandibular cork, all set to screw other corks. But Angelo does not want to pick up any information about Armando, even indirectly. Photography! Sure, à la Four Seasons. He thanks him and leaves. He takes his shoe off the typed pages, puts everything back into the tote, and makes an about-face pointed toward the central station of the Terrazzine, mumbles something like "Oh ho! Oh ho! *Oh* or *ho*?" But modesty prevented him from taking the tape from the safe-deposit box and listening to Edda Lometto née Napaglia's solo.

Immediately after Rosenheim, Lometto had stopped his transatlantic diesel on a lot covered with birch trees and, opening the trunk, extracted from it a bobble of hard-boiled eggs in a small plastic bag. From another bag, a bakery bag, a well-curried salami, and a large jug of wine. During the trip, to make the pleasure of the air-conditioning system fully enjoyable, he raised it so high that Angelo had to cover his knees with the car rug that was lying there and stank of horse manure. The conversation did not stray from General Insurance: policies, partial car thefts, fire, etc. Lometto and Nicola sitting in front, limply, display an enviable stamina in not choosing any subject whatsoever and cruising around it for hours without ever getting tired. Angelo is fed up with hunching forward to listen to ineffable Masonic idiocies. Between the two partners there is a subterranean exasperation, an acrid gaiety when they laugh about a certain evening in which the clumsy services of a Thai girl in Frankfurt resulted in an inflammation that lasted two weeks. The excuses he had to invent for his fiancée. Lometto whenever he can leads the conversation back to pantyhose, and whether Nicola's commission for introducing two customers shouldn't be conditional.

Nicola has duly sighed, conceded something, requested something else in exchange, a guarantee for the future. Lometto asks Angelo the meaning of what is written on the road signs, and the two of them are back where they started: Nicola brings up again the subject of his cabin cruiser, over there in the harbor of Peschiera, oh, to take off the tarp and head for the open lake, where nobody breaks your whatcha-ma-call-its, take the sun, your little drinkie on the rocks, your slice of ice-cold melon. Angelo stays out of it, waiting for something to get into. He's tired of putting on polite smiles for these two raconteurs of stale jokes.

"Did you hear this one?" Lometto suddenly says. "This husband comes home and goes into the bedroom. His wife is under the sheets. He goes to the closet and sees a stark-naked man. 'What are you doing, locked up in here?' 'You won't believe me' the man says 'but I'm waiting for the train.' Ha, ha, ha!"

There are some that go on for twenty minutes, between three and six o'clock on this afternoon trip begun too late. Twenty minutes of good manners, with that stinking rug on his knees, the undaunted servility necessary not to break into sobs or yawn because Lometto watches his reaction in the rearview mirror.

"And what about you, don't you know any jokes?" says Lometto, examining Angelo from the bridge of his nose to his hairline.

"Yes, the ones I'm forced to listen to. Unfortunately, I can't forget them, that's the problem. One would be all right but . . ."

Lometto, still in the rearview mirror, flushes deep red: Nicola slowly turns around and stares at Angelo with dismay.

"At any rate, I'll tell you one. Two friends go on a safari together. They leave their wives home and go off to the Congo by themselves. Suddenly in the middle of the forest from a liana a gorilla leaps on the closest one, pulls down his pants with one big paw, tears off his shorts, bends him forward with a smack, sticks it in his ass with a single stroke. His scream calls back his friend, but at that sight, instead of intervening, he runs away, terrorized. In such cases one usually says that one is going for reinforcements. The gorilla is not content with buggering him once, but he stuffs the unfortunate guy in rapid fire like a Christmas turkey. Rescue arrives—much too late; you know, safaris . . . The victim is hospitalized in shock and mention is only made of an accident while hunting. The dreadful truth is kept secret by the friend and only the doctor in charge is informed. Two, three months go by: the poor fellow, transported back to his hometown, is still in bed, his eyes and mouth gaping, and since that day he hasn't uttered a single word. His friend visits him every day, suffering because of that silence and feeling guilty because he got scared and ran away. Well, at the end of the fourth month he arrives at the hospital and sees his friend's expression is more bitter than usual, and like every other time, without expecting an answer, he asks him how he feels. Miracle: the guy opens his mouth and begins to speak: 'Well, how do you expect me to feel, after what happened to me?' 'Well, I know what you mean, the condition you're in.' 'Don't say a word. I don't want to talk about it. Nobody knows how it feels. Four months, four months! Not even a phone call, not even a postcard . . .' "

The reaction of the two up front is fishlike. They exchange glances.

"Am I supposed to laugh?" says Nicola.

"I didn't get it" Lometto echoes.

"And neither did I."

"There's nothing to explain. Either you get it or you don't."

And Angelo has once and for all stretched out on the back seat and is immediately reprimanded by Lometto.

"Look out you don't dirty my seats with your shoes."

It is obvious that he is very tense, over the seat and due to that joke he didn't get.

"Four months. Not even a phone call, not even a postcard . . . Oh, now I see!"

"Explain it to me too!"

Nicola is finally filled in at the service area before the border where Lometto, in Austria, has stopped to get some gas. Nicola laughs, not quite convinced, and his only comment is: "Oh, he's become like you, huh?" turning to Angelo with a smirk. At the self-service there is only a man behind the counter and another at the cash register. Tourists swarm in like locusts in a single sudoriferous fumigation and jostle each other with shoulder blades peeled by the concentrated trip to Italy. The locusts increase in number, hundreds of objects are touched and taken off and put back on the shelves, Lometto is drinking and Angelo notices that he snitches other people's receipts from the counter and sticks them in his pocket; then, before leaving, he puts under his arm two magazines, slips in his pocket a jar of salted peanuts, hands Nicola a bottle of tamarind-juice concentrate, and they walk out. Shocked, Angelo remarks:

"Say, Lometto, you forgot to pay."

"It's not my fault, let them hire more personnel, they can't blame me, I can't hang around here until they're good and ready. Time is money."

"I'm sorry but what's that got to do with the juice?" Angelo retorts, sore at having been made an accomplice.

"It's for my boys. They like tamarind juice. And even better if it's for free."

"Well, when I'm around, try to avoid making this kind of present, right?" Angelo said dryly, ducking into the car and slamming the door.

"But Nicola here told me that you can take a joke."

Lometto: he too one of those who insist on having the last word.

And now there he is, in his usual sloppy shorts, as he pulls out of the bag a dozen eggs, slips them onto the rim of the spare tire, and begins to cut the salami. There are no glasses, not even paper cups. The two of them drink from the jug, Nicola for "just a taste" and Lometto heaving powerful sucks and gurgles of utter satisfaction. Angelo has noticed that Lometto's teeth are in excellent condition and the arc of his gums is purplish; every time he turned from the steering to ask him something, Angelo was invested by a putrid pyorrheic cloud. Angelo barely touches the food and, irked by the familiarity imposed on him, he asks for a glass that doesn't exist. Lometto, who has just wiped off his sweat, wipes the mouth of the jug with the same hand and holds it out to Angelo.

"No, I don't drink straight from the bottle."

Lometto squints at him, annoyed by this further impertinence, and then stares at Nicola fixedly: did or didn't he explain to him *who he is*?

"And anyway, listen, Lometto, this is the first time I go on a business trip for a firm and we stop on the side of the road to eat bread and salami. This isn't a school outing with teacher. No, let me tell you, this won't do."

Angelo wants to be clear: he has understood that Lometto with his very calculated manners of a wily rustic must be kept under control instant by instant, inhibited in his false liberality of someone saving on a dinner he owes (just look how he proffers the eggs, with what insistence he cuts slices of salami and says 'Eat, eat, there's plenty of it,' flaunting a generosity which would have been exaggerated even right after the war). Lometto at the first opportunity—when he really will have to give something of his that "costs"—will force you to fathom the full depth of his programmatic peasant avarice and will not scruple at using you as integrative dung for his jovial imperialistic ends. But Angelo isn't Nicola. And neither does he have such interests with Lometto as to tolerate even the slightest rudeness—no comradely games of brown-bag dinners to skip the white tablecloth and jump straight into bed.

"Don't you like salami and bread? It's all homemade stuff, you know."

"Of course I like it, but when I pick it, not when it's an imposition. You can impose on me only with salmon and red caviar."

"How about some crackers?" Lometto asks, suddenly conciliatory, blushing a bit, perhaps with anger at being caught between the rock and the hard place, between the *informal* bread and salami and wine refused because truly *informal*—something which to this day nobody must have realized and must have saved him the cost of any number of dinners.

"What are you talking about? Salted peanuts! With another five hundred kilometers ahead of us! Nicola, why don't you eat those saltines since you like them so much. Come on, let's go, let's not waste any more time, we must get there before midnight, you haven't even made hotel reservations. And if there is some trade show in Frankfurt, we're screwed, we'll end up sleeping in the car."

"A lot I care" says Lometto, quite game, perking up at the idea of also saving the cost of the rooms. And as he starts up the car he tears the plastic cover off the jar and begins crunching peanuts with a noise of open challenge. Angelo knows Frankfurt very well: one hotel serves a very abundant breakfast, another should be avoided because the eggs are cooked earlier by the night porter, another near the Stall means saving two taxis. In another there was a Tunisian at night who finished off the jobs started elsewhere by others.

And halfway there Angelo got the car to stop at another service area, told them to follow him, made straight for a restaurant, set them down, and, while deadly pale, stuffed with eggs, salami, and peanuts, they burped, he ordered a goulash soup, pepper fillet, a giant blueberry yogurt, and two glasses of apple juice. Lometto paid without a word, traumatized by that demonstration of absolute heartlessness. Then Angelo leafed through his memories and called Frankfurt.

"We'd better make reservations right now. If it's not too late already."

"Remember, I don't go in for a lot of baloney."

"Neither do I, but it's got to be good."

"Even if it's three beds, even if there's no toilet . . ."

"Done. A double room with a sink and a single with a shower. Now I feel better. No searching half dead from hotel to hotel."

"What do you mean *two*?" Lometto says, putting his hands on his hips.

"Yes, of course. I can't sleep if there's another person in the room. Much less two."

"But I thought you slept with Nicola?"

"Not me."

"And now how am I supposed to wash?"

"Well, didn't you say that it was okay without? There'll be a bathroom down the hall."

And then, Angelo remembers, at the restaurant they insisted on getting two checks for one drink, one each, they got the waitress to increase the figure, and then Lometto didn't even want to leave a tip of one mark and he had to do it. And having satisfied all their little fiscal-fraud gratifications, Lometto nudged him in the side with an elbow and said, still looking for more:

"Ask her for another two stamped chits of paper like these."

Angelo refused, blasting him with an irritated look because of his familiar tone.

After Mannheim—it is already night—since Angelo isn't asking questions and doesn't seem interested in knowing how many "boys" there are, Lometto opens the paternity compartment and shakes Nicola by the shoulder. Nicola was snoring beatifically.

"Did I show you the photograph album of my first boy's first communion?"

"Yes . . . three years ago" Nicola says laconically.

"And the album of my second boy?"

"I think so, yes, last year."

"Then you're missing the one of my third. And the confirmation of my first."

"No, but show them to me some other time."

Angelo, at coming across the first tiny monk's habit with a wooden cross on its breast and tiny joined hands, says, irritably "Please, keep your eyes on the road."

"Don't worry. I look at that too."

Days of confirmation, of first communion: the two older boys dressed like friars in beige, the other, the youngest, in a little dark suit and a tie that covers his entire shirt. As they go into church. At the altar. With the basket—lilies. On a fence. Here comes the priest's car. The priest—a blatant Wall Street face, long hooked nose, narrow eyes, something of the porcupine. Everybody around a festive table—sausages, cutlets, cookies, Marsala wine. Habit hoods fluttering in the wind, Lometto and Signora—with a vulpine look, eyes inspired by a superior ecstasy, in keeping with a first checking account opened in church, a ray of sun that descends from a stained-glass window and comes to rest on the fuzz of the upper lip. Lometto in a blue suit, with an expression of deep feeling, one pound of flat knotted tie. Obviously in the first pew. A situation that is repeated three times, with savings on habit and wooden cross.

"My wife got the bishop to change the date because that day she had her curse, and she also had to have her douches. Democratic, right? What do you think? Are they handsome or aren't they?"

Angelo remains silent, he doesn't know what to say, they all look like so many goitered puppets, with the good intentions of saving on everything, recycling their little carnival outfits. But the boys, even rigged out like this, reveal a substantial disobedience to all that repugnant mise-en-scène of knights of an entrepreneurial god: they are very beautiful.

"How old are they?" Angelo asks, just to get off the hook.

"They all have names ending in 'ario,' I notice" Nicola says, being properly trained.

"Now twelve and a half, eleven, and ten."

While he's at it, he asks for their names.

"Ilario, Belisario, and Berengario. They're crazy about animals. You know, in the country . . . What do you say, eh?"

"And this is your wife?"

"Yes."

"She looks like she's from the South."

"Hh hh."

"Where from?"

Billboards floodlit like the large streets and boats below.

"This is Frankfurt. But what does 'am Main' mean?"

"It's the name of the river. Where from?"

"You are nosy, aren't you?" And he turns off the inside light and puts the album back into the compartment.

"They really are beautiful, all three of them. They don't even look like yours."

And they all burst into liberating laughter. Then Angelo, tired of inveighing in an undertone and certain he has given Lometto enough lessons, doubles the dose, invents a syrup of compliments worthy of a popular beauty manual. Lometto drives as if in a trance, swept away by the description of faces that are *his*. In the rearview mirror Angelo sees his eyes sparkle milky blue in the intermittent darkness of the streetlights and in a cracked voice Lometto says:

"And they're very smart in school, and if there's a need to give a hand in cutting or bringing in the hay they don't shirk. Not because they're mine . . ."

Of course, Angelo thinks, Pincario or Pallinario were not *Aryan* enough for Lometto.

"And just think, my wife prepares their menu every week, never the same thing twice. She does it all by herself. And then swimming pool, gym, soccer, in school they don't even know what sports are. The oldest one already has a pair of shoulders like this."

"And we get eggs!" Angelo exclaims. "Get off at the next exit, follow the arrow that says '*Stadtmitte*.' "

"But is he always like this?" Lometto says. "He isn't a Red or a Socialist, is he?"

"And so now you're also repeating what I say. I am Bazarovian, with a tendency to the sinister."

"Sinister? Left, you mean to say, Angelo."

"No, sinister. And stop calling me Angelo."

And now there they are, the two buddies in the double room *with bath* because it was available. Lometto and Nicola, bushed, undigested, the wine jug on the dresser and the bag of eggs and salami on the armchair. But Lometto does not let go and as soon as Angelo looks in on them again to see if everything is okay, he rushes to the bag and says with his usual alert malicious amiability:

"Come on, eat, Nicola, because you won't see salami like this for ages" and heroically it is he who sets an example of obstinacy. "Would you like some?"

Angelo doesn't bother to say no with his chin. He impassively watches Nicola swallowing while Lometto cuts slice after slice and shells egg after egg like a solicitous daddy on an Easter picnic. He drops shells and skins all over the place, into the wastebasket, on the floor, in the ashtray. And he clacks his tongue and squints his eyes, under the illusion that with a glove of yoke and gristle he is giving a slap in the face to that cunt college graduate who is standing there at the door and at thirty rides a bicycle because he doesn't even have a driver's license, doesn't have a proper home of his own, and at one hundred and eighty kilometers an hour clings to the door handle.

All the faucets in the bathroom are running, Nicola is waiting for Lometto to take his blessed right of precedence.

"Sure, go ahead and take a bath and then drop dead, stuffed as you are."

"Nobody's taking a bath. You didn't have to get a room with bath . . ." Lometto says with his mouth full.

"I thought you were going to. You have all the faucets running."

"Damnit! It makes the water cooler. It's included in the price, isn't it?"

"Well, good night, it's almost time for breakfast and they're stuffing their faces with bread and salami. You're crazy."

Nicola looks at him with a beseeching expression.

"I've asked them to call us at eight-thirty. Since our appointment is for ten."

"Are you going to sleep?" Nicola asks in a tiny voice.

"Not me" Angelo answers curtly.

"And where are you going? Are we going too?" he says, turning to Lometto.

"I'm going to get it up that place. After one thousand kilometers—not a prick, not an ass" Angelo says impartially, accompanying his crack with a gelid little laugh because he does not want it to seem a crack intended to make them laugh.

"Oh, really? Aren't we lucky. Come on, Nicola, let's go too."

"Yes, come on, it won't take us long to wash up. You'll knock for us, okay?"

"All right. In five minutes. If you're not ready, I'll see you tomorrow. It's already half past one."

If Nicola and Lometto think that he'll go to some nightclub with Oriental, Rumanian, and Bulgarian women, they've got another think coming. He knows nothing about this type of time killer in Frankfurt. Nor in other cities either. Even if he's been a few times to these nightclubs for men only, to accompany some fat entrepreneur. Sequined little broads who lift their little legs over the table with the ice bucket are stuff for the Valenvaska gang. One of the gang was killed on the highway along the lakes. Tattooed on his right arm was the sentence "All women are whores." In block letters. Certainly for him everything must have been much easier. Women, alienated, removed from humanity, rendered contemptible by being attractive, were sculpted into the male's flesh like an impure syntax of abstract bestiality. They were whores even if, during a striptease, they didn't so much as cough. Angelo, instead, would have liked to throw a blanket over them and say to them "Let's go, my dears, it's all over," as in a horror film with a happy ending.

At the Stall the two straight Italians looked at each other ill at ease, in their striped shirts with knife-edged pleats, summer gabardine pants, their slightly loosened ties—Lometto's sprinkled with crossed shields, oh God, was as big as a baby sheet—little sweaters over their arms. Angelo, instead, conformed.

"But there's really only men here, all of them!" Lometto exclaims, scratching his head. "Not even one German broad."

"And I thought he was joking" Nicola remarks, holding on to his glass with all his might. Two guys arrive, bare-chested with tasseled rings threaded in their nipples. Lometto's eyes pop out and he jerks forward with a gasp.

"Oh, this is something, this is really something."

"But who are they, neo-Nazis? Look at all those birthmarks."

"No, they are up-to-date bank clerks, hosiery salesmen from the city, and those things on the arms aren't birthmarks, they're cigarette burns."

Angelo feels like dumping them and going about his business. The club is large enough for him not to meet up with them for at least a couple of hours. Customers keep arriving by the dozens. The Stall is the last to close. Still more leather, jeans, studs everywhere, ornamental piercings.

"They've all got earrings stuck in their lobes. And not even one cunt, eh?" says Lometto, already with a touch of a reporter's detachment.

"Oh course there are. Plenty of them. After a while you catch on. Do you see the one with his buttocks sticking out, with the droopy mustache? She's a transvestite. Trying is believing."

"I don't believe you!"

"Eight kilos of gash, guaranteed" Angelo insists with a serious face. The two display obligatory pouts of amazement.

"Oh, but here you have to be sure to hold a hand over your ass, right?" Nicola says, starting to laugh nervously. "Oh, this is the first and last time you fool me. Where the hell did you take us?"

"I told you, didn't I?"

"But I thought that . . ."

"Oh, shut up!"

"Heavens, this is the end."

"But why are they looking at us like that? I hope they don't have bad intentions, eh?"

"No, don't even hope for it. It's just that dressed up like this you look like two roasted penguins."

"But how am I supposed to know? It's that idiot there: let's go, he's taking us to get whores. Some whores! With a handle and no shopping bag!"

"Who, me?" Nicola retorts, flabbergasted by a cramped smile that meets him face to face. A baldie lays a hairy hand on his neck. Nicola is stunned. He regains his speech.

"Angelo, what's he doing? Angelooo."

"Nothing. He thinks that the way you're dressed is some new perversion. He says you're cute. Do you want to go to his place? Do you like dildos?"

"First of all, tell him to take his filthy hands off me, and then who are these dildos?"

"Japanese marbles. Oh well, it's too complicated to explain. And you can push away his hand yourself, politely. And stop making those terrified faces or else he'll think that you can't wait."

Then Angelo left them enchanted with the amenity of the place—they had no desire at all to leave, they laughed through their teeth at their reciprocal expressions of encouragement and amazement. Lometto, however, seemed to go along absentmindedly out of solidarity among mutineers, not out of conviction.

"The two of you, it's better if you don't go in there, agreed?" Angelo said.

It was a dark, U-shaped room dimly illuminated by a red light suspended above a large-meshed military net that hung from the ceiling. "Why? What's in there?" Lometto had asked, with the neutrality of someone dying of curiosity.

"It's the site of the sacrifice. The sacrifice of those who are too curious" Angelo said, smiling at saying something that could not be understood. It was not a sacrifice in any sense and for no one, it was like going to a bar and having a glass with friends after work. But Lometto and Nicola were so far removed from all metaphors, and you can imagine how far from those that weren't metaphors at all.

"*Ciao*, see you later. Or in any case you know the way back to the hotel. Or take a cab, you've got the address."

At a certain point outlined in the fine red dust of bodies, he saw the silhouette of Lometto, alone. His hands in his pockets, his lips in a heart-shaped pout as if from one minute to the next he was going to whistle, curses rising because of where he put his feet. Damn him! His greed was unlimited. There was nothing that for him was not already included in the price. He did not have to pay an additional fee to go in there. No extra was required for that profanation perpetrated purely for the sake of profit and the Complimentary Coupon.

"How about it, Celestino? Do you like it?" Angelo whispered to him, irritated by his disobedience.

"It's okay, it's okay. But I've never seen anything like it. They're sticking it to each other."

"Get out and wait for me at the bar. Or offer the other buttock. Stop bothering me, goddamnit."

But he didn't leave, he changed direction and ended up in the corridor across the room. He leaned against the black window, arms crossed, transforming it into a bay window turned the wrong way. It was impossible to make out the expression on his face. It must have been the usual expression of a person who having ended up in a place by mistake has not the slightest intention of leaving. Angelo moved toward the window and smiled furiously at the protuberance—he looked like a whale pup, not out of water really, and when he gave signs of wanting to be sociable, Angelo lay across his mouth a finger so straight that the other shut up forever. He knew that Lometto did not lose sight of him even for an instant.

Several hands lifted Angelo's body onto a swing, other hands and arms jostled and pushed forward, Lometto was shoved aside with the cruelty of someone who is doing something against those who aren't doing anything and are an obstacle if only in thought. Flight jackets and jeans were flung out of the melee. Strident sounds of zippers, some of them getting stuck. Angelo's curly head emerged and disappeared in that reddish breaker. Above those heads two feet hovered, tendons like red arrows strained against the metal grating. Something was being lifted. Angelo kept seeing things from Lometto's perspective even when he let out the final scream that made him unique even in Germany, and he heard Lometto say:

"Oh God, they're doing him in" while Angelo continued to rave and immediately began to laugh uncontrollably because of that "doing in."

"Come on, Lometto, let's get the fuck out of here, it's late" Angelo said, hooking his arm in his and pulling him out of the melee.

"Oh God, they're feeling up my ass!"

"It's good luck; I'm choking in here."

"Oh God, it was you with the legs up in the air, wasn't it?"

"I think so, there were so many. Did Nicola leave?"

"Nicola is talking German. With both his hands on his balls."

"You sure picked up some goodies" Lometto said.

"You're not jealous, by any chance."

"Look, dearie, I leave all those nice little items with the handle to you."

Lometto pressed him lightly with his arm and squeezed Angelo's elbow into the blubber of his waistline. It was an offhand declaration that there was no need to say anything. Angelo found it so extraordinary that Lometto should not have any specific opinion—or moralistic notion on the subject—that this empty space—or rather: free from the normative little traps of "acceptance," "tolerance," "condemnation," "nature," "procreation," "what if everybody acted like this?" etc.—was filled by him with sudden admiration. Lometto was touched by grace. By his not taking a position he revealed an unhoped-for vascularization, and none of the solid citizen's hematophagus bedbugs. For him, sex was not a social value. No diagrams to be drawn around it, no *more* or *less*, nothing at all. No property laws, no instructions for use, no advice à la Kipling engraved from the navel down. No particular use and every use, if one felt like it. Pee-pee and poo-poo, depending. One could use anything to obtain one's aims, but not turn to sexual tastes to humiliate or exalt someone in his social ascent or climb. It was permissible to trick someone or step over his corpse in so many other ways without resorting to Soviet or English government expedients.

Angelo, after a decade of snobbery or smug anthropological notions, if not true martyrdoms of conscience, in order to be on a par with hairdressers and fashion designers, was totally overcome by the astounding agnosticism of a hosiery merchant with a fifth-grade education, a real con man without the slightest scruples. He gave him the highest grade: a certain style. Lometto was the first *to be true* in his *non-opinion* and, moreover, true in not having anything to say on the subject. In fact, an embarrassed remark made his mental void on the subject more sacred.

The next day Angelo investigated on tip-tongues. Lometto showed surprise on hearing that there were people who did not think the way he did—that is, that did not think anything at all. With that instinctive, pneumatic farsightedness of his, typical only of the beatific in spirit, able to touch on any human matter without its concerning or not concerning them, Lometto drove back wearing above his head a halo of unacknowledged grandeur as dazzling as it was invisible. Which Angelo, however, if only because of the dismay at finding himself for the first time in his life confronted by such a phenomenon, was always ready to strip him of at the first incautious definition or defloration of that miraculously virginal space.

Back in Verona on Via Verdi, tearing off a check and unscrewing the cap of his Bakelite fountain pen, Lometto said:

"A hundred thousand, do you really want all of it? Come on, just for a nice little trip in good company! And then all those nice little items you picked up thanks to me! You should be paying me!"

Angelo did not come down a single lira—in vain because Lometto had already written "ninety thousand" on the check and all on his own was turning the business into a joke.

Perhaps that space was not at all empty, probably it had never even had the possibility of existing. In Lometto everything was occupied by the hundredth fraction of a hundredth still available on earth down to the last histological millimeter. No nuances for him: by detaching that treacherously reduced check he revealed the uniformity of the passion which devastated him at every instant. He had no opinion on other people's sex because he was not the owner of whorehouses but of shares in a pantyhose factory, and he had no interest in drawing up a table of costs and earnings in sex beyond his strict matrimonial benefits. He had no prejudices about the sex of others, not by divine grace, but because he was too committed to having them about the nylon, cattle raising, and dairy farms of others. And Angelo had the sensation that there was a personal shading in this hemocoelum of Lometto's, an advance payment of self-interested, long-term magnanimity toward himself . . .

Angelo, confronted by ten thousand lire less than had been agreed upon, had to change his mind, if only in part. The Never-Never Land of the Pure Spirit did not exist. An empty space was such because one was vigilant that nothing ever should come to contaminate it. An undertaking which rarely leaves room for others. This was not the case with Lometto. Freedom remained a laborious nuance: it sucked up all energies and yielded no results, much less a profit. Angelo's disappointment, in realizing that something that had cost Lometto nothing should now cost him even a single lira, was such that he pocketed the check and in a detached tone closed the door on both of them, saying:

"Well, this time I gave you a special price, for you, Nicola, *una tantum.* I'm always here, like those Cambodian ladies, the first to show up gets me. But I'm not going to move again for less than my normal fee, a hundred thousand a day plus expenses. I hope these ten thousand lire stick in your craw, Lometto, you prick!"

Lometto began to batter the door with his fists and begged:

"Open up, open up, I'll give you your ten thousand fucking lire, damnit!"

Angelo opened the door again. Lometto was rummaging in his pockets full of marks and couldn't find the ten thousand.

"Will you take ten marks?" he asked, trying to make himself small.

"Now listen, stop trying to make a fool of me. Ten marks is less than half. And at the bank they won't accept foreign small change."

"Here, twenty, but no cursing. I've already got one at home that gives me the evil eye."

This last detail seemed to have slipped out of him together with some coins that were rolling down the stairs.

Angelo said nothing, he took the two ten-mark bills with his fingertips and closed the door in perfect silence, without saying goodbye again. One must never pretend to grant someone the luxury of pretending to give, in the hope of getting one's own back later on: there never is a *later on*, if one starts so badly. One must make one's demands. No coyness where capital is involved. Lometto's wallet was the only true terminal of his nervous system. Strike there in order to strike at the heart. And banish all nuances. Now, as he went back inside, the room was filled with the stench of decomposing melons. Gino had gone overboard again. Angelo sighed and dragged onto the landing a crate of melons that were ripe but not rotten. He had added the decomposing out of nausea for this railroad-vegetable octopus constitutionally impervious to any tentacle of ridicule.

"Hey, *fratellini*!" he began to shout down the stairwell. "Free melons today for everyone. Melons worthy of Mother Nature! Come and get them, cheeseheads! Hurry, hurry, little black faces! Free Melooon! And you too, daddies and mommies! Kit and Caboodle, with no wit in your noodle!"

They were almost all small-time Fascists and Catholic Communists, poor, lugubrious, and Angelo wanted to stick to the calembour, so as to make his compulsory generosity more easily acceptable: that is why he offends them as he hands out a gourd brassy with double meaning. He was the thirty-fifth enemy plane that that bunch of pupils was not going to shoot down: too ethereal for them, too subterranean, too down-to-earth.

What a crowd today on the kerchief cut out among the reeds right behind the villa, all the little shrieks, all the little flutterings of muffled propellers, declamatory, ready to lunge or resonating with the patient hum of a reconnoitering mission which will last for quite a while before deciding to accost.

The transvestites have shattered the peace of this place. Their perfect breasts have been a gold mine for the rowboat renter down there on the Lido. Their aquatic processions around Grace's pink rubber raft. Grace, however, is not working but only exhibiting herself: she is a tall product of surgical witchery from head to foot. Her copper-red curls hang over the edge of the raft and their tips sway in the water like tropical algae, the angular face is perfectly made, marmoreal, thin, long lips covered with brick-colored lipstick, knowledgeably throbbing nostrils, breasts devoid of the least wobble, and that tanga of fake leopard regurgitating with a provocative male member of arbitrary proportions on which are focused all the regatta's pantographic gazes.

Grace never smiles, there is a good reason for the fierce expression on his face. Anyone approaching this floating yum-yum will notice that from the massive silver chain which cuts into his neck below the pointed ear hangs an uncommon charm: a full denture. It's his. Now he's a specialist in the "gum job," but this is a result, not a point of departure. As a token of love for a young man from Virle Tre Ponti who had problems, in the space of forty-eight hours Grace had all his teeth pulled out in Rotterdam so as to be able at last to satisfy him. And also in order to be able to make sure that nobody, ever, will steal him away. His mouth is not simply toothless: it is the site of a competition on the interprovincial level that never does and never will come to an end. She is the Turandot about whom marvels are told between Brescia and Bergamo, and all those who believe they are more richly endowed than Grace's current lover risk both journey and humiliation in the hope of beating that record. Grace, reclining in the psychic pink of the inside of his cheeks, has only one dream: that the day will come when he will be compelled to have an operation on his mandibular bone.

Now the little girl in the bright blue tanga, with the long black hair, the small hard body, the tiny, well-toned muscles, is combing Palmira, about whom she is crazy. Palmira kicks and whines, but the two are always together. The little gorilla-girl is a protectress in love. Palmira is the oldest of three brothers, he's only nineteen, and he has brought up the seventeen-year-old and the sixteen-year-old appropriately. Together with Carlina and Nicoletta, the three of them form the

Pasionaria trio. They have slim bodies, tempered by work in the fields, finely drawn little faces, no aggressive feature. It's a pity that Palmira has this problem of a thick, very dark beard, which with the use of depilatory creams and greasepaint has spoiled his complexion, so that now he must always sit there with a veil over his head to avoid getting too much sun.

Last year the mother of these three, a not very practical woman and also despite her internationalist faith very hostile to the turn taken by her offspring, renounced forever trying to "straighten" them out and expired because of cardiac arrest after pursuing the trio with a sickle in her hand and a hammer in her mind. The father, very modern, perhaps in reaction to such a wife, has given up the land, granted full freedom to his sons, and now is the one who stays home to do the housework. He takes care of everything. He's the one who escorts them to the station in Brescia at ten o'clock and during the midnight break shows up with thermos and sandwiches. He hangs out in the neighborhood until two, when he finally loads them all in the car and starts adding up the proceeds. Now, if they get a phone installed at the farmhouse, they'll no longer have to go to Brescia so often, especially in the winter when it's very cold. They have many steady customers. But the three brothers are also very cautious: no silicon injections, no alteration in their chromosomal endowment. They're so young, perhaps one day they'll decide to start a family and then, with a couple of sons, their old age would be taken care of. And besides, as the father says, everything being equal, a well-painted piece, with a working bird, turns more tricks than a real quail or one of those operated-on morons whom nobody wants any longer and who all end up alcoholic and jump over the banister. If his wife had known about this, she would not have given them all those Communist names, because what's the point, the names of the past mean nothing in the present.

The little girl insists: "Come on. I'll make you corn rows. I can do them well."

"I look like a dog in them, just give it a good brushing, tease it a bit. Ouch, what are you doing? Not like that."

"So how do you want me to fix your hair today? All on one side?"

"Yes, but not on the left, on the right, I look better in profile. But don't you smell something burning?"

"Yeah, I think so."

"It comes from over there. Look, there's smoke. But where have my sisters gone? Carlinaaa! Nicolettaaa!"

"But what are you worried about? They probably set fire to another stretch of the escarpment. The usual pyromaniac acting macho."

"Stop pulling like that! Pyro what?"

Beyond the reed *séparé* there are several anxious mature gentlemen lying on their towels, their brows fatigued from vainly focusing on the young bodies perambulating by with indifference. All ready to tear each other limb from limb if the gerontophiliac from Rivoltella, who here has become a legendary hero, should appear. Unfortunately he shows up rarely, once, twice a season, but he leaves indelible marks on the aged little flesh of his fortunate choice.

Last year Angelo talked with him, apparently he was the only one under sixty who managed to get close to him. And what's more: to interrogate him, and make him talk willingly, since he couldn't do otherwise. This man from Rivoltella is the depository of one of the most haunting stories that Angelo ever picked up—he picks up stories in the way that connoisseurs pick poisonous mushrooms. The man had been raped by his grandfather at the age of seven. His grandfather had a small neighborhood barbershop, he always kept his brush of pure bristle dipped in the soap mug. One day he grabbed him, pulled down his short pants, passed the brush over his little hole, and raped him. With one stroke. The child stayed in bed for ten days with a fever without saying a word. Grandpa had threatened to kill him. The relationship, which had all the soap-and-water appearances of tender affection between grandpas and grandchildren in a barbershop, had continued with the same brutality until the grandfather died five years later. The child had grown up very taciturn; in fact, so much so that as he lay on one of the rare grassy patches along the shore, he was surprised at himself: this was the first time in twenty-five years that he had told his story. As he spoke, he ripped into shreds everything within reach: pages of porno magazines, twigs, leaves, flies, grasshoppers. But naturally that hadn't been the end of the problem. He had lived until he was twenty locked up in the house, without a friend, without a girl. He was turned on a lathe of darkness. There had been a moment in which he believed his parents had known everything from the start and it had been a horrible moment. The darkness of attics and cellars and natural inland caves had endowed him with a cavernous dark beauty which seized you as by concentric circles and inexorably captivated, like the flight of a bat in full daylight. People on the street turned to look. His eyes emitted dolorous enchantments which left you breathless. Of average height, with dark blond kinky hair, and a hard body of stone. And, in telling the ancestral story, he had become excited. Quite offhand, he had pulled down his bathing suit, the same as he had as a boy, and, to impart the correct dimension to his confidences, he had added:

"My grandfather had one like this, like mine."

In a flash, Angelo again saw the sprightly, puny barbers peeking through the beaded curtains of his childhood, he felt in his throat the dryness of the dust on the roads of past summers, razors gliding over ribbons of leather, shiny as silk, and he shivered and felt pity and admiration for that youth, a worthy aspirant to the mandibular shafting of Grace. The man said that—he didn't know why—at a certain point he had begun to go out in the evening and remain nailed to the metal fences around the bocce alleys in the neighboring villages. At times he had ejaculations while standing there, contemplating. He liked skinny, bony, not very tall men, with silver-sprinkled hair and a face full of good humor. Until one evening, four years ago, he had stood as if struck by lightning at the fence around the wineshop with the bocce alley. In front of him, target ball in hand, bent over to throw, the incarnation of his dreams. There was a questioning glance on the part of the distinguished old man as he straightened up and went to check the opponent's bocce ball. Since the young man kept staring at him, the old man had smiled at him amiably and must certainly have thought that he was being complimented on the accuracy of his throw. Old people, like young, are often grateful precisely for trifling things, it is those in between who are never grateful for anything and easily offended. Well, our budding gerontophile began to court him discreetly but assiduously, managed within the space of a week to become his partner in a bocce foursome and at card games, to accompany him right into his house and meet his only unmarried daughter. The old man was a widower. The young man knew the girl by sight. She was a few years older than he, she was pretty enough, and she had been more than happy at his visit. To make a long story short, the two men were always together; at times the daughter dropped in at the wineshop to look for them and said, "So do I fix dinner for three?" They got engaged. But just as at the beginning he had recovered vitality and appetite and the wish to live, so with the passing months and years he had wasted away and lived in a state of anguished tension and, on the sly, had become dependent on barbiturates. He made love to the girl, but he had to imagine that under him he had his future father-in-law. He suffered from dreadful headaches which lasted two, even three days plus the nights. He had seen many doctors; he slept no more than three hours a day. He had become even more beautiful. She kept telling him that she did not believe in his illnesses. Perhaps, by chance . . . but he couldn't say . . . he had let the father's name slip out during "intercourse," the daughter had understood something perhaps. Perhaps, like his mother in her day, she pretended she didn't know anything. But she no longer was as importunate as before; often, with some sort of an excuse—bingo, her girlfriend, her married sister—she went out and left them alone. The two men, left to the fantasies of a dim living room, sheltered from all indiscreet eyes, immediately changed their way of communicating: slowly they locked eyes and remained that way. What there was in the old man's eyes, he could not say. It was a complicated situation. If he had any doubts about the daughter, he had none about the father: he had caught on. There was this lingering with spasmodic expectation in the mercurial immobility of hypotheses overturned by themselves, a vain grasping for help from each other, skimming over the snow on the windowsill or a chunk of moon at the window. One day a cat showed up in the house. A stove-black tabby with yellow eyes. The animal imparted a wavy movement to the atmosphere, discharging it. The two now confronted each other from two opposed armchairs and the cat came and went from the lap of the old man to the fly of the young man. Both in turn caressed the cat, staring at each other like beasts, gliding their hand beneath its "bun." They said to it, "You never get enough, eh?" "What a dirty tom, look how he enjoys it." "He's excited, this beast." "We're all animals."

And the cat was again sent to the sender-addressee, who, after having taken note with his fingertips of all the lascivious caresses conveyed by the beast, sent him back to the addressee-sender always a bit more languid than before. Their hands stroked the same fur, the same butt, belly, were inserted between the sharp little teeth without the six eyes ever leaving each other for an instant. Then the daughter came home, or the old man told him that it was time to go to sleep, showed him that the cat was going to sleep next to him, and the spell broken, gave him a smack on the shoulder and said "See you tomorrow." That is why he came sometimes to the Terrazzine: to pour out his heart, to stop thinking about it. He picked the most emaciated, a man with reasonably white or gray hair and a bit fat even, or with a receding hairline or bald but skinny or rubicund with black hair but distinguished, in short he picked up any old man, lured him into the thicket, and did to him what his grandfather had done to him. Eight times in a row. He had with him the brush and a can of shaving cream.

Now Angelo gets up to greet people here and there, checks the ripening of the last blackberries which are still too green, he's a glutton for them. Having reached the wild fig tree which separates these two stations, he is welcomed by the habitual hum of admiring disapproval.

"Here comes Pica della Mirandola! Here she is, preaching one thing and practicing another!" Carmencita shrieks in falsetto. "Did you leave the pulpit behind?"

Angelo laughs wholeheartedly and stretches out on the stones. This isn't the smell of burnt twigs, or even if it were. He always and only experiences this remembrance of pharmacopoeial smells, and within it there is a streak of burnt straw. Manias. He has spent ten years asking himself how it is that, from time to time, he smelled under his nose a scent of watermelon just taken out of ice-cold water and eaten with bread. During the winter, in Oslo, or on a Caravelle, in situations that had nothing in common apparently except a feeling of being lost forever, away from a non-specified place. Only to discover what it was a year ago, at the end of March, standing before a coffin. The watermelon and bread had been sacred viands of the only afternoon of truce, or passable communion, with his father. He was little less than an adolescent. The watermelon sat in the stream and his father dozed beneath a plane tree. It had been his surprise: a whole watermelon for the two of them! Angelo chased the flies from his face and arms, taking care that neither he nor they should wake him. He looked now at him, now at the gleaming dark green half-moon in the water, and was perturbed by the sumptuousness of the two beauties there, beneath his fingers, terrifying. Then the watermelon is quartered, fangs sink into it, the bread is broken, swallowed, defecated, the brook freezes a spore in some cell of the brain, flies and coleoptera devour the rinds and crumbs of that horrible happiness on the pebbled shore, and for decades nothing is heard about that final doze beneath the throbbing armpit of that unknown corpse which has invaded the anteroom and laughs inside a refrigerated drawer . . .

Not one of these bathers bleeds any longer. Everything is coagulated, as though embalmed. Angelo is jolted by this echo which strikes him in the drowsiness to which he was yielding.

Angelo knows, as he takes in fragmentary sentences, what Moschina will do now: she will rise on the tips of her toes, fling up her arms, bump and grind, and cry: "Miss Italee!"

Everything has been recorded once and for all. It is there, clear, scratchy, but in the end it is the black on white of a case dismissed.

They made a second trip at the beginning of September after what was a vagabond August for Angelo, since during that month the university apartments were closed down. Nicola went along, but he seemed to have lost much of the already meager importance he had. Angelo had imposed his cachet. He must put everything on the line: he had enrolled in a driving school and was going to cough up for the third learner's permit. He was completely untalented, even worse than a fledgling nun. This was pure Germanic philology aggravated by pistons and exhaust pipes and gears. On that trip it was Nicola who slept in the single room and he with Lometto.

"This is between us: it's the last time we take along Nicola. Some balls! To do the foreign market using an interpreter I pay and he pockets the commission! For free. And besides, I tell you, the customers can't stand him. That slowpoke. Anyway, don't let on, but I'm unloading him."

"But why are you telling me all this? What do I know about the agreements between you two? What do I care? You need me, you pay me; he needs me, he pays me."

"Oh no, my friend, this is exactly what I meant: that in the future if he asks you, you mustn't go with him. You're mine, exclusive, all right?"

"Oh, we'll have to see what's in it for me."

"Well, then, do as you like. This trip and no hard feelings."

Everything was clear enough: after getting him to introduce him to these two customers, he had no more use for Nicola, just costly ballast to be unloaded.

Angelo had been so good at dealing with these two Germans worth half a billion between them that they now wanted him as mediator. Back in August, Lometto had asked him to make a couple of phone calls. He'd come to pick him up by car at Montichiari and had taken him to Toigo, to the factory, had locked him in the office and gotten him to make phone calls for four hours. Not only to Germany, to all of Europe. Angelo basted, mended, ironed, put back in place. A job of haute couture via the telephone wire.

When he had asked about Nicola, Lometto had shrugged: "He's probably on his motorboat with some pretty tourist."

Four years earlier Lometto had been elected managing director of the company of which he owned thirty percent of the shares. He had sunk into the leather armchair behind the desk and, from an initial business volume of three hundred million, almost solely through his weight, which enlarged everything and in many directions, the last billing of '78 had been almost four billion lire—practically an annual turnover of ten billion lire. He had almost immediately begun to build new concrete wings, had increased the investment in machinery, he was waiting for the new balance sheet to realize the dream of every sock knitter: his own dyeing plant. Now Lometto planned to eliminate all salesmen one by one, since his portfolio of customers had already become an accordion encompassing every European meridian and parallel, and personally to take care of the commercial side. With the help of a secretary for the correspondence abroad and a free-lance interpreter. Angelo had calculated that, besides taking "human" possession of the customers through direct relations, even using him every day of the year, he would save four hundred percent in commissions, and certainly even with the rosiest calculations, Angelo could not hope to put in more than fifty actual working days, not counting little bites into mornings and afternoons for sudden customer visits to the plant. Lometto's savings, even though he now had to contribute his own time, were incalculable. They returned from the second trip with Nicola scowling and Lometto driving as if he had a carton of panty-hose discards at his side.

What importance Angelo had acquired! By adding some ideas of his own to the arguments of his two temporary employers, he had managed to corner two customers, he who while translating also advised on the next move to make because there was an untranslatable nuance which hung there over the accuracy of the linguistic reproduction, like an Ortega y Gasset sword, and, according to him, should be interpreted "this way." Angelo set before his two companions a whole gamut of hypotheses, barring none: one of them contained the appropriate spring trap for that particular commercial fox. What did they think about it? Lometto and Nicola always staked their money on the most toothless. Angelo pointed out to them that, in his opinion, taking into account the times, the competition of Israel, not to mention the internal one from Castelgoffredo, the short-term increase in orders, the hypothesis to espouse was another and that, indeed, one could, one must come down a few pfennigs, for the "entry." From nuance to nuance, the negotiations never missed fire, neither over the phone nor in person. The facts proved it. Not that afterward Lometto would tell him how a certain contract for a certain quantity of that particular item had concretely taken shape via telex, but the office girl was explicit: the orders poured in. Lometto only said: "Yes, a few items, nothing much."

But already since those first few times, the two or three partners who worked on the inside of the factory treated him with such consideration that there could be no doubt: Angelo was important, indispensable. For everybody save one: Bananone—Big Banana.

On the third trip in November, he and Lometto alone, free, and full of their respective secret forecasts and certainties of profit, decided that they would be on a "honeymoon" and would quarrel only to make the driving time go by, intentionally. Angelo helped him to discover a number of things: Chinese restaurants, how to knot a tie, the small pills to dissolve in the mouth against bad breath, Lake Starnberg, on the way back from Schöngau. They arrived at the Chapel, where a tiny man spoke about Ludwig as if he were his current gamekeeper. Lometto was in a hurry, what did he care who had drowned there a century before? Obviously, you drown in water, not by doing gymnastics. He kept saying that he was cold, wanted to get back in the car. Angelo, who felt exactly as he did, did not find him more odious than necessary. He thanked him at any rate for having stopped. But Angelo did harbor a certain resentment: Lometto, in other words, made it clear to him that that half-hour stop was a waste of time. And that in the future he should abstain.

Angelo understood and went on the attack, from the flank: "Say something, because whether you do or do not talk one can smell your shitty breath anyway. Take a pill."

Lometto refused to bite: he kept driving disdainfully, in a turmoil because someone had dared tell him that he stank and full of admiration for letting himself be dragged by the sleeve into a pharmacy.

"But really, now look at the face he's making just because of a twenty-minute stop. We stretched our legs. It's as if you had walked down Via Wagner."

"Great stuff. Just to show off. I know plenty of things that you don't know. Go there by yourself next time. You made me spend two marks to look at some dirty water and a bunch of photographs."

"I don't care, if you stink you stink, that's all. The lake's got nothing to do with it. The fact is that you want to drive thirteen hours a day, do customer after customer, exploit me as much as you can."

"But I do pay you."

"Yes, but if it goes on like this even a hundred thousand a day isn't enough, if I'm supposed to stay awake twenty-four hours a day at your beck and call."

"But you didn't specify that museums and churches should be included—just look at him, the little intellectual gentleman with egg on his head! We're not out for a stroll. And besides, there's Edda, I even asked her, what bad breath are you talking about?"

"One exhalation from you and goodbye customer. Just as when you sleep: there's no point in your insisting that your wife says you don't snore. You snore, you snore like a cement mixer in full swing. So make up your mind to get single rooms!"

"You didn't specify that either."

"Well, from now on it's a hundred thousand plus meals and single room."

"I bet you'd like to lay down the rules afterward."

"And ten hours running around a day is tops."

"Oh, what a sweet sugar-lump mouth! No, darling, you'll sleep with me. And you can begin right now to behave as agreed. And if you're a good boy, between the light and the dark, you'll pick up an item . . ."

"Come on, Lometto, you know very well that I'd never give it to you. You're not my type. I like fat men whose breath stinks and who snore at night. All the things that you are not, you just said so yourself."

"Watch out, I'll throw you out right here. An icicle, that's what you'll be by the time they find you."

On the road it rained and hailed and snowed all at the same time.

"You'll be surprised. I'd find something to do even here, with my inventiveness I'd make snot Popsicles."

"Yeah, you'll turn frozen tricks! Of course, to make a bit of extra money and pay at least for your fucking pepper fillets you could even turn a couple of tricks . . . and what's more, look, I'm ready to go broke: I'll give you the pantyhose, oh God, oh heavens! Those lacy orange ones that Pfefferman got me to make up: you'd pick up some items, some first-class items!"

"Why don't you wear them! Or I'll take the orange ones, and you the ones with the seam in the back. Shall we go together to the fancy-dress ball come carnival?"

"Did I tell you the one about the iron cunt?"

"Yes, beloved, yes. At least twenty times. Look out, you're swerving, be careful."

"Hey, you, you'll end up breaking my windshield. Look at all those pine trees and fir. They've got plenty of timber."

"Don't you see that two out of three are rotten?"

"I see, I see. I don't need you to teach me what chemical rain is, eh, Angelina, my little cunt!"

"No wonder. You all did the same thing with the waste water, you included. Only in Italy the forests aren't rotting, because there aren't any left."

"And I'm going to tell it to you anyway. There was a wineshop in the open countryside not far from Madonna della Grazie, the owner was a . . ."

"Celestino, enough, take pity! Tell them to your partners. To Bananone!"

"I know where I would give that one a big banana."

They called him Bananone because he wore a fat round curl like a banana on the top of his head, like a country tough, thought he was irresistible to the women employees, and only put on pinstripes. The more the new trends in entrepreneurial adventure pushed him back, the more he insisted on his role as a Communist frantic to show who he was. He didn't even know how to draw an O with the bottom of his glass. Lometto knew that Bananone was splitting hairs in four, using every means of persuasion, to entice nine more partners to his side, based on the fact that Lometto was a thief when it came to the dividends, probably, or that he was expanding, expending, and never paid out a lira at the end of the year.

"But why does he have it in for you, Lometto?"

The nights they had to while away together were many, the dinners, the stops; one after the other, all subjects had to be touched on, from the most important to the most trifling and unconfessable, until the nth "iron cunt" popped up again, and it became necessary to start inventing another wrangle to bring on the evening and kill those four more hours of travel decided on—by Lometto—at nine o'clock.

"Ask him."

"He doesn't even say hello to me. He looks at me as if I were a worm. What did I ever do to him? He should be glad that the customers like me, right?"

"What do you mean, what did you do to him? You were brought in by me, no?"

"Big fucking deal, but you're the commercial and managing director, you're the president of the company, or aren't you?"

"He wanted to pull in a cousin of his, to put a spy on my tail. Just think, he doesn't even have the right to set foot in the factory if I don't want him to, and I should hire one of his flunkies."

"But what is he complaining about? I don't get it. He too must see that dividends are increasing every year, right? Let's even say that you steal a bit . . ."

"As for stealing, nobody beats you. It's envy, jealousy."

"But of what? Of you?"

"No, you. Of course, me! First for actions and then also for words."

"Because of your fast talk?"

"I bawl him out at the board meetings. I don't let him get away with anything. He with his banana curl on his forehead. A company is not a whorehouse, two tits and that's all. You need incrementation, productivity, to keep in step. And if once more he takes the liberty of calling my girls 'cutie pie' and using their first names, I'll have him thrown out."

"But then, when you call waiters by their first names, isn't it the same stuff? As far as manners go, look, I assure you, you have no reason to be envious of him. Between you and your partners, you're all a bunch of oafs. It's enough for somebody to wait on you for a moment, and you're on first-name terms, just like Comrade Bananone."

A quarrel followed. The quarrel was followed by threats of farewell forever. Then there were contests regarding primacy of intelligence. In a didactically nineteenth-century spirit, Angelo told him: "You see,

Lometto, you are shrewd, you are, and an expert in economics—that is, making things all go one way. Intelligence is not applicable to the laws of profit. Intelligence becomes subtle and loses. You, on the contrary, make money and arrange things so that you always make money. You are on this side of reality and your shrewdness screens you from the other side. You think that there are no demarcations, but there is a nervous barrier beyond which you cannot go. However, I am really intelligent. I do not capitalize and then always look back at those who are worse off than I. It isn't that I'm more intelligent than you, or vice versa. These are two different things, two irreconcilable conditions. You are shrewd, call it astuteness and I leave the palm to you in all conscience, together with your billions et cetera. But intelligence, no, in all honesty no, I cannot do you the injustice of considering you more intelligent than me. It's like adding figs and watermelons. I could let you believe it, but then I would prove that I'm not only more intelligent than you but also shrewder. I don't do so because I have nothing to gain from leading you down the road to perdition: you would really lose yourself. You're too stupid."

"For me, you're full of complexes because you haven't got a lira and you can't do the things you'd like to. For example, it's since I know you that you've been dreaming of going to Egypt."

"You too, unfortunately, are full of complexes because, and you show it, you're neither educated nor intelligent. Your shrewdness doesn't let you, it doesn't let you see your mistakes. I could even decide to make money, you cannot decide to understand the beauty of a lake and the mystery of the suicide of an imbecile linked to history. At the age of forty-two you can't decide to become intelligent. You see, an intelligent person, if he wants to, can even become shrewd, the shrewd cannot become intelligent, nor can the intelligent person once he has turned shrewd go back ever again."

"Oh God, all this blah-blah for nothing. Cut it out."

"And anyway, what do you need intelligence for? It doesn't sell pantyhose. Go on making pantyhose and buy yourself intelligence or education or any quality you lack on the market, as has been done since the beginning of time."

"Let me tell you, nobody has ever insulted me like you. No wonder you didn't last long on your jobs."

"Obviously, with all those jubilant ignoramuses that surround you! Did I ever meet during these six months, among your customers, suppliers, partners, employees, anyone who slightly stands out from the mere animal condition of making it to payday? No. So don't be surprised if nobody has ever offended you openly: they lack the gift of speech, they only know how to say yes. But—I don't say all of them—just take Bananone and that other one from machine maintenance: in my opinion there's a whole lot of people who smile to your face and meanwhile dig the ground from under your feet."

These conversations were dropped after dinner and often resumed at two in the morning when Angelo came back. Hearing the knock at the door, Lometto emitted a more intense grunt and came to open it, rubbing his eye like a big whimpering baby with an ugly dream on his forehead, but he never cursed. He opened the door and threw himself back on the bed, making the springs sing, and while Angelo slipped under the shower in the dark or with only the light in the bathroom lit, Lometto began to comment in a faltering somnolent voice: "There he comes . . . at this hour . . . what time is it? Stark naked and he takes his undershirt off in the elevator . . . his shorts as he goes along the way . . . he makes a goddamn racket . . . Yeah sure, laugh, laugh . . . Did you catch some little items, eh? Wash her off good, you better . . ."

"All right already! And you?"

"Me, not even one. I telephoned Edda. I've got a headache!"

"So jerk off."

"I don't know how, I never . . . not even when I was a kid. I'd need a stranger's hand."

"Poor thing . . . use your shoehorn . . . Night."

"If you guess what I've got in my hand, I'll give you a piece of it."

"A chocolate cream!"

"Getting warm, getting warm!"

"A stick of licorice!"

"Lukey-warm, lukey-warm!"

"A slipper!"

"You, do me a favor, don't call my business a slipper. Cold, cold . . . Night."

Away from Nicola, Lometto was different: more relaxed, without a touch of night-wandering at all costs. He wanted only one thing: get back to the hotel, call home, and fiddle with the calculator until he keeled over with fatigue. He counted the pantyhose sold or projected, usually until twelve o'clock, then until twelve-thirty he metamorphosed them into marks or florins, and from that into lire. And from lire into houses or stables. Then, if he got a "headache," into rents, milk, cheese. Then into ministerial armchairs for his sons. Angelo had only been able to get that far, but certainly there must be many more links in Lometto's commutative chain.

The trip lasted a lifetime, the longest yet: Munich, Augsburg, Stuttgart, Mannheim, Frankfurt, Cologne, Krefeld, then off to Dortmund, Hanover, from there to Berlin and down again to Munich.

From Munich, with a sour look, Lometto continued alone on the way home because Angelo took the opportunity to stop off at Jürgen's. Jürgen studied architecture and lived in a studio apartment in which there was a bed, an enormous white table, and a small marble angel that came from the grave of a great-aunt, and three chairs, two of them garden chairs removed at night from a beer hall and one, very precious, almost a rocker from the twenties, bought from an antique shop. The two garden chairs were broken, the other too decorative to sit on. One always stood up or sat down on the rug. Resting against the only free wall of the cubicle—beyond which were more narrow studio apartments inhabited by spinsters, old homosexuals, students, and other very colorful singles who lived dejected and burdened with problems—a framed poster of *Iphigenia*. It had hung there since he received it as a gift from the director of the production two years before. The space under the bed and under the table was occupied by a stack of books and small wooden puzzle toys for children, which he loved.

He found him reading the fifth volume of Casanova's *Memoirs*, which he alternated with *Oblomov*. If they were standing they changed position by touching index fingers and embroidering a nimble minuet around the small heap of dirty laundry in the center of the room. Jürgen began his highly literary sentences with: "You see, my dear girl, here at Versailles . . ." accompanying them with a sweeping gesture of his free arm. Then he started to complain about "the help these days." Jürgen was a hand taller than Angelo and had a cool delicate complexion. He sniffed his finger every ten seconds. He stuck it everywhere and in any situation. Whenever Angelo attempted a sociopolitical switch to find out more about Germany, Jürgen pulled his finger out of somewhere and, sniffing it with expertise, said: "Oh, my dear Charlotte, *je vous en prie pas de quoi merci beaucoup*"—that is, all the French he knew.

They walked along the banks of the Isar, through the snow, the first Christmas trees already glittered through the windows. Since he had just been in South Africa—his mother supported him magnificently, which was a secret to his carpenter father, who gave him a fixed stipend—Angelo wanted to hear something "narrative" about apartheid. Jürgen opened his eyes wide and answered the same thing he answered when the subject was the Bader-Meinhof gang: "Regards to the girls at Johnny Müller's bar." Together they built a snowman.

It was fun to stay a few days with Jürgen, to stroll with him through the picture galleries and the Cinema Museum. But Angelo had to go by himself to see an exhibition that had just been moved in bulk from Wiesbaden and purged of all its elements of high military technology so it could be opened to the public. One could have called it the supermarket of the twentieth-century spy-at-the-keyhole. Micro radio transceivers, minuscule recorders hidden in matchboxes, ordinary eyeglasses with an enlarging device inside, cameras encapsulated in lighters and lipsticks, a whole congeries of Distrust and Suspicion within reach of the man in the street. In the exhibition hall there was the electrifying happiness of people trying by all means to discover what others will do anything to keep hidden. Angelo was not interested in all this, he did it reluctantly to keep in practice at not doing only the things to which he felt attracted. After all there were times when one must get on the ball and rush to spy on what the *alien* was doing, the sprite of "the world such as it is." And he managed to do so, but there was no way that one could drag along Jürgen, all taken up with his microbiological experiments on himself; he did not give a damn about the Japanese and Americans. He was dialoguing with Voltaire and the Hohenzollerns, Gropius and Artemidorus, and dropped an LSD tablet a day. At night he attached torture instruments to his nipples, a novelty to increase their turgidity, and two eye-openers, certain minuscule silver traps that imprisoned his eyelids and prevented him from falling asleep. He gazed fixedly at the ceiling and didn't bother anyone even for a moment. Two days later he received an extra six hundred marks from his mother, whom he had just convinced to give him a tattoo for a Christmas present. They went together to a huge Dutchman who had a shop at Schwabing and there Angelo witnessed the puncturing of the tail and the tracing of the entire design. The buttock bled copiously and it was decided to stop there for that session. Jürgen revealed to him that he was doing this to obey his new friend, a plastic surgeon, a person about Angelo's age—Jürgen was seven years younger.

Everything in Jürgen was so delicately insensate that all by himself he resembled a nation in decline. He had a sense of commendable measure in all the abuses he perpetrated on himself. He had this gift of exceeding in everything without overdoing it, every time bringing himself home all in one piece. Angelo was enchanted by his proximity. It was not easy to find him at home, most times he was in a hospital. Strange brainstorms, which did not actually aim at suicide but at a prolongation of the sensation of death: chlorine, muriatic acid, freezing. Jürgen was the only person to get every venereal disease before and better than Angelo. But there was no bacterial jousting between them, it was a simple alternate passing along of the torch, the gas torch, to fix the slides of the allergy tests. Both of them waited for the appearance on the market of new antibiotics, because their bodies produced nuances of ever more complex momentary cancers.

This time too Angelo managed to tear himself away from the serpentine coils of his aspermatic friend and, reluctantly, he returned to Verona. It was becoming increasingly difficult for him not to attend to those echoes of self-destructive blandishments and delve again into the nightly engine studies, in the small classroom of youngsters who needed only a bureaucratic certificate, while the little nun giggled foolishly at every mistaken X on the tests. Angelo thought about Jürgen, his somewhat fishlike beauty, and of where he would go to procure for him ten "hand-polished" olive-wood eggs—the kind used to mend socks. Many surprises came and went in the standard existence of a temporary pantyhose salesman on the brink of getting his driver's license and his degree. Some had been deposited once and for all and now showed all the droopiness of habit: Imer, Demetrio, Gino, cyclical like the changing of linens. They were the shorts and undershirts and socks he took to his mother to be washed: always a bit more worn but not to the point of being thrown away. Taking turns, all three would come to Via Verdi to masticate the aria of their inadequacy at living. They were the most frightful Catholics, those orphaned by the orthodoxy of confession. A priest was no longer enough for them, they wanted a devil of flesh and blood. Angelo lent himself out of weakness which he knew how to transform into logorrheic complacency and he rested his ear against the grate of their bogus inappetences. When they left, he was exhausted from all that "listening." His voice was gone.

Since, despite telephone calls and hints, Lometto was not making up his mind to show up with a check, he called him again and told him clearly: "What about my money?"

"What money?"

"What do you mean, what money? The money you owe me for the trip."

"But didn't I already give it to you?"

"Listen, if you're trying to get me mad, tell me right away."

"But look, with the advance and what I gave you day by day, we're even."

"But you're crazy through and through, you owe me four hundred thousand lire and a bit more."

"Really? Well, I don't have the time now, I'll look into it."

"What are you saying, look into it, look into it! You're going to bring me that money before this evening, and either you figure it out now or we'll settle the score when you get here. Listen, Lometto, no tricks with me."

"Or else?"

"Or else I'll show you something. I expect to see you this evening at eight o'clock. Make sure you're on time."

The "or else" had been clear to both of them; or else he would call the customers, drop a corrosive moth, a competitive red ant, a hyena that commercially would have done him in.

On time came Adele's oldest boy, around eight o'clock, with a sweaty little note from Lometto announcing a sudden engagement / but tomorrow at eleven / luncheon at his house / could he be at the Verona South exit, a thousand thanks? (The "thousand thanks" was Adele's thoughtful contribution.)

Oh, finally Lometto was presenting him to the Family; it was self-evident that he had looked into it, and thoroughly.

The rain had swept away the morning's veil of snow, carried to the middle of the highway by the wind. At eleven there was a blinding sun that entered through the silver metallized body of the car. With a whistling glance Lometto plugs in the Fred Buongusto cassette, the object of so much intolerance during the trip to Germany.

"Are you trying to give me a bellyache? If you don't change it, I'll throw it out the window."

"You wouldn't dare. It's my wife's."

"But are they all like this?"

"She bought it wholesale. She lets me have one a month."

"That's just great."

And here goes Lometto doing a hundred and fifty in the center of Toigo, on his way to Penzana, the nearby town where they live. A traffic paddle bobs up and down. The brownish uniform approaches. Lometto lowers the window.

"Oh, Engineer. Lometto, sir! I didn't recognize you! You've changed cars! Beautiful, just beautiful. This one doesn't skid even in the snow. Go on, go ahead."

Lometto's chin does a triumphant *ralenti*, his eyes have a kindly expression.

"Since when are you an engineer?"

"Like that . . . And everybody notices that I've changed cars, everybody but you. Didn't you see it's not the same I had two weeks ago? Where do you live?"

They start up again, a bit more slowly. Along the highway several factory sirens shriek. After a sharp turn which runs into the open countryside, Lometto sticks his arm out into the damp wind and makes a one-hundred-and-eighty-degree gesture. Penzana. Angelo thinks such an all-encompassing gesture must have been made the last time by Satan during the Temptation of Christ. The rain which falls from an illuminated sky renders the ostentation laconic: fields, farms, building lots, and an enormous sign, "Gonzaga Consortium." And then the index finger points toward a building in the middle with three sloping roofs and, above the highest, a battlemented tower of very recent construction, certainly an addition of feudal whimsy to the restructured farmhouse. They drive along a ditch full of rotten reed mace, reach a low building, "kindergarten," plaster gnomes, and the skeleton of a car whose protuberances are topped with clumps of snow pop up along a track of beaten earth—for tractors, threshers, and carts: and there they are, the farm machines, with their noses sticking out of the large hangar windows to see what the weather is like. On this hybrid Mikado's threshing floor no stench of manure, loud moos isolate it on several sides, enamel it with a no-nonsense silent Lombard religiosity.

Edda Lometto stands at the door under the portico, the root of her eyebrows so typically that of a woman from the South, and she's hurriedly drying her hands on her apron. She wears a dress of inexpensive black wool. Tall, abundant haunches, aquiline nose, short mouse-colored hair cripsy and unkempt, tight mouth, receding lips. Not a shadow of make-up. She is very excited. "Calm down" her husband orders. "He isn't the prime minister."

"Oh, delighted, my name is Edda. I'm not ready yet. I wanted to prepare a surprise for you, but you know how it is, run here, run there, and the maids are always up to something. The duck is a bit . . ."

"Don't worry, he'll eat the duck just as it is. And the boys?"

"They'll be here any minute. Could I offer you a slice of salami?"

"No, thanks."

"We've had the masons until yesterday. We're always building here."

They've already gone down the hallway, enter a large room with rustic, massive furniture, the dining room, where every edge is beveled, chairs that seem in suspense in their leather and straw; one feels that nobody has ever eaten here.

"Walnut?"

"Yes, all custom-made for me. My father-in-law is an artist, he chose the kind of wood that will last a thousand years. Come, let me show you the fireplace in the next room. You set the table meanwhile."

"Here?"

"Sure, where else?"

In a huge room crammed with stacked cartons, reams of cardboard inserts wrapped in transparent plastic and piles of bleached pantyhose, there are some slabs of pink Garda marble inserted in a hole in the wall.

"Do you like it? Wait till it's finished."

"It's very nice marble. And in here?"

"This is an office, I've got my phone, do a bit of private accounting."

"Why all those cartons?"

"I have my own workshop, don't I?"

"Oh! And what has it got to do with Mire, Inc."

"That *and* the workshop. Everybody has got an extra workshop, my partners too. Other outlets . . . in the wee small hours, with the north wind . . . all black, under the counter!"

As they climbed up to the second floor the smell of fresh-chipped lime diminished and another smell wafted over, indefinable, which brought to mind hospital wards stumbled into for a moment by mistake. The odor of musk inspired the premonition of a crèche. Lometto flung open the doors: the boys' bedrooms, the bath, the storage room. Then his own bedroom, but just a glimpse, without letting go of the door handle, closing it again on a crack through which appeared the side view of a small wax Madonna covered with tiny hearts and red amulets under a glass bell. Everywhere something was missing: a tile, a balustrade, a molding, a shelf. Not a plant to be seen.

"Up there, in the tower, there is the room where they cook up their stuff. At least this way they don't break our balls. They'll take you up." He stared at Angelo perfidiously and added, "But watch your step, right?"

"Listen, Celestino, you prick, get off my ass. I've told you a hundred times that I'm not a pederast and besides I'm allergic to sons in general. What I want to do is settle our account. I'd rather spoil my appetite than my digestion."

"All you think about is money. You're just a moneygrubber, not a friend."

"Some gall."

In the small jumbled room adjacent to the big room downstairs the accounts were finally settled. It was as though the accounting of God the Creator expressing his wrath was unleashed. They could hear Edda moving back and forth between kitchen and dining room: she must have heard their stubborn clashes over a thousand lire, the creaking of chairs mixed with the grating of the old manual adding machine starting again from zero. From moment to moment Lometto fine-tuned his enervating tactics so that Angelo, worn out, would throw in the towel and let go of twenty, twenty-five thousand lire. Or, perhaps, he meant to force Angelo to do his accounts properly, taking into the right *account* the whimsical deductions by the employer, and thus learn to list them additionally, as Lometto did whenever he foresaw a *discount*. This was Lometto's aim: to teach him the ABC's of corruption, to begin to steal in order to obtain what is right. It was a modest first step, Angelo did not even want to think what the second might be. He did not accept the procedure. He never would accept it. He wanted his due, what was agreed upon, factoring in the cost of his intelligence or ability to render services, he saw no reason—or interest—in obtaining it by shrewdness. He wanted this line of separation to remain fixed, almost physical, between himself and Lometto.

"It's ready!" Edda took the liberty of chirping. The gaiety of her announcement was forced. It could also have been the finale of a roundelay hummed to herself, or a curse in Sunday dress.

Taking his seat in front of the stretch of tablecloth that partially covered the 3.5-by-1.3-meter table, Angelo saw the steaming tureen held by two worn hands sticking out of cheap black wool material, now all pilled. Edda had gone to change, and she was the same as before. But without an apron: her large black navel was outlined beneath the glitter of chipped porcelain and an unexpected hole that sucked in his direction struck Angelo as the most ferocious part that had escaped from a chained-up beast. He shivered, thanked without lifting his head, and had the impression of sinking into the fleshy maw of a crater hovering in the air. Edda's navel was an eye, lying in ambush, blind and obtuse, with something ferocious and brooding and incommensurably obscene. Angelo sensed a prehensile, vindictive divinity that issued from there to judge him and then coursed through Edda's internal veins, her softest parts, a sacrality of her blood, on whose prejudice such a woman bases her pitiless certainties.

"They're homemade" she said, dishing out the large pumpkin-stuffed ravioli. "My mother-in-law made them."

An adolescent voice, uncertain whether to go down or up. Angelo noticed that she accompanied every gesture or sentence with a glance at her husband, from whom she sought constant confirmation that she was fulfilling her task properly.

"They are exquisite. But aren't you sitting down with us?"

"Oh, I have to look after the boys, they eat inside. One of them wants it with sauce, the other with butter and sage, the other doesn't like them, a madhouse. The wine is my sister's, you've seen the vineyard behind the stables."

Edda shuffled away. It was not very warm in that room.

"But what's this businesss of the evil eye?" Angelo could not stop himself from bringing it up.

"What evil eye?" Lometto asked, calmly, emptying the bowl of grated cheese into his plate.

"In Verona, remember, when you didn't want to give me the twenty marks. You said that you already had enough with one at home, cursing you."

"Who, me? Never said anything like that. You must have misunderstood."

"Oh."

Shouts from the hallway, the rustle of plastic capes, joined feet jumping up and down on the doormat to shake off the rainwater. Television set turned on immediately in the kitchen. Clatter of crockery and dishes. The door thrown wide open, while Edda takes the last orders.

"Hello, my name is Angelo."

"Bring me the mineral water!" Lometto shouts.

"There's always something missing. How was school? What about the Christmas vacation?"

"Fine. Pleased to meet you: Ilario."

"Fine. Pleased to meet you: Berengario."

"And what's your name?" Angelo asked the smallest one.

"Belisario. Fine. Am I hungry!"

On the road outside Angelo caught a glimpse of a number of women of subnormal beauteousness who were getting on their bicycles and riding to lunch in the teeth of wind and drizzle.

"Who are they?" he asked.

"The women from the workshop. Some more?"

"Yes, yes. And where are they going?"

"To eat, at the parish house."

"Oh."

Under the windowsill a chicken landed by chance on a wooden base roosted stock-still. He concentrated on that strange apparition, while begging Edda not to overdo it with the duck sauce. From that hard beak and those slightly ruined feathers again shot out the shrapnel of that hospital-like odor he had noticed before, going upstairs. The names of the boys became confused, after an instant he no longer knew which one of them was Ilario, Berengario, and Belisario, and immediately he registered the diaphanous beauty of the oldest, the masculine beauty of the one in between, and the urchinlike beauty of the smallest. A crew in which the blood of the Gonzagas and that of the Aragonese were locked in combat. Seeing that Edda probably was from Caserta or Naples, or thereabouts. Watching her clear the table in silence with those sudden shy smiles of a young, uncertain girl which alternated with the sidelong glances of a hag, her body made one think of two silky morning glories stuck one inside the other. They started from a thread of smoke—slim calves, fragile ankles, small feet as though contracted—and expanded into the first flower at the height of the pelvis to then become narrower and commence the second flower, which slowly blossomed at the hips and opened up around the breasts, broad and flat. The head, minute, was the third inception of a further flowering, which came to a halt at the forehead and hair. In this head, in fact, there was something unfinished, the distrait traces of an inner pruning. All in all, it had the morphology of a fountain of the Fascist era: conoidal seashells inserted into each other and regurgitating with the stagnant life of the mollusk, on high a spurt of nervous pupils between narrow cheekbones, a low forehead, a prognathous chin. Now, assailed by the three sons, who raved around her and touched her ecstatically, Angelo saw, through the crack of the door which led to the kitchen, that that sharply honed gaze tried vainly to assume rotundity and softness or feminine humility. Edda gave an impression of obstinacy. The sons adored her because they knew how many and what soft spots there were inside the hardness of her façade.

"What are you looking at?"

"Your sons are really masterpieces."

"Oh!"

"And your wife is a woman who's on the ball."

"My wife is a woman on *two* balls, since you bring it up."

Angelo realized that Lometto was furiously and complacently both jealous and proud of her. They laughed at his crack. Angelo imagined the fuzz on Edda's lip as she bent to place kisses on her husband's hairless, hebetudinous lips. Her navel, rising and falling like a crab detached from the rest of the body over his, its claws small and in repose, the two soft hollows of admission into the world fitting together and sucking in, like two wounds or two valves of the same mollusk. He did not see any contraposition between male and female but rather two faces of a single creature that rolled upon itself by its own motion, the fact that their three sons had then come out of her womb was an insignificant, clinical detail.

At the end of the meal all the adjoining relatives came in for coffee. The authoritarian and bristly sister who took care of raising the milk cows, the servant brother-in-law, Lometto's father and mother, and two small nephews. They all sat down around the table gaping at the interpreter who knows five languages and has snared two customers worth half a billion. Their expression was reverential. Angelo, in his jacket and tie, knew how to make an impression on the popular imagination in overalls and housecoats: letting himself be worshipped by supplying for the winter conversations only the material they already had. Everybody knew everything about their trips, Lometto had never been stingy with artfully reembroidered anecdotes. The sister offered to uncork new bottles of wine, the fruit of her experiments—the soil there was most unsuitable for the production of those qualities but she insisted year in and year out on extracting Barolo, Amarone, Pinot: all megalomaniac for success in that family, Angelo thought, consenting to taste this one and that one and proclaiming its excellence, while doors opened and shut and little boys took turns going down to the cellar. The old mother with the light blue gaze whimpered over her troubles: the work shifts, the *poor* girls, the pantyhose, labels, problems with the dyeing plant, with plastic bags, with boxes, and then came colitis, arthritis, her back, the thermal baths, depression. The father was large and seraphic, drank without listening, a sparkling smile disporportionate to the events, a chunk of stogie in his mouth, a shirt with rolled-up sleeves, rubber boots as though it were spring outside. Lometto repeated events of the trips they had taken, adding details which to neither of the two had at the time seemed funny, inventing out of whole cloth when the stories in reality had not condensed into meaningful finales, attaching to them appendices and fanciful entrails so that the anecdotes could indeed be called that. When traveling, the things that do not have the time to assume a shape outnumber those which offer the pretext for a conclusive story. But everybody wanted fairy tales, and Angelo did his utmost not to send the audience away disappointed with itself. Lometto was happily enthroned with his straight man at his side.

"What a nice man! What a a nice man!" the mother repeated. "What a card! What a card!"

They all shook hands with him and disappeared, some into the stables, some into the underground workshop—and here came the bicycles of the wonder-women workers, halting on the little road beyond the window, all of them like crows cloaked in black clothes—the boys went into their rooms or up into the Tower. Edda had remained on her feet, holding out glasses, straightening out napkins. Every now and then she pulled down her dress of thin, prickly wool which climbed up her hips. She was somewhere between fourteen and forty-two. Of a sudden, the dining room emptied of shouts and laughter-at-all-costs and half-full bottles. Lometto shut his eyes and began to snore. His elbows on the table slipped sideways and in a few instants his head nestled between his arms.

There was a lovely sound of rain and wind. The check safely tucked away, despite the thirty thousand lire less. The little glassy eye of the chicken charged with ambushing antagonism. But what did Angelo care? His stuffing was only temporary.

"Do you want to see the Tower?" whispered the oldest boy, sticking in his head. Lometto let out a roar and rolled over onto his other arm.

"Go, go" Edda urged him. "He always dozes off for ten minutes after he eats."

And she gave him a childish smile, turning from the sink.

The Tower had a winding staircase and the other four children were waiting in front of a door at the top. The in-between Lometto was showing the way. The smell was becoming increasingly intense and precise. But it had no name in Angelo's sparse notions on the subject. The five boys were winding up the iron spirals in religious bickering. There was a second floor, which they passed quickly. Then, at the third, Angelo was confronted by the dull gleam of various implements, retorts and beakers on shelves, plastic aprons with large advertising slogans—"Napaglia Furniture decorates the house of your dreams"—a case full of very finely honed small knives, and a small gas range with an outdoor picnicking gas tank, glass eyes in a shoe box. On a shelf, a domestic zoo: a weasel, two owls, a dozen green lizards, a marmalade kitten a few days old. Plastic bags with handles smeared with clotted blood. And many small ampules.

"But what's this smell?"

And the in-between Lometto removed the cork from an ampule and said:

"It's phenol."

So that's how Lometto's boys were crazy about animals.

". . . pitch, we've been using pitch" said the in-between Lometto, the spokesman, holding up a dove with sparse feathers around the neck. "It came apart, we didn't strangle her right."

"Who taught you how to stuff animals?" Angelo asked, picking up from a small bench tufts of hemp and pieces of straw more dehydrated than normal.

"Our grandfather Ardito!" the trio cried in unison. The two cousins didn't make a peep, underlings.

"Who? The grandfather that was downstairs with the stogie?"

"Oh, no, the other one, grandpa Ardito. When he was young he used to cane chairs. He is self-made. Don't you know him?" the small Lometto asked.

"I don't."

"He's the one who now has the furniture factory."

"He has three of them. See this apron?"

"Oh!"

Angelo noticed that there must have been an escalation: at first animals caught in ditches, along the riverbanks, in the meadows, wild animals that didn't cost anything. Then the kitten, something already perhaps belonging to a neighbor, the chicken downstairs in the dining room. A waste of edible meat. A true and proper investment. He thought he could see Lometto sigh and admit his fatherly weakness with a hand over his chicken coop.

"But they seem to stink, or are they supposed to be like this?"

"You see?" interjected the middle one. "I told you so, there's still something that doesn't work. In my opinion we're not opening the jugular well enough. Damnit, these too will have to be thrown out."

"I think you leave too much guts inside."

"I'll dig the hole!" one of the two cousins offered.

"You shut up and stand at attention" the in-between one ordered.

"Well, meanwhile we're practicing, aren't we?" the small one said.

"Yes, if we continue like this we can kiss the piglet goodbye!" the oldest Lometto retorted disconsolately.

"Sure, we practice. When will we catch another weasel? And the owls? And when do you think Papa will give us another chicken, eh? But they are beautiful, aren't they? Try and hold your nose."

"Yes, well, I . . . as a hobby, I mean . . ."

"I'm the one who makes the trestles!" exulted the little Lometto, coming forward. He was covered with freckles and wore glasses.

"Oh yes" said Angelo "the trestles are important, they suggest the environment. And what is your role?" he continued, turning to the two children of Lometto's sister. Mario was three years old and his eyes burst with merriment as black and immense as his extraneousness. He had not yet learned how to talk, perhaps he was destined to a great unconcerned intelligence.

"We look at them" said Dario, the older cousin, somewhat disconsolate.

"When they're finished" specified the in-between one.

"When they're finished, not before" the possible competitor admitted. And turning to Angelo: "They're afraid I might learn too. And maybe mine wouldn't even stink."

"Why don't you go to your own grandfather, get him to teach you something, if he knows how. Your grandfather was in the Resistance, not like mine! Mine, my dear, was in the war, and look what he's been able to build up from nothing."

"He's from down South."

The in-between Lometto delivered a good smack. Angelo protested, amused. The cheek's sonority echoed down the stairs, where the whimperings of a puppy came running up. The rain and wind had stopped. Through the skylight he saw the fog invade the precocious sunset. All the boys began to play with a small muddy and frenetic little thing.

"My father named him Gelo, he's three months old" said the oldest. Partly because of the caresses and somersaults, which those fledgling executioners put him through, partly because that name reminded him of something vague, a sound, Angelo shivered. And then everybody rushed down the stairs at breakneck speed, with the puppy underfoot, barking happily. Who knows for how much longer. And perhaps he wouldn't even turn out well.

When after his swim Angelo slips through the opening in the reeds, there is a rubber boat obstructing the passage. Four men stand around watching the card game, and Zizi entertains them with his grimaces and appropriate wisecracks. They've come by to have a laugh. Angelo approaches one of the two who is mistreating a transistor radio.

"Can't you stop changing stations every minute? It's years that I'm coming here and nobody's ever dared to bring transistors. There must be a reason, don't you think? If you want a radio, go somewhere else."

"Who do you think you are? the owner of the airwaves?" snaps the knob manipulator.

Very quietly, Zizi says:

"Sooner or later Bazarovi will end up by killing all the fairies. Two of spades."

"Oh no, you can bet somebody else will see to that. Someone who isn't afraid of getting his hands dirty."

There is much excitement around the four men, clients of the Bordello. Engaged. Married. Normal.

"Hey, pretty boys, do you want to go for a ride in the boat?" proposes Messalina, turning on his thighs like an obese lizard.

"Oh yes, if Calcinculo comes too. She said she was coming here today" the more assured of the group says. "Didn't you see her?"

"Calcinculo isn't here" Zizi says curtly. "She's most likely fixing up. She eats fruit garnished with heroin. She likes pears! Are you crazy, why don't you play clubs? My partner is always thinking about pricks. Concentrate instead on picking up my friends' bundle."

"Do you know what cocker spaniels like to eat?" Larousse emerges from the mist of his crossword puzzle.

And now Amanda goes to the trouble of asking: "What?"

"Fresh eggs. Come on, Magra, sing something for us. They're crazy about them."

The little aria from *Traviata* rises all around. Magra dei Veleni—veteran basketball player—has placed on his chest a hand with tapered fingers and very long nails and sings. He keeps looking at one of the four dudes, the one about six feet tall. He is more inspired than usual, his flesh-padded armature which extends upward imparts more color to his superannuated repertory. The beanpole laughs and, convulsed with laughter, loses part of his charisma. Magra dei Veleni stops and turns his head to the other side without taking the hand off his chest. He removes it to bend over and pick up a handful of rocks.

"Watch out, Magra, don't start throwing rocks, because today you'll end up like Tosca" Mandinga threatens, the only one who has some ascendancy over him, since he is gigantic.

"And what about Svergola?" one of the other three now asks.

"She was here before. She's probably on the knoll working away. But she'll come, she'll come. In any case" Zizi suggests with a heart-shaped pout "there's always me and Messalina. And we like the *rubber boat* so much, isn't it true, Messa?"

"A-tisket, a-tasket, hop into the rubber basket."

"Hey, Zizi, Messalina, Mandinga, Larousse, Amanda, Evita, Culaton-sur-ton, how about founding a kind of Pink Brigade? Arm ourselves with pistols and bombs and sawed-off shotguns and avenge the comrades beaten to a pulp by your beautiful machos?" Angelo proposes. Culaton-sur-ton works at the Dalmine steel plant and always wears gray, from eyeglass frames to bathing suits. Angelo feels a prickling in his hands, his temples throb intensely. It is not like him to go looking for trouble. Then, turning his eyes toward two men with a haughty bearing: "We could use these two with their eyeglasses as lookouts. And so your four machos will have the opportunity to cover us from the back in the service of a good cause."

"What's he talking about? Did the sun go to his head?" Moscina says. "Finally something sensible. Count me in. I look good in pink."

"Assholers! Assholers! There are many other ways to catch the boys! And a little beating never hurt anyone!"

"Yes, sure, go right ahead, you and those like you, Angelina, at least they'll do you in once and for all!" Carmencita goads. "They all want a union, all of them!"

"It's more likely that they'll do you in first" Angelo says, dissatisfied with the modest result of his provocation. "You should be happy that somebody goes to avenge you because he takes the beatings you receive at face value and doesn't know you like them. Isn't it true, Carmencita? We all know they tied you to an electric pole and shoved a jack up your ass. You've forgotten all about it, haven't you? Amusing, eh? You bring charges against the doctors who didn't sew you up properly and not against those others, right?"

Carmencita lowers his glasses, furious.

"And what about you, Zizi, the time they pumped air into your intestines with a bicycle pump so that you almost croaked? This too is part of being macho, right?"

"Well, *ciao*, we're leaving. If you see Calcinculo . . ." says the Bordello's spokesperson.

"But no, stay, come on, we'll go too" Messalina squeaks, jumping to his feet.

"Come on, stay" Zizi echoes. "Don't pay any attention to him, he's just talking. He has it in for everybody."

"But why don't you let them go? Didn't you say you like 'males'? What can you do with those four closet queens?"

Angelo has jumped to his feet, by now ready for anything. Not only to get beaten up but also to rave.

"Listen, boys, don't take offense, keep calm, it isn't worth it" Zizi says, gettting in the path of their menacing forward steps. "It's because this one here never gets buggered by anybody."

"If they go with you, they're faggots like you, certainly not like me" Angelo retorts.

"You and I will settle this some other time" Beanpole says.

"Anytime" Angelo answers. He's made a great effort to gather the indispensable minimum of adrenaline. Say he meets him some other time, Angelo may not even remember and collapse under the punches, spellbound by a question—but what did I do to him? and who is this guy?—and he would have to connect up too many things before being in a condition to react. This is a lingering consequence from when, in the family, he was passed on from one to the other and beaten up by all of them: *one* was already a multitude. The rubber boat moves out into the open water amid the splashing of a thousand beg-your-pardons on the part of the three or four dainty rowdies.

Here, in this open-air cage, sunset risks becoming an inner choice and never setting, so it takes a decision to leave. This torpor of limbs, this wish to let everything go hang and do oneself violence until no speeches exist any longer but only preambles and comforting bars that separate in your stead a *here* from a *beyond*, must now be doused with ice-cold water, and one must pick up and leave, resist the spell of right and wrong.

At home he collects a change of linen for two days, translation and original. His mother is out. He gets to Verona by car. He leaves it near the station, takes the train, overcrowded with emigrants coming home for the mid-August holiday, and when he is more or less almost at Bologna, he thinks that he might have left her a note to say where he was going, tell her that he would be away for only a day and a half, she shouldn't get her hopes up.

On the train, another piece of luck, he gets to stand up, even though crushed. Perhaps his mother will think that Lometto has suddenly turned up again and will keep him away for a week, at least.

On the train, at night, if you can't sleep because you don't have a seat, true enough, you gladly think about "love."

A train is ideal for summing up . . .

Monday night.

Tuesday.

Wednesday, dawn.

A train is ideal for summing up the distances one has covered and which rise before this other distance yet to be covered. If, furthermore, it is a vacation night and one finds oneself squatting among suitcases and footwear, skirt hems and bare ankles between the door of the toilet and that of the compartment, the very position of extreme concentration in the lower part of the world determines the course of hate-filled thoughts. Only in the jostle of the stops, when nobody gets off and others get on, Giorgina Washington squeezes through, at the beginning a thought fragile as a little angel which then immediately slips away because of the lack of space. Angelo cannot materially welcome within himself that spirit as he does whenever he finds himself in the open, because Giorgina Washington, like the frozen twenty thousand dollars—which he himself froze—needs the open air to uncurl and assume an outline beyond the unexpressed, smothered life represented by both.

It is therefore with all the ease of the constriction suffered in a milieu saturated with smoke and sweat and empty cans and butts which roll under hands and feet that Angelo thinks that the only power left him to feel alive is to withdraw into some crevice and begin hating. He only has to think for one instant about "love" to exhaust it and find immediately behind it mountains of hatred to demolish at his pleasure. Until arrival at the end of the world. In a few hours he consumes all the expectations which had been waiting day in day out throughout the life of which he has memory and, invariably, he compresses them into a hovering little motif articulated by sloth and resentment.

Angelo did not have the good fortune to know what these emotions of belonging to someone would have been if lived once in all their temporal and sentimental vastness and to what point this subitaneous deteriorating of love into hatred and depression was determined by external causes or by his deliberate intervention. There had been a continual pruning, a story made up of veils of salt so that everything should end up *there*. His mouth, in those solitary brooding crises, produced caustic words which burnt away every possibility of words less bitter than the ritual ones, both whether he lived or remembered. The one thing was almost simultaneous with the other. On the castrated part was spread a brackish layer of aggressive melancholy on which all resumption of germination, of vital grafting was impossible. He felt over and around himself this brackish metaphor change into rotten blood on his palate, in his nostrils and eyes, while he kept on slashing with ever more decisive strokes at that amorous bud which he wanted to amputate from his body. He gave himself many reasons.

It seems to him that he has left open more than one door and that if he wished that man could have entered and started the embrace. Every time, however, something had intervened, even though it seemed to him that he did not only leave door and window open but that he ventured to the threshold, went past it, held out his hand. But no: the man had changed into a mailman and delivered a telegram with a thousand apologies and a blank check to be signed. Unacceptable.

So it was not all that simple: one had to undergo a struggle and win it before receiving the authorization *to give oneself*. The gratuitousness, the readiness of his love did not interest any of those who interested him, had no credibility. It gave the impression of being a populist slogan, the lover felt confused with fate, demanded to be *himself*. But *he was* himself, precisely due to the fact of being *this* or *that* one by chance.

Angelo did not feel misunderstood or rejected, he didn't have the time: he felt irreparably insulted, mortally and forever. A love-passion was difficult within an open democratic structure: picture and frame did not go together. It was like trying to circumscribe a conflagration inside a glacier. Not that his need for warmth was reduced: the fact was that one must give the fire the possibility of having a limit to overcome, to melt before devastating ad infinitum, set fire to the whole being and consume it. He negotiated limited passions precisely because of his thirst for the infinite. But it turned out that his farsightedness was mistaken for lack of reflexes and readiness to throw himself into the fire. But a pyre did not exist per se. This nobody understood: a man is always so convinced of being a volcano by divine gift that it seems to him degrading to compare himself to nothing more than sparks. Others had a genetic patrimony, the unconscious pride of belonging by rights to a *species* human par excellence. He had the bundle of the day by day, time by time, instant by instant, the negation of all indisputable heredity. Angelo was as boring as a Martian once it is established that he is one and that fantasies about him are no longer possible. He was left in his down-to-earth comet: thus everyone had a need for something *concrete*—that is, incommensurably fatuous.

He withdrew, turned into salt, and no longer offered any possibility to the man who had told him "Shoo, shoo" with a few affected apologies. Angelo swallowed him in the long esophagus of hatred, abstract in its total absence of expression and, staring straight ahead, saw him engulf himself in the wattles of his mental grinder, behind whose transparent membrane the man of the moment squirmed and groped, perhaps crying out, unheard, some of his inessential reasons which were rooted in his instinct for survival.

With a start Angelo woke from this cannibalism as if purified and placated, once again strong in his uncontaminated solitude of an Adamitic terrestrial, splendidly taut in all his nerves and muscles, appeased by his recovered freedom no longer threatened by nostalgia for a lost paradise and a bit dazed as though under the anesthetic effect of an oblivion procured by self-hypnosis. He resumed his place among his non-fellow men, to whom he was now disposed to concede every reason because they had not a single consistent one for him. He performed feats of great diplomacy so that the ghosts among whom he was forced to live would not realize that they had no body, had lost it through their certainty of being *flesh and blood*. But it had cost him a great effort to deny himself to "love." The halo of suffering discharged during these hours of concentration into his own blood and purified by the *heart* to destroy at the root the simulacrum of his current betrayed or rejected and by now impossible love accompanied him through days and nights, bloating his eyes and cheekbones, making his hair grow limp and sticky in sudden sweats, injecting the whites of his eyes with cobwebs of broken capillaries. He felt exceedingly tired and resigned to a useless pride. His pressure, at its highest, touched its usual lowest: ninety-eight. He enjoyed the thought that it would happen even to him to faint from sorrow, he who had never fainted. There were people who fainted from cold, from hunger, from too strong an emotion. He would faint from hatred.

Very little sufficed to trigger in him this desire for destruction—which, not unfolding in any form of external vengeance, destroyed only the illusions that preceded that psychic process of the desire for love. A discourtesy, even involuntary, or a lack of attention, or a clumsiness, or a mistaken relative pronoun—anything whatsoever not determined by him but at the mercy of the others' procedural lack of consideration—impinged on his expectation of sudden perfect harmony, emotional maturation *à deux*, as perfect as it was instantaneous. With Italians this was possible only if you owned a big car or a villa in Positano.

Angelo considered vulgar all forms of seduction, direct or indirect. All calculation concocted to create for oneself something mysterious and inaccessible only at a certain price—and *never* right away—was inadmissible. How to make it clear that also ten months from now would be *right away*. The theory of time had become the appanage of the cosmetic industry. He felt a bit sorry for all these humans who, wanting to consider themselves interesting *in time*, managed to do so. He couldn't even understand courtship between cats, much less between others. All amorous tactics were vulgar, if they were indeed amorous and not intent on a convenient arrangement. He felt that he did not have enough energy for both moments of the undertaking: he could not conquer and then go to the trouble of plundering. His strength would leave him after the conquest and he knew that out of weariness, animal boredom, he would turn his back on all plunder anxiously waiting to be picked up, to be hoisted on one's shoulder, and to *belong*. He could not do too many things at once. If he had been a thief, he would have confined himself to unhinging doors and windows and safes and at the very most, before leaving empty-handed, he would have plucked something from the refrigerator, uncorked a bottle, to leave some trace of his work and his incredible credibility. Exclusive love could not avoid the vulgarity of experiencing another person as one's own.

Whenever he believed that a form of love might be possible, let us say, a particularized love *around* that individual rather than *for* that individual, instead of relaxing his reservations, at least at the commencement, and waiting to see how things would turn out, Angelo became even more intransigent, a kind of guardian of form—his own, obviously. His immunological system against legendary but traditional loves was so well contrived that he managed to saddle *destiny* or *chance* with a will and a conscience, succeeding in denaturing them, bending them to the exigency of his super-rational style. There must not exist things that happen by chance, are done by chance, much less those which are the fruits of absentmindedness or negligence. The candidates must be candid and thus have well drained in themselves the Machiavellian ink of the chapter on *fortune*, so as to leave a white space between chapters XXIV and XXVI. Then indeed one would be able to talk about *The Prince*, Charming.

He posed preliminary conditions in which the time/space factor must be annulled. Loving one could and must set everything aside: from the place where love happens to fall (if necessary one must be able to organize love's change of address in a space of six hours, the time to call a moving van) to the instant in which the looks of that instantaneous amorous maturation were discharged (he was always on the lake: the person pirouetting with a tray full of beers would have done well, once struck by his glance, to let go of the tray, take off his apron or white jacket, and go for the door and follow—he was very attracted by waiters with black curls on the nape of the neck). One could not discuss or haggle over the mover: pack and load the past life, that physical abstraction was so delicate that it demanded there and then an island and eternity. Those ten minutes that it would last would last *forever*. One must act quickly: had it not already happened to him to live for ten years on the income from ten minutes and in the wide world after having lived them on a sod no larger than a sofa? One could not wait for closing time, the day off, love was a pied piper, one must follow it immediately all the way to the catastrophe or the impatient desire to go back and be alone as soon as possible. He made fun of himself because of this, though not too much: but he demanded that those fulminated by his passion should behave like this, for this is how he in fact behaved.

A lover—the candidate lover of the moment—who, for the sake of his lightninglike love, already ripened by the entire process from blossom to comestible, did not prevent chance from impinging on his expectations, was already no longer a candidate worthy of being taken into consideration; his etymological guise began to be pocked by invisible, irritating blebs which retracted and swelled, and revealed in the élan's texture the spongy contortions of pros and cons. At that point hatred intervened, flashing and blind, a whitener that acted in depth, washing out the spots and also corroding the garments.

If he expected the miraculous event, if he found himself in one of those rare and eventually vain crises of held breath, the world of his possible interlocutor no longer had the right or need to go on turning: it must stop, be alert to its slightest movement of arrest, for the more abruptly the brakes were applied, the more inevitable were the vexatious jolts. It never happened. There existed other stars and satellites which attracted from some undesired place, which crippled the straightness of the trajectory, of the molecular immobility shared together with him—a wife, a fiancée, a stuttering friend, parents, people, the thicket of condominium expenses. There were friends, relations, investments, projects, with a deadline so out of proportion to the duration of life itself that this was obvious: every life is completely programmed all the way to immortality, not the smidgen of an unforeseen sprite could slip through.

And Angelo retreated into a corner and hated that man so absentminded and negligent as not to have understood that, as in slow motion there is projected the wonderful scene of the tray which tips and the foam which spurts up while the goblets shatter on the floor and splatter all around a fine dust of ground glass, he had ceased breathing and was there motionless and in need. Hatred, with the passing of minutes, became reflexive, the dike poured upon the object of his yearning was transformed into a slime of self-reproach sealed by the same slogan, "at my age . . ." Starting at thirteen. And for days and days to come he suffered an obtusely memoryless insomnia; he laboriously rose vertically to evaporate and reenter in a circle, with less excoriating and bitter words for himself.

In Florence the train slides a few inches to a stop with a breathless sigh.

Until Lometto gave him the alarm with one of his phone calls.

"Hello? Is this the Dwarf's Umbrella Factory? How is the cockologist today? Listen, girlie, we ought to call Pfefferman and Badakowitz. Tell Pfefferman that the arabesque samples are ready but it is impossible to dye them in those cuntlike Hitlerian colors, that the barbed-wire color costs an arm and a leg, and tell Badakowitz that it's either a letter of credit or zilch with this trouble in Poland, I don't see why he should ask me of all people for *Solidarnosc*, right? And remember that when the country calls, all the items answer."

And Angelo ran to the bar in the piazza if he was in Montichiari, or to the public phones at Piazza Bra if he was in Verona, to scream at the top of his lungs in a passage full of video games the orders specified in pounds, marks, crowns, florins, and francs. And with this call to telephonic order, Angelo again became integrated in the role of éminence grise of Mire, Inc., only too happy to find respite from hatred-generating melancholia in the instantly elicited exaltation of having to earn a living. He picked up the phone, dialed the international prefix whenever possible, gave his surname to the secretaries, preceded by the title Doctor, which he did not yet have—per instructions from Lometto, who set great store by it, and in his interlocutory telexes he always announced that "OUR DR. BAZAROVI CONTACTING YOUR FIRM BY PHONE SOONEST"—and Angelo slipped into the pantyhose what he had not been able to slip in elsewhere, without any of the managers experiencing the slightest confriction.

Pantyhose are not like men, they are always made of nylon six or nylon six/six and come essentially in two types: with or without gusset. To love them desperately and rhapsodically for a little while, the time long enough to sublimate a rejected love, was not impossible. Angelo proposed the pantyhose *with love* and, except for Russia, all of Europe reciprocated. Thus, the science of strands, of the alimentation of mechanical looms, the ironed or full-fashioned or *chiffonné* pantyhose, the sewn or tubular toe, the heel to be eliminated because of its additional cost, slowly swallowed the memory of that sudden jolt of love pressed into a host of hatred tabernacled in the recondite site of global amnesia. If hatred served to cancel love for a while, the pantyhose served to cancel hatred for another little while. He felt that the circle of life was becoming invulvaed in a pantyhose gusset and it did not displease him.

But then it happened that a sudden hint from the past poured into the memorylessness of the present—a phone call or a postcard—and insisted on stimulating the memory of a person whom it was no longer possible either to love or to hate because deprived of mnemotechnical dimensions. The effort to de-memorize had been vehement but rewarded by a captiously total erasure. The mind was cluttered with pantyhose or North American idiomatic expressions to be translated, without equivalents in Italian. Or memory peeked out through the interstices of the noble snobbism of the offended party, who was willing to dig up the insult and feigned a cordial indifference.

That person came to you with myriads of data on the management of your existence—ideas, anecdotes, rumors, tales—that you did not know how to fit in, jibe with what you must have been at that time. To Angelo it seemed impossible that he had devoted himself with such a wealth of ideological detail and emotional nuances to someone whom he no longer could want to remember. All that belonged to another life, and this other life, absurdly credible and confirmed by a thousand guarantees lavishly expounded with impartial precision, must have been lived by him, Angelo, told by him, and yet it belonged only to the memory of that sender, that voice at the other end of the line. The anguish deriving from it was indescribable, he could have described it only with Homeric essentiality. It seemed to him a conspiracy plotted against him by ghostly, inverted Lotus-eaters. He frantically tried to diminish the recriminating turns of the key in that door to the salt mine, to let a ray of genius enter that flat and even quarry. Everything corresponded in the description given of him: physiognomic traits (tall, thick hair, Michelangelesque or snub-nose, depending, the drawl of the mouth affected by slight paresis due to partial deafness) and other details: that the nail on his middle finger was deformed because crushed by a methane tank when he was a little boy, that he always went about with a book in his hand, and a number of juvenile misdeeds that he probably magnified in order to tell them in utter sincerity.

Angelo, instead of cursing, let them talk and ended by apologizing. No, there were no past realities that could tinkle in the present, not so far as he knew. He turned the postcard over and over in his hands, the interpunctuation of the telephone call between tympanum and hammer, like an enchanted and moronic key faced by a thousand different locks, all occluded. He tested them gently: he sifted cities and trains and countries and works and gardens and the steps of monuments, the dead spermothèque of the past. What, for example, did this mean—"you've been the most human monster I ever met and I did not understand it in time"?

He liked to work for Mire, Inc., while it lasted, there were no memory gaps there. One always knew, at any time, that if a pantyhose was *without* gusset it should have been *with*. Perhaps a round gusset or a dorsal one for women suffering from rheumatism. Or with a seam or a minuscule clock at the ankle, but the substantial Manichaean dualism of nylon was a comforting, indisputable fact. Nothing from there came to alter one's rhythm, apart from a growing rancor against Lometto, who saw life only as a system of familial economic relationships and himself as guardian of order (his) and or meritocratic justice. But even this rancor was not overflowing; Angelo, for hygienic reasons, released it against Lometto periodically. Lometto was interested only in increasing the *bulk* of life, not its value. The latter was only a consequence of the former. Angelo thought otherwise. Lometto said that by thinking too much one did not think at all. Thought had neither weight nor measure nor *numbers*. And so on. Who would have the penultimate word between them?

Getting off at Castiglion Fiorentino and waiting for the bus that will take him to a hamlet where a Japanese professor will come to pick him up to lead him to a remote hill lost in the mountains where the American professor lives, Angelo is confronted by the dawn of another day of labor, without surprises. In the disk which rises from beyond landscapes of fir groves, as if it meant to bounce tenuously on pillars of aspen fronds, he sees again Lometto's bulk on the hotel bed when, in the evening, all appointments taken care of, or at first light, while waiting for breakfast, he began to go pip-peep with his calculator and compared currencies, played the stock market by mumbling to himself, indifferent to all that did not concern nylon and his family, his cattle farm, his milk and Parmesan consortium, of which he was the major partner, and he feels a certain tenderness for the uncollapsible self-assurance of this bulk of lard sprawled in his shorts on the foam rubber of his *values*. Lometto's loves were generic, legitimized once and for all in the night of time. He had on his side History and Capital and the Constitution and he could make them interact positively without whimsical crises: three male children from whom he expected many successes in high finance or in free professions of great prestige, and his wife, whom he loved in an exclusive manner and by whom, so he said, he was loved in return with inexhaustible erotic imagination. It was as though that couple owned the patent for the wheel and the discovery of fire. It was asking for trouble to say, instead, that this was just warmed-up water, and nothing more. Celestino had chosen once with great care and now he had everything there, surrounding him, and forever, nothing would be dispersed, his hold was as elastic as the bulk he proposed to extract from hearth, bank, and church. Everything else aroused his curiosity without ever tempting him, or so it seemed, and he visited the world to confirm his proverbial philosophy: "for every chump there is a shrewd man who chomps him up." This was *solidity* for him, the kind that obtains smiling acknowledgments at the windows of those institutions human par excellence—banks.

Perhaps, though with great difficulty, in the certainty and social grounding of his few but resonant values, a malicious thought, immediately suppressed, had wormed its way into Lometto: that he was so unappetizing to any woman less than wretched that were he to want an extra one he would have to shell out. This unacceptable perfidy of his consciousness had been transformed by him for his own use and consumption: that he was a definitely interesting, likable man full of resources and charm and that he did not need another woman because his own suited him fine and was quite enough and fit within the overall expenses of a married man, a father, a husband, and a proper person. Lometto was faithful—and satisfied out of avarice. He only had desires within the reach of his stinginess. But was there never, never even a "free" feel of one of the hunchbacks or dwarfs working in his den and afraid of losing her job?

Angelo gets on the bus, a big comfortable belly completely at his disposal, and at half past six it is already full daylight. His somnolence takes him back to the light that entered through the shutter at the *pensione* in Rome—how long ago?—on the top floor. There were Somali or Mauretanian squabbles in the hallways. He had waited and waited and waited. His two travel companions slept, they had come back to the *pensione* and he had pretended he was asleep. The hour—two o'clock—was a good hour not to have to give explanations to their curiosity. Between snores, Imer kept asking: "How did it go? How did it go?" It had been his love for assignations that had once more led him into a room in the city to endure the night with wide-open eyes. It had also been the last love assignation in his life and the first time that he had in the end asked Lometto for a definitive remedy. Angelo had written eighty-two letters to this Italo without receiving a single reply. Then, over the phone, the proposal for a meeting halfway, which Italo immediately accepted. The meeting had been set for Rome. Angelo lived in Verona and he lived at Anguillara Sabazia. Five hundred kilometers as against thirty. Angelo, with wings on his feet, thought that when it came to halfways he had never done so well.

He had asked Demetrio to take him by car. At the last minute they had been joined by Imer, who happened to be in the neighborhood of Via Verdi and whom Angelo couldn't convince not to drop in by chance too often. Grimacing, Imer had insisted, he had never been to Rome. The three of them had landed in a cheap *pensione* full of African maids and old pensioners. The telephone rang in vain in Anguillara. On the third day of stressful waiting for this Italo, whose face, seen only once a year ago, Angelo could not even remember, they had left at night. He felt he was pursued by the primping gestures of his figure in front of the armoire mirror in the room: his image which examined itself, which had washed, freshened up, decked itself out to bring on the dawn amid the torments of a deadly hoax. Now, in the car, he could not get away quickly enough from those two friends of his, so laconic and defeated, who hung from his solemn despair, adored him like a guru, useless, lost in the deferential insolence of their passive contemplation of a poor bastard transformed into a god only so that he should offer a lair for their anguish, the anguish of dogs in need of a master. At that time he wanted to get back to Verona as quickly as possible, because the only point of this debacle was to tell it to Lometto at the first opportunity. He delivered himself to nylon and its celestial prince as to a suicide. Lometto had been so overcome by this neurotic interest suddenly dropped on him that, sensing in it a special commercial opportunity, he decided to accept Angelo's proposal to prospect in Scandinavia, but at a reduced fee. By plane, and in the spring. Instead they left immediately, at the end of January, and by car. Angelo's ghosts, aching from all that coagulated pain, faced by all that snow, put on their chains and sank agilely into the ice.

"It's like being at the North Pole" Lometto said, aware of the mission's absurdity.

On their return the ghosts had melted completely. A new era was beginning, the Bazarovi-Lometto era. They were two profoundly divided continents, with different and not always complementary resources, climates, uninhabitable for each other, and neither of the two wished to recognize the livability of the other's hemisphere. The attraction was due to an absolute lack of respect made precious by admiration.

For Angelo nothing was born, but he clung to this distance—which removed them from each other in a definitive manner—as to a set meeting point, as to a form of abstract intimate life. Lometto had probably felt flattered by a number of concessions regarding restaurant expenses and hotels and some half days of work. But he was not ungrateful. He bought a collection, *1,069 Jokes of TV Comedians*, and made an effort to remember which ones he had already told. In the morning Angelo found on his pillows thick locks of hair, all of a sudden he was going bald, he didn't care, it was useless to look for a reason. He told Lometto that it was because of his jokes, and they had fun interpreting his sadness. Hatred, and self-hatred, was a stray mine that exploded now in the capillary bulbs, finally destroying something at the roots. For Angelo, who kept silent, it was a relief: the thing that was dying on his head was for him the signal of an end. To a curly past filled with bilked expectations in *pensioni* for Ethiopians, a middle-aged, white-haired half encounter, half sex, half feeling was preferable.

As evening falls the Japanese professor accompanies him back to the bus stop; in the train Angelo has a seat all to himself, air enters from all windows and there is a landscape.

Tight-lipped as he was with information about the state—flourishing—of his finances and of his strategic plans to increment them, Lometto did not stint on confidences of an intrinsic nature that might amplify his image of full happiness steeped in the flesh, his, Edda's, Ilario's, Berengario's, and Belisario's. Angelo told Lometto everything he would have told anyone, he had no particular reservations or theories about "someone just met." Lometto's euphemistic expression was "to get one's due." Edda got her due almost every day, several times a day. She always invented something new, she was solicitous. He might get a headache later, during his trips. Better to take care of it in advance. And now she demanded an advance on the advance. The formulation of happiness was also well tested: "every time it's like the first time." It was like a game with prizes: "will this time still be the first time?" There was this biblical suspense of pieces of clay and ribs which came together, moved apart, wished each other good night, having sanctified that day too.

"Hey, look, Laurel and Hardy are here" his mother whispered to him last year in March, opening the door to the terrace where Angelo was doing his exercises, while in the house there was the silent bustle of death. His mother with jubilant tears in her eyes had added: "She really looks like a stepladder. Flowers have also come."

Celestino and Edda, their faces long ovals of circumstance, dressed in dark clothes, appeared on the terrace and were simultaneously seized by a burst of laughter which they choked off with their heads.

"What is going on here? I don't believe it! When you told me yesterday over the phone, I didn't believe it at all. I phoned the florist at Montichiari to find out whether it was true. And there he is, look at him, look at him! In his little shorts jumping up and down. But this isn't a joke, is it? Where's the bottle you said you would open?"

They really did look like Laurel and Hardy even though Edda was not actually thin but certainly, even so, she was half the size of her husband. And she wore the shrewd expression which at moments of southern gloominess contorted all features, rendering indecipherable the knot she carried inside like an imploded birth pang. And if one listened to Lometto speak about his wife, one had the impression that he had built her for himself in his own image and semblance, like a garage or a privileged mortgage or a writing desk on whose crinkly leather top no unemployed person's plea would ever leave a mark.

In that gloominess of Edda's, Angelo had, however, sensed a profound rebellion incapable of expression itself, unexplained and without visible consequences. They were two caricatures, and the wild woman who mewled at the bottom of Edda had adjusted to being the straight man for the lead caricature, the civilized man of responsibility. He was almost always the one to speak when somebody asked her something, Edda did not mind a ventriloquist sanctioned by the sacraments, so much readier than she with yes and no.

Also the crass cracks had a certain official quality useful to their interchanges. Every so often Lometto demanded that Angelo translate one of them for some impeccable customer just because he was Jewish. Angelo was reluctant: Jews did not like stories of the "iron cunt" variety, he told him, they weren't as subtle, you'll make a bad impression. Tell him anyway, he ordered. Angelo obeyed. To the letter. Lometto also knew a lot about ruinous bankruptcies. He always had something in reserve. The name of an agent, a corporation lawyer, an attorney specializing in international law, a certain story of fraudulent bankruptcy on the Ivory Coast.

The few times that Angelo had seen Edda he had noticed that

within a matter of instants violent shadows passed through her eyes, extinguishing the tawny color of shrewdness trained to handle any situation. Edda broke off sentences with the same absentminded promptness with which glasses fell from her hands because she always had her glance fixed on her husband, waiting for instructions. If he laughed, she laughed too. He must have once said to her, at the moment of the contract, "You do as I do, and you'll never go wrong," and she kept to this scrupulously. Everything worked marvelously: sons, money, local power. Lometto was sincerely enamored—he had been so from the first moment—of that blind but active, not lazy obedience of mind and flesh. One time in Oslo, Angelo had encouraged him to go with one of the girls in the hotel lobby, since he had such a headache and they had to spend another four days before returning home. Angelo was taken up with the reckless watermelon scent of his memory, he wanted to be alone to surprise it in its hidden lair.

"It would be like taking the bread out of my children's mouths" Lometto apologized.

"Always them. But what about your wife? You never mention her, ever. If you had to throw her or one of them off the Tower, whom would you opt for?" Angelo flung at him, almost as though to punish the immovable mass on the bed, and afraid that he might resume one of his usual rigmaroles about the goodness, skill, and obedience of the three animal lovers.

"You."

"Forget about me. So whom would you throw off the tower?"

He did not want to answer, tried to wriggle out of it, cursed.

"Well, if you don't answer me, from now on I will behave likewise. Just think of the kind of questions you always put to me and whether I ever abstained from answering you even once . . . So?"

". . . my wife."

"Why?" Angelo pressed. He wanted to know what motivations went through Lometto's mind as he climbed up the Tower chewing his nails in search of the answer as to whom to fling down with his eyes closed.

"You can always arrange for a new wife, not a son."

That "arrange for" covered a Pygmalionesque latitude which was as infinite as it was practical, untainted by cynicism, traversed by the hasty longitudes of a not long yet sorrowful widowhood.

At that moment Angelo had experienced a great personal feeling of kinship for Edda, to whom Lometto, forsaken, seemed to deny the uniqueness of life, overwhelming it in the hope of a freewheeling repetition of wives.

"No whores then? No furry aspirin?"

"Aren't you going to the sauna?"

"There isn't any in Oslo, at least not what I consider a sauna."

Lometto, strong in the fact that his actual and untiring desire for his wife prevented him from appearing hypocritical, had once in Paris gone so far as to propose to Angelo to go out looking for men, to do him a favor. The steam, while Angelo indulged himself in his labyrinths, had probably calmed his headache, and perhaps he himself by reflex had felt a certain relief.

He knew how to make his indifference for any human being who was not Edda appear as a further economic effort at guaranteeing a brilliant future for his sons. It seemed, indeed, that the idea of another woman horrified him, it seemed that the universal eternal feminine was directly connected with his wallet in particular. He had preferred to remain there in the sauna with a shiny eye, perhaps envious that there existed categories able to satisfy each other at a cost equivalent to a pound of grana cheese, and he took advantage of it with Angelo to add the final touches to his image of a European who has escaped from the bigoted mire of sexual intolerances.

His headache drew enormous benefits from his indifference to every moving virile magma. It was he who said, passing a hand over his forehead: "Let's stay another ten minutes," the non-desire and envy over the low admission price must be acting as a cold shower. He would never have any of the qualities of the charming swindler who risks his skin in a criminal feat and then squanders everything for a bar girl's beautiful eyes. Too cautious and distrustful. He was not interested in things that can be bought with money, but in money per se. Similar in this to Edda, who had been trained to become like him due to calculations of a higher order. Angelo had sensed right from the start that they wanted lots of it, that they always wanted more, and that, therefore, they would give up everything—except eating, and not even all that well but hastily, as he had already noticed on his third visit.

In chaos one proceeds chaotically. Lacerating ecmnesia . . .

. . . There was not a flower in the house, nor a garden outside—

not even a tree—nor a valuable knickknack, nor a picture—even though Lometto indulged in stock-marketish considerations about certain *ex-voidos* by Mantegna—nor a crystal glass nor a set of china dishes, but instead this atmosphere of a polar cap lined by a firmament of millions and billions which studded the magnificent future owed their sons. Meanwhile, everything was unmatched. From cups to saucers, from forks to spoons, and the sugar was set on the table in its original cardboard box. On one side there was this future with the iridescence of a rainbow, the color of immortality, on the other a jokelike present, the color of a mouse.

In May 1980, Lometto's greedy doltishness had hit bottom: he, who would have let himself be castrated rather than be hit in his right-hand back pocket for anything involving women, was ready to splurge if the certainty of a grandiose deal at bargain prices flashed through his mind. It was a matter here of buying smoke in the eyes for people as incompetent as he on the subject of art, for the "chumps" whom providence set on his path in such abundance.

After much insistence, Angelo—whose eyes had almost popped out of his head two weeks earlier on hearing Lometto brag to one of the women employees that in Bavaria he had visited a castle built at the order of a certain Ludovico "Il Moro"—had convinced Lometto to give up his bed, the room's tepid fug, underwear and open faucets and *pip-peep*, and go with him to the Rijksmuseum, since it was Sunday and they must inevitably adjust to the inconceivable condition of waiting. Oh, the endless disputes over these days of forced leisure that Lometto did not want to pay for, or pay only half, or pretended to forget, Angelo's tantrums, the sinister fury of his threat of reprisals, the hours of reciprocal prostration before beginning again to insult each other. Lometto wasn't interested in anything; neither museums nor the theater nor the cinema nor music nor opera, nothing at all that wasn't nylon, and its technology. Was there a museum on the subject? No, except for a small section in the Science and Techniques Museum in Munich. Was there a museum of the Financial Page, the Stock Market? No, answered Angelo, but you can draw your conclusions all the same by visiting any other museum, from pile dwellings to Picasso. And one on Artificial Insemination, with tableau vivant? He demanded custom-made museums, the existing ones were too dispersive, too roundabout a way to get there. He preferred to stay in bed with the crossword-puzzle magazine bought as long ago as February, or a *Corriere della Sera* or *Il Giornale* brought from home. And why, instead of setting up a useless and expensive embassy full of incompetents, why didn't the Italian government set up Dante Alighieri Institutes for the divine grana cheese? For Lake Garda olive oil? And so Lometto betrayed another branch on which he put forth buds.

Angelo had to promise that he would pay for his admission and also for the cab, because Lometto was not up to walking.

He dragged himself through the rooms with an expression of infinite patience, and when Angelo tried to involve him in admiring a Rembrandt, in order not to be outdone by any other visitor illuminated by that *Night Watch* Lometto burst into loud expletives, using, in order to get back at Angelo, the same jargon used by middlemen to appraise a head of cattle at an agricultural show. Or, on purpose, to punish Angelo, "who forced him to walk," he extrapolated from the canvases the most fleeting details, with the air of a great connoisseur, thus thwarting every didactic effort on Angelo's part to convey more general data of a historical nature but limited to a pleasant dusting of information so as not to kill the pleasure of his shamefaced amazement. But this sort of behavior from which a stranger might have deduced that they were both art historians, this snobbery typical of the *faux naïfs* who always want to have the last word on things they do not know, soon got on Angelo's nerves and he ended by ignoring Lometto and continuing on his own—when Lometto said to him, "You can tell that this Rambran is one of ours, not one of yours. He paints only handsome people!"

When they met again in the lobby, Lometto carried under his arm cardboard rolls of varying lengths—many, at least fifteen. He had bought that many prints and meant to have them framed and hang them on the walls of his house, which were so bare.

"Do you approve, eh?" asked Lometto, who expected the admiration due a disinterested patron of the arts.

"You really are a ninny . . . one would have been enough, as a souvenir, to hang in the toilet, or three, even, one for each of your kids' rooms, but eighteen! . . . You can't even carry them."

"Give me a hand . . ."

"You can carry them yourself. I'm telling you, nobody is going to see me walking around with that stuff under my arm. Not even in Amsterdam. It's about time you bought yourself a few *true* paintings.

Eighteen reproductions . . . a painting by Tirlindana would be worth more."

"What does *gevis bride* mean?" he asked, unrolling the one he probably liked the best. His eyes brimmed with tenderness.

"Even you know that. 'Lometto and spouse at Via Reggio carnival.' Come, get moving, we're going back."

Considering that neither of the two was exactly philo-Palestinian (but how divergent their reasons!), Lometto was too anti-Semitic, even though politically philo-Israeli, to accept hanging in the nuptial chamber, next to the oval of the Holy Family with the little flames behind the head, a perfectly circumcised print. The Israelis in the pantyhose sector were the only ones who gave the Mantuan manufacturers a hard time, and the Jewish wholesalers aroused unqualified admiration in Angelo for the rocklike politeness with which they refused both the jokes and the inflated price list palmed off as fire-sale bargains. And so Angelo had switched the subject quickly in order not to disappoint him right away and waited for the print of the "Jewish bride" to be first framed and hung. On their way Lometto clutched the rolls like lodes of gold, and whenever one of them fell to the ground Angelo quickened his step, pretending he was flagging a cab, and let him struggle by himself with the other seventeen.

At The Hague, near the railroad station where he had parked, at the mercy of a consumer frenzy verging on lasciviousness, Lometto bought a teapot, cream pitcher, and sugar bowl in fake silver, demanded that they be wrapped in gilded paper and velvet ribbons—also fake—and tried to persuade Angelo to ask for a discount. Lometto didn't even know how tea was made. Edda dropped the bags directly into the tin pot on the stove. A full-fledged non-essential expense. Angelo, who had a lot of time also to be ashamed of him and for him, already saw him casting about for a pretext at five o'clock—an "English" notion very widespread in the provinces—to force some neighbor or a somewhat distinguished relation to drink a cup of tea instead of a glass of wine so as to display his *set of pure silver* . . . And the cups would be paper because he didn't have any others, nor did the thought of them even cross his mind. If only Angelo had been more understanding in cases like this! Instead he lapsed into a tomblike silence and imagined Lometto's enjoyment when he would twist the arms of his dependents or chosen guests until he managed to wrest from them an appreciative comment on this silver set that everyone knew to be false. But subordinate workers, although instinctively influenced by the fascination of gold and silver and platinum and diamonds to the point of being unable to be fooled, also know the difference between accepting as true a precious metal that is false and being fired at the first opportunity. This tea set would hyper-realistically become the purest silver in the world just by the fact that it belonged to Lometto.

In Bologna the reconstruction work at the station is in full swing at night too, and Angelo realizes that he has involuntarily drawn a line between proletarian submission to the falsity of that tea set, and the waiting rooms and the bomb that has blown them up . . .

. . . There were plenty of domestic animals all around. Animals did not cost anything, apart from guinea hens, but one could close an eye, they strolled about with the autogenetic imperturbability of sewer rats. What mattered was that the boys should feel love for their home . . .

They had everything, the Lomettos: butchered meat, butter, milk, eggs, gasoline, and diesel oil. When Lometto, at Angelo's insistence, agreed to invite Pfefferman, that snobbish, megalomaniac customer, directly to his house, Angelo translated for him: "The Lomettos only buy matches, they've got everything else."

But Lometto's lunches or dinners were not all based on pumpkin-stuffed ravioli and duck and homemade ice cream and *Irish* coffee that he, not keeping whiskey in the house, made by dropping bitters and grappa into the espresso pot. Edda in fact apologized, she hadn't had the time—the warehouse, the bills of lading, he who hadn't phoned her to give instructions, the bogey-girls in the workshop. She went to the stove at a quarter past twelve, and at half past the food was on the table. For condiment, tomato concentrate and butter in quantity. Yesterday's bread, local wine gone sour—that forced wine should be drunk a whole bottle at a time immediately, as soon as it was uncorked; in an hour it was ready to be thrown out.

Edda, in Angelo's opinion, out of pure jealousy, just as she had never wanted a maid, had chosen for the workshop only monster women, who worked there under the sponsorship of the parish, of one woman in particular, the *perpetua*, the priest's housekeeper, whom Angelo had once seen in long skirts with a few bones inside to hold them up, a disquieting, rabbitlike face. The women who got on the bicycles might have been headed for a circus performance, and not to the parish mess: warty, bald, with jockeys' legs, lame, one a dwarf, and even a mongoloid.

Edda did everything by herself, including the nonsense about proteically calibrated menus for her sons, for whom she had, in fact, very little time.

There were several discrepancies between the Edda as told by Celestino and the Edda who, through sudden gaps in a quickly closed curtain, showed herself to Angelo. He felt he had been deceived by this beatification of the exemplary spouse to which he had to adhere when speaking—that is, listening to Lometto talking about her. The role into which Lometto had sunk her for the delight of his audience of singles, separated, childless, widowers, divorced, the messed up in general, was of no use to Angelo except to not understand, not know Edda, be deflected from any possible psychological reality of this woman, this unwitting impersonation of herself. And in fact Angelo felt a trifle less "temporary" in relation to Lometto's enterprise, more compromised than before, fallen a little further into the trap of life's total mystification which Lometto set, in good faith, for all those who, not being part of the Family, nevertheless served his purposes and must therefore be theatrically cast into it.

Everything had a price, one could even renounce the authenticity of one's pronunciations if from this one could draw a pecuniary advantage. Why not? Why shouldn't Angelo ask for a more substantial return for this *falsification*, which the Lomettos could not do without? To demand more money was the only way left to him to reaffirm a distance in style. The Lomettos did whatever they liked in full daylight, it would seem, and defrauded on taxes and contributions and unions in cahoots with the tax collectors and union delegates and the workers themselves. Even Edda was defrauded of herself, the first to be in cahoots. Not Angelo, at least not for free. So he might as well plunk down the request for an increase since it was he who covered up everything, at least a good slice, with the legitimation of a sprinkling of social prestige. Lometto turned down his requests, sensed the most provocative design that it implied.

"No, that's too much, no hard feelings" was Lometto's indifferent conclusion.

"No hard feelings, Celestino. Go back to your clichés" Angelo replied, just as impersonally.

He had two final exams to go and his thesis on John Ashbery was coming along well. Moreover, he had obtained his driver's license the first time out, by changing at the last moment the place of four X's in the boxes on the test. He even had some savings, he could hold out for a few months without pantyhose. One mustn't give in, the only thing that impressed Lometto favorably in everything was contractual power, especially if one invented it by declaring oneself ready to renounce all negotiations. In Angelo had clicked the sacrosanct mechanism of a question of *principle*. Invented there and then and not part of his baggage because he had never been sufficiently well off to impose any sort of morality. There was nothing that he did or did not do out of principle, he evaluated things as they eventuated, even though very attentive to their contexts. Principles were, if anything, unconscious and all of a celestial levity: not, however, of such a bright blue as to become princely. At any rate it seemed to him he had very few of these either. To demand more money was proof of character, of a better-articulated basic morality, and this impressed Lometto, since "chumps" were beings who deserved to be screwed because of their absolute amorality in offering an open flank to exploitation. They never even discussed it again. Lometto would get another interpreter. Very well. Lometto, however, was convinced that Angelo would give in and as soon as he did he would, to punish him, immediately deduct twenty or thirty thousand lire from the hundred thousand a day he had received until then. No alternative but that of triumphing. Angelo knew that Lometto was going to cough up when faced by the remonstrances of his *faithful* customers, and how! Only he had to prove that he knew how to beat him at holding out, and meanwhile convince him that he would not give him anything more than the reasonable remuneration for his irreplaceable services. He must, indeed, hold out the prospect of a further increase.

Lometto called on him a few times, because, in the meanwhile, Angelo refused to make phone calls for him and he came to see what was what, to test the ground of that laudable obstinacy.

Angelo had told Adele not to send her sons galloping any longer and that there was no message so urgent that it could not be delivered by herself the next day.

Angelo invented new commitments, other firms sprouted like mushrooms on the faculty notice board, and one truth: he had begun to translate a novel for a Milanese publishing house. But he did not tell him that he would barely get the cost of a two-way train trip in order to gain admission to the dream of dreams—printed paper with his name beneath that of the other, the translatee, and nothing more.

"You always put everything on the plane of dough" Lometto had reproached him months later. There was a stalled situation between them, a resistance that lasted beyond the foreseen. Lometto was attacking the third persimmon, hothouse or imported from God knows where. Gino insisted that he must always have the first of any fruit from the General Markets, and at the same time he expected some fucking gesture of gratitude.

"You've got your nerve, look who's preaching! After all, Celestino, I don't see why you should make hundreds of millions thanks to me and I . . ."

". . . thanks to my merchandise and my organization, you mean to say . . ."

"Listen, bullshit and bullshit. Your merchandise is exactly the same as everybody else's from Castelgoffredo to Viadana. It has the same shitty commercial value, since there is so much of it. It's as though everybody in Mantua had decided to make shit and were now trying to sell it. All that differentiates it from the cesspools that are collapsing all over the place while yours is going great guns is that yours is being sold by me. You can't go on making all those millions and pay me less than a maid and try to chisel too . . . The stench I have to put up with is too much for that, believe you me. And besides, I have a thousand commitments, and I have Paris too."

"But you won't even write me an invoice. Do that and I'll give you more."

"Listen, that's enough. I can't register with the Chamber of Commerce, pay two and a half million in dues, to write you an invoice for six or seven million a year."

"We all have our problems, my dear."

"Look who's talking! And you, what about you, with your alternative channels, all that black dough you make going back and forth from Penzana to Padua and Mestre with the van at night? Invoice! Do me a favor, just shut up, will you! And anyway, look, I answered an ad in the *Arena* for a position as sales manager in Mantua, how about that. They've answered me and I already went to see them. I'll probably start with them as early as next week."

"I wouldn't believe it if I . . . Who are they?"

Lometto began to squirm on his chair while, leaning against the backrest, he spat the persimmon pits into the kitchen sink.

"Gallinone's, china and glassware. I don't mind telling you. Actually he'll probably call for references, I gave him your name. I don't think you'll have the gall to say something against me."

"Does he know that you pick up all those little items? And that you don't go to mass? And that when something doesn't suit you . . ."

"Why, do you ask your workers? What the fuck does he care? Anyway, unless you give me fifty thousand more a day and guarantee me sixty days a year plus meals, plus single hotel room, I'll take the job."

"No, this is where you're crazy, you don't have everything at home up there. Mine is a poor product, you know that I have to scrimp on pennies."

"On the pennies of millions and millions of pairs, damn you! And anyway, you've never shown me your cost schedule."

Lometto stood firm, polishing off the crate of orange-colored fruit left by Gino. Angelo did not give in, unable to touch a persimmon, in fact detesting them, almost thankful that Lometto liked them. They set his teeth on edge, on principle.

On the first of December 1980 he officially began work at Gallinone, Inc., even though no one outside the family owned a share. He settled down in a third-class boardinghouse. He wanted to save. He had left his old secondhand Volkswagen in canvas trousers, and he too needed to renew his wardrobe. The first day his jacket with the kimono sleeves had elicited a whistle of wonderment that spread through offices and hangar and perhaps had already reached the Rotary Club. But he had signed a contract that never stopped amazing him: it went on for four pages, at the end of which they were giving him a monthly salary to make your head spin and he committed himself to be so free as to breathe only enough not to faint. By day he memorized the cards—origin, composition, cost, retail price—of the fifteen thousand items on sale with particular attention to those made of porcelain (china clay, quartz, feldspar; in which percentages according to which manufacturing process); late in the evening he returned home rigidified by the gentlemanly mania that Gallinone demanded of him, and from the Volkswagen Angelo had the impression of ushering into the stinking miasma of Mantuan mist a very elegant gentleman of middle age and more, looking older, who had been asked for thirteen consecutive hours to act as the shoulder supporting the fate of the terraqueous globe, whose axis, naturally, was maneuvered by Glauco Gallinone himself.

Gino and Demetrio came only once. Angelo gave them some very beautiful presents to shut their mouths and not tell him what they thought about his condition. He was visibly run down and the contempt he felt for Gallinone consumed him. The mists, the officers' club environment, the members of the Inc., bigoted and reactionary as is proper for objects of great classical and imported tradition, were draining him of his not inconsiderable energies. The employees were up to par, they had been raised in the double faith of secret, gossipy hatred and unconditional admiration in the light of day.

Cavalier Gallinone, fiftyish, went in for fiddle-faddle in the English style: on his walls hung prints of fox hunts and new locomotives ready to be inaugurated by a buxom lady at Victoria Station, he came to the office in a charcoal-gray suit and bowler hat.

He gave him a lecture on the military origins of his dynasty, he outdid himself in singing modest praises of Franco and Salazar, wanted to know what Angelo thought of them.

"They are obscene. They do not know how to do their job" was Angelo's single concession. Gallinone demanded that the present tense be used when speaking about certain dead persons.

"Yes, good heavens, I too am anti-Fascist, but with certain people a firm hand, right, wouldn't you say?"

Six porcine saleswomen clustered around him, exuding the incense of a past spent and withered in the porcelaneous hope of becoming his consort. It was they who had accustomed him to an uncompromising submissiveness which had then contaminated also the supplementary hours of the new arrivals, men and women: everybody stayed at the plant three hours more than they had to "because one can't leave things half done, Signor Glauco." These faithful deluded creatures had initiated that practice some ten, some twenty years before in order to become matrimonially appreciated. All of them religious odalisques extinguished in a servitude which had no other upshot than that of attaining, year after year, the nullification of every spore of female moistness. Not even mist and snow managed to deprive them of the dryness they clutched between breasts and legs, and which crackled even in the steps of their feet shod in low-heeled moccasins, like those of hysterical religious in expectation of a summons always a trifle further removed, more divine because wisely withheld. Not even the fact that Gallinone, having just passed fifty, had gotten married and was the father of two brats had assuaged their vocation.

Gallinone, perhaps to prove to Angelo that he too, behind the mask of the good family man, was a person with certain definite weaknesses and perhaps an abuse, almost immediately got him to translate the instructions for a Chinese pharmaceutical product that had arrived especially for him from Hong Kong, a product which cured, besides anorexias and prostatic feelings of heaviness, also the "slowdown of desire." Gallinone had opted for the youngest and prettiest of the girls armed with feather duster for the shelves, leaving all the little old things gaping, this one without molars, that one with dentures. Here too the proverb applied that he who dies dusting dies hoping. Their fideism for Glauco Gallinone was inflexible and severe, like a hatred hard to replace with something else. Time was running out, so one might as well gather with it around this bankrupt but nevertheless corporate chimera. Oh, what nostalgia for Lometto seized him as he slurped his broth or took off his shoes in a deluxe disco and rested his feet on the table, a defenseless braggart, not an ill-mannered child, who always got away with it. The one thing he would have liked to hear in that mortuary was a fart or to smell a poisonous breath, the tangible sign of a malodorous but human presence: Celestino Lometto.

At Christmas, Angelo collected a dizzying salary, which, however, no longer justified the Mephistophelian pact stipulated with Sir Gallinone. Every morning Angelo had the impression of having to slip into the black tails of a bad-luck crow and to bring down on himself misfortune by playing, aged and exhausted as he was, the young Faust, all energy and corporate enthusiasm. Then came a very cheerful phone call from Ilario.

"You know, we've all become a little better. Papa had promised us a suckling pig if our report cards were good. You know, there's been a bit of plague. No, not where we are, up at Marmirolo. And now he'll have to keep his promise. We've learned to stretch the skins and clean the wounds properly. And how are you? Wait, I'll put him on."

"Hey, baby, I have to go to a fair at Sarbrook, at the beginning of February. Will you come?"

"I don't think you realize, Celestino, what you're asking me."

Lometto began visiting him at the boardinghouse and calling him every day, using his boys and Edda.

"*Ciao*, Angelo! Do you know that they've sent us an Indian doctor! He's almost a Negro, and I don't want a Negro to put his hands on me. And I'm also very dissatisfied with Don Nocciolini. Do you know what he did Christmas Eve? First he had as usual reserved for us the first pew with the tassels, which at any rate we paid for, and then, because we came five minutes late, we found it occupied. And you know by whom? If my husband knows that I'm telling you, I don't know, I don't know what . . . Bananone with wife and kids. A Communist! He's got to go, I must have him transferred. . . . Who? The priest? No, not Don Nocciolini, the Indian! Did I ever tell you that I have an uncle who is an archbishop? And how are you? Wait, I'll put him on. Yes, yes, my dues are coming in . . ."

"What's going on? Did you ask for the week off or didn't you?"

"I wouldn't even think of it! I've been here a month and I should ask for a week just like that? We're in the middle of inventory, we must set up the warehouse on the computer."

"So what am I supposed to do? Would you like to come, yes or no?"

"Celestino, do you know what my price is today, after deductions? One hundred and fifty thousand a day, I'm awfully sorry for you. Sure I'll come, if you manage to convince Gallinone, but wouldn't it be more convenient for you to take a beginner who'll cost you half as much? You've always said that you have dozens of interpreters at your feet . . ."

"Yes, thanks for telling me" and he slammed down the receiver.

That very same evening he was there, at the boardinghouse, submerged in overcoat and mufflers and gloves, a textile avalanche with a cold. Angelo showed him the breakdown of his December salary, which was inflated for that month; for some mysterious reason, that first month he did not have deductions of any kind.

Lometto, ignorant of national contracts in commerce, gulped.

"Never mind, if I manage not to croak from a nervous breakdown, I'll also give you your cunt money. One hundred fifty thousand lire a day! Where is this all going to end!"

"One hundred and eighty, Lometto, one hundred and eighty."

"You should come with me for nothing, because I'm the one who gave him the references . . ."

"But aside from the one hundred and eighty thousand lire and not a lira less, that's not the problem, try to understand. I have assumed responsibilities. Do you realize what risks I'm taking to do you a favor? What am I supposed to tell Gallinone, leaving him in the lurch in the middle of inventory?"

Angelo was secretly enjoying himself; he had learned to complain about his good fortune precisely from him. He liked this whining vulgarity, it was a return to simple folk origins that he had never had.

"I'll take care of it, I know what to do."

"Look, leave me out of your little plots. But tell me what you're planning to do."

"Well, since we're sponsored by the Chamber of Commerce and I'm a friend of the president, no less, and the president also knows Gallinone, it will be like a favor between companies, right?"

"So that in Mantua you will look good."

"You always have to add an extra piece. Look good, with a cunt umbrella maker like you."

"I don't think it'll be enough."

"Just leave it to me. Gallinone hired you thanks to my guarantee, he owes me the loan of you."

"Not bad, I'm flattered."

Gallinone, on the contrary, did not want to hear of it; he spoke to Angelo, asked him whether he had debts of any sort or *moral* ones with this Lometto, and why did he insist so much?

"No, not at all. I'm not insisting either way, it's a matter in which I too am instrumentalized by the Chamber of Commerce. You know, they already know me from before, they don't trust somebody else for Mire, Inc. . . ."

"Oh, if that's the case . . ."

"Oh, you can refuse, of course. I don't mind at all."

"I could do it as a personal favor . . ."

"For whom? Me? Definitely not! Three days at the stand where I don't get to see the German smog and two days traveling. No, actually, let it ride. If anything, you'd be doing a favor to the president of the Chamber. Tell him no, and that's the end of it. In any case, I can't drop the inventory halfway through . . ."

Lometto and Angelo, together with a group of the most prominent local manufacturers, left for Saarbrücken. The idyll was blossoming again. Lometto draped his arm over the back of the seat in the airplane, slipped two fingers into Angelo's shoulder blade, and gave him a small but intense squeeze.

Angelo mesmerized more customers, set up a series of encounters to be programmed later on, in the spring when there was less of a rush. Angelo filled an invisible breach in Lometto's life and Lometto glistened with pride. Angelo always made sure to push him to the proscenium, make him shine with reflected bluish light like every charming prince cut short by his secretary, down there, in the prompter's box. Other manufacturers stepped forward guardedly, they wanted to know what Angelo's situation was professionally, and whether by any chance . . . They left calling cards with the circumspection of thieves.

He kept Lometto minutely up to date on these advances, and Lometto took the cards, flattered and irked, and tore them into tiny pieces.

"Don't you dare give *it* to the competition" he said, looking him straight in the eye.

He had to make an effort to remain serious.

Angelo couldn't wait to clear away the somewhat formal exultation of the renewed encounter to resume as soon as possible talking about this and that, as usual.

For example, about the last of his "little vows," which Lometto called "Franciscan," obviously, and Angelo, within himself, Wildean. They consisted in allowing oneself to be seized by the aestheticizing whim *of giving someone a hand.* In other words, as one might have put it in such cases, *helping him.* In truth, with the consciousness of wasting part of one's energy and one's meager savings in an unheard-of luxury for a weak and poor person like himself: to throw oneself to the wind, concern oneself with the credible needs of others, knowing that one would never enjoy any west wind in return. The cause of these generosities, which were more complex than merely disinterested and had that basic pettiness that all things have which *truly* do not want anything in exchange, was that he, now, with his very serene existence, as much food as he wanted, rooms to sleep in (in Verona, in Montichiari even a house in his name, in Florence at Tirlindana's), a car outside the gate on Via Verdi on alternate days (on other days in Mantua or at the mechanic's), was ashamed because reality contradicted with facts his basic existential ideology; if he was there, it was because he had *looked ahead* and had been more than happy to be in a position, for once, not to have to *look back* at those who were much worse off than he. This sudden affluence, these roofs over his head, these waiters hovering at his back, were his work. It was the first time that he was mortally ashamed, and did not know how to make up for that affluence. He would have liked to know from whom he was taking what was coming to him so that he could enjoy the superfluous. This kind of talk would send Lometto up the wall, so he couldn't wait to have a conversation.

Already in Florence, during the year in which he had attended a private institute to prepare for the university, and had rented the small apartment at No. 1 Via del Inferno, he had five keys made to distribute them to hobo acquaintances or occasional friends of friends, so that they could go there to do as they or anyone else, save for him, pleased. But it was different from now: then there was a feeling of guilt about being kept by a woman who had continuous breakdowns, a woman whose candied and untouchable cherry he was. Now the same thing was being repeated with an aggravating circumstance; this affluence was not fallacious because it was not procured by his ambiguous charm as a *male* homosexual to be converted, but risked becoming lasting because procured by himself for himself. He suddenly realized that he had a will, a tenacity, a strength of character, a discipline which were monstrous, and that was the hidden end of everything, unbeknown to him: a position as a sales manager whose duty it is to look down on people, especially when he must pretend to put himself on the same visual level to obtain the last little droplet of marrow from underlings to be sacrificed to the Moloch of corporate patronage.

Angelo was beside himself with delight at the very thought of conversing with Lometto on these topics; he was sure that, if he wanted to blandish him all the way by exasperating him, in order to be understood he must not leave before giving him a belly cramp, and then a definitive declaration of love that would liberate him from Gallinone, Inc.'s claws once and for all.

Angelo fulfilled his philanthropic whims without irony, but with the seriousness of a wellborn adolescent who, having reached his crème caramel, kicks the maid, throws away his initialed napkin, and decides that something must be done in order to change the world for the better—have *two* portions of crème caramel, change desserts, maids, everything but the status quo. This is how revolutions must start: as a whim, investing someone else with one's own unavowable needs, calling it all the *thirst for justice*. Every so often an unthinkable basic Fascism popped out of him, which delighted him, making him feel doubly ashamed of this capricious instinct to *think about others as well.*

Anyhow, he preferred it to the risk of taking his impulses seriously, which was like offering the sacred side to the already poised spear of the poor enemy to be helped.

For example, he had already told Lometto about the trip to Morocco with Demetrio and that they had come home practically in their underwear because they had distributed everything: camping tent, never used and brand-new, sunglasses, clothes, money, everything, except for what they needed for gas and oil to return home, and that, not having anything else, they had been forced to promise to send parcels to various addresses from Casbah Tedla to Marrakesh. Baby clothes, if possible, and Bogart-style raincoats, white if possible, had written one of the recipients of their bounty, as well as money to a student of great intellect for tuition fees and textbooks. It seemed that Angelo lent himself to such things out of sadism toward Lometto and that he never had reneged on any of these comic commitments for the pleasure of being as faithful and sincere and abundant as possible in recounting them.

Lometto had objected that the two of them, "worn out by handles," in so doing had simply augmented the "natural tendency to beggary," to use Tirlindana's aulic words, of Arabs in general, and that theirs were exploits of phony philanthropists, that their hands should be cut off, that they were corrupters, and that they were everything that he was not. This is not generosity, generosity binds to a rendering of accounts, to due dates, and so impels man toward enfranchisement and freedom . . . one mustn't hand out fish which were already caught but teach them how to make fishing poles.

Lometto, in short, faced by people who were dying of hunger or on the point of drowning, advised the shipment of old Lonati machinery, by now obsolete for Europe, or the construction of bridges over water which was pulling a raft to the bottom—that is, he advised negotiations prior to any reckless gesture of brotherhood. "No one can die of hunger all of a sudden, he must think about it before and in time. If it then happens to him anyway it is because he deserves it. Yours are no arguments" he said. With his financial vision of life and fatalistic vision of death—the death of others—it was impossible to trip him up: Lometto never made mistakes of this kind because, if they were mistakes for Angelo, for him they were bizarre abstractions that even if he strained his sight could never reveal to him some mistaken aspect of his premise. They were the whims of a spoiled child, nothing more. And that is why Angelo presented them to Lometto exactly in this guise: to give further relief to the self-sacrifice. Among the stands of the exhibition floated a very appropriate Mozartian sound, the whimsical *Eine kleine Nachtmusik*: Angelo broached another of his horrifying but fabulistic philanthropisms.

". . ." Angelo went on.

Now Lometto was trying to move away from that state of petrification, he wanted to burp at all costs to show that he was about to vomit. Not true. The Italian Commercial Institute's section was emptying, the exhibitors were putting away their leaflets. But Lometto mimed these signs of nausea not so much because of the story but because of the final moral, in which he already foresaw the usual smack of the hammer on his avid and avaricious fingers, his respectable egoism, the healthy egoism of an entrepreneur who activates the balance of payments abroad because he imports prized currency and does not ride around in the night on his bicycle to pick up faulty merchandise, drugged human devaluations who have filled their pants.

When the exhibition was over, after Angelo had scheduled a series of meetings between April and June in Holland, France, Belgium, above all Germany, Lometto found himself more Basarovi-dependent than before. Angelo, in any case, went to Paris before returning home to Gallinone's Anglo-Saxon fogs, and there he did three days of Salon Europe Homme Mode for Jeff Sayre. He no longer cared anything about Gallinone, he invented a pretext to get back as late as Monday. On Monday the yearned-for phone call from Lometto came.

"So with whom am I supposed to do these trips you set up?"

"But what do you want from me, you always say that an interpreter, et cetera et cetera, go get somebody else, I'll introduce Imer to you, if you want me to, he's from Trento, he knows German better than me."

"And who is he?" Lometto asked, interested, literally.

Angelo backed up slightly, told him that this Imer, yes, when it came to German, but he didn't know much English and almost no French . . .

Oh, to be able to be back traveling all over Europe with Lometto as soon as possible! Only when he had him there did Angelo feel most profoundly called upon to sing out reproachful arias.

They negotiated again. Lometto banged his fist on the table, saying, just for a change, that it was like taking the bread out of his mouth. Angelo ignored him, they were both doomed, there was a magnet that drove them into each other's claws, and at the same time, the angel of one fluttered in the celestine element of the other. They seraphically complemented each other.

At the end of February, Angelo tore up his blood pact with Gallinone. Rushing to gather together his things in his room at the boardinghouse, he did a bit of reckoning, happy. He had the money necessary to pay the notary for the purchase of the house, money to finish the university, money for a little trip—the money to give himself three weeks of irresponsibility after so many years of atrocious scrimping. The only thing he would miss would be the lard and crushed garlic on slices of toasted polenta that were prepared for him by a friend he had made in Mantua, Epaminonda, a brisk little old woman, a pipe smoker, spiritually a Red Brigader, at whose house he went to watch the one o'clock news whenever he could just to hear her comments.

He had a great deal of time before beginning the new trip with Lometto. He called Demetrio, the lowly employee of the Postal and Telecommunications Services, the clerk in charge, taciturn, obedient, another of those human-interest cases who feel they are somebody only if one decides to exploit them like lackeys, and asked him to come along on a trip to Hungary and Czechoslovakia. Demetrio liked to drive, it was the single quality that testified to his belonging to a species endowed with psychomotor reflexes. In this sense he had reached the end of the Darwinian evolutionary process like everybody else. And they left. Good weather and excellent driving. Angelo talked to himself out loud. End of trip.

"You see, Demetrio refuses to grow up" he was now saying to Lometto immediately after the end of the Modena-Brenner highway as they headed for the Austrian border. "It's three years that I've been trying to convince him to think with his own head, and he listens very carefully and lets me talk a blue streak and then relapses into his usual refusal to have a head. I would like to build him one myself, any old head, and then let him use it as he likes, cut it off, but do something with it, for heaven's sake. But like this, at the mercy of the first person who comes along, how can that be?"

"Oh, you'd like to unscrew people's heads and then screw them back on as you like. Like all *comrades* . . ."

"Not at all! Do you know what he used to do, what his mother made him do when I met him? Well, I met him on a New Year's Eve at the station in Verona. I was there on my bicycle, I liked to watch the transvestites in their fur coats, but most of all the men who picked them up. I believe that I was foaming at the mouth with rage then at the thought that transvestites could, they could, not I, you know what I mean, bugger those miracles of flaunted virility. I was so fascinated by the evening sexuality of bank employees, mechanics, and soccer players! I had become friends with some of the transvestites, they gave me special treatment, I mean, they respected me, how should I put it, they liked to talk with me. They liked, perhaps out of exhibitionism, my furious envy disguised as ethological interest. Let me explain what that is . . ."

That road seemed always the same, and the moment in which one was on it as well, and also the conversation inside that auto body seemed pleasantly recorded. But here one never knew how it would end, the recording in the present tense of a section of the past was unpredictable. What mattered was that there should not be the usual disgusting Buongusto cassette.

"Do you understand? They talked with me between one trick and the next. I waited for them to return, caught a glimpse of the stern face at the wheel, was overcome by dizziness at the thought of ever by chance running into one of those males who *paid* to be buggered! I wasn't at all interested in their childhoods: I wanted to know, just like any other turd journalist, which of the two fucked the other, how much they paid, who were their faithful customers—and I who had seen some of them felt my throat clutched by a lust which in itself came close to orgasm. But I could not ask them about all this too directly: that's what everybody did. And they told everybody a bunch of lurid tales, or chased them away with shrieks and curses. One had to touch them on the soft spot: childhood, the mother figure. I've had to put up with so many boring childhoods, bad mamas, good mamas, papas like this, papas like that, I wanted to get immediately to the jailhouse ravishments . . . They had almost all been in jail for one reason or another. I liked to hear from these divas, Loredanas, Fijones, about when they grabbed those handsome big machos, all cunt and tits, and made them bend over upon request. Oh, you know, my sexuality was quite simple in those days . . . Well, I was there at the station, as I was saying, oh yes, Demetrio. I'm going into all these details because we still have a long ride ahead of us."

"Go on, go on. I like this. As long as you don't end up in politics . . ."

"Demetrio was there in his little red sports car, smoking and looking out through the lowered window. He had timidly struck up a conversation with me, actually no, of course I must have asked him something. He laughed continually, always at the wrong time. He had a syncopated way of gesticulating and speaking. Making strange pauses that I did not understand right away. In fact, they were not pauses for things about to be said: they were periods with nothing in the next paragraph. Those lips which stopped in the middle of a word were a sly invitation for his interlocutor to steal speech away from him as quickly as possible. He never had anything to say in his mind. He told me he had been to teachers college, that he had also begun teaching, but that then, during confession, the parish priest had warmly suggested that he compete for a job at the post office and give up teaching because of the temptations. He had one of the many nervous breakdowns in his life because of all this and passed the state exam. While we chatted in the lovely cold frost full of *honk-honk*, some acquaintances of his arrived, two carloads of respectable little men headed for a discotheque near Parma. He asked me if I wanted to go too. I locked up my bike and joined them. During the drive Demetrio asked such precise questions that I felt like playing the most varied roles to cut short immediately his need to know *who he was dealing with*. The first transformation that came to my mind was, of course, that of an occasional transvestite. When he raised objections because of my mustache, I told him that I was in fact nicknamed Big Mustache, and he wriggled, laughing and clucking, and enjoyed himself immensely. I had found someone who had less identity than I, who had none, this touched me as an extreme. His was a stripped lack of identity, mine was a rich lack of identity. He began to come and see me on Via Verdi. He would stay there evening after evening, unable to initiate any conversation whatsoever; I showed him my books, I described to him the exams I was taking, I introduced him to my co-tenants as the Pocket Venus—Demetrio gave the impression that he could fit in one hand. He blushed virginally and became flustered. The subject that most interested him was the frequency of the sexual encounters I'd had while traveling, not, I mean to say, once I had gotten to the place, but on the means of transportation, trains, ships, trucks, cars, motorcycles, hay carts, bicycles. All that was missing was an airplane. He was enchanted by sex as a means of getting somewhere by car. He always played dumb when I turned his questions back to his past. He always laughed. But he laughed on the other side of his face, like a victim. And when I entered into more minute details on the motor behavior of my and other people's sexual organs, he asked me what I thought of God, if I believed that there is an afterlife. I mean, you talk and talk, you make a minimum amount of sociological analysis precisely to get yourself out of the Grand Guignol, the center which you believe with all your strength you occupy in life . . ."

"What? What a mouthful!"

"Yes, in short, a social analysis of the things you experience, that happen to you, it's like saying that you see the problems that you consider personal in a light that embraces more people than yourself, a group, society in some way. You don't individualize them, but try to understand how others at the same moment are living your same problem and to know how they see it and why, and if there isn't a possibility of drawing from it some general consideration that might be of benefit for everyone, to get away from the attitude of the victim, from the Catholic centrality of the *mea culpa* . . ."

"Oh, what crap!"

"Crap or not, to transform a *problem* into a question of conventions accepted or rejected for the moment is a function necessary for knowledge. You live better when you have reduced yourself as close as possible to nothing, at least you no longer suffer nervous depressions. You have depressions of another kind, professional, for example, and you are already on a very good path to breaking the balls of a whole lot of people . . . The tragic thing in Demetrio, for example, was indeed that, incapable of reducing himself to the lowest common denominator of a situation which is almost general for all homosexuals who live at home, he had allowed his sixty-year-old mother to convince him that he was sick, and for years he had been going to a psychiatrist *to be cured*, that was the cause of his fear of everything, of his waiting for someone to rob him of his speech: he had been robbed of it completely. This is what I found out after he had been going back and forth from Via Verdi for six months."

"And what was wrong with him?" Lometto asked, holding out his passport for a second time. But Angelo realized that it was a shrewd question just to please him, to demonstrate that he was not like everybody else. Angelo overlooked it: it was already better than nothing, or perhaps it was a great deal that Lometto should feel duty-bound to apply his shrewdness to matters that he could have swept aside by silence or a shrug of the shoulder.

"Have stockings?" the Austrian customs agent asked.

"But isn't this something, they already know us!" Angelo said. "Give him a box, he knows that you don't have a temporary export permit. Fuck it, they still remember us."

"Throw box in booth driving" the young man said, returning the passport.

"Damnit! This is nothing to laugh about! They've got the picture of this car printed on the brain!"

"What do you mean, what was wrong with him? He was a faggot like me, right, and he went to get ripped off, fifty thousand lire a throw, because according to him and his mother he was sick. I cursed him out, ordered him to stop immediately or stop coming to suck my blood in order to nourish his mother's theories and those of that Nazi analyst pimp. Whom I denounced publicly in letters to the papers which were never published."

"Nazi what?"

"Yes, these people who listen to you, who tell you that certain things must be lived surreptitiously in other cities, that the family is sacred, etc., and in exchange for these wonderful discoveries of theirs pluck you clean like a chicken. In the meantime I convinced him to invest the biweekly hundred thousand lire in the draftee section of the Diaz barracks in Verona. There was a bar for the meetings, there were also rooms upstairs, soldiers aren't expensive, certainly they don't *cure* you but they boost your morale, I tried to convince him. He was foolish and depressed because he believed blindly in medical science only because, infallibly, it did not yield results, nor would it ever be able to yield any. And if he was still where he had started, it was not medicine's fault, it was because he was very sick, do you see the trap? He went every night from eleven to dawn to the remote rest areas on the highway to cruise the truck drivers, and by day his life was hell again. Oh, perfectly free to enjoy all this, but then, I told him, don't come to me to have your depressions recycled, go to hell, stay as you are. No, I can't take it any longer, he told me. He had an idiotic fear of being discovered. Just imagine, discovered! He had it written all over him; he moved like a hapless little woman, you could just see the sneers of his post-office underlings. Oh, his undeclared love-passion which had lasted for years for a mailman, a telegraph operator, a collector of first emissions! I talked to him for hours and hours and then all he came up with was 'It depends' or 'Everything is relative.' He enraged me so much, I thought I could no longer do without it. Then one fine day, at last, there came a hint, why didn't he get married? There was a woman employee who was crazy about him, why didn't he make a move? Or did he perhaps prefer Carlo's mustache and beard? He had begun to cry and scream in front of everybody, he, with his position *as director*, of who knows what. I urged him to become a bit harder, more square. If he wanted to get his employees to toe the line, he had to overcome his inoculated nature of a little female, all home and church and post office and rig? If he wanted to stay there, or else he must change professions, become a sacristan or a hairdresser, not aspire to being an office manager to all intents and purposes. And how did they take it at the Central Office? How would they take it after his department inevitably had become a madhouse due to him, to his weakness? So let him continue to go to the truck drivers but let him also learn some tactics to keep order if he did not want to be demoted to stamp licker or something like that . . ."

"That's why you advised him to go with soldiers?"

"Anyway, I gave him *a head*. He said that it was useless, that he was weak by temperament, that I was sucking his soul. But it's impossible, I kept telling him, you haven't got a soul for somebody like me to be able to suck it. You don't have words of quality, only so many, a few words that don't correspond to anything: soul, God, sin, people, grief, illness, cure, et cetera."

"You always mix everything up together. Leave God out of it."

"Don't get started! You use God like a threshing machine, at least keep quiet . . ."

"Just be a little respectful, I'm a Catholic . . ."

"That you certainly are. Nobody knows how to use threshing machines like you."

"The way I see it, you were using him, destroying him. He was in no condition to react. He made you feel important, right, baby?"

"Just listen to him! I was only telling him that he must come to terms with common sense, that it was very exciting always having to live with a guilt complex and an inferiority complex ready to hand, but that then the years go by and, precisely, at his age, almost forty, *defeat* becomes less and less exciting, the victimized attitude no longer makes the tiny wrinkles of your asshole sizzle . . ."

"Did you hear the lastest one?" Lometto proposed. Demetrio was a small parcel without postage. It didn't reach him.

"Is it another one of those that your sons learn in school? Or did you get it from your conversation manual?"

"It's the one about the figs."

"You already told it ten times."

"And the one about the slut who got cramps in her mouth?"

"But don't you think you've taken enough advantage of my ears with your witless jokes?"

"And you of mine with your witless friends?"

Yes, Angelo's friends were witless, they seemed to have been flunked even in the courses of salvaging life.

They pretended to quarrel for a while. Ten uninterrupted hours of driving were exhausting, a bit of feigned irritation was good, relaxing.

Lometto drove, Angelo too, alongside. Usually he could not sleep in a car, it seemed to him cowardly while the other hung on at the wheel.

"Hey, baby! Baby!" he would suddenly start to bellow the rare times Angelo closed his eyes for five minutes. "I'll tell you the latest, come on, let me tell it."

"Oh yes" Angelo consented, offhand. "Begin at the end and tell it backwards."

Lometto told the same joke word for word, reversing it. This produced certain backgrounds worthy of a Gonzagesque slum, certain bloodcurdling scenes of vaginas tied to tavern tables and covered with salt to whet the customers' thirst.

Lometto told him the usual rigmarole, though he was tired of hearing it, and all he could do was laugh at it, defeated. Perhaps at the end of everything, at the end of existence itself, there was this laugh of weariness and despair which enveloped the car's hood and the road junctions of the trips back and forth, the epigraph of a joke.

Angelo, with a slight headache caused by two nights with hardly any sleep, comes out of the Verona station and heads for his car. How beautiful this sensation of swooning, of being physically weak, of being able to yield to everything and for good reason, now or never.

The Volkswagen acts up, a run-down battery. For ten thousand lire a taxi driver agrees to attach the jump cables. One after the other the rear lights are extinguished in front of Angelo, who has entered highway traffic. It is already hot. Beyond the wire fence women and children arrange boxes of peaches under large umbrellas.

There are stretches of road like this beneath the radiant light of a singing dawn where only dark banalities come to mind: that life is a vale of tears, unemployment, drugs, illness, weariness, and the sense of having been forever abandoned to oneself, after having been thoroughly taken for a ride. And with each umbrella that opens, Angelo makes the accelerator hit the floor and remembers aloud: "And so what, and so what, and so what?"

There were several trips during the spring and summer of 1981, but Angelo was all the same able to take his orals in English 4 and decided not to take the written exam but to leave it for the next academic year. By so doing he guaranteed his lodgings and the course.

To live in that pretty little house which was in his name but in fact less his than the room he occupied on Via Verdi was a traumatizing experience. His folks kept alive by mutual howled hatred seemed taken up by a mesmerizing activity that threatened to last another thirty years.

After the daily round of appointments was completed, Angelo was intractable and unrestrainable. He flew up to his room and changed into neutral-looking clothes, in all seasons and in any weather, and he ran out toward the mating of his modest but ravenous desires. He cared for quantity and silence.

Lometto, already in his undershorts, had opened, as usual, all the faucets in the bathroom and was lazing on the bed, intent on reading the daily newspaper he had found at the International Press stand at the railroad station. Once, at Malmö, Angelo played a trick on him. He had gone out purposely to buy him something to read—*Il Giornale* or *Corriere della Sera* or *Il Borghese* or *Candido* or *Gente*. It was strange but at Malmö station the only Italian publication that one could find was *L'Unità*. He bought it, already rubbing his hands over Lometto's spasmodic reaction. Who changed color as if he had been insulted or beaten up in church; refused to open it or even touch it, and yelled after him all sorts of insults for having financed that "cunt of a party."

Angelo was sorry that Lometto in the evening, unable to exploit the indecent hour to pounce unexpectedly on unscheduled customers, had no way of amusing himself. He was not interested in anything, he never even brought along a detective story. One doesn't know how it got there, but one day out of his overnighter popped a sexy magazine with a pile-up of males. Lometto, who never did anything by chance, commented on the large size of the *handles* and from there went on to the torments a persimmon must undergo to "take in" those *businesses*, invariably stuck not in vaginas but in the behinds of sailors and crane operators. He did not seem to attach any importance to their posterior specificity. Some newspaper dealer must have slipped it to him by mistake, Angelo thought, amused; he did not want to touch this subject, he did not want to glimpse in Lometto the direct intention of reconciling his headaches with his faithfulness to his wife, with his avarice or thriftiness. Angelo himself did not find anything exciting in those pictures, and even less a reason to laugh about them. Pornography was a terribly serious and wonderful thing, but so frustrating: *they* were always the actors and he was not satisfied simply to watch. But he had a profound understanding of those who could not or did not want to do better or more. He felt a great tenderness for Lometto and his migraines, that too a way not to *watch*, a reverse pornography.

It was in a moment of this kind, in an atmosphere of not-seen/not-said/not-heard, with Angelo already at the door, all set to leap into the night, that Lometto asked: "When will you be back?"

Angelo turned around and came back into the room. Perhaps the fellow felt like taking a walk, at last, to go and lap up a quart of ice cream at the café. He pretended that he did not see the hand that was manipulating inside the underpants.

"I don't know, the same as usual, before eleven or tomorrow at dawn, if I stay and sleep out, as always. Did you want to go and have an ice cream? You know, it's all the same to me, as long as I tire myself a bit physically so I can sleep."

Angelo was deeply surprised, like a son who realizes for the first time that Mama too has sexual desires and what's more outside the family. He saw him collapse so shamelessly, there now with his prick, in his fist, him, Lometto, who was staring at him with an anemic, professionally inquisitive expression, as if he were Churchill at Yalta intent on putting a further signature to a further imposed pact. As if everything were the obvious outcome of events which had gone a certain way, as if he expected he was owed just another attention from a servant, who is never obliged to speculate on his master's undressed attitudes.

"If you want to come along, I'm going to the sauna."

"What am I supposed to do in a sauna? No . . . How long are you going to stay?"

"Well, an hour, two, as usual!"

"I don't have anything to read . . ."

"Listen, you could buy your own newspapers, you know, you don't need an interpreter for that. Shit, I have to be your valet too. Okay, do you want the crossword puzzles? Do you want *Rinascita*?"

"Oh, you're not going to fool me this time. I'll go down myself, I'll buy my own papers."

Angelo patiently waited for Lometto to get dressed again. They were at the Bahnhof Hotel in Cologne, as always. Lometto did not find anything that suited him, and yet this time he could choose. He hesitated. They drank *Apfelsaft*. They took a tour of the corridors. Angelo, seized by haste for *himself*, was forced to face the situation. They took a taxi with Lometto cursing because he always pulled him to *his* side. Angelo didn't say anything, this too was part of his porno-tenderness.

"Please make sure, ask for an extra towel" Lometto said once at the Römische Bäder, beneath the same Intercontihotel where Angelo had once been with the George Rech collection.

Not even with two towels was Lometto able to encircle his hips. He had a body devastated by stretch marks thick as tent ropes. Angelo saw him for the first time in a certain way, deeply sorry for him, a huge adipose window coagulated in its will not to open up onto anything so that nothing from inside should transpire and spend the rest of his existence prone, spying at the landscape of others through the keyhole. Those others, who despite themselves would be forced to include him, would be carnally precluded to him. At least here, the annex club of many body-building guys.

"Don't leave me here alone. Which way do we go?"

"Oh, you'll find the way by yourself. You won't get lost, you'll see."

Angelo had already exhausted his patience, the sauna closed at midnight. He was tired of this full-time assistance, during which Lometto demanded to be treated as a hapless *bon enfant*. Oh, if he could only dump him and do what the hell he wanted! So that at least for one hour he would be spared the trouble of satisfying the untiring greed typical of those who rent by the hour.

They met after a while in the small room where American movies were showing on the television. A distinguished old man and an effeminate youth on a couch in front of the one that Lometto occupied fully all by himself, and on which he seemed at ease, were caressing each other ineffectually like little old nostalgic *Blumenstil* ladies, all too happy at enjoying some sort of audience for their decadent cabaret number. It did not escape Angelo that Lometto was watching with great interest what was happening on the screen: in a prison a vicious guard forces the convicts in their long flannel underwear to bend to his lust. While a gang of convicts is being taken to the work site, there is a mutiny with many close-ups, so that while the guard violates a man with a beard, this man imprisons him with all the strength of his anal (?) muscles and for so long that the others have the time to: (a) break their chains with rocks; (b) escape into the woods; (c) reenact the showers in boarding schools. Then comes a scene in a leafy hut: under the threat of weapons, two of the escaped convicts force the gamekeeper to give them shelter for the night and prepare food for them. The gamekeeper puts a sleeping draft into the bean soup, etc., etc. In short: the only female presence is disclosed by that joker John Cage, who passes himself off as Janette Cocky, the script girl in the closing credits.

Lometto fidgeted slightly on the couch, victim of an erection that he did not understand, perhaps understood even less than the preceding one displayed in the hotel room. Those guys were not even remotely comparable to Edda, aside from their determination to get down to business. They were males. They had, sure enough, mustaches, but also robust *extroverted* sexual apparatuses. So explicit. But Angelo did not worry too much, and neither did Lometto, seeing him at his side, do anything to conceal his erection and he began to comment on the pictures of the film that was starting all over again.

"What items, what handles! Poor convicts, what items you have to accommodate if you go to jail! A paradise for you, baby."

"At the end that one kneeling over there" Angelo said, even though he hadn't watched to the end "repents and becomes a nun. That's how it always is. Did you or did you not realize that it is the same? Why don't you take a little walk?" Later on he again met the ever more disconcerted bulk in the *mannerist* section, a huge labyrinthine room crowded with wooden piles and iron bars which divided the space of darkness into alleys, holes, corridors, cabins with peepholes. Lometto was, as always, at the tail end of things. He observed, or sounded out, a small group of an indefinite number of City *clerics* busy signaling to each other tribal transactions so very unlike his own at home. This time too Angelo saluted him discreetly, smiling at him, noticing that Lometto, statuesque, did nothing to hide under one of the towels the usual, incomprehensible protuberance. He attempted an ironic observation and Angelo cut him off.

"No comments on the activities of others. Nobody forces you to stand there and look. Take a sauna if you want or go take a rest or do your sunlamp or go drink in the bar. You're not at the movies here. People risk their health for certain things. Show some respect."

Lometto would have liked to justify himself, but he did not really have excessive feelings of guilt about anything. An amateurish legacy for an industrialist who must produce and sell and keep informed, who must not overlook anything that is there to see. In the space of a few months, he became used to a lifestyle that previously had been for him almost totally unknown or exceptional. He accompanied Angelo to clubs and saunas, even of the *brutal* type, with the same jovial indifference with which he called on customers, old and new. Lometto wanted to "boost his morale." Angelo never told him that he did not in the least need him to go and "boost his morale." These were small ploys to snoop to his heart's content. Between them there never was an explicit allusion to what Lometto was up to in the sauna. Probably nothing. Whether this nothing was due to him or his unattractive body, one does not know. There are, however, frail youths who swoon over bellies and rubber rafts of gelatin, just as others love only athletic physiques or ephebes. So *beauty* or *ugliness* never had anything to do with sex and the other cynical things of life. Lometto never did speak about it, except when referring to what Angelo did or did not do. He continued to suffer headaches. And to rave that he wanted to get home as soon as possible because of Edda. He telephoned her only when he really felt bad.

Angelo was with him that time, he had not yet gone out. He had asked Lometto if he preferred that he go somewhere else while he was talking. But no, he said, and why?

"Hello?"

". . ."

"And what are you doing there?"

". . ."

"What do you mean, Mama lets you? Where is she? Come on, tell her to step on it, it's expensive."

". . ."

"What's Ilario doing in our bed?"

". . ."

"What are you talking about, children! You tell him, do me a favor, and get him out of there right away, he isn't three years old anymore."

". . ."

"Yeah, if you think this is hard I'll give it to him soft. This is nothing to laugh about, he'll soon be in the army and he . . ."

". . ."

"Ah, I see! One evening each! Great, just great!"

". . ."

". . . Oh, that's how it is! Well, now you tell all three of them that it's time to stop all this. They're too old for this foolishness! The Indian said so!"

". . ."

"And how are you, my precious? Did you hear anything about the dyeing plant? And did you call Novarini about the inserts for the Belinda? No, no, we can't ship on the thirteenth and besides for so little. And then let them figure it out, we deliver the merchandise paid at the Italian border and we're already doing them a favor. What? Internal revenue? And when? Oh, the day after tomorrow they told you. Very well. Take it easy and don't get excited, please. Pull out those two ledgers, the gray ones, and use that orange commercial envelope, in the first drawer at the top behind the dossiers. No, not yellow, the orange one is enough, the one that's left unsealed inside the second page of the bigger ledger. No, I don't want you to do anything. Mum's the word. How am I supposed to tell you? Nothing and nothing . . . Get it? They take the bait better. Yes, how many times do I have to tell you? . . . But no, they'll take the bait, they'll take it . . . Yes, I'll phone them myself . . . And how are you? And the children? . . . Me . . . the usual headache . . . If you don't know why . . . why are you laughing? He's here, he's here, the *umbrella man of my cunt*. But really, come on, a little headache. Yes. Yes. Yes

. . . day after tomorrow, I hope. Yes, a little something, we're making the rounds . . . a couple of orders . . ."

"Four! Two for you and two for Mire" Angelo shouted. Lometto, while he was making the rounds, competed on the sly with seventy percent of Mire stock that didn't belong to him.

"Yes! What else is there? Yes, when I get back you can go to the spa. You had your fortune told? All for free? Fine. And *take care of it*, keep it on ice meanwhile . . . Come on, *ciao*, yes, but come on already! This costs money."

Edda had *discharges*. She went to the spa for *irrigations*. Poor women, shabbily treated also linguistically. Angelo could not help but imagine sulphurous rivulets in flood entering one sewer and issuing out of another. The National Institute for Social Security and Health used obscene expressions almost as though to get back at the mothers of families who had recourse to the benefits of its participating waters but in recompense gave everything, trip and hotel included. This was a special health insurance held only by those who knew a certain bureaucratic route. The wives of lawyers, dentists, and industrialists used it, a first-class insurance. Like Lometto's sons: they went, yes, to the "fresh-air fund" and paid seven hundred lire a day, everything included, together with nuns and social workers, but it was a fund, so to speak. "Everybody" could go there, obviously, but especially the sons of lawyers, dentists, and industrialists. Subsidized by the Region, it goes without saying, which when it wanted to knew how to do things very nicely and "without too much publicity." Lometto was radiant when he described these nasty truths to Angelo, indeed, he encouraged him to take advantage of them, oh, no problem, he knew into whose ear he must drop a little hint. Angelo refused, he had no desire to be "irrigated" by all that privileged nectar produced by the intestines of workers on a fixed salary. Lometto, dripping cheerfulness from all pores, called him a boob, and said that one lives only once and one must take advantage, etc., the kind of cheerfulness money assumes when, from the transcendent value it maintains in *one's own* pockets, it descends to the immanent value of money taken from the pockets of others. After all, he said, somebody had to pay, didn't they? And how can the rich remain rich if they are forced to come up with the money? Who would keep the nation going? It was much more sensible to extract it from those who, in any case, would never become rich and had nothing to lose because they would always remain poor, and you wouldn't expect a poor person to assume also the responsibility of keeping the nation going, right?

Lometto went into a lather of delight regaling Angelo with these finely chiseled sophisms, and exaggerated them to see him shocked and gasping, but there was no need at all to exaggerate, they never managed to become paradoxical satire; because, even reduced to the lowest denominator of collegiate buffoonery, they betrayed the disarmed, ineluctable, leaden conception of the social pyramid. You were either on top or underneath. He sided with and hung around the peak. He could afford everything because it was those on top like him who dictated *democracy* to the bottom. He was very democratic because he was very much the boss. He saw himself in no other role than this. He was born to it, he said, apologizing. The more he was a boss, the more contributions he made to legalize the just injustice of this democracy. He seemed to enjoy an impunity of a superior type: it amused him to chatter about these monstrosities because he was certain that everyone wanted him to get away with it always and no matter how. That is why he was respected by the unions and the Communists as well: because he knew how to respect the rules and make them work to his advantage, and he had demonstrated that whoever had dared turn these same rules against him, viewed from an eccentric perspective, that is, let us say, Marxist, had his fingers smartly rapped first of all by the Communists and the unions. He gave examples to demonstrate that his was not a personal cynicism but a collective coercion in the system, the true law that he was obliged to read between the lines of the merely formal laws, made to look good not in life but in the typographical characters of the *Gazzetta di San Luigi Gonzaga*.

"Take the business with the grana cheese. Every time you get to a border station you hand over the bank documents, the bills of lading, etc., and they're checked and stamped for approval. And for every pound that you export the government gives you a subsidy of seventeen hundred lire. Of course you can imagine, it goes without saying, what happens to the hundreds of agricultural products within the Common Market, oranges, for example, olives. But forget about that. Let's stick to the grana. Say a truck goes through the Domodossola. Well, you take a little ride on the other side, you have an aperitif and you come back to the border. Nothing to declare, did you or did you not unload? Everything is checked, stamped, everything is in order, etc. You go to Chiasso . . ."

"With the same truck?"

"Of course, that's the point. You've got ten duplicate sets of documents in your attaché case, dummy! You go to Chiasso, I was saying. You buy yourself a cute little watch or you go to take a look at your bank account . . ."

"Your bank account, you mean to say . . ."

"There's no doubt about that, baby, just imagine your having a bank account in Switzerland. Well, you have a chat about interest rates and you come back through the same border. Then there is Vipiteno, customs posts are a dime a dozen. At every entry-exit the government subsidies are multiplied by two, by three, by four, by as many turns as you want to take in this game of snakes and ladders, you understand? Certainly, every so often you can't avoid leaving behind a round of cheese, you mustn't look too greedy . . . At the end of the day you've earned a truckful of rounds and, since you won't be so stupid as to go back and unload it in your own warehouses, you'll go down to volcano land with this grana cheese which has already been exported ten times and paid for by the state ten times at one thousand seven hundred lire, which, wholesale, is its price, that is, twice as much. In Naples, Salerno, Caserta, you sell it slightly below cost but for cash: all of it net and clean money. And do you know how many millions a truckful of grana cheese rounds amounts to? There is no game, there is no trick, even a one-year-old child can do it! There, you cunt-faced intellectual. And everything, but everything with the blessing of State and Common Market, which are perfectly aware of it, understand? Who would be offended if you, the producer, were so stupid as not to take advantage of it. Then the State, on the strength of so much hard phantom currency, don't you worry, will settle everything with the banks. Of course, you need to have contacts there too . . ."

"And what if I were to talk, blow the whistle on all this stuff?"

"They'd think you're crazy, dearie."

"And what if I denounced you to the Public Prosecutor?"

"Go ahead. You'll be locked up for slander, not me for fraud."

"And if I had made a tape recording of everything?"

"Well, then there . . . in that case . . . it depends whether you're serious or not. So many people disappear and nobody knows how they ended up . . ."

"Go fuck yourself, Lometto. You're a megalomaniac."

"You cheat more than I do, since you don't even write me an invoice, a receipt, and I can't even deduct you!"

"Oh, oh, there we go again with the invoice, enough, have mercy . . ."

"You, you're the one who works off the books and you're not entitled. In my case it's the system that demands it. There's your difference. In your case it's necessary because you're a nothing and a nobody."

This because, halfway through the week, on Wednesday or Thursday night, Lometto took off with his van packed like an egg and went to unload along the Adriatic coast. It was Edda who had told him once on the phone.

"He returned at three o'clock this morning too. If he isn't at Mire either, he certainly isn't here. You never come to see us."

"Well, you know, I'm almost always there at Toigo when they need me. I never get a chance to go through Penzana."

Edda, recently, talked a lot. Angelo inspired confidence in her. So much so that once she said to him:

"When you tell something to anyone around here, at the plant, or in the piazza, the next day everybody knows everything. You listen and I never ever heard anything come back."

"Indeed. I wasn't born yesterday," Angelo answered; he loved gossip too much to spread it. "If you want to confide in me . . . Not even Celestino will ever hear anything about it. Just as you will never hear anything about the confidences he makes in me."

She had burst out laughing and certainly had passed a hand over her belly, lingering with her thumb inside the large navel outlined on the cloth.

"Don't worry, he does the same with me too! For instance, that you show up in the room naked after walking through the hallway. Why don't you ever introduce us to one of *them*?"

Lometto told her everything, skipping the *gender*. It was for the sake of the travel anecdotes; they must be told in front of the Family.

In August, the Via Verdi apartment being shut down again, Angelo said goodbye by phone and left with Tirlindana on a cruise of the Anatolian coast. Angelo had placed a few of Tirlindana's authentic pictures, so much less important than the fakes produced by the Tuscan painter in his youth. Indirectly, the cruise was financed by Angelo.

Angelo's role on that "boat" (about which he had a very strange idea, all oars, before stepping on board) was most confused; it was so grotesque having to condescend for hospitality's sake to a hysterical weirdo who was a legend only to himself. Angelo consumed in silence and even with secret irony his growing rancor toward the venerated, perhaps "venerable" maestro. Angelo looked around at the passengers on the yacht without knowing what to say or what to listen to. They were run-down dolls full of the ticks which precede the battery's total exhaustion. And he was there with them. But he had sensed everything from the very first instant and had not pulled back; these were "upper crust" and one must get to know them from close by, the opportunity was unique. How was it possible that everything, social prestige, money, the forging of existential models—there was a dwarf owner of a couple of unlicensed television stations—had ended up in the hands of these, and only these, representatives of the most sinister supermanist and Masonic bourgeoisie? "Heavens, what a fuss for a bit of kneecapping!" was Epaminonda's sentence that Angelo repeated to himself whenever he masked his homicidal instincts behind a conventional smile.

He felt repaid for the group's hostile contemplation only when he had before him the fish just caught by skin divers and already steaming on the dishes. Those delicate fishbones between the teeth made up for the torture of stifling his rage and forcing himself to maintain an abstract, etiquettelike patience without betraying his feelings. Even the ladies' bikinis irritated him, the fluttering of eyelashes and the other customs of the incense wafters of the offshore *beau monde*. Tirlindana, always so much the prima donna, profoundly set his nerves on edge; the thought that he would be there in front of him also when he woke up prevented him from getting a wink of sleep. Tirlindana did not swim well, but this was not enough on which to embroider some sort of hope. At the first port Angelo indulged in that most perfidious sin, masochism: he wrote the eighty-third letter to the mute apparatus in Anguillara and mailed it. "Why didn't you come to the appointment?"

In an envelope, enclosed in the sheet, he dropped locks of hair, dry, dead, some silvery and electrified by brinelike filaments of burnt-out light bulbs. The lucid folly of this gesture, which announced a further uncheckable series, imparted vigor to his melancholy wearied by the boredom of his company. From every place where a postal service existed, climbing by bus and donkey all the way to Izmir, he sent letter upon letter and hair upon hair. He would stop when he had become completely bald. He did not care at all whether Italo read them or tore them up without reading them, received them or not, was dead or alive. They did not concern him. But to know, oh God, to know why he had not come to the appointment! This was the thought that peeked out between the thousands of mindless lines written at every hour of the day and night. Those letters were the sole black consolation that kept him alive during those days of humiliating sociological enrichment and individual nullification; they were written in the exhausted but happy spirit of a miner who comes back to the light after a day's labor in the darkest lairs of the human spirit, and too bad if outside it was already night and the light lunar. He would never forget Turkish stamps. At his awakening they flashed through his mind like scimitars moving from distant space. As for writing, he would write, hating his hand tight around the pen, hating himself and his fixed thought on that lazy, pusillanimous boy, but this was nothing compared to the labor of procuring stamps. Oh, those little licks! Between him and this Italo there had been no turgidity, unfortunately. The more the fellow, from the very start, had not answered unless forced by a phone call, the more the letters had multiplied in a desperate, ever faster, fanatical, mortifying, autochthonous merry-go-round. All of them special delivery. In the end they had become letters of hatred which Angelo wrote and did not mail. He had a folder full of them, he begged him to give a sign of life, to break the malign papery spell that nailed him to the chair. Sometimes he picked up the receiver, dialed one more digit than the time before . . . Until finally he arranged for that appointment and that hoax.

In Istanbul, Angelo, with his admirable divinatory gift, had ended up in Taxim Park with a dagger dug in his side and had managed to get out of it thanks to the usual slightly euphoric cold blood with which he emptied his pockets and unbuckled his watchband, and returned to the hotel cursing. He wanted to leave the next day. But they had group tickets. Tirlindana was against it: he had run into a soccer team and had just now begun to *do the portrait* of the left wing. He sponsored the sport. Angelo waited for him to score, tired as he was of translating their mercenary obscenities on the Sheraton's terrace. The poverty of the city and the stereotyped luxury in which he spent his nights had stripped him of even that touch of enthusiasm inspired by the discovery of a new city.

The cruise had been a catastrophe, just waiting around for the meals so as to break the monotony of the barrier which separated him from those people, only capable of complaining about the services of plumbers and waiters, and the school, and the telephone service, and the railroads, which "are no longer what they used to be." The very rich, harmonious dwarf, who forbade even the slightest familiarity with himself and his wife, in terror of even the slightest hint of his gnomishness. His wife, a woman all tendons, androgynous, very hard and almost beautiful, clamped shut like an oyster afraid to reveal its origin as a mussel; their little boy, with legs, alas, crooked and stumpy like his father's, serious and he too distrustful as a clown. Then there was a morphine addict, bloated like a moonfish, a very sweet, harmless, playful man, lost in memories of an Olympian youth in whose inflated physique he did not recognize himself: his was the typical bonhomie of someone who, for one reason or another, had suffered a leak of gray matter, solicitous, warm, and useless; an actress always on deck, her small post-Sunset Boulevard, the face of a goat stretched by many face-lifts and a body maniacally subjected to the massage of an old Turk brought on board for the purpose, who expired on the fourth day of navigation, leaning on a lobster trap, had moved his bowels there, in a corner, with open eyes, mortally in love with the sea. Then there was a small ministry employee, timorous, maladroit, who skipped about like an elf at the mercy of seasickness. Always hanging on to the morphine addict, he had gained forty pounds in two weeks, was unrecognizable at first sight. A smaller boat followed with a famous judge and his young intellectual mistress with the air of one perennially trampled by fate, plus adolescent son who grudgingly endured the little discomforts of a corps of servants not at its best. There was only one brief docking, at the insistence of the painter, who returned on board late in the evening, saying that it had simply been an aperitif. He was anxious to get to Istanbul, where he looked forward to a real gorging.

With the excuse of the portrait he began to call into his room the young deckhands and undressed them and sucked them off and then chased them away in a hurry, prey to the soul-saving guilt feeling that seized him at the hour of the collective tea. At dinner he skipped dessert and started up again till late into the night. His success was incredible. He picked up men in bars, on the street, in cabs, and Angelo negotiated for him.

The hotel management put a detective in the hall so that nothing should happen to him, at least not there. Then something awful happened and Tirlindana asked Angelo to go with him to the manager's office. The manager reprimanded him amiably, there was too much coming and going. Discretion, if possible. And the number of them too. Tirlindana apologized profusely, sketched majestic bows, opened wide the entire denture of his savoir-faire, drooled. He started up again that very same evening. The next day they were again in the manager's office; a young waiter had been fired on the spot because, seen by the detective coming out after too long a time, he had been reported to the head of personnel and, in view of the insistence with which the boy proclaimed his innocence, the painter had been called in to provide an explanation. Tirlindana gave way to panic, poured all the blame on the youngster for having the impertinence to show up in his room for a small portrait and then make obscene proposals, and he had angrily thrown him out. Angelo thought of the tragedy of the young man thrown into the street by the customer who is always right and was overcome by an uprush of nausea which risked shattering his painful discretion maintained until then despite everything and everybody. Tirlindana was the typical homocratic artist who's arrived. They were all made of the same stuff.

Angelo acted as cashier and the painter did not stint on expenses, he laughed loudly about the incident which had befallen the young man, saying that he was young, had the world before him, right, what did Angelo think about it? Angelo shrugged his shoulders, he felt definitely befouled, short-circuited with himself. Tirlindana became even more openhanded with Angelo as well as with the tricks and he often urged Angelo to buy himself a Turk, but in Angelo there did not exist the precedents of the "artistic" homosexual rear guard, which, being able to crystallize a libido around the appropriate use of money, had given Italy so many minds worthy of anthologies, museums, publishing houses, cinema, and theater, and not one sensible man. What a bore!

Finally, they got back to Italy. At Rome airport he was about to telephone Anguillara but was already hoping that Italo wouldn't be home. He might as well save the token. He returned to Verona with his entire dream held tightly between his teeth: that he had not been able to come to the appointment because he had suddenly died. This would also explain in part why he had never answered, even once. Arrived in Florence, before leaving Tirlindana, Angelo presented to him his theory on intelligence, in whose most beautiful and exalting phase he, in his opinion, happened to be: the phase in which one has the energy to defend necessarily not only what one *has* but the right of others to have in equal measure, independently of their *intelligence* or technical ability or cunning. Nothing was so unjust as the merits acquired by so-called *merit*, just think of those acquired by *cultural* and *artistic*, that is, economic and political oppression.

Angelo, when he expounded these ideas to the paint dauber, received question and answer at the same time: "So what am I supposed to do? Throw myself in front of a train?"

And Angelo, with the same dolorous discretion maintained till that moment, had answered a laconic: "Yes."

Angelo bid Tirlindana goodbye with a Judas kiss, he did not crucify him immediately because it was obvious anyway that his fate was already sealed and someone else would take care of it. Angelo would also have been willing to make it clear to him that the only way for him to be reborn was to throw himself in front of a train once and for all, without so much fuss, but Tirlindana was too tightly clutched to his schemes to accept this advice.

Legal Italy, from industry to university, from culture to politics, was an immense geographic basin of thefts. Life was falsified in total complicity in order to better plunder it, enslave it, derail it.

At the end of summer he showed up again in Florence. Angelo dragged these ideas of his into more than one home into which he was invited in Tirlindana's company. He went because he was interested in social forms, which, no matter what chamber-maids may say, are visible only if one enters through the front door. Here he deposited, on gigantic platters of jumbo shrimps and sea bream, his sympathy for the Sardinian kidnappers, well, of course, always depending on what new egregious son of a respectable leech they had sequestered, what other innocent sacred life they had tortured and killed. And here he dropped a praline according to which the so-called Sardinian shepherd worked in the underground under great environmental hardships, while the others worked in insurance, the registrar's office, public works, agricultural subsidies, real estate speculation, and unemployment assistance. One could—oh, that dish of fisherman's rice, so steaming, under the star-studded arbor!—make certain distinctions also as regards the sacredness of life: not because he made them but because the system itself established tortuous nuances by which in the end one life was more sacred than another which evidently was less so. Elsewhere he delighted the refined coterie—was it in Arezzo? oh yes, that old-fashioned *ribollita* with small pork ribs, in the garden, those Gozzano-like waitresses, dressed in black with their frilly white caps—by saying that all of Italy seemed to have become a chaste caste, a private circle, Freemasonry, and those who were not part of it, those indispensably dispensed from this obligation to belong, were those who by not activating the means of production were jam to be spread in layers on beautiful progressive words and bank accounts. And the boys to lure into one's room—Tirlindana gave a start, dribbling a rivulet of very liquid currant cream on his ascot—with the excuse of doing their portrait and politely and haughtily shown the door, clutching a bank note. Whoever buys always buys a brand and the price includes the impunity and anonymity of the customer, who is a non actor, therefore any possible complaint always hinges on the defectiveness of the bought or buyable, which is by nature mute and cannot ever say anything to exonerate itself. Oh, these arguments about the world's oldest profession were cretinous and lent themselves to easy ironies and smug shrugs, just because one persisted in always seeing them from the point of view of those who, having the money and therefore the word, have no interest in reversing the approach, in letting some of the speechless speak, the *non gratis* people.

And that the State closed one eye to wink with the other at God's little lambs and that . . . But the lady of the house said that it had gotten very late.

If Angelo did not disappear by himself so as to preserve some doubt or hope about a snobbery more prominent here than there or elsewhere, he never was invited to the same house a second time. Perhaps nobody was giving parties anymore.

Angelo, having returned to Via Verdi, took long rides on his bicycle to the small wood near the Adige, stirring in the cauldron of his anger and frustration. He had plunged headfirst into a truth. His frankness and restlessness closed all doors to him, and he noticed that the "grand" and "middle" bourgeoisie was suffering its most catastrophic loss, snobbery. It really had nothing left, aside from money. And if that was the future, the future of an intelligent and frank man like himself, he wanted no part of it. But he also detested the thought of becoming a dishwasher with a degree. Yet there must be *a way in between*. No, it did exist: that's why it could be found easily, he had only to lift for one moment that pitiless gaze of his, *look ahead*, resign himself to a certain corruption of his style. The unhappiness, discomfort, and sadness of others did not make him happy, they humiliated and inhibited him. He wanted to affirm his intelligence and merits by synchronically affirming that intelligence and merit, admitting that they existed beyond the convenient social postulates of the moment, must refuse to be sources of privilege. And in Marrakesh, one time, he'd had a rebellious outburst, his body in revulsion had turned into one hundred and forty pounds of dynamite at the sight of that Rolls-Royce escorted by dozens of mounted policemen with whips hissing down on the crowd to clear the way, while the children who had not been able to sit down with him—he and Demetrio by now had only their underwear left—crawled under the chairs and benches to snatch up morsels of bread and mutton like dogs. What a thirst for blood to be avenged he felt in his veins! But was he or wasn't he about to sip some Veuve Clicquot? And so for how many more damned years would he have to cohabit with that continuous clickety-click knitting in his head the names of heads to be chopped off? Angelo had felt definitely alone, with a self that offered him no truce. The only thread of life that kept him pedaling trustingly toward the bonfires in the wood was his hatred and the hope to organize it without debasing it, by weaving a carnivorous, thick net à la Madame Defarge, not psychological and full of gaps. Soon the first autumn trip would begin. Also Lometto and his family were part of those who had taxidermized the world and the world, which knew nothing else, had not expected and did not expect anything but being taxidermized.

Angelo's mother is watering the geraniums on the terrace.

"*Ciao!* Did you just get in?"

"*Ciao*. In central Italy, down your sister's way."

"Where have you been?"

"Did anybody call?"

"No; yes, I don't remember who. You got back here already?"

Angelo can't fall asleep. All she can do is predict the weather because of her leg. He gets dressed again in a hurry, looks around: Giuditta isn't there, already having breakfast in different houses. He starts the motor. He'll sleep at the Terrazzine.

Lometto was fully happy only when Angelo, artfully, pressed him to spoon-feed him his knowledge of economics. His economic theory was simple, refined, commonplace: profit. With a dignity all his own: Lometto detested the welfare state and did not understand—that is, understood it very well, but the thing made him sick—why one should keep alive sulphur mines whose maintenance cost more than the income from the production and which lost twice as much as one would have earned—that is, have lost—by paying those workers to stay at home to strike matches from morning till night. And the steel-producing monster cities kept alive in the teeth of all international marketing laws. When he happened to pass in front of a Communist Party branch, he crossed himself. Now he said he felt no pity for those who resorted to the trick of arousing pity—it was like underwriting the certain bankruptcy of any business—in order to arrive at any goal whatsoever, and even less if workers or unemployed or unwed pregnant mothers or unwed teenage mothers without means of support did so in order to be hired—did he say rehired? This dissertation was a trifle vague, always seemed to be on the point of becoming something else, indecisive. It was the middle of September: Lometto, as said, had begun to talk about economics, etc., in a very soft, assured voice. Then there was a fact that kept popping up, but what fact was it? Many were the divagations. In short Angelo noticed that there were certain tortuous circumlocutions and many ramblings and salacious cracks but that Lometto was about to say something which he perhaps felt strongly about. He wandered and trained his vocal cords, sharpened them in search of the proper tone, a silvery modulation of preliminaries with sudden grim notes. It was as though he were trying all the door handles in a house in order to find the most appropriate on which to tie a nylon thread and pull out a tooth with one jerk—cautiously? If one more or less adroitly put together these fragments—the door handle had squeaked, the nylon had broken, the tooth ended up in crumbs, and the root was left inside—the *fact* had been as follows: One day during the winter of 1978, that means before knowing Angelo, a woman had shown up at Mire with a babe in her arms asking for work or something along those lines. She wasn't just anybody, in the sense that in Penzana everybody knows who is an unwed mother even if, as in all small towns, one often doesn't know who the father is. She was not from those parts, she came from Campania, one of these . . . well, anyway, you know what I mean. She had settled there about a year before, two years, something like that. Oh, some sort of a vagrant, an orphan, ugly, a beggar, and with a bum leg. Don Galetta, yes, Don Nocciolini, the priest, had tried to give her a hand, etc., and . . . to make a long story short: Lometto had preached her a little sermon and told her that if she had really been anxious to work she would never have shown up at the plant with a child in her arms, and besides with the crisis there was for *normal* girls (?). No point in begging for understanding now; if you dabble in mud, you should know beforehand that you're bound to get dirty. Et cetera. She had begged him, and so he had said "And who are you going to leave him with when you work? In the churchyard?"

"Don't worry I'll . . ." etc., etc. "Perfectly capable of staying home every other day after being insured. What a wonderful example! An invitation to our daughters to make children too . . ." (He did not have any females.) He'd had his secretary accompany her to the door, but he had been adamant, a company has expenses that it must balance at the end of the month, it is not a charity institute, why didn't she go back to where she came from? "And between you and me I also gave her a hundred thousand lire, so much for you saying that I'm stingy." Et cetera. And then the story had crumbled, pulverized in a dust of sentences and monosyllables from which Angelo now no longer was able to disentangle what Lometto had sighed out from what he himself had added, impelled by the fervor of the shock that had tied his tongue. So then: the woman, humiliated and undone, you see, so humiliated as to feel to the depths that she was guilty, that very night on or below the church steps had killed herself, slashing her wrists. And the newborn baby, right beside her, until morning, could have died of exposure or pneumonia. All the consideration at any rate, of this he was certain, had been hers, not Lometto's.

If she had chosen the churchyard—the appointed place—only to draw attention to herself and so stage a true and proper suicide attempt (which is most unlikely in a small agricultural center practicing and respectful of the rules, and besides at night there isn't a soul on the streets after nine at night even in Mantua!), she had really been unlucky. Nobody had come by . . . The baby, a few months old, had been sent to a temporary orphanage, and Mire, Inc., had underwritten a certain monthly sum for a certain amount of time so that it would be sure to receive every assistance beyond the obligatory, etc. Lometto was very proud of this result, he felt he had to demonstrate that he and his partners were just men and that he had behaved as any other sensible manager would in his place.

Angelo was disconcerted by this story and had not been able to get out a word. The monstrosity of Lometto's certainties was of a Vedic altitude, over which he had not felt he could glide. But his bowels squirmed at knowing that perhaps with his astonished silence he had helped to infuse some sort of pride in Lometto, the insidious silent approval that he had acted in *conformity* with his responsibilities, his position as a *sensible* man.

Angelo had spent several nights reflecting on this disintegrated story and could not make head or tail of it. What was Lometto aiming at? precisely at that proverbial silence of his? at consent? at the confirmation that he had acted properly? was he bribing him to obtain the official probity which a definitive lay absolution sanctions? let's not kid ourselves, creatures like Lometto have no need for any kind of absolution, they never make mistakes, just as well not to play around too much with the complex of guilt or repentance applied to profit. And, above all, why had Lometto decided to tell him a story that was so ambiguous for him? And Nicola, did he know it? Angelo decided he didn't, otherwise who knows how long ago he would have rushed to tell it to him, as a revenge for having been shoved aside. Lometto never told anything about himself, only unimportant things that would easily have wearied any stranger: his military service, the first car, the first million, the first communion banquets for his sons, his exemplary wife, a real trooper, "not too democratic," dissatisfied with the Indian at the health insurance, the veterinarian, the priest, the bogey-women, the pharmacist, the bank employees who, just because they'd studied a bit, often forgot *who she was*, etc. Angelo broke his head over this story, and renounced forever, it seemed to him, understanding its ultimate reason, and did not arrive until much later at the simplest explanation within easy reach of comprehension: the fact that now at work Bananone was very friendly and had something on the tip of his tongue and that Lometto had certainly noticed this. Undoubtedly he had preferred to be the one to tell him how things had gone because, even though Bananone and the gasoline woman—who had smirked when Angelo explained why he always tanked up there—did not breathe a word while dying to do so, the event must be a matter of public knowledge, and if all the people in Penzana when telling a story added as many embellishments as Lometto did to his travel anecdotes, Angelo would hear some lurid versions of that nasty story. That perhaps the poor spastic had also approached Edda before, asking to be taken on with the handicapped women in the cellar, or perhaps that she had been thrown out from one place and had hoped to find refuge in the den of Mire's other half. Or that one bum leg guaranteeing *for free* also the other . . . or perhaps one should listen also to what the other local women had to say, without, however, relying on the office girls ranged compactly around Lometto. Any two other women, at least two, would have guaranteed two completely opposed versions which render a real story credible; Angelo and time would add the edge which holds together the two faces of the same coin and for many years the truth would have been available. But two women were fundamentally necessary, women were always so divided by nature. This, then, Lometto had meant to avoid: the indomitable coloration and coloratura of the anonymous voice of the populace.

Lometto added details, but Angelo no longer was listening: this was too much for him; he already saw himself, deaf to all explanations, flung into a vendetta. He held his hands clasped tight between his knees, as if he had slept outdoors, but the tendons vibrated, the vise yearned for Lometto's neck, how dare he involve him morally in such swinishness? And yet he sensed that he did not have sufficient elements to form an idea, he followed a maelstrom of emotional hypotheses and kept staring ahead, calm. But Lometto must have remained on tenterhooks, or perhaps not. Angelo never went back to the subject either then or later, gnawed by the certainty that Lometto, instead, had applied a proverb and now slept the sleep of the just, having obtained absolution even from the man most difficult to corrupt: the *cunt umbrella man.*

Angelo dumped the thought of Lometto—pompous behind his desk, preaching morals to a girl with blood on her wrists, rivulets like water from the leather desktop onto the travertine slabs, and this little bundle of snot and nocturnal mist broken by whimpers on the steps of the deaf church—dumped it into the depths of a mental storage place created there and then, and made an effort to set above it an ecstatic stone with a cross. But there had been nights during which he had felt, while awake, the shiver that must shake the buried alive when in the enclosure of the coffin they begin to break and then rasp their nails against the hermetic boards. He was burying also himself in the composure of that merely inner rebellion. Had that tea set of plated pewter become true silver for him too? Was it to this admission, shouted or silent, that Lometto had meant to lead him trip after trip? Another blood pact on the blood of others between Angelo and *an authority*, before the *authority*, Lometto, allowed him to parade his simplistic full-daylight honesty?

Lometto had had the prints framed in the most gilded, most curlicued and outdated frames, spending at the carpenter's a sum certainly ten times greater than the cost of the prints themselves, and one day at the beginning of October when Angelo too was there for lunch—the piglet embalmed almost a year earlier prominently displayed on a chest, arranged artistically: a tiny trough under its snout, a curly tail, but it was hopeless anyway, all the animals that ended up among the little knives and fine needles of the junior Lomettos had the same scrofulous appearance of badly packed salami—Lometto took a distant relation, a peasant woman doing well in real estate who lived on overcooked rice without television or heating or savings, on a tour of his gallery. Although the poor woman didn't understand a thing, it did not escape Angelo that when Lometto's voice suddenly dropped it was to tell her that they were all oils and all antiques, rare pieces.

"But how beautiful, how beautiful!" the little rice-shaped woman exclaimed, rapt. "You made a great buy, you did just the right thing. The frames are really beautiful, after all you live only once, good for you."

But a couple of days later when Pfefferman came to dinner again, the most touchy and haughty customer in the entire portfolio, who justified his stopping at second-class hotels on the lake by saying that they were second-class because they were six hundred meters away from the center of town and that if they had been six hundred meters closer to the center they would be first-class, and he had come to Italy with the Renault because the Mercedes attracted too much attention, and what's the big difference if you have to do six hundred meters more or less in a Mercedes? Teapot and milk jug and sugar bowl were proudly displayed beneath the lamp in the center of the table, which was not yet set. Around the larger prints Lometto had had small spotlights installed, which Angelo was seeing lit for the first time. Angelo already had the premonition of something very embarrassing: the sock maker had in his own fashion ingested some of Angelo's talks on art and now would attempt the impossible, ignorant of the fact that old Germans who have survived Hitler were either totally nostalgic or knew a lot anyway and that if, on top of it, they were Jewish, they always had that additional grain of pepper for survival and prosperity at all times that only universities like Heidelberg or Berlin could have ground up and sprinkled over them. Not even a salamander like Pfefferman could have safely traversed so many crematoria without a minimum of sacred fire of his own. So then Lometto was preparing to extort an *aesthetic* falsification and was maneuvering to force Angelo to act as his accomplice, to support this sudden collector's spasm with a polished and convincing translation: to make Pfefferman believe that that 16mo *Night Watch* was an original contemporary miniature by an anonymous Flemish painter. Obviously, there was protective glass everywhere and the Rijksmuseum's very perfect reproductions even gave the tactile sense of the surface crust. Angelo was sweating a bit, he had to translate that flight of lies from Mantuan into German, make them *his* own. He tried, cursing and swearing in sad and cordial tones, to convince Lometto to desist from coming up with such enormities, he reminded him, with the most nonchalant air in the world so that Pfefferman shouldn't notice anything, that if now he could boast of a china set for six he must thank him who had given it to him as a present in a moment of weakness. But Lometto insisted that he obey and Edda too tried to convince him, bearing encouraging looks back and forth from kitchen to dining room. The falsehood was translated, reproduced, and Pfefferman, pleasantly surprised, approached the print, extracted a monocle from his vest pocket, smiled, and turned around wagging his index finger at Angelo, not at Lometto.

"*Bandito, bandito!*" he exclaimed, amused. There was no need to translate for Lometto, who, still laughing and backed up by his wife, gesticulated and gargled to Pfefferman that the whole thing had been Bazarovi's idea.

"*Dr. Bazarovi, bandito bandito bandito!*" bellowed Lometto, unloading the attempted hoax on the flabbergasted Angelo.

He had a tremendous desire to slap his face for him. Lometto knew that he must never take the liberty, not even in jest, of saddling Angelo with his lack of common sense, in this instance the brazenness and full-fledged ignorance of things which, recently, he tried to appropriate because they added refinement. Lometto had been enchanted by words like *miniature, 16mo, Flemish* and decided to reproduce them himself. Lometto ignored Angelo's frosty expression, shrugged, and said through clenched teeth:

"Stop making that face, I pay you for this too. You like ricotta tortelloni? Wine good? *Gut, gut? Ah, bandito!*"

For the second course Edda placed on the table a stainless-steel platter covered with slices of veal in tuna sauce. The dish was translated, Pfefferman said that it was one of his favorite dishes, that he liked white meats, "ideal when you travel, so long as it isn't pork." Before they sat down at the table there had been a discussion which, starting from Lometto's cows, had arrived at the boys' taxidermic activities and then gone on to the current prohibition on importing into Germany sausages and pork meat of Italian origin, not that the matter concerned him personally, he had no use for it; it probably had all been propaganda to slow down imports, they agreed (Lometto agreed all by himself, Pfefferman sharply dissented), but the suspicion or the actual existence of the swine plague that year would prevent all German tourists, under the threat of very heavy fines (he had pulled from one of his pockets the customs notice distributed at the border), from stocking up and it was even advised not to consume them on the spot. And in fact Pfefferman had accepted, for hospitality's sake, to have only one slice of their homemade salami, declaring it good and a trifle "sinful" for him. Usually, however, Lometto remarked, he himself did eat salami, just one slice each at a time.

At the first mouthful of that white meat smothered in cream, Angelo recognized pig meat disguised beneath mayonnaise, tuna, capers, and olive oil. As usual, the Lomettos, considering cheaper the pork which they had in quantity, had had the nerve to offer a customer worth three hundred million veal with snout, simultaneously mocking his porkish taboos and his gluttony for our local salami.

"This pork is delicious, juicier than veal. Is it loin? My mother makes it too all the time, to save."

Lometto blasted him with a glance, Pfefferman said "*Wie?*" and Angelo was about to translate deliberately when he apologized and went to the toilet. He vomited the tortelloni and the mouthful of tunaed veal, not because it was pork, but because he was nauseated by the use those pigs were making of him, rubricating him to perfection to give him those delinquent touches of a Mafia underling which he so much lacked. But why? What was the need for it? None, the mutual co-interests were, after all, already perfect and circumscribed! But Angelo did not ignore the fact that the Mafia, like ignorance or an assumed behavior, justifies itself and in itself finds all the decisive elements to reproduce itself *sympathetically*.

It was while vomiting up his soul that into Angelo's mind leaped many details of this implicit annexation which had been dropped here and there by the Lomettos, details which Angelo had taken lightly because he did not understand them. Such as the two bank managers who one day had shown up there at the Lomettos', an agent of the internal revenue who on a Wednesday evening had telephoned and given the green light for certain roads to be chosen by avoiding others, or Edda, who answered the phone and then returned and said, "Naples," "Salerno," "Catania," and Lometto would sigh and amble without haste to the phone. Then there had been the two local secretaries of two parties disapproved of by Lometto, and an assessor of public works whom Angelo had met in the farmyard or at the front door. Lometto, later, always explained to him who this or that one was without ever specifying what they came there for, and then lapsed into an allusive silence . . . And then the names of business administrators, of corporation lawyers, of unspecified "presidents," of mayors of nearby towns, let drop, as if by mistake, along the workshop-stable-office route, charitable ladies who in their leisure time, not much, took an interest in the workers in the cellar, especially that woman glimpsed from afar, in very long skirts, the priest's housekeeper, his *perpetua*, skin and skeleton, and that priest whom he had seen in the confirmation photos, in black trousers, and with white hair bristly like porcupine quills . . . Had he too, Angelo, already become a pretty figurine in this crèche of conspiracy?

"Excuse me, but I don't feel well and I'd like to go" he said in both languages. "If Signor Pfefferman doesn't need me anymore . . ."

The orders had already been given, everything was taken care of, Pfefferman had devoured his huge dish of pork and was taking his leave together with Angelo, perfectly satisfied with the honors of the house, and thanked him for his cooperation and warned him not to tell any more cock-and-bull stories to him, who knew Greek and Latin and owned a fine Van Gogh self-portrait. Lometto was about to say something stinging, but he stopped himself, as though just in time.

Angelo left, determined to go back over everything point by point the very next day and establish sharp boundary lines between collaboration and complicity. He slept on it as best he could and in the morning his admiration for the immense energy released by this prankish and pushy couple had already gotten the better of his intention of dotting the *i*'s.

Thanks to the pantyhose he could afford the luxury of translating American metaphysical poets, squandering his own money for the pleasure of racking his brains over a fatalistic stream of consciousness financed by a certain Guggenheim Foundation. In any case, the Lomettos let him go about his own business, accurately decanting his increasingly confused remonstrances and then telephoning him with the most nonchalant and brazen attitude in this vale of licit tears to tell him that there was a stuffed duck waiting for him—and a trip to be taken.

The phenomenon produced by money which most appealed to Lometto was impunity. A man, a family of that kind, could afford to do anything and what's more had the pleasure of boasting about it—at least in a restricted circle, either of people such as small intellectuals or of big politicians. After a certain period of time one obtained confidential access to braggings on the fiscal level, of mortgages, regional subsidies, etc., of the Lometto & Napaglia enterprise. Defrauding was not enough for him—"the law passed the deception is found" was a proverb that before this had never made much sense to Angelo—Lometto wished to proclaim it, discreetly of course, but flaunt it proudly to those who like Angelo, at bottom, felt more intelligent and important than he and did not fail to tell him.

"I don't think that anyone is above me, not even the Pope" Lometto had once said.

"Not even Andreotti, our prime minister?"

"No. They need a whole lot of Celestinos to get where they are, I believe I'd be here no matter what, with them or with others in their place or without them."

"Well, I hope you never delude yourself to the point of feeling superior to me and swallow me down in one gulp as you've done with your mayors and assessors and priests and lawyers and bankers. I allow you to give me a tiny bite at a time, remember that."

"What do you mean?"

"That recently you've been disrespectful, you permit yourself liberties that you're taking on your own and that I never ratified. It seems to me that you're skipping any kind of negotiations on the liberties you're taking and you're taking too many things for granted, almost as owed to you. I don't owe you anything, Lometto, try to remember that."

"That is?"

"You understand perfectly. You didn't buy me for all eternity, you're not giving me any dividends, I'm not your partner, let this be clear: you pay me each time for *the* service agreed upon beforehand, and if afterwards you want something more or different, don't always start out from the presumption that I am in agreement no matter what. Is that clear?"

"But work is work, situations change, there are unforeseeables . . ."

"Your unforeseeables are not mine, remember that. You have to win me over each time. And actually, while we're at it, let us get one thing straight: there are things on which I have not expressed an opinion because at the moment I was prevented from doing so. But don't you believe that my silence means consent . . ."

"I don't know what you're saying, are you raving?"

". . . and that my true opinions will hit you between head and neck when you least expect. For instance, to touch on the first thing that comes to mind . . ."

"Let's hear this."

"You pretend you listen, Lometto. You ask a whole lot of questions in silence and then you answer them by yourself on my account. You're making a mistake. One of these days you'll register clear and loud who Angelo Bazarovi is . . ."

"If I'm not mistaken I've always paid you, and plenty."

"Sure, but you pay, you give yourself your own discount and then you demand something more, in addition. This doesn't work with me, I'm not an employee of yours, not one of your lackeys. I insist on precision from you or I'll cut all bridges this very moment. I'm passing through, I'm temporary. I never married you, remember that. I don't have to follow you wherever you go, and for free . . ."

"Oh, you're just a prickomaniac . . ."

"I'm as bad as you, worse if I feel like it. Economics is not everything in this world, and remember that there exists something that beats even the taste for power: the taste for madness. And that when it explodes, like the revolution, for quite a while there's no calculator that can hold it back."

"Just look what I had to pick for a friend!"

"That's enough. Everything is all right with you so long as everything contributes to keep you in the warmth of your certainties, wrapped in your blankets of institutional perfection. You aren't worth an old cigarette butt as an individual, without your wife you'd already be half. And if you were to weigh all three of your boys, we'd suddenly see that you weigh as much as all three of them put together. All you lack now is to begin buying stock in newspapers and then you'll be the perfect industrialist who's got it made."

"Who tells you that I haven't got them already?"

"Oh, one more or less, at this point . . . But your power depends on too many people . . ."

"So does theirs too . . ."

"Today things are fine for you, tomorrow you'll bite the dust."

"Eh, life is a jungle . . ."

"Someone on the inside of your system can suddenly go crazy . . ."

"You?"

"You see, you give yourself away. I'm not part of your system, only in your diseased head, Lometto. And besides there exist collective madnesses, swerves of the system, but I insist on saying that a single unexpected madness can be unleashed, by someone you would least expect, which will send you flying. For all I know, you and Andreotti and Wojtyla could even end up as transvestites in the port of Trapani a week from now."

"What are you trying to say, intellectual cunt? I buy you, I'll give you even more . . . oh, don't kid yourself, you've still got to eat a lot of polenta!—but I buy you whenever I feel like it."

"Just a moment, you're renting me. I don't have any contract with you, I'm a daily. If one day I don't feel like it, you're not entitled to send one of your inspectors to my house as you do with your workers. I can drop you when I want to, when I've eaten everybody has eaten or everybody's eaten but me but never mind."

"Oh, sure, I really like to see that, you, you cotton-pricker faced by an offer of a person I can think of . . . A concrete offer. An international office, for example. In Luxembourg . . ."

"I do not have material ambitions so boundless as to need you or that person. With all your power you'll be able, yes, to wear me out, but not to buy me, annihilate me, but not convince me to come over to your side . . ."

"Which side, you fanatic?"

"You know, we understand each other perfectly. The only side there is. Well, I'm not for sale. And you certainly aren't my first opportunity or even the most enthralling."

"Oh, sure, who would stake even a cent on you? Only a *madman* like me . . ."

"I ask for only one thing—that you reflect on some of my silences in recent days, and you'll do best not to assume it means consent. Don't depend on the idea that you can do anything you want with me. You know very well that I am crazy by design and that in five minutes I can do what I haven't done in three years."

"But you know how to up the price. And you like pepper fillets . . ."

"You pay me because I produce accordingly, sweetie, neither more nor less, and always less than I intend to ask you for come the new year . . ."

"Forget it."

"Paying me well is a guarantee also for you, so that when one of your competitors calls me to find out how things are in Germany and what your price is on packaged merchandise, I politely send all of them to take a crap. I am incorruptible because I do not feel frustrated, period. Or they might even be people whom you yourself tell to call me. Spare yourself the effort. I cannot betray you because it would mean that you own me. I am faithful to you because you pay me and because I belong only to myself. I do not want to go to the trouble of being dishonest: those who betray bind themselves forever. It's to your advantage, after all. If I remain with you and do not go over to the competition it's because I like you, yes, you have an ideal incorruptibility all your own, an obstinacy all your own in accumulating power which very much resembles an intellective ability . . . The logic of one who sets down what logic is . . . for everyone else. I am moderately fascinated by this quality of violence, but it is not and never will be *my* logic . . ."

"And so I'm supposed to be the violent one . . ."

"Not only, you're sly, Celestino, like an oil slick . . . I've seen how you act with others, but you're not going to dress this salad . . .

If you manage with everybody else to convince them that this here in front of them is not shit, for example, but an omelet, with me you end up grabbed by the ass and I make you taste it. When you least expect it, just like one of your kind."

"Are you finished? So we've had this fine discourse just to tell me that you want a raise . . . You cute little mouth stuffer! Your father is right when he says that the real Fascist in the house is you. You would always like to have the last word. You, with all your cuntanthropist's pretensions."

"Philanthropist, Celestino, philanthropist."

"And anyway, why in Trapani?"

"An eye for an eye, a tooth for a tooth. Stuffed for stuffed."

At nine o'clock in the morning, nine-thirty . . .

Wednesday, morning and afternoon. Thursday.

At nine o'clock in the morning, nine-thirty, there's rarely anyone at the Terrazzine. And Wednesday is not a good day; even from the name assigned to these twenty-four hours one can deduce that they will be more repetitive than usual, as regards a severe official reproach slowed down by the fatigue accumulated Monday and Tuesday, fatigue disturbed by the rustle of still too many animals among the brambles and bushes. With each step along the escarpment Angelo thinks aloud a time-honored, old exorcism: "Now I'll find him."

His is a fixation on a child's superstitious path: that sooner or later he must bump into the corpse of someone who has died a violent death. It has happened to a lot of people to find a man's mutilated body in a field, in a car, at the bottom of a canal, in the toilets of a movie house—never to him. The fantasies are already triggered: what he could do in such a case, how he would take it, and the subsequent stages. First: to think up an alibi to prove that he's not the one who killed, even if the fact of not knowing him, never having seen him before when alive nor even having had anything to do with him, would certainly not be in his favor. Second: that he did it, the evidence he would concoct in a flash based on an irrefutable premeditation that goes back decades earlier. Third: that the corpse is not his, the judicial quibbles in court to convince himself and others of the evident.

Angelo spreads out his towel this side of the "accursed" villa, his eyes hurt too much, he cannot keep them closed for longer than thirty seconds as he counts. He already sees himself surrounded by the rats, who want to know from him why he has broken the rules of the day's divisions. Whether Armando, the photographer Neapolitan style, comes or not, he has before him hours and hours of listlessness and deliquescent pangs. There is nothing any longer that comes to his mind unbidden, and, as he sometimes happens to choose a dream before falling asleep, he now makes a list of the things to think that must be given priority.

When he was a boy he liked to go and smoke in the cemetery, in the underground passages. When he shook the ash from the ember, he felt a shiver, something of his which from his fingertip came into contact with the pints and pints of ashes entombed there. At any rate, he had no other links with the image of death. Death did not interest him, it never had interested him. Not even with his father, both of them so taken up with life that death seemed almost an indifferent prize to those who, in the ardor of their days, had thought least about it. Both had been filled with ardor; the father, feeling it arrive, had clung to the wrist of a daughter-in-law, letting go of his bicycle, and had given the demonstration of sudden panic exhibited by people hit by lightning, but his face, when dead, mockingly declared that for an entire life he had been faster than that lightning bolt and had never spent precious instants fending it off when it was not necessary. Angelo was also like this. It is twenty years that he hasn't set foot in a cemetery. He had caught a quick glimpse of the funeral procession from the marble cross on the hill of San Pancrazio, intermittently, making torso-neck-foot twists. He does not even know where they put him in the end. His mother complained about a small ladder that she always had to go and look for, of her fear of falling when she put up the flowers. Then she had bought plastic ones for safety's sake.

It is the first time that it occurs to Angelo that Giorgina Washington inaugurated the family chapel—*of steel and marble*, Lometto had emphasized. Never had been there either, never had thought about it. But as a boy he had spent days and days talking to the little dead girl of a woman-mother in his neighborhood.

She had been a tiny little girl, perhaps less than a year old, laid out in a room that smelled of mulberry leaves, because there on the upper shelves of the tall cumbersome chest of drawers silkworms lived. Who knows what he told her, and why this embarrassment at remembering now such a thing, so close to a form of love. Perhaps he had done it out of exhibitionism or to spite those relatives who did not like the idea of his always hanging around that small rectangle of piled-up earth. He remembers that he attributed to them, to some of them, the blame for that death, unjustly, what did he know about it? But actually, of one thing he was certain: that if that mother and those other women relatives had perhaps never felt that newborn baby girl to be *theirs* when it was *alive*, they absolutely did not want it to become someone else's when *dead*. Not even a little boy with a small nosegay. Excavating in here, in this memory of decades ago, it seems to Angelo he's going back over paths opened no longer by him, obligatory routes of a memory that belongs only partially to him. But also to that little girl, by now unknown, forgotten, he must have given himself with the same ardor with which he has espoused the cause of Giorgina Washington: from the living to the living. Of this he is certain. Death having arrived, it really had no importance that for many years he had gone to visit that little grave—removed by now?—and not even once Giorgina Washington or his father. Now Angelo also understands the reason, one of the many which explain something that one can even go without explaining (but this sun, these burning eyes, the brain which *hurts*, how to stop all this?): he remembers that he had smothered that very small friend with caresses, had combed her, given her unending little kisses, carried her out in his arms through streets and courtyards. Theirs had been an intense physical love, it was beautiful and exhausting to rest a cheek against the tiny little face. With Giorgina Washington he had not been in time, with his father there had never been time. His visit there had been a physical continuation of his strolls with her, only that instead of holding her hand in his hand, he now held her by a fistful of white stone or the rim of the glass in which he put daisies and gladiolas that were broken off short. Because of this he has never thought of visiting Giorgina or his father: these were two rigidified farewells which dug down inside him continually in the impossible search for a caress to give, to receive. Two thoughts without rest, the opposite of dust. You cannot visit someone who inhabits you.

A majestic belly surmounted by two very long divergent mustaches appears. Oh, the paterfamilias from Verona who renders him Carthusian services since the time of the university. A sort of after-work affair, with phrases of circumstance about the weather while he struggles with his zipper. Not very exciting, but certain. A somewhat laborious release, but so well mannered and always better than nothing. What for

Angelo gives it the decisive touch to prefer it to any waiting for something better is that mustache wants nothing for himself, that Angelo does not have to reciprocate even with a rubbing of his fingers, even though he once turned him over head down to get a good look at his big sumo wrestler's ass and take advantage of it.

Now mustache is there on the rim of the escarpment, no farther than ten yards away from Angelo. Angelo does not feel like talking about the weather, nothing is being forecast. He goes into the grove of reeds, out of the corner of his eye he sees him squat down and jump off the small wall. Angelo stretches out in the low mud and says "*Ciao*" when mustache pulls down his shorts. He possessed already in those days a real expertise, a sense of rhythm and salivation. Now he's even better. So good that, a bit because they haven't seen each other for a while, a bit because Angelo does not have sufficient energy to have recourse to sustaining fantasies, the business is unexpectedly exciting as much as any other thing that attains the barest minimum.

There were salivas that hurt him, yes, caustic salivas, that's it, like douches of Clorox. Instead, that of mustache is sweet—it has this well-practiced power to summon from the depths in a honeyed, gradual, homogeneous manner. It has always seemed to Angelo that there is a lot of love in the final swallowing of this man, an affective lust. Once, in the highway parking lot of Sommacampagna, Angelo had decided to stay and chat with him, an ogre if properly viewed. The ogre couldn't have been happier, intimidated. That time too Angelo had the confirmation that the world was a congeries of first steps that it would always be his lot to take down roads which others should have gone down alone. Well, mustache had told him about his passion for his son, a seventeen-year-old whom he spied on through the keyhole of the bathroom when he took a shower, or when he masturbated on the edge of the tub. He followed his spurts with the terror and admiration of a helmsman who sees a storm advance and recoils with a gesture that exposes his bare chest. Mustache came up with some beautiful images. He watched him on the sly from a skylight in the hayloft, when he climbed up there for the same reason of peace and quiet. The father clenched the inner flesh of his cheeks between his teeth. He was only thirty-six years old, four years older than Angelo, he was not a grandfather. His description had gone into the minutest details: the color of the skin, shiny like brown shoe polish, of the eyes, also brown, a tracery of veins on the "pompous" prick, on the arms, legs, and belly, the wheat-colored fuzz in the armpits, on the scrotum, the legs, the burnt-blond color of the hair, like the hairs in the ears, on the knuckles of the hands, the perfectly rectangular shape of the nails. You would have said that he was a mythical beast not yet soiled by the necessity of having a character. In the end big mustache had wiped his eyes and nose with the sleeve of his shirt. From then on, every time they met, he added details about his son, sang the praises of his prick, which he dreamed of as multiplied in his ass and in his mouth and nostrils and eyes day and night . . . and every time he was always more grateful to Angelo, and his saliva, impregnated with the gratitude of a new installment of narrated passion, became magically more honeyed, more magnetizing, more orgasmic.

"For you time has stopped" mustache says, smoothing his mustache, while Angelo rises and runs into the water. "For me instead, just look at this belly."

"And me, look at these stretch marks" Angelo says, showing his back, furrowed by striations of abused skin. "It's because I start all of a sudden to do exercises, wear out body and soul, and then stop."

"You're still a very handsome man, come on, don't be coy" big mustache insists. "Look at those shoulders, those legs. You've got a mouth that looks like it's carved in marble. Like my son . . ."

"You still haven't managed to make him?" Angelo asks, out of politeness.

"I wish it were true! No! Now the fool has returned from the army and even wants to get married. At twenty-one! There's a guy his age who's after him but only I have realized it, not he. With only a woman he's wasted. Goodbye."

"Keep on the ball."

He would have liked to have some coffee, a bit of water, he never does remember to bring some from home. And today on purpose he hasn't brought anything to read, just to see how he can manage. It's like giving up cigarettes. One suffers because the liver suffers, the lungs, the blood suffers, the salutary lack of nicotine is lethal like the lack of printer's ink if it suddenly occurs. Angelo has no inventiveness, he swears to himself that he will never again repeat the experiment. What he manages to think left alone with himself interests him less and less, bores him, one can never escape an unlimited cage, one is forever a prisoner, only the comparison with another person's bars frees you from yours. That other person is not there. Nobody to help him unhinge his false infinite. All that is left to him is to exhaust another layer of the Lomettian library shelf inside himself.

"You got to come right away" he yelled over the telephone at the end of October or just after. "I've got this big whore here, an Austrian madwoman with her stud, you should see these types, and what teeth! They want twenty millions' worth of stock. Where am I supposed to get a stock of twenty million? Get a move on, hurry, because here we can't understand shit."

The "crazy dame" was about forty, a bit more, with a definite dash of export blood (Turkey, Armenia, or thereabouts), and her name was Jasmine Belart. A gaudy one, dressed in white, not fresh linen with a narrow slash down the front—it was hellishly hot, they had again turned on the air conditioner—with something sumptuous in the hips and brown arms, braceleted with Indian things. Tall, light chestnut hair with red streaks gathered untidily in a spray above the neck and let fall, or left tousled on forehead and ears. Some strands probably still greasy with suntan lotion were stuck to the bare left shoulder—a dress like this could be described as "slave style"—and didn't move, looked like the plastic snakes children use to play a joke. The olive skin of her face shone under not recent and very slapdash makeup. There was more ash-colored dust over the left eye than over the right, the lipstick of a brilliant pink had oozed into the dimples beside the lips, and the first thing Angelo thought was: how can *he* not tell her, since she does not seem to be aware of it? He could remain silent only for two reasons, one look at him was enough to understand that he was not the kind of person who owned a third of anything. Jasmine Belart was sitting sideways, on one buttock, and she rested one foot without pantyhose on her shoe—stiletto heels. Alongside, standing, he "the stud": a blondish, washed-out thirty-year-old, certainly of Yugoslav or Swiss origin, oh much younger than she, very tight white pants with a swelling that made the eyes smart just to look at it. In the space of three minutes he changed its position three times. He looked like somebody who has just set up house and is asking around for advice on how to arrange the furniture. The gold cross, in the wide-open shirt, attached to a chain thick as a finger among the thin blondish hairs bounced with all the certainties he had attained on the concept of "how to make an impression on women," without ever asking himself of what type. As soon as Angelo saw, compared, subtracted, and pretended he hadn't noticed, he already had a thousand reasons to hate him, though without for this reason feeling any sympathy for her. The office door was thrown wide onto the big room filled with employees and there was a to-and-fro of eyelashes that fluttered as high as they could while leafing through dictionaries on the desk, at the height of the continually fingered white pants. Many cries of "*Nein! Nein!*" had echoed like shots as he came through the main door. At hearing Angelo, who greeted them correctly and cordially welcomed them both, the woman heaved a sigh of relief.

"You tell them" she said immediately after the introduction, panting to get down to the "nitty-gritty." "This is what it's about, it's very, very simple."

Bundles of Austrian schillings held together by yellow and green and red rubber bands had already been poured out onto the desk, and one had the sensation that everything must take place quickly, as if those bank notes were the booty of a holdup just carried out around the corner and they could sprout wings at any moment. Belart, with an emphatic gesture, one of many, took Angelo by the hand, pulled him up to the handle of the door, closed Lometto's office, and stared into his eyes, sighing. She began to speak slowly now, with a slowness at the limits of impatience, while Lometto smiled sardonically at the sudden familiarity and fondness that that sort of madwoman poured from her hand, which he must have clasped, into the hand of *his Dr.* Bazarovi. Angelo did not listen to her, displaying all the proper signs of professional attention: he remained spellbound at length by the two gold canines which glittered in the woman's soft and bedaubed mouth.

Angelo clarified and reclarified the situation between the two parties, the stud confined himself to saying only "*Ja!*" "*So!*" "*Sicher!*"—jerking back his pelvis a few inches to execute the shift without moving his feet.

The pair wanted an immediate shipment to Switzerland—where they had an address, one among others, it seemed—of pantyhose at fire-sale prices, seconds obviously, enveloped or boxed, it didn't matter, and in all available colors and sizes, with or without double gussets. In any event, they were for Hungary, an emerging Communist country and therefore enthusiastic about everything. First of all, the price must be low low low. They were paying cash, here it is on the nail, Lometto's word was enough for them, and now also Bazarovi's, they had sufficient references and "connections" to trust him, and besides if a certain ministerial crack would open up for them *over there*, they would always need plenty of merchandise like this. They talked a bit about Poland: never had an industrialist—an Italian—been so much in favor of a serious workers' insurgency—abroad. They all agreed, they fraternized.

"Lometto, watch it now" Angelo said. "Take care of them properly because you have found the hyenas who will dispose of the warehouse carrion." The pair did not want the documents to indicate the actual quantity, but they wanted them reduced, on paper, to one-fourth of the merchandise and the price listed accordingly lower. Moreover, the truck must arrive at Chiasso at a prearranged time, they would be there to give a hand if necessary, they had "connections" there too. This term recurred several times, like so many clips which, though small, managed to hold together bundles of papers that have nothing to do with one another and impart a temporary but useful order to disparate phenomena in a reality presumed to be hostile. There were other insidious clips here and there, such as "*kein Problem!*" faced by obstacles of a customs and bureaucratic nature which to Angelo seemed insurmountable. When you had connections, reality did not present problems. One small clip, and the Babelish archive of reality became a simple, clean, quick little affair. Reality was for the others, poor things. Jasmine Belart seemed to be able to dispense with it in all senses and did not even have sufficient imagination to apologize for it. Like Lometto. She did not give Angelo any impression of brazenness; Jasmine Belart set out from the acritical certainty that reality had been invented by her. She was well "connected" with it, no problem.

Again and again Angelo caught the twinkle in Lometto's small azurine eyes with their golden irises, which stealthily enjoyed themselves by darting about that small mound of purplish bank notes on the desk's green leather and almost already in his pocket, black, under the counter. Angelo secretly shook his head: Lometto was going to pocket all the money and then ship somehow. One must never give money to Lometto like this, before the merchandise; unless it was "dirty" money, this Belart must really be a madwoman. But dirty in which way? No, no, Belart was mad-mad, and that's all. Mad because she was taking a fall that couldn't be worse, her naïveté imparted cleanliness, if that were necessary, to that watermarked paper. At that point Angelo, twisting free from that hand, large and clammy but not unpleasant in one's own, decided that, within the limits of his possibility, he would protect those two half-ass smugglers, who were certainly less cunning than they were in the habit of thinking. If they too had in mind screwing a third "chump," these were matters which did not concern him. Here St. Anthony's chain of an individual's responsibility came to a halt, and Angelo, proud of having rediscovered the borders of his island, looked at Lometto impassively, threw back at him all the blood of others that for years now he had splashed in the face of his contemptuous collaborator, whom he had perhaps subdued once and for all by wedging him into a production cycle which was larger, infinitely larger, and at whose invisible origin there seemed to be necessary victims, necessary also for a temporary interpreter. Lometto must have sensed that at that instant in the midst of a dictionary, a pile of money, beyond his armchair, something fundamental was taking place in Angelo, something which, after silences and compressed waverings, alienated him forever and nailed him to the weight of responsibilities which were only and exclusively his, not humanity's. Angelo felt so good in those final moments of the contest that he showed some special courtesy toward the woman whom he considered had inspired that gulp of fresh, unpolluted water which as though by magic gushed into his throat. The "chumps" were a sign of providence under any flag and in any system, the blood spilled was not. Now, Belart could even consider herself shrewder than the next person, and she had this gift of slipping two fingers inside the elastic which supported her left breast in order to make it looser by pulling it down, and also show three horizontal beauty spots just above the rim of the nipple satined with suntan, she might have the "involuntary" endless mannerisms of a woman who practices seduction at the wrong moments to mortgage the most appropriate moments and do so for financial gain, yes, but Angelo sensed that Belart, were she to fail in all her attempts, would be capable of stopping in order perhaps to start all over again. Lometto, no, he did not give in. If he had not even been able to give in to the supplication of a wretched woman alone with her child in a strange small town, what could ever convince him to accept a loss even though slight, as slight as hiring one unneeded worker? Lometto was finalizing everything, Belart—and Angelo now watched her rummage together with this Hans through a bunch of inserts with German, Italian, French, and Dutch captions—a kind of a madwoman completely in the throes of an unpredictable mechanism that she would have certainly called living. One felt that she wanted to impose a false image of herself, even of someone possibly vicious and resolute. But she was not, and besides when Angelo took a woman to heart he was never mistaken, and if he was mistaken it was only because it eventually turned out that she had been mistaken about herself. Belart and Hans drove off in their mauve-colored sports car with the understanding that two days hence the truck would be in Chiasso at the stroke of noon. Belart, with her usual nonchalance, once the last bundle was removed, had sufficiently spread open her midwife's bag, so that Lometto and one of his partners there by chance, a guy from Parma who was short of breath, as well as Angelo, should see that she had a predilection for ivory. Not only her elephant-tusk earrings and bracelets and necklace were of ivory set in gold, but so was the grip of the small and pretty revolver inlaid with mother-of-pearl. The two men were slightly startled, Angelo noticed only that the final handshake had been longer for him than for the other two and that Belart had regaled him with a tickle on the inside of his palm with the nail of her middle finger. She was definitely some type. Angelo was careful not to say that in his opinion it was a toy pistol for some little nephew.

Lometto immediately gave orders to amass twenty or more thousand pairs of *first-class* seconds—he needed sixty thousand—from the warehouse under the portico, and everybody, even the office women, came to fill the cartons, also secondhand, of all sizes. This activity, obviously, had continued late into the night, while Lometto phoned right and left to put together that shipment fit for an aboriginal souk. As a matter of fact, he did not have much stock and he adhered to a policy truly distinctive in the sector: he produced only against orders and did not create an artificial inventory which would force him to sell below cost like those who coerced the law of demand and supply. He knew that knowing how to lose *immediately* signified in itself a source of insured profit, on future losses. Loss for loss, one didn't amortize machinery if one didn't risk, but if necessary there always was an integration fund against which Lometto was dead set only in words, but in recent times even he was not always able to lay off without notice.

There began to arrive at Mire, Inc., vans of merchandise forgotten in the broom closets of family workshops and perhaps for as long as ten years, all of it handled on a lump-sum basis of so much per van (a pittance but in cash: Lometto had decided to make a splash with other people's money and great was the amazement of these small artisans with water up to their necks and tears in their pockets), and everybody trusted everybody, nobody even glanced at the merchandise, nor the quantities, nor its condition. It became necessary to call for a trailer, and the trailer punctually arrived at Chiasso. Lometto wanted Angelo to take "an outing" at the trucker's side, "a beautiful hunk of meat," for free. Angelo refused, and did not go for the outing. After that first delivery, there were phone calls to Belart, as though between the best of comrades, and she acted as though she were dealing with one of her Casbah acquaintances. Angelo was disturbed by this familiarity, as though plunked down among old one thousand and one brothel glories who meet again in a rest home for belly dancers. On the phone Belart did not proffer words: she naveled them, warbling them in dirges into which slipped strange commercial requests: could he get his hands on three million blue jeans, never mind pattern, size, top price five dollars and fifty cents each? were they for Nigeria, Zambia, the Cameroons? Angelo reported and Lometto did not bat an eyelash: he told him to say that he'd have a look around.

"But are you serious?" Angelo asked, finding himself before an unexpected Celestino connected with Italy's most diversified products. "You've got all of Nigeria and miles and miles of savannas to dress for thirty years, proportionately speaking."

Lometto phoned him the results of his search: the annual production of all Italian jeans factories put together was five million pairs. He had managed, nominally, to put together two million of them, from those with the skinny leg of the sixties to those with the high Spanish-style waist of the seventies. Twenty years of jeans that no one, here, would ever wear again, not even to escape from the South. And, by the way, the unsold production in inventory of the submerged economy from Prato down. Altering them costs more than making new ones. It was true: didn't a good pantyhose whose production cost between two hundred and fifty-three hundred lire a pair cost between three and five thousand lire in the store?

Another appointment was arranged, this time at Innsbruck. They went there by train, the appointment was in the station restaurant. Belart, still escorted by her stud with gold cross and little hairs in the V of a skimpy angora wool sweater, arrived considerably late. This time beneath a short lamb coat she wore a black suit with borders of metallic embroidery, much below the knee, gathered around the shoulders with a deep, heart-shaped neckline which spread from her neck down to the furrow between her breasts. She wore no brassiere, it goes without saying, and at the sides the heart gaped. In sitting down she bent over not at all casually and on her left breast the three beauty spots appeared. Angelo could have sworn that he had seen them in a horizontal deployment the other time, he must have been mistaken. The neck did not have the uniform color of well-stretched and natural skin, it was somewhat like tissue paper in the thin veinings of a layer of powder which did not properly cover the irregular crimpings of full maturity. Her nose had just a slight curve, and it was not thin, it was the beautiful nose of someone who has always breathed deeply, and the nostrils' irregular flutter gave it delicacy. Her lips still with that pink lipstick which would have sorely tested even the face of a Miss Universe. Belart was alive, she had the somewhat melancholy avidity of one who is sure of having always filled the surrounding atmospheres without ever having been filled by them. A very beautiful woman, plundered and inexhaustible, like a cult site at the end of a ritual. Hans didn't say much. He moved a lot, fidgeting on his chair.

Belart said that the top price for jeans was now five even. Lometto said that, alas, he needed at least six. Discussion. They again arrived at five dollars and fifty cents. But it looked like a deal fated to fall through: either three million pairs, to fill up a ship, or nothing. The ship seemed to be essential. And a letter of credit, underlined Belart, anticipating Lometto. Angelo made a few calculations, the dizziness began to balance again around the three beauty spots carefully hidden from the light of the sun which poured in from snow-covered mountains. When a woman had three so "movable" beauty spots, she could also manipulate ten million dollars on the nail and have a big grease stain below the last button of her mohair jacket. That too enhanced her credit.

Now Belart was beginning to rummage in her big, slightly worn Western midwife's bag. She did not wear perfume, but the one he smelled came from Hans's little hairs. But how could *she* go with a guy like that?

"You see" Belart said, holding out to Angelo a small pharmaceutical box like those used for aspirin tablets. "This is, let's say, an excitant. Oh, nothing particular in itself, but in Germany a decree of the Ministry of Health has taken it off the market because it is toxic. Now it is forbidden. But people of a certain kind, especially seniors, pensioners, and students, you know, to stay awake and also, ahem, call girls in the nightclubs who put it in the customers' drinks. An old practice, it came on the market immediately after the war, to relieve 'depression.' An institution, like the Wall, rather than a drug: one can no longer tear it down because of the fine arts, you understand? Well, now those who have a bit of it set aside sell it on the black market and make a fortune. Would it be possible to make it in Italy exactly the same?"

Angelo, ecstatic, stared at Belart; he read the name on the small box, Coptafuk, and did not permit himself to laugh. In Germany and in other German areas it was like saying XY, a name like any other.

He hid the writing with his hand, hesitated, did not know how to communicate the whole thing to Lometto. By making her turn and turn again several times around herself in a bed, he was certain that he would have been able to seriously sodomize Jasmine Belart *in front*. But now he was afraid that in reading the name he would burst out laughing because Lometto would have laughed and then it would have been up to him to explain to the Armenian Turkish matters linked to the Italian mentality. Whichever way you turned, there was always a fuk underfoot immediately after getting through the Brenner Pass. Laboriously, showing that he had to gulp to get ready, he translated everything, uncovering the small box in the palm of his hand. Lometto read and looked blank. He asked him to translate also the ingredients. Angelo said to him in dialect, smiling: "I hope you're not going to start making uppers, this is a full-fledged drug."

"I don't care one way or the other" Lometto said in a harmonious, low voice. "If it's made in Italy, fine, otherwise amen. Tell her that we probably have a different name for it."

"In Italy it doesn't exist at all, under any name" Belart said. "It's a matter of producing it from A to Z. If necessary, we can give you the boxes and the printed tinfoil."

"Oh, that's the least, everything can be done" Lometto interrupted.

"Perhaps with a different type of excitant" said Belart, who, however, did not actually use this word but a paraphrase which would have to be translated literally as "pick-me-up." "Somewhat different ingredients could be all right too, but not with this. The palates are used to it for more than thirty years, there is a small, how can I put it, sizzle under your teeth as soon as you put it in your mouth, and if that *ouverture* is missing, we've had it."

Did Belart know French? Angelo asked himself. No, he answered himself through his teeth, but she loved music.

"Why has it been abolished?" Angelo asked after this parenthesis of an almost personal intrusion. He understood so little about all this, certainly much less than Lometto, who in a flash managed to put together hypotheses and reality, eclipsing every one of Angelo's imperfect syllogisms. If Belart had her clips, Lometto had clamps and clothespins. Connections versus connections.

"It's supposed to be carcinogenic" sighed Belart. "Fashions. Now cancer is fashionable. Well, who knows why? And what about this coffee then, these cigarettes? By selling cocaine the state makes a larger profit and saves face officially by passing laws to combat it. Anyway, people don't give a damn whether it's carcinogenic or not. At their age! On the Berlin market alone . . . All that matters is that they can no longer find it and that eight million habitual consumers have seen themselves deprived of their darling cocalina from one day to the next. And there you have eight million potential outlaws presented on a silver platter to the person who gets there first. A great opportunity."

"May I keep the box?" Lometto asked. "So everything's all right with our pantyhose?"

"Well, no complaints up to now. You know, Hungary . . ."

Angelo pointed to the coffeepot.

"*Gern*, I adore coffee. There are millions to be made with Coptafuk."

Angelo translated mechanically, he was thinking about a supermarket at Tenerife, he saw it for the first time with new eyes.

"Tell her that if she needs them there are a few more of those pantyhose, same price, same terms."

"How many?" she said, interested, crossing her legs again because by now the crack had closed up and it was again necessary to uncover a stretch of thigh. Incredible: she wore a black garter but no pantyhose. She was a woman to take prick right to the bottom, one of those who all their lives assume the burden of leading men by the nose to distract them, and so be free to think of something else. Angelo would have liked to ask her if it wasn't too tight around her thigh, if she didn't feel like taking it off for a while, while she was there, if she didn't want to take the opportunity for a moment of relaxation.

"Forty thousand, give or take one or two."

They negotiated, very little. They seemed to understand each other instantly. Angelo was asking himself where he would ever be able to come up with another forty thousand pantyhose at that price, one-third of the current price list. He always let him in on things at the last moment, Lometto did, without giving him the time to form an opinion on things that were better translated *at a distance*.

"Interested?" Belart said after a while, tucking away in the big bag her small blue notebook and pencil and calculator and now pulling out a zipper. She looked like a free-lance salesperson who has rung all the bells in a condominium. Hans and Angelo saw to it that Belart's cup was always kept full, since she herself was polishing off a pot for six.

"Are you interested?" translated Angelo, by now so dazed by that continuous display as not to give further explanations or ask for any. Now he would have indeed liked to start laughing uproariously: are you interested in a zipper? really, what did it all mean? But Lometto had become so serious, almost pensive and reserved, as to take the dentelated tape in his hands and say, "How many?" as if he already knew the goal of that sinuous, unbelievable woman out of a photo-romance in which she plays the part of the Dutch broker's woman in Taiwan, the one who always shows up with very long oval cigarettes sparkling between her fingers as though they were candy canes, even in the scenes when she brushes her teeth.

"Three hundred thousand. All sizes and one color only: black. If you know some pants manufacturer . . . without pretensions . . . there's money to be made. They're Czechoslovakian. Two shipments. Via Greece."

"How come via Greece?" asked Angelo, almost offended by all these incongruities, which were such only for him.

"Via Greece, no two ways about it. By ship. Payment in Rome. Possibility for a short extension. Only for you, obviously, not for third parties."

Lometto showed little interest. Buying and reselling did not interest him much, and besides, zippers. He definitely preferred to sell other people's stuff, but never to risk his own on behalf of third parties. Angelo was beside himself. Lometto spoke as though in a trance: "Well, I can look. But not I personally. If it goes through I'll leave it to you, it means we will agree on a commission. But I put you on the right track, then I get out. It's not my trade. I produce pantyhose, tell her."

"All right" said Belart. Hans did not take his eyes off her for a moment, it seemed included in the contract. Angelo was exhausted and wanted to finish as quickly as possible, because he wanted to go on to Munich. In a small bag he had ten onyx eggs of all colors, Florentine craftsmanship; those made of olive wood, Jürgen had told him over the phone, were not suitable, they stuck, and besides, two of them had two small chips.

And then, as Angelo and Lometto are looking at each other, satiated by now with Belart's birdbrained commercial proposals—Lometto is happy as a lark with those forty to seventy thousand pantyhose, ninety percent insured. Belart, who in ten days or so would drop by to bring the money if it goes through, "and it will go through," she had said—Belart flings them another word: "Vises?"

Angelo makes her repeat it clearly, he is afraid of not having grasped, he had this handicap of being a bit deaf, of not grasping complex sounds like "vises" outside of their natural semantic sphere, such as a mechanic's workshop or a machine-tool plant. Vises?

"Yes, vises, vises, like this one" Belart had insisted with a slightly resentful tone. This interpreter was a bit thick, did his work badly, she must have thought, he is not fluent in his reactions, indeed he has reactions and he shouldn't. And perhaps she had also concluded that he wasn't so much and only an interpreter . . . and here with a sudden movement she extracts a vise about thirty centimeters high from that big conjuror's bag of hers and begins energetically screwing the two clamps on the edge of the table, while Lometto lolls in his chair with a small backward bounce and Angelo makes every effort to keep the waiter at a distance with a telepathic order.

"Do you understand now? Ten thousand vises, at a fire-sale price. All made of this alloy here, iron and zinc, all the same. German Democratic Republic."

Without changing expression (he had none left), only his pupils a trifle more dilated because of the blinding reflections pouring down in that outmoded bar, all decals behind glass, Angelo said, involuntarily lowering his voice: "Celestino, are you interested in ten thousand vises? Do you have ten thousand blacksmiths handy?"

"Ten thousand? I can try. What size?"

"All like that one. She is screwing it tighter, she's wrecking the table. What do I tell her? Come on, hurry. The waiter is coming."

"Can I have it?" Lometto asked.

"Gern!" Belart said, and with one wrenching movement of the hand she detaches the vise without unscrewing it. She smooths the tablecloth nicely and with a thrust of her heel she makes the chewed-off piece of wood disappear under the table. It seemed that they would remain sitting there forever, until the table was destroyed either by time or by Belart's further empirical demonstrations.

Hans started to pour coffee in her cup, ordered another mug of beer, liter size. But where did he put it all? Angelo was startled at the thought that now coursed through his mind. Hans twiddled himself for the nth time. He must have his leather pants sewn to his body. A dandy convinced to his depths of being mother earth's gift to women.

Despite his haste to finish and climb on opposed trains, Angelo experienced, and almost against his will, sympathy of a well-nigh sensory kind for Belart. She had power, speech, disquisition, gall, and the charm of one who knows she has already lost much and can continue to risk and live like a madwoman. He was sorry that she spoiled the image by the propinquity of that freckled man, so passive, servile, vulgar, and inefficient, so *male*. But Angelo admitted that about *Kupplung* he didn't understand a thing, for him there existed only self-pluggings, solo couplings, relationships lacking a partner, single shoes, never unmated, because he saw every individual as if he had a single leg and was forced to believe that he had two, to buy a pair of them and to live conditioned by that other neither worn nor wearable, the chimera in the drawer, always within foot's reach in the expectation of, the hope that, dreaming that one day . . . Angelo had understood the swindle and he had thrown away his extra shoe, even if in its time he had let himself be convinced to buy it. Perhaps the phantom shoes of Hans and Jasmine Belart, together, formed a thing that walked by itself, a creature so well put together in its dovetailing of desire and paltriness as actually to sprout wings. They were a *couple*, a two-headed monster created thousands of years ago which always popped up again in new guises at every step in the street, the bars, stores, even domestic hotbeds. Something like this really existed, indeed had replaced all the rest, and original man, alone, single, sustained by himself, had ended by becoming a by-product. Angelo saw Hans and Belart, Lometto and ideally Edda at his side, as a sort of paired Martians who had managed to deceive everyone and pass themselves off as true humans even to themselves.

But Jasmine Belart had a strange demeanor that still left room for hope: now she was there with *him* but tomorrow? She did not seem to be the sort to harbor illusions. She seemed, how should one say, detached from this, from all those men who must have passed through the eye of her needle; precisely, she was something more vast and complete than the eye of a needle, she was a needle: she must be threaded in order to continue pulling the thread through. Yet Angelo saw her capable of that exclusive original quality of being or remaining "empty" and stuck by herself in a spool of thread for the rest of her life without feeling either deprived or enriched. Jasmine Belart did not care whether her eye was filled or not, or if she could continue sewing something thanks to this. Of course, catching another glimpse of the swelling of Hans's fly, as long as it lasted, she could even insist on being threaded properly. She was not a woman for half measures. And such a woman, sooner or later, is a woman forced to be free. Available for another thread. Angelo decided that at least in the dealings with Lometto she would be his personal protégé despite him, Hans, without of course letting either her or Lometto know about it. But here on the spot this business of the German's "pick-me-up," the zippers and vises, went beyond the limited possibilities of his competence and therefore of his ability to watch over her. So they fixed this other tentative meeting at Toigo, because she had to come to Italy for other matters, she had to contact certain wine importers on Lake Garda. Well, were they finished now? When would come the dampish handshake, a trifle longer and intense for him? He watched Belart as she got up and adjusted the slit at her side. Once on her feet, she slipped her hand with a swift movement into her big bag. Angelo, darting a spiked glance at the clockface on the wall, realized that he would miss his train for Munich. Belart was rummaging in the depths of the big bag and saying mumbled words, as though they only half concerned the things that had not yet completely appeared. At last her sentences were illumined: her hand had fully seized the things on the abysmal bottom of her big bag.

"Rolex, Cartié, Bo Mersié!" Belart listed, putting them on the tablecloth, rooting in the innards for things tucked beforehand into a small corner.

"What is she saying now?" Lometto for the sake of appearances asked Angelo, who this time was unable to hide his bewilderment.

Belart smiled, from her fleshy lips two golden glints shone through. She held out a watch and waited.

"Now, really . . . I don't have to translate, you can understand this by yourself."

"But you've got to translate everything and right away, thank you" Lometto said in dialect, hiding his irritation.

"She wants to know if you can get your paws on . . . if you can procure . . . Look, I don't want to have anything to do with this sort of thing. This is getting to be a criminal conspiracy, it's too much even for someone whose only regret is not having studied Greek."

"No, no Greek ship" Belart interjected. Angelo apologized, he was talking about something else.

"But what the fuck . . . ?"

"Coptafuk," she corrected. Angelo apologized again, they weren't talking about that either.

"What do you think you're doing? Translate, and that's it . . . Beautiful, imitated perfectly" Lometto commented, leaving Angelo dazed: so those weren't stolen watches, they were fake brand-name watches, but actually bought and in all likelihood paid for in cash by Belart.

She craned her tall and slightly too abundant neck around the semi-deserted room and was now displaying three watches on the palm of her hand. She had also studied the farce of circumspection. Gold? And next to the watch faces appear, deposited by those nails covered with pink, slightly chipped polish, pins, necklaces, earrings, all valuable jewels, whose design has already been vaguely seen elsewhere even by Angelo, objects copied faithfully but different "gilded" alloys, whose worth in the original derived not so much from the noble metal used, nor from their uniqueness, but precisely from the number of a limited series engraved inside.

"You, Signor Lometto, and also you, Dr. Bazarovi? Do you know around your parts or a little farther down, in Naples let's say, someone who might be able . . . *nicht wahr*? we understand each other."

Angelo was very much disturbed by that plural, even though dubitative: he did not know any fences and did not intend to begin now, not even to show off. He felt sorry for the humanist gangster, the myth of the P-38 pistol with which one tried to redeem the shame of having obtained a degree cum laude in sociology or political science or architecture or the performing arts. Having received such a degree, all one could do was assume the responsibility of a grim respectability to the end of one's days. But few had resisted the temptation of 7th of April snobbism. It did not involve him: his was going to be a serious degree beyond all temptation. It would be of no use to him because there was nothing for which a degree could be of any use. He would never be tempted to soil his penal record or ruin someone's kneecaps only because of a complex caused by an unfortunate subject. Let Lometto fend for himself, if the business got out of hand, and without him.

Indeed, Angelo wanted it to be clear immediately that he was no longer having any part of it from that precise moment. And besides, there were too many things that Lometto caught right away and he didn't. When Angelo pronounced the word "fence" Lometto gave him a human-interest smile. Angelo tried to parry the blow.

"But it seems to me that the Cartier and the others can't possibly be authentic."

"Thanks a lot" Lometto cracked, repeating his mocking smile. "But just look who I have to hang out with to have things explained to me. One of these days I really must take you down to Salerno, to Milan . . ."

"Yes, Naples, Como, around those parts . . ." Belart said, on her own.

"No, I tell you right now, you can go to Salerno by yourself, you don't need an interpreter. Pantyhose, Lometto, remember: only pantyhose!"

"Yes, those too, what's that got to do with anything now?" asked Belart, who did not understand private conversation in public.

Lometto remained vague with Belart, yet she seemed satisfied. How could there possibly exist a sympathetic language able to negotiate the translation barrier with a secret "allez hop"? Whether those two had winked at each other or made a grimace or some sign of complicity behind his back, Angelo could not say.

In Munich, Angelo apologized to Jürgen for not having been able to participate in the seminar he had led from an isolation bed during a relapse of hepatitis. Jürgen's illnesses were followed by a few elect all wearing pince-nez glasses, students of architecture, apprentice psychiatrists, opera extras who attended a course in transcendental medicine. His organic debilitations were considered an almost fashionable event, something that was programmed partly by autosuggestion, partly by frequenting environments particularly rich in bacteria (gyms, cutting and sewing classes, courses in body-language maieutics, courses on signs, midnight saunas never disinfected during the week, etc.) or by eating food gone bad, taking infusions of poisonous herbs, licking boots just polished with a patina an inch thick, and reading against all natural predispositions the chic works of Stefan Zweig.

Jürgen's nearest and most longed-for goal was a form of napalm-induced intestinal amoeba imported, as usual, from the United States via Vietnam, highly infectious, lethal in seventy percent of the cases—this is what Angelo thought about every time he drank from the same glass as Jürgen or wore his veronica towels when he had run out of T-shirts or shorts.

Now Jürgen was waiting for him with a vast white smile in a white face inside a white duvet. They were always so happy to see each other alive again, beneath the kindly gaze of the small marble angel. Jürgen immediately expected to be waited on: not because he was convalescing; he was always convalescing and Angelo had gotten used to it. He ordered tea, sent Angelo to buy English jams at the corner, whole-wheat bread made by Hare Krishnas, spinach-and-soy omelets, rhubarb juice. Angelo knew that visiting this highly imaginative patient cost a mint and he was always well supplied in order to be able to keep up with the alimentary choreography of a suicide researched with an aesthete's punctilio in every gesture, word, and *nourriture*. Angelo was convinced, however, that Jürgen would continue to commit suicide until he was ninety: would become a complex-suffering Midas impervious even to atomic radiations. Jürgen's dream was to possess a mesmeric body, a marriage of mind and plastic, something absolutely protean that was never on this side or that. He wanted to reach a degree of corporeal insensibility that would distance him from the contingency of mortality. Perhaps he simply wanted to live, and could not manage it. He loved everything that could crystallize him and deflect him from the constant token paid to his nature as a human: from TB to IVs to LSD to cocaine—ingurgitated through the anus—to Madame de Staël, never read but often heard mentioned. In his cubbyhole he held out his hand to visitors like a princess habituated by protocol to do only this. His psychedelic-polystyrene trips had by now become daily, and all the while his mother thought that the money was being transformed into so many steaks. He was more than ever enamored of the plastic surgeon, who had the upper hand with Jürgen, who was totally subjugated by his friend's money pouch. The two of them spent nights prey to hallucinations in which they flung themselves onto a hammock stretched into the void from chimney to chimney on the eighth floor of a baroque palace, and chased each other with a flashlight across the roofs and let themselves down again through attic windows into the surgeon's large apartment. They could make love satisfactorily only after assorted perils of this kind, and not even by themselves. It's not that they were not enough for each other, they found each other inessential for this purpose. Jürgen on the phone recounted romantic motorcycle rides dressed in leather helmets plugged into rubber apparatuses something on the order of gas masks, or how they crossed a mountain and a forest in Thailand for eight days and eight nights without saying a word to each other, immersed in the silence broken by parrots and the cellophane of the whole-wheat crackers taken out of their packs. Having reached the temple, they had slapped each other's face in a dispute about who had finished the crackers.

"I'm guttering out, come" Jürgen said prettily after having gone *tick-tock* with his tongue for a quarter of an hour over the wire. He imitated time. He did not have a Teletimer.

He had less hair now than last time: he'd found a pomade that burnt it slowly and which, if used with regularity, would filter into his skull within three months. Jürgen pushed aside the duvet (he was always cold or he forced himself to feel cold, and it was one of those Novembers like the beginning of spring one rarely sees) and he got up only after the white angel was shifted and tea served on a free corner of the table.

His long naked body was now adorned with the yearned-for snake head greening amid the pubic hair. Jürgen's smile was one of puerperal felicity: the tattoo cost, besides money, much pain and blood and an infection and the not yet finished snake had produced a purulence around the scrotum. Jürgen touched the diseased part—probably because infected by feces—and lifted his finger to his nose, then inviting Angelo to sniff: it was quite a peculiar odor, a mixture of ether and mistletoe sweat. He said that it was the smell of the snake at the time it molted, the smell of a transition between two states of vivified death. They ate. Standing up, as usual, touching indexes, bowing and twirling.

They went out for an nth visit to the Neue Pinakothek, where Angelo tried in vain to track down a reproduction of a painting by Boecklin mentioned in the novel he was translating. The painting had been destroyed during the war and no one had ever thought of photographing it beforehand. Then, from there to the Türkendolch cinema, where a punk film was being shown. Afterwards they went into ecstasies over an interview granted by Beuys to the *Abend Zeitung*: that man was inexhaustible, a most serene volcano of intelligence. He was sensible, cultivated and not at all sibylline, and everything he said was frankly so genially banal and without double meanings that, even though Angelo had never wanted to see even one of his works in the flesh, one could conclude that he was the greatest living European artist. Jürgen resembled Beuys physically: emaciated, with calculatedly shabby and identical clothes, the shaved head, the soft hat pulled over the forehead, and the eyes, set laterally, which by their blinding light accumulated as much light as four or five Italian artists put together, to stare at you. Then Jürgen went home alone to wait for the phone call from his friend, who at that hour was probably pulling off his plastic gloves and picking up from the dispensary the evening supply of pills of various kinds for himself and his friend. On the subject of the sexual avant-garde the ethereal Jürgen had already surpassed even Angelo, too fast by now in everything to know at what point in sexuality's painful kitsch he stood. There were days in which even the time spent going in search of sex seemed stolen time to him. He strolled for miles and miles along the Isar, sour, starved, visiting latrines in the hopes of getting back to where he had started as soon as possible. To accept the burden of sex was the only way to let things slide with some measure of success.

Jürgen's cubbyhole was enriched by the most recently published books bought at the Sodom bookstore, strewn about with the most premeditated carelessness, and by dirt from the sink to the small bathroom to the balcony. You had to be careful where you put your feet in the dark—the single lamp was near the window and the bed against the opposite wall—so as not to cut them on the crested tin of a can of mango or peanut butter or on the can opener itself. Jürgen, on the average, read ten hours a day, and one could forgive him even the tetanus and his non-populist populism.

On the evening of his arrival Angelo was just about to go out when he received a phone call from Jürgen, who as usual was sleeping over at the surgeon's:

"Come here and join us; Wilhelm is inviting you to dinner. Then you can also make a survey. Thanks for the eggs. These are perfect."

Angelo rushed over, without too much curiosity, to get a look at the battlefield on which the two of them operated under the influence of hallucinogens. He was much intrigued by the trapeze number blandly described by Jürgen but by now discarded, due to the fact that one could expect to wait ten years for the natural wear and tear of the ropes tied to the chimneys to take effect.

The entire mansard of the apartment's two floors had been set aside for maneuvers. The young surgeon, the same age as Angelo, had spent his youth in Berlin and as a child had seen nothing but soldiers. Jürgen only went along. The parquet floor had been covered with a military tent and strewn everywhere with sharpened daggers, muskets, Kaiser Wilhelm helmets, leather boots with incrustations of mud and whips, two helmeted gas masks, and the brand-new onyx eggs. From a dough bin began to spill the phalluses of synthetic resin, in all dimensions and colors—from pale pink with light blue veins to black with red urethra, and one the color of café au lait—one of them had a glans at each extremity to be used simultaneously, back to back, while reading aloud passages of *The Elective Affinities*. This last was Jürgen's touch, surgeons do not read the classics. Angelo stood on the threshold holding a candelabrum in one hand and an apple in the other. All one expected from him was to shed a bit of light on the double secret in order to attend the premiere of their first depositions. The beautiful milky bodies of the two friends—the surgeon went to the gym every day and aside from a tiny voice was an athletic and sexy man, shorter than Jürgen, huskier, with something feline and lustful in his green eyes, which were always pointed at people's nipples—and they began slipping the onyx eggs into each other's sphincter. Angelo saw all the beauty of this ante-post gesture and watched the performance in an affectionate, discreet spirit. They wanted to reach five eggs each. There was a great use of Crisco, a cream which was originally used by American colonists to milk cows. The light of the red candles imparted to the scenic apparatus the correct dose of twilight, whether rising or falling is unimportant to this existential experimentation between two such intelligent, beautiful men sticking eggs into each other's bottom (from the egg to life?) as an aesthetic conjecture of an absolute form of sexual dignity (and, seeing that they called in witnesses, civilized) independent of received canons. They aimed at aristocracy, unaware of the fact that millions of scions of the upper middle class were performing, in their own way, the same practices at the same moment, having recourse to sadomasochistic rituals not so much in order to climb up a step as to be pushed back down into the lower middle class of a sex canonized by the Thursdays, Saturdays, and every month's paydays. There was undoubtedly a class argument to be made about the interpretation of sex and a special one, worthy of a separate exegesis, on homosexuality, but, leaving aside the role of bilious humors in all "melancholy" human activities set on conjoining two desires with the psychic means of "sexual blood," Angelo decided out of sympathy that it was better to rise to the position of back-straddling rooster than having to endure the sheep-humping catechisms of Latin sexuality. Better Prussia than Mount Goat anytime.

For him, observing with his mind as free as possible of mirrors was the highest form of life interpretation, the thought which, invited to violate an external reality, takes the opportunity to pay it respect.

There was a certain romantic weariness in the gestures, two corporeal spirits so rationally sexual, so programmatically and publicly *animal*—were they roosters impregnated by an alien procreation and did they admit without shame the hysteria of a fertility denied them?

With eyes glittering as at the sight of a new toy, Jürgen let the eggs be inserted with the smiling grace and curiosity of a child trying on his gorgeous first communion suit. Angelo, who was chewing the apple and getting a cramp in his arm because of the candelabrum, thought that the scene should be immortalized in a film of octosyllabic verse with alternating slides. There was more poetry in those calculated gestures than in a heartrending declaration of love beneath the moonlight. No passion guaranteed so much per star.

They were very happy, as though they had extracted the hoped-for result from a formula. Angelo, then, returned by himself to the cubbyhole, cursing the ten years of his youth wasted running after a couple of little he-cunts capable only of "yes and no" and slipping back on the phony wedding band as soon as they got up off the bed. Shit is better, he said to himself, it may be not quite right but there's no comparison. Out of friendship he just barely toyed with the thought that also the sewers were garrisoned by a bureaucracy, like *love* and the "yes and no."

The next day the three of them met for *Frühstück*: eggs, milk, honey, bacon, orange juice, freeze-dried rice, apple juice, Gouda cheese, toast, and Rossinian symphonies. This was the life! To have one's awakening prepared just so, without fear. A friend of theirs had joined them, someone called "*das Pferd*," the horse. He was six foot two, corpulent but proportionately, weighed two hundred and forty pounds, a mass of muscles without a thread of fat, static and rather sinister; he'd had a motorcycle accident a few years before and had a bad leg which he dragged a bit; he gave the impression of wanting to avenge himself for an iron shoe badly nailed under his hoof, when he walked he seemed to be moving calmly but inexorably toward something to be torn apart with his teeth. His hair, extremely short, with a small tail on the nape of his neck, the arc of his teeth large and rather English, conferred on him the studied wildness of a horse trained at Oxford. Also his equine manner was not unaccompanied in its ways by English pretensions. He too was a doctor. His enormous hairy hands had nails in proportion: broad, rough, hard as horn and very well cared for. He was dressed in black leather from head to foot, high forehead, dark red eyebrows without interval above the bridge of the nose. His eyes, so terrible and stagnant at first, became most amiable when crinkling in Angelo's direction. Angelo was struck by the refined manner with which he sat at table, almost mincing, and by the exquisite way he had of putting ethologically embarrassing questions. Did Angelo like to be buggered by two men simultaneously? Had he tried the arm? up to the elbow? Did he get excited by licking the shoe polish on boots? buttoned? with laces? The centaur was very disappointed by the equally circumstantial replies he got from Angelo, who kept saying no and apologized, even when the other continued with the questions, taking for granted the "yes" which was "no." Angelo gave him all of his man-of-the-world's attention: but he would never have liked to be even grazed by that dark mass of flesh which devoured the space of the table and the room and did not touch anything edible except tap water. The eggs and the rest were handed around the beautiful embroidered linen tablecloth while the conversation ran on pleasantly and inevitably about the slanderous denigratory campaign against small geranium pots which fall from the world's windows and kill helpless passersby, a campaign called as a whole Acquired Immune Deficiency Syndrome. Jürgen already fantasized about black blotches produced by Kaposi's sarcoma, egged on by the applause of the other three. He must definitely do all he could to get into the NATO bases.

Angelo at times felt so strong an affectionate impulse toward Jürgen that he could only express it in the old manner: paternally, something that bothered him more than his friend.

At the Munich station while waiting for the train, he almost telephoned Italo at Anguillara: it seemed to him that he was safer there, with more kilometers of telephone line between them than when he was at home. If he were ever to make up his mind to call him, since he did not answer his letters with a single line, would Italo ever tell him why he hadn't shown up in Rome? Over the phone he had *always* been so polite. You couldn't have two without a three.

Then there had been a change in Belart's plan: she said that she could not come to Italy, and something weird, that her must was still on the high seas, so ship the other sixty thousand on trust. The proposal translated, Lometto simply raised his index finger to his temple and signaled that she was definitely crazy, and through and through. No, it was not possible. And as for that "other" business? On the high seas here too, Lometto was looking around, it was a matter of a few days, there were possibilities. Who knows into which of all those "other" businesses the two of them had flung themselves, there had been so many of them. Angelo translated literally, he did not arbitrarily specify messages which were already so clear in their ingeniousness. In fact, Belart seemed to glimpse a certainty in these vague simultaneous answers and confirmed: that the truck must arrive on Saturday, same procedure, and money on the nail. Angelo saw Belart's neglected nail toying with a pile of Swiss francs and Austrian schillings. Lometto was not too convinced: if things went wrong, he would get stuck with all the expenses for assembling the goods and the useless freight. But there was no choice: Lometto had already set aside the seventy thousand pairs, sure of what he was doing. Saturday where? At St. Gallen, near Lake Constance. They looked at the map. Damnit! Would it not have been better to meet at the border and take care of the merchandise-money exchange there? Considering the miserable price of those stockings, wasn't it a pure loss for him? In fact, either this way or nothing. Lometto held his breath. Belart accepted. And all of Mire, Inc., began boxing those thousands of pantyhose which dated back to the experimental invention of nylon.

Belart was not at the Splügen. Hans was there alone, apologizing because she couldn't come and he would make the exchange. Rubbing himself in the crotch with both hands. The driver of the truck, with the morning half over and still stuck on the lot together with dozens of other trucks, was hopping mad, because he had been paid for something that was supposed to go quickly and instead was already lasting too long, and he wanted to be guaranteed that Lometto would shell out the difference. Since it was Saturday the owner had been chosen over the company trucker, who, because of the overtime and holiday and the air of irritation and indispensability he would have assumed, would have cost twice as much and besides would have stuck his nose into the papers, realizing what was going on. Lometto asked Hans for the money. There was only fifty percent of it. So, no customs clearance, and zilch for the other deals. But the merchandise is already sold, Hans expostulated, and the banks were closed. Sorry, but they should have thought about it before, this wasn't what was agreed upon. Hans ran to the phone. Now Belart was asking that despite everything they go to St. Gallen with the truck, it was only a two-hour drive. But was the money there, or wasn't it? Sure, no problem. Meanwhile put the merchandise through customs and let the rig leave. Lometto did not accept: he himself would give the truck instructions to leave after pocketing the money. The driver was foaming with rage, now they were telling him to stay there and to phone this number in Switzerland in a couple of hours or even a bit later. Hans led the way with the roadster.

"Lometto, here they'll rub us out if we don't watch out."

"Don't worry, they thought they could screw me. They'll see."

After three hours they stopped—the two cars slowed down by miniature shower-deluges—in front of a modest-looking condominium. Lometto and Angelo were brought into a room that was also modest on the first floor, full of lineoleum and plastic shelves and Bakelite glasses and the smell of dogs. Was this the den of Belart's pirates? And that Germanic couple, she slovenly with a sheen of greasy plastic on her cheeks, he fat, with a belt under his belly from which his navel peeped out, making an effort at conversation, did they not look like smugglers addicted to the elderly liqueur from boxes of spoiled chocolates? Angelo sat on the edge of the bench and looked at Lometto and told him the things said by those two and Lometto answered, turning down the corners of his mouth.

"Ask them if they have shat in their pants here . . . Don't you smell the stench? But when is she getting here?"

"It's the smell of the dog's basket, it must be this bitch here . . . All we need now is a police raid and they should find a kilo of pure heroin hidden in the tits of this puppet here . . ."

"Try to touch them, maybe she's made of wood . . . God, what a stink . . ."

"It's just what you deserve; the trouble is that I'll end up in the omelet too . . . No, look, Lometto, you're not screwing me again. I can't work for almost nothing and run this kind of risk . . ."

"Are you getting started?"

Belart arrived vindictively late and Angelo hated her because of this: she was not out of breath. The second telephone appointment was about to fall due and they still didn't know what to say to the trucker who was watching the rain and the roadside shelters with the motor running because of the heater. Here it ran on kerosene. Belart had a red plastic raincoat cinched at the waist with an extraneous belt, a man's belt, and green rubber boots. Hans followed behind her. Belart gave orders to open a bottle of champagne, Veuve Clicquot no less! So there.

"Don't go to all this trouble, let's get to our problem, please, tell her."

In a tomblike silence—rendered even gloomier by the painful realization that Belart had not brought along her big cow-midwife's bag—bottles of champagne of various brands appeared on the wax tablecloth. Little smiles: they must had been caught in the net. Was he interested? The price? A little more than a fiasco of Chianti. Minimum quantity: fifty thousand units. It would deceive even the most refined palate. Bubbles, color, flavor were identical.

During the trip, Angelo had been unable to get anything out of Lometto, he didn't know a thing. Neither about his search for zippers, nor the vises, nor in the field of "brand-name" watches. Even less in that of underground pharmaceuticals. He was consumed by a curiosity that gave him stomach cramps, because it was mixed up with the mortification of seeing prosper, with his ill-paid complicity, people without scruples, proprietors of pieces of the world, the owners of the "chumps." And his proud weakness, honesty, was the link, the below-cost translation which made possible the agreement on fraud and deception as forms of enterprise.

"Well" Lometto said, since nobody said a word. "How about the pantyhose, the money?"

"Signor Lometto, at least this time you could treat me with the same trust I showed you. Half now and the other half in fifteen days."

"That's not what we agreed on. And with what guarantees?"

"By now we're almost partners, right, Dr. Bazarovi? There should be some goodwill, the wish to meet halfway."

"I don't own the company by myself, tell her. I too have my instructions" Lometto said: it wasn't true, and who would have ever dared instruct him? "There has to be at least seventy-five percent in cash, the balance in postdated checks, but certified by the bank."

"But what bank, Signor Lometto, on Saturday!"

"Oh, Signora Belart, I'm sure that for you Saturday is a day like any other, the same as for me. Why don't you call Dr. Heinz at the Kommerzbank?"

Belart changed expression, as if she'd been struck by an unexpected karate blow in the teeth. Her canines sparkled on the green glass of the bottle. The other three remained with their glasses raised in a static photo-comic pose. Lometto slowly sipped the drink made from apples and carbon dioxide and clacked his tongue against his palate.

"Not bad, how much did you say a bottle? Same price for all brands?"

Belart made a very long, somewhat imploring phone call. Twenty minutes later Heinz, the manager of the Kommerzbank, parked a huge gray car alongside the pink-purple-and-mauve roadster and let the four into the building through a side door. The two parties demanded mutual guarantees. Were Swiss checks all right? I should say! Belart and Lometto always went the manager one better when it came to quibbles in high finance. While he was countersigning the bank drafts, the manager behaved with TV-script dignity. He even sat down at the typewriter to type endless statements, etc. Belart, in her outfit designed for a leaf-covered shelter from which to shoot thrushes, on and off dropped her hand into the manager's but simultaneously bent over Angelo and grazed him with the tip of a nipple under the black sweater or with a hip encased in moss-colored velvet pants with men's fly buttons.

The trucker had already phoned three times, and he'd been told to call again. The negotiations lasted an eternity, to their mutual satisfaction, as though the two were playing a chess game and Lometto had dug in his heels in an effort to checkmate the madwoman.

God, how obstinate and petty he was in some ways, he and his matters of principle! Angelo almost regretted that Belart, had she really intended to do so, had not managed to do a job on him. Finally, in view of the bank's certification, Lometto had ended by being grandiose and satisfied with sixty-five percent in cash. Belart ordered Hans—

oh, goodness, he was there too—to go to the roadster and bring back the three-bottle package. Moët & Chandon. The manager apologized, he could not accept, he preferred a promise that anything like this would be avoided in the future, he was watching *Dynasty* with his family. But Belart forced him to accept the three bombastic labels, fruit of technological and chemical inventiveness, and lingered with her hand—her index finger—in the manager's hand, and the small, bald, and self-important man craned his long neck and stood for a moment as though lightning-struck under the rain with the car's door open.

"But listen, Lometto, don't you think that when you give the go-ahead to the truck, and it comes here and unloads, these people will follow us, will do us in, grab the cash from you and the checks too?" Angelo asked, sick and tired of always having to travel carrying so much cash when by operating properly one could avoid it and not worry.

"No, there's nothing in it for them" Lometto said, quite certain.

"And what if they check you out at the border? if they take away my passport too? if you start saying that you don't know a thing about it, that you've just picked up a hitchhiker, I wouldn't put it past you."

"Stop fussing! I'm not taking even one cent into Italy."

"Of course, today is Saturday! The banks are wide open! In Switzerland! For you! Why don't you just drop it."

"You've finally got it. Don't you believe me?"

Back in the den, Lometto was immediately reached by the nth exhausted call from the trucker: by now it was half past four in the afternoon. But yes, he could get started, what was he waiting for, he was still there? hadn't they told him an hour ago? what do you mean who? when he had called! hadn't they told him to go, to call that other number there at the bank where he was? clean your ears out! wake up! instead of wasting time counting every second! The trucker must have been absolutely flabbergasted and Lometto continued to talk to him like a machine gun in bursts. Stunning him and when in the end he said "Never mind," Angelo understood that the owner had ended up by apologizing to the boss. Lometto always won, oh God, what shits all these workers were! the owner of a truck, with right on his side, and he apologized, let himself be fooled by a loud voice, or a promise or hint! was it still not clear to everyone that Lometto was here, in this world, in order to take everything away from everybody and make them feel guilty for still holding on to too much?

Between Belart and Lometto not a word had been exchanged about the other deals, probably Lometto had condescended to take an interest in them only to stick her with these *x* thousand pairs of pantyhose, period. Or was he using another interpreter for *those* deals?

Angelo was hungry now and he could no longer go on with the eye-mouth playacting required to make Belart understand the uselessness of hers: her fluttering eyelashes, careless knee touchings under the table, laying her hand on his in front of everyone, and he also could no longer endure the hammering of Hans, who, with direct, theatrical looks, mimed jealousy and a puss-in-the-middle distress. And Lometto's acting the wise man, making no reference to vises, or zippers, or watches, and his well-mannered silence seemed to constitute the most difficult role in the whole domestic comedy. The Germanic couple functioned as ballast, so that the four of them could fly higher behind hidden curtains. Who knows which one would make the first move to lower the gas flame so as to redescend to depths more solidly infernal than these, so celestial and ineffectual for the purpose of sales. They floated freely for a more down-to-earth study of each other. Lometto waited for Angelo to take the initiative in talking about Coptafuk, because that was the longed-for island, the utopian happiness pill which all of them sighted in the distance. Angelo might initiate the matter and then Lometto, if things turned out badly, would be quite capable of accusing him of taking an arbitrary initiative. Let them take care of it all the way by themselves. So there wasn't a separate interpreter, he too was still involved. Angelo felt better and worse at the same time. It wasn't possible to always stay in the middle of things by staying out of them, too easy. It wasn't possible here to find out about things and vanish: here you either stayed with it or you didn't. If you didn't stay with it, still you had the right to write a book about it, and certainly this was not what Angelo needed. However, it didn't suit him either to be in it too deep: he didn't make enough from acting as the go-between at so much a day, the risk was not in proportion to the curiosity and the profit. He decided to play dumb and wait for instructions, enraging Lometto, who was giving him instructions galore, staring at him for long periods and emitting "Copta" with his left pupil and "fuk" with the right one. Not enough: Angelo, for those few cents, required the official word, exemption from formal involvement beforehand, the black on white of enunciated vowels and consonants chosen in the first person. He would not cut for them the ribbon of the definitive inauguration of the economic exploitation of Evil's toxicity. Actually, they meant to plan in opposition to the new health trend which had sapped the waking state of eight million people. Lometto counted on Angelo to avoid admitting officially his total availability to debauchery, and Belart, already debauched on her own, counted on it so as not to arouse the suspicion that she was a woman of half measures. Those two were profoundly and philosophically in agreement on the *depressing* destiny of humanity, they were only waiting for Angelo's "go-ahead." Angelo was not fazed for a moment, he seemed to savor his importance, refusing to accept all allusive injunctions. He saw strewn all over the Italy of ministries and underground "piecework" forges a handful of tiny, soot-covered men, deceived and happy, stamping out carcinogenic pills, ready to swear in court they were simply peppermint to stop bad breath.

"Come on now, tell her about that thing there" Lometto threw in, wiping a corner of his mouth with the napkin; they had stopped at a pizzeria in the vicinity for a bite. As if he were telling him: ask her what she thinks the weather will be like tomorrow.

"Which thing there?" Angelo said, delightedly twisting the knife in the tender flank of this man who supplied him with work and easy riddles.

"The thing, no, how many things are there?"

"Oh, the vises."

"No."

"The zippers then."

"Noooo."

"The watches? The jewelry?"

"Keep those for later, the thing, the pill."

"The pill? A contraceptive, for you, Lometto. At least call it by its name: that piece of carcinogenic hallucinogenic. I thoroughly checked out the formula, you know. There's cocaine disguised under another name, erytheoxylaid alkaloid, and formaldehyde, Lometto, and camphor and some Benzedrine, and then there's an aphrodisiac, the . . ."

"You have some underdeveloped subproletarian mentality. It's impossible to get anything done with you, you continually try to throw a monkey wrench into the works. Cut it out, get moving, tell her that . . . that for the Coptafuk . . ."

Belart perked up, and so did Hans, and so did the couple of retired smugglers.

"Oh yes, I was forgetting, the Coptafuk!" exclaimed Belart, completely shameless. "Any news?"

"Everything is possible" Lometto said, without looking Angelo straight in the face.

"*Alles ist möglich*" Angelo translated, blushing, and he thought of Goethe.* The next step this guy will force me to take will be white slavery. Then into the market of illegal adoptions and thence into pederastic pornography. Angelo got up, said he had to leave immediately, probably by now the highways were completely iced over. Angelo asked for the check: but neither of the parties pounced on it. The check continued to lay embarrassedly on the small nickel-plated dish. Lometto was calculating that at the going rate, with all that coffee for Belart, it was the same as having had dinner in a real restaurant in Italy. One way or another the dinner got paid for and Angelo also managed to slip in an irritated sentence for Belart—he told her that he didn't want to know anything about their business because he had not been informed beforehand. And he refused to translate anything that did not concern the new shipment of pantyhose. He repeated this word for word to Lometto. He was the first to say goodbye and left by himself, heading for the car.

As soon as they were inside, Angelo told Lometto that from that very instant he would never again work for Mire, Inc.—for that local hero Orso le Mire, to whom was dedicated the street on which stood the *Manifattura Italiana lo miRE*, and one of the father-in-law's and brother-in-law's furniture factories, for that *hero of the Resistance*, as the enameled iron plaque at the beginning of the street said. Angelo explained to Lometto that, swindles and domestic or foreign commercial piracy aside, he no longer felt like coming to the office ever since he had found out who Orso le Mire was, and that it had been Lometto's father-in-law who, during the years of the boom, had forced on the local administration a street named after the hero and friend Orso le Mire. For otherwise he would build his furniture factory somewhere else, and refused to take no for an answer. Orso le Mire got his street and was declared a local hero because the depressed areas all

* "*Style is restraint*."

around were too many and one mustn't let an investment program such as Napaglia's escape. And, at any rate, he had to be satisfied with "hero of the Resistance" and that's all, and not, as he had envisaged from the start, "hero of the Resistance cut down by the murderous hand of the Partisans." In short, Angelo wanted no more of it, there were just too many things, details, hidden traps, an unheard-of mire into which he sank because of Lometto and without the slightest warning.

"And who told you the story about my father-in-law?"

"I have my informants too" Angelo said smugly.

"Tell me."

"Not on your life."

"It's your duty to tell me."

"I feel sorry for you."

"Bananone? The other one? Nicola?"

"Forget it."

"Maybe you should get out here" Lometto opined jokingly, as he was again pushing in the Orietta Berti cassette.

"As you please" Angelo said, taking him at his word. "Actually, this is what we'll do: I'll make you a present of my day's work. Add it to your kids' savings account. That way your conscience will be even more at peace."

Lometto thought Angelo was joking. At a red light he got out of the car in the rain without slamming the door, with the naturalness of someone who has seen a line of cabs in front of him. He transferred to one of them and asked to be taken to the railroad station. Lometto, who yelled something which bounced back from the already closed door, tailgated them.

After a three-hundred-meter pursuit the discussion was resumed in front of the ticket counter.

"How dare you involve me in this sort of thing? Some collaborator! You expect me to become your accomplice, not only without paying me but also without asking me beforehand whether it's all right with me."

Angelo shouted like a man possessed when he was forced to repeat the same thing a dozen times; Lometto, to the extent that this was possible, tried to make himself small. Angelo erupted, dug up details stored away months ago and apparently forgotten, other pieces of the puzzle in which nylon pantyhose seemed to be transformed into balaclavas. He threw aside conventions to which he had never subscribed, destroyed, was like an unleashed fury. He made a tabula rasa, reappropriated himself by expressing himself.

"I, my dear man" Angelo said, having recourse to a very popular regional theme for affirming one's levity "have never killed anyone, or even suicided anyone, I haven't! Why should I risk going to jail without getting something in exchange? And stop telling me to shout in a lower voice. I'll shout all I want to. Too easy 'everything is possible'! Too easy! If I had been working for someone for whom everything is possible I would not have waited until now and not under these conditions. Just look at him. Do you think I've been interdicted! You, with your smiles of a bread-and-salami good-time Charlie, you've become a burden for me, because you're a capitalist idiot and you don't know that only a couple of things in life are possible, not *all*. You are dangerous, Lometto, for my good name, for which I care above all else, because they wouldn't touch you no matter what happens but I'm the first they would get their hands on. And I don't want to bastardize my name and end up in jail for an idiot who thinks he's God Almighty and makes me work and then gyps me out of twenty thousand lire each time. Is that clear?"

Lometto, bundled up in a powder-blue coat, leaned against a grille and looked in all directions whenever a rare traveler appeared in the lobby.

"And besides, Belart, remember, can be a troublemaker on a Turko-Babylonian level. A fuck-up of the first order. And she's convinced that silently I'm your partner, understand, not a hired hand . . ."

"Hired hand?"

"Paid by the day! And you take advantage of this ambiguity and use me in a thousand sauces besides the one we agreed on to season the personality of your overcooked macaroni. Beat it, Lometto, get out of here, because I'm going back by train. Period."

Now Lometto was gasping for air, as if he'd been the one shouting all through that long half hour. By now Angelo had touched the bottom of extreme exhalation. That's it: now, as after a good run, he took a five-minute rest, exuded the last bit of leftover sweat under his skin. A few more moments and it would be possible to pour a nice shower of boiling, fizzy water over it.

"Excuse me, sir, you know, I'm just on my way through here"

Lometto started. "Would you be interested in two aircraft carriers? Just a moment, I have them here in my attaché case. I'll let you have them freight prepaid. By ship. Have you got a pier? Or a pear? Would you also be interested in three truckloads of bayonets? And eight hundred thousand three hundred and twenty poisoned darts? Real Brazilart!"

And so now he had turned on the farce tap, another three seconds and Angelo would be forced to catch the ball on the bounce and pretend to laugh. Translations don't take you to the end of the month, and the savings from Gallinone, Inc., were almost gone.

Lometto skipped around him, imitating Belart, grabbing his hand and pretending to put it between his legs, and he hadn't realized that he was losing the belt of his coat, a soft tail which followed him everywhere while trying to reattach itself to him. He looked like an animal hot-air balloon which puffed and was unable to take flight. Angelo made an effort not to immediately concede the quarter-inch of uncovered teeth that would lead Lometto to believe that he too was ready to turn the whole thing into a joke. He cornered him, pulling himself together.

"That's it, Lometto, you've given me enough laughs for today. Go ahead and do what you want, but get yourself another interpreter for certain things. I don't want to always play the part of the moralist and the bigot worried about the health of the universe, but the fact is, you do not pay me enough for me to want to continue being your Cyrenian."

"My Cyri what?" he grunted.

"And aren't you the one who sits in the first pew in church on Sundays, ha? Can you tell me why I should lend myself to risks of this kind so you can earn millions and I get crumbs?"

"You're not risking anything. You've got no capital invested" was Lometto's curt reply.

"What do you mean I don't have capital invested? What about my brain, my life?"

"Those don't count. They are something that is taken for granted, like one's arms. By themselves, my boy, they're worth nothing, nothing without the numbers, nothing. Is that clear?"

"But brain and life *are* a number."

"Well, in that case I've got them too and on top of them I also have the *other* numbers" Lometto said in a suddenly managerial tone.

"Then we haven't understood each other at all, thanks to spitting it out so loud and clear for once. A number oriented to making numbers isn't exactly what I regard as brains. The brain is an infinite number and it is zero."

"See, that's what I told you. Zero is not capital."

"Well, your capital does not pay enough for my zeroness, does that suit you?"

"So then you see that it is not only and always a matter of intelligence but of dough?"

"Let's say it's like that, I'm trying to follow you. Certainly, but what am I doing here speculating, discussing, not speculating as you understand it, about the concept of the gratuitousness of intelligence? Let us confine ourselves to demand and supply and the work it provides: I suit you, Lometto, because I sell you with my personality and also with my knowledge of languages. You like this and profit from it, and pay little for it. Let's look at it this way, as to the wherewithal. Let us negotiate a figure for everything, and let us meanwhile make distinctions. Then I might even tell you no, in fact I would tell you no if the business offends me morally. In any case I do not go along with certain things. So not only don't I go along but I also get sore as a pup, because you pretend nothing is going on and take it for granted that I will go along and that you don't have to shell out any extras. As if I were one of your chumps. And look, I even want to break a lance in *your* favor . . ."

". . . it's about time . . ."

". . . if the economic-political world is made up exclusively of relationships like this, between one party that can see and another that one must not see, and nobody says anything, you all fit into it marvelously, you too and Belart and Cutolo and the Grecos and Marcinkus or whatever his name is and those poor slobs who must continually pretend they're smuggling arms for their governments. All of you are protected by fronts. Internally by you know who, externally by decent people like myself who give you luster and staged dignity in exchange for a good hunk of bread and by those others, those whom you have reduced to slavery for thousands of years now, the contented servants, and we won't even talk about them. In short, too bad, I'm nobody's executioner but don't ask for my participation, because in that case I too can come up with some numbers."

"Hey, you're not trying to tell me I'm a Mafioso, that I have anything to share with Neapolitans and Sicilians?"

"No, nothing to share. I'm sure you already grabbed their share too."

They both burst out laughing, but it was a nervous laugh, not really definitive.

"And then, from the way you behave" Angelo resumed, cutting off the laughter in the other's mouth "how do I know in what pies you have your sticky fingers? There, in that concoction of tiny ivory revolvers and luxury amphetamines and zippers and vises from the East and French and Swiss jewels made in Naples. I don't, I'm sorry, feel at ease. By dint of being forgers, one becomes false. Leave me to my own business. I started on pantyhose with you, I don't want to end up in the CIA or the Cosa Nostra."

"Listen, in that case, do you think that they would come to you and ask for your permission? Come on, this is going on too long, let's go, I'm cold, let's argue while we're driving. You know that I have to go to the b . . ."

"Go, go, what are you waiting for?"

Angelo was cocking his good ear: no noise from a train, this was like a station rebuilt in a television studio for the annual *Karenina*.

"*Ciao.*"

"You, Lometto, are insatiable for adventures, emotions, because nothing can filter into that fat heart of yours. You are impermeable to everything. But not me: my rate of need for emotions is among the lowest in the world. Your love for industrial counterespionage makes me yawn, you like to think you are being tailed and two eyes are not enough, you would like to have twice as many because you feel targeted by the world. Not me. For me the dangerous life or on the razor's edge is a tiny petty-bourgeois concept. But, as it happens, you do not like to risk in the first person, after all, you delegate the truly dangerous actions to others. The dishes you eat you first want them tasted by me to see whether they're poisoned and you hope that I croak in order to give yourself a bit of importance and have some reason to feel persecuted. That's ridiculous, don't you realize that you're on the wrong track, that with me you're trying to bite off more than you can chew?"

And at this point, seeing a group of young Italians coming in, who were slipping off backpacks, mountain climbers or skiers, he raised his voice and approached Lometto menacingly: "Why don't you try to choke the little rabbit you've got in here, huh? here, in this tiny heart, choked by your *always more at all costs*? When will you decide to go out and take your own risks, if you're up to it?"

"What are you trying to say?"

"That you're scared, scared shitless! That the last time you saw me taking an injection at the hotel you almost fainted. That you have clay feet, Celestino, you half-assed colossus, and that you are sucking me slowly to build them up without paying the toll to my *marble*."

"Whose feet?"

"In short, you are a clump of quicksand not only because of external factors but because in my opinion inside you are cowardly in character. You've gotten away with it for so long and you've convinced yourself that you're a tough guy. But you're mistaken, inside you know that you're a little fish that leaks from all sides. You're held together by your scales"—and yet Angelo knew that Lometto was tossed between rage and fascination with the incomprehensible images he used in yelling at him—"because I'm the one who gives you the glue, you play peacock with my feathers, and you have no one of my moral and intellectual caliber in your circle, not even the priest, and don't think you ever will have. You suck my soul, I can feel it, and all you're able to do is despise this bellyful of Dr. Bazarovi, and ask for a discount and not pay much and then slip away, leaving his bones to the dogs. No, enough is enough. When I'm gone you will go back to being the little Commendatore you are, with your compadres at Castelgoffredo. Did you ever see anyone who is just a little more than a discotheque owner? No, you're all the same, you're still there, all of you, all stinking from hoof-and-mouth disease just dug up and sold retail and eleven o'clock incense and nobody, obviously, is superior to you, not even the Pope, you bet. All of you there giving orders to unemployed college graduates whom you wipe your ass with in front of everyone to show how much someone with a degree is worth when he does not have the *numbers* . . . You don't even know how to speak correct Italian, Lometto, I'm more ashamed when I'm with you than with normally dishonest but educated people. It makes me sick to be with an ex-cowherd with money and a three-pound knot in his tie. And stop saying that's it! I'm the one who says that's it. And stop breaking my balls, go and get your Swiss bank manager to tuck you in, what use do you have for me? You stick it in sky blue and may even pull it out navy blue, but not in me. Do you want my culture, my gambols around your customers because by itself your merchandise has no attraction, because there's ten thousand of you making it when one hundred would suffice, and you need the doctorate I haven't got yet to give yourself class? So pay for it, then we'll see. There are people galore who ask me to work for them, your competitors. And then you expect me at the same price to become your pimp with fake watches and drugs? Oh no. Pantyhose, Lometto, pantyhose!"

"And who might these people be who come to ask you to work for them?" demanded Lometto, satiated with all the cuticles of all his nails.

He did not expect Angelo to begin yelling again and now he played the insulted one: "So I'm a coward, an ex-cowherd with money, you're ashamed to be seen with me, fine, excellent, I'll remember this. Keep it up."

"I will! What do you think you had become after not even three years that I do you the honor of my collaboration? The Begum? You're a yokel in his Sunday best, that's easier for you to understand. When shit mounts on high, it stinks to the sky . . ."

"The Begum, that's you, baby. Are you through now putting on a show? Can we go home? Come on, you can set up your carousel somewhere else."

They left the station. It was raining, a thin Swiss rain, very dense, refined, silent, from incognito billionaire clouds. First they shook off the water, then came some shy little laughs, the kind generated by nervousness which evaporates the moment it is put in gear.

"Oh God, the names you called me! the insults! to me! Step on it, step on it, because with all that yelling he might lose his cunt along the way, his persimmon! Oh, you should see her here in Locarno, turning tricks at the railroad station! And me running after her, to save her from perdition, this cuntarussky!"

"Stop simplifying me all over, I'm not philo-Russian! I've never even been there, in Russia."

They waited for a while, enjoying the downpour without saying anything, driving slowly, both of them exhausted. The branches of the trees in the dark revealed gaps of a filigree green, William Tell watched over the stock of apples of the rapacious world within and without the borders.

"It's definitely strange, I'd say, to bring pantyhose here for Hungary" Angelo, conciliatory, said.

"Who knows where they take them! But they're for Austria, aren't they? Didn't you get that? They go in that way, stop off at stores, and with a drawn pistol politely ask them to underwrite a shipment of a thousand at a time. The same as down our way . . . understand?"

"Down *your* way, if you don't mind."

". . . And who might these competitors be, eh, who might they be who want to hire you?"

Angelo cut him short, forget it once and for all. Did he tell him everything, perhaps? No, on the contrary, always the indispensable minimum, the least possible, and every time he put him before the fait accompli. He had learned his lesson quite well, he too would do exactly the same. But he did not tell him so.

In Lugano, Lometto dashed out of the car for a moment. Here, at eleven o'clock in the evening, not only bank managers could be tracked down on a Saturday, they could even be pulled out of bed.

The sun is at its zenith and of Armando not a shadow. Angelo looks around, livid from the lack of sleep. He would so much like to see a yellow beard tangled in the briers, something external to tear him forcibly from this story that he can tell only to himself and whose conclusion not even he knows and which nevertheless is already concluded: Giorgina Washington, born and dead and buried. One would have to have the corpse exhumed, demand its pathological anatomy. Here comes the fellow with the toupee: even the message "It's raining today" would be misinterpreted when delivered by someone like this. No, he hasn't seen him around either, he says, passing his tongue over his ceramic teeth, which are too long for the encaged tongue not to want to flicker out at the slightest pretext.

"Do you know where this Manerba pizzeria is?"

"I've been there many times. It's right in the center, there's a little wooden horse outside." The copper-blond is now waiting for the fatal question and holds his tongue peeping out between his teeth, ready to shoot.

"Did you tell him yesterday why I didn't come?"

"Oh, sure. He told me to tell you where he works."

Angelo thanks him. He is happy with this syntony, even though detoured through this stranger so out of tune altogether, so out of place. But this vulgarity of set passages does not displease him, even though it removes much of the charm of a direct, personal discovery.

Angelo gathers his stuff, tottering with sleepiness and fatigue, makes an appearance on the other side of the small wall, gives the sign of his presence to those from the central station, beyond the wild fig tree; the usual wild murmur, and he turns right about and climbs back up the escarpment as though parts of the lake were tugging at his heels, pulling him back down to the shore. And he goes home. He closes the blinds, the double curtains on the terrace, and does not sleep. He switches the light on and off, exhausted. By now it is night, his mother in the other room grumbles each time, satisfied because she has been awakened from a sleep she didn't have anyway. The mosquitoes and sultriness render the intermittent dream flights even more sour. The telephone has remained mute all afternoon.

Toward the hour of milk and coffee, five-thirty, the cock-a-doodle-doo of a rooster in a cage, the bark, the bell, his mother, who picks up the bowl from the drainboard and slams it down on the table with the kind of racket that only she knows how to make, and then the ear pricked because the torture of the spoon that will be turned inside it must first end—Angelo keels over and sleeps.

This is the ideal hour to go down to the Terrazzine: half past two. At three, half past three at the latest also Armando might be there for a swim.

He isn't. Angelo lies down on the low concrete wall in front of the boathouse and waits. Those statues of gangrenous tufa in the villa's garden must have cheered the flights of the children of some Fascist big shot, pursued by maids in black with cups of hot chocolate and ladyfingers at four o'clock. Now it would no longer be possible to flee, it has become so overgrown and wild and full of ghosts. Armando will not come today either.

Well, if that's how it is, Angelo will have recourse to the extreme vulgarity of an on-site visit. Pizzerias are enemy territory and par excellence hostile to love, with their smell of garlic and oregano, the mugs of beer which always depart and always arrive at their destination, and he is left there with his tongue hanging out and foaming with rage.

In Manerba he finds it immediately. A Nordic boy is shouting "Giddyap!" on the small horse outside; he drives past him and begins the tribulation of finding a hole to park in. The lake is full of tourists, the dog-day sun makes the search rich in illegal parking places. And this weariness of the past days is not yet digested, the effort of forcing oneself once more to go all the way to the bottom.

Certainly the chapel in which Giorgina Washington rests—it'll be a skyscraper with a facade like the Central Station in Milan—must be full of coolth and shadow, and on a day like today the cemetery is probably deserted. The living are all about. To smoke there, with a big fat bunch of lilies in the other hand. Lilies, if they don't cost so much, dangle so well inside the tissue paper and in the damp heat they would dangle like chalices down against the knee, preparing for the vibration of many funereal caresses once they are arranged in the vase. Provided there is one. There must be a vase after all, even though empty. Who knows if family tombs are always open, or if one must call the custodian. Or perhaps he would leave the lilies on the pebbles at the entrance and would go away burning mad at the family who owns the chapel and wants locks there too. Who knows. Next mirage, a big house trailer in slow motion, a godsend for the two cars already waiting there. Drive around again. In front now a bus loaded with blind children, in the large rear dial a number of little heads driven around by "City of Cremona—Association Visit to Lake Garda—Parents of Blind Children" turn and the young woman incites them to wave greetings with their hands, so slow, like clock hands that are not pursuing time.

As he enters the pizzeria he immediately sees Armando—he's wearing a yellow T-shirt and, against the yellow wall and the black unlit counter, only the two red cheekbones of his face are visible. Armando does not recognize him: he stares at him for an instant and continues to walk toward a table with a bowl in his hand, his thumb in blood-colored liquid. Angelo approaches the counter, recognizes the youngest boy of the trio, who was at the beach on Monday. Armando comes back, opens his eyes wide and shakes his head.

"Give me a bowl of that too."

"Come, sit down here" and he goes to get a bowl of new wine.

There are only four customers, the crowd is still at the beach.

"I don't want to waste your time" Angelo says right off. "I've come mostly to tell you . . ."

"I would like to show you my photographs. I have a lot of difficulties, I tried a show here and the police stepped in, I have a charge of corruption of minors hanging over my head . . ."

Both sit on the edge of their chairs, ready to dash away.

"Are you married? Do you have children?"

"An eight-year-old boy."

"Married men are fuck-ups. And arid. Their gestures and gesticulations are always more orotund than the things they mean to say and give . . . You look like a beast, a not completely domesticated animal. I am inside as you are outside."

Armando must like all this, it sounds artistic to him. He must feel at the center of a cultivated man's interest, this probably doesn't often happen to him around these parts. Humanity is completely geared to tourism here.

"I like you a lot too. You're very profound" Armando says, using a tragicomic adjective, unfortunately without realizing it.

"I hope it's not only because of that. What I need least is a brainy seduction. For me sex is too important for it to come on the heels of something else, its dignity is justified by itself. To fuck is noble. So it's best not to waste a good dose of blue blood among professionals. Or am I wrong? I'll leave you my phone number."

Armando returns with an address book. The A page is full of names. Angelo's barely fits on the last line, after that of a soft-drink supplier. To Angelo it seems obvious that there should be no need to give telephone numbers: why doesn't he come up with some excuse and make himself available immediately? But it doesn't happen, one is inserted in a probable program. Castrating.

"Next week my wife is going to the beach with the boy. I'll have more time. You come to my house. She knows all about it."

Not only doesn't he come right away, but one must even wait for his wife to go on vacation, as in an American movie. Angelo makes a gesture of protest.

"Fine, anyway you can tell me at any time. At night too. *Ciao*. Even tonight."

"*Ciao*, I can't promise you. See you soon."

"As soon as you can" Angelo says, brushing the fly of his pants and bringing the back of the other's hand clasped in his up against a most aristocratic erection which has tormented him for the last ten minutes. Armando, with the nonchalance typical of a waiter used to doing everything in public without anybody ever being aware of it, clutches his prick in his hand, talking about this and that with his father-in-law. Incredible, what a formidable tactician. And now, rushing to masturbate will involve a tolerable headache. His name is at the bottom of a page of the San Paolo Bank Address Book, together with the suppliers of soft drinks and bacon, anchovies and olives and artichoke hearts. Only a few years ago this sort of thing would have seemed unacceptable to him. But at that time he didn't even have a telephone. Now he's a bit older and more patient about the seriality of numbers to which even love at first sight must be subjected. So his emotions must go on the waiting list, as when he was young. Commitments, recondite interests to change and diminish them. Rendered them too real, vulgar. Another missed appointment for which he had been punctual, and this fellow too, here, and it's the same disappointment.

At the beginning of December, Angelo picked up the receiver and dialed Italo's number. It was the first time he heard his voice after an eternity, he was moved. He squeezed out the question, trying to sound ironic.

"Oh, you're alive. You know, I waited three days for you in Rome. Frankly I didn't expect this. I'd like to know why you didn't come to the appointment. That's what I also asked you so many times in my letters. I've come up with all possible hypotheses."

"Yes, but not the right one."

"That is?"

His heart was pounding, he felt that something definitive like an ax had been suspended over his head day after day. Now it was about to plunge down on him, overwhelm him. Angelo followed its movement, could do nothing about it, and until the very last instant it seemed that the ax must be made of papier-mâché, he found it hard to believe that it was all true, and that it was aimed at him.

After taking the blow, he felt nothing else and for days continued as always to do the same things, fainted with his eyes open. No, that hypothesis, *that* reality, *that* truth he had never taken into account.

One day in the middle of December, Lometto called at the Central Bar, left a message for Dr. Bazarovi to get in touch with him, with Mire, Inc., as soon as possible. The bartender always said "Look, the big frog from the mire has called." Angelo snorted and thanked him.

"It's about time. Didn't they tell you to call me right away?"

"But it's not the public telephone service, they don't rush to my house to tell me."

"Belart called, here nobody understood a thing. She seemed a bit high. She's talking about 'holes.' Maybe they poked another one in her. Find out what she wants. And let's not have so many silk ladders, right?"

Angelo did as ordered. It was so embarrassing to telephone in that gut without a booth, with all ears straining in amazement to listen to that usurper tongue, having to wave one's hand to chase away those who stuck their noses in your face to get your attention and asked you if you were talking Turkish. Belart was very cordial—with him personally. Through the wire she extended her hand and laid it on his cheek, touched his earlobe and rubbed it. But then quickly she went on the attack. The merchandise was rubbish, thirty, forty percent of it, who knows, maybe fifty or a hundred percent. Thousands of pantyhose not even in envelopes, still tied in bundles of twenty in the cartons, open tips, holes, ladders, and ordered lots which kept being returned, thousands of undyed stockings, gussets coming apart, unraveled, a crime, a loss on all fronts (the borders?), of image, money, future deliveries; her customer—the only one, it seemed—making serious threats. And she too threatened very effectively. Precisely and concisely.

Angelo immediately called Lometto.

"So then, the devil makes the pots but not the lids"—a boomerang proverb against Lometto, the proverb specialist, must have resounded like a smack flung at him, sprinting from centuries of peasant wisdom always and only *imposed*. "Moral of the fable: she wants a forty percent minimum refund as of today, probably fifty percent, and immediately . . . *Or else*."

"Or else what? but what's the matter with her, doesn't she know how to sew the tips up herself at that price? and what did she expect, also the tips? or else or else! or else what?"

"Stop opening a big mouth. Who knows what merchandise you gave her? Look, I don't even want to get into this. You tell me what I'm supposed to communicate and I'll transmit. Only Marconi, and no tricks for you, on your behalf."

"Tell her to go to hell, that gold-toothed viper. You figure out something with her."

"Me? What have I got to do with it?"

"Well, I don't know, invent something."

"What, for example?"

"You people want to take power with your imagination? Then this is a good time to show how."

"Hey, listen, Lometto, one more sentence like that and I'll hang up and you can see how you put on your lids, I never thought such a thing about power. In fact, *ciao*."

Lometto called back immediately but Angelo had already left the café. He caught him at coffee time.

"Listen, you don't hang up the phone on me, you understand?"

"And you don't take me for an ex-sixty-eighter or a son of the flowers, get it? And I'm not your ass kisser. Either you have an answer for Belart or you don't. I personally don't have anything to do with her. You do. I'd warned you."

"She said *or else*. And then?"

"Nothing. Nothing and everything, as you prefer."

"But according to you, what did she mean?"

"I'm under no obligation to squeeze my gray cells. She said *or else* and that's it. I give it to you as I got it. It is an *or else* that concerns not me but you. She gives me blow jobs over the wire."

"You tell her that we are willing to refund ten percent, so long as that's the end of it."

"Ten percent on the postdated checks?"

"Yes, here comes the great mind! Who knows where those are! On the money, ten percent cash."

"Very well. Ten percent."

More phone calls. Belart intimated that Angelo himself might be an imbecile.

"She repeated *or else*. She wants all of them, forty percent, *or else* . . ."

"Oh, really, threats, in other words, actual, absolute threats. Ah, some bunch. And you even seemed to side with them . . . It's all your fault . . . I knew I shouldn't trust them, and you kept insisting."

Angelo removed the receiver from his ear. This wasn't the first time that Lometto unloaded his rare failures on him.

"Listen, Lometto, shipping that merchandise in that condition . . . who are the crooks, you or they? and you expect them to sit down with needle and thread to sew up the tips, dye the raw pieces. Belart gave you the money, and good cash too. If anyone is devoid of scruples it's you."

"Ha, you're even siding with them now! And she probably even gives you a cut!"

Angelo slammed down the receiver. Lometto called back immediately. He had the woman at the counter say he had gone to the toilet, to call again. Angelo knew he would say that he'd rather wait for him to return. After keeping him waiting for five or six minutes, Angelo picked up the receiver and yelled into it "Go get it up your ass" and left.

At lunchtime Lometto was already at his door, downcast, chewing his nails and asking "May I?"

"Just tell me, who pays you, me or her?"

"She not at all and you too little."

"Beat her down, beat her down, get her to make it twenty percent."

"Look, Lometto, there's nothing to beat down. You'll do the beating when you see each other, if you want. She said, 'If I were in his place I would give it a little thought.' This is an exact translation of the last sentence of the last phone call. It's up to you."

Angelo dropped in a pause, studied the collar of Lometto's coat, where a spray from the gutter was melting. Now he could have sworn that Lometto was laying that little thought like an egg and that within it imploded the name of his favorite: Ilario, the beautiful Ilario. Lometto could hardly breathe. He had a sudden shortness of breath.

Angelo resumed: "The appointment would be outside the Vipiteno exit tomorrow at eleven. She'll bring you a truckful of stuff to see in case you're not convinced about the crap you sent her. And you must bring her three million and a half at least, now, right away. Then she'll see about further complaints. They may even become five, six, who knows. She said to be careful, to toe the line, and that her name is Jasmine Belart and not *die kleine Heilige* . . . not a saint."

"The same as saying she's the bandit Giuliano."

"Neither more nor less. It'll be a relief. Anyway, in my opinion, this is all money you've earned, almost net, money that in your wildest dreams you couldn't get for such merchandise. You'll take a small loss on the net profit you've made off her and that's the end of it. I've got this Belart up to here, if you must know. She'd be perfectly capable of threatening me too because of your greediness."

"Don't make such a big deal out of it. It's all a bluff."

"Well, I'm through with her. This is the last time. And what if she asks me about Coptafuk?" Angelo asked, hesitant and distrustful.

"That it's no go" Lometto answered with determination and a touch of venom that did not escape Angelo. Angelo did not want to go into details, or hear more about it, he took him at his word. But Lometto's chin remained thrust out toward a further, probable question of Angelo's. In vain.

Before leaving, very early in the morning, while shaving, depressed, Angelo, after Italo's cruel answer, also checked out his hair: apparently within a week it had grown back fairly well. Angelo was ashamed of the insouciance of his capillary glands. At eleven, Angelo, Lometto, and his partner from Parma, a whiner who spoke all the time about palpitations and fiscal audit, got off the highway at Vipiteno.

The two of them had talked a lot also about Bananone, who was rallying around himself all the partners to push Lometto out of the management and therefore his position as Mire, Inc.'s commercial director, because of his continuous investments. Angelo withdrew into himself and again thought a lot about that Roman wait. Every step, every ring, every time the door opened, for three days of unspeakable pain.

"Why didn't you come?" Angelo had asked him after months and months of paralysis at the last digit of the telephone number and an nth impossible conjecture. And that unexpected executioner had brought down the most horrible ax: "Everything about you is so false." His hair had probably begun to grow back at the moment that Angelo had started to justify him.

Belart's roadster lay in wait like an enormous gillyflower behind a field of small sand hills. You would have said that a distracted washerwoman had passed by, small piles of dirty snow were strewn here and there like shorts and T-shirts not wrung out and threadbare white . . . Behind the roadster a van with two men never seen before in the cab, flannel undershirts with long sleeves despite the frozen laundry of old snow all around. Lometto stopped his car at a certain distance from Belart's. Oh God, now lances would appear and the joust begin. Angelo did not say anything because of the guy from Parma in a state of pre-collapse, and irritated by this high-noon standoff, he immediately knew without going into polemics what was expected of him: to cover the discrepancy by himself, go and negotiate. Up to a maximum of four million and a half, including the mortgage on any future complaint. He risked absolutely nothing, of this he was certain. And anyway he would have liked to die, extinguish the echo of the hypothesis about him presented over the phone by that torturer. But certainly he could not count on Belart, she was all pantomime. Belart had the superior morality of powerful women capable of hurting indefinitely without ever wounding mortally and, above all, not so hysterical as to mistake a palfrey for the true and proper knight. Angelo would have been able to entertain some dread and hope if Lometto, so impressionable, incapable of sangfroid even in Lapland, had been in Belart's place.

He got out of the car, turned his back to the two partners, and began to walk. He immediately started smiling at Belart, from afar, a comical smile with the radiance of someone so immensely unhappy that he was unable to restrain his giggles.

She was at the wheel wrapped in a white fur coat with her hair hanging loose and she seemed extraordinarily young. The cold became her. Hans got out of the roadster, moved the seat, and let Angelo get into the back, where there was not even enough space to rest one's balls and take a deep breath.

"So" Angelo started "we could come to a preliminary agreement . . ."

"We could try . . ." Belart said.

"Point one: whether you believe it or not, Lometto has no intention of paying me for this day's work and I'm already climbing up the wall because of all the arguments we've had."

"Dr. Bazarovi . . ." broke in Belart, who did not believe a word of all that sincerity poured over her.

"He says that these are the hazards of the trade and I owe him a day's work, at least fifty percent. Incredible. As I told you over the phone, I was coming only if you guaranteed me at least half of this day's money. You accepted, right?"

"Absolutely right."

"Fine. So then, in this whole story I've earned my morning milk and coffee for a month, and you, both parties, enough to buy yourself true champagne and smoked salmon every day of the year morning and evening, correct? And, Signora Belart, if you please, I'm only an interpreter hired by the day *and that's all.* You who know so many things . . ."

"Yes, I know now. But you know, it's hard to believe that you really are just an interpreter, you do everything . . ."

"Only in appearance . . . Now, I know exactly the final, the very final figure that Mire, Inc., is willing to disburse, reimburse. It may be a little higher or even noticeably lower than the one you want, and nevertheless it is understood that, such as it is, it includes any possible future claim. After all, come on, even if that van over there is full of defective pantyhose, this does not mean that you are actually in a position to prove that there is an infinite number of others in the same condition. And what will you do? Lometto wants the evidence, at the cost of counting them one by one personally. Or are you going to send them back and forth, ship them, begin counting them yourselves? That's senseless. The amount you want, going by that van, might be, in truth, excessive and impracticable. You need an awful lot of discarded merchandise to make up a million, certainly not a small van! So let's not waste time and interest, agreed?"

Angelo spoke fluently, without pausing for breath, as if he had memorized the business and now had the advantage of making someone else go over it.

"I'm not double-crossing anybody, my involvement is so limited, and besides you already know, I told you over the phone, that if there is a complaint I'm not under any obligation to side with Lometto, always and under all circumstances. He pays me a pittance . . . Well, you now, in my opinion, should be concerned only with the final and definitive outcome of this complaint. You want three million, then four, and then five, and then six: this is not a valid argument. How many cartons of rejected merchandise are there in that van?"

Belart looked at Hans. "Four? Five?"

Hans scratched, he must have felt very cramped, uncomfortable, his affectation had become a necessity.

"Five, six" Hans said, with a grimace of adjustment.

"Fine, five or six or seven cartons as proof of the condition of the overall merchandise. But not as proof of three and a half million of rejected merchandise. If I talked to him, for four and a half cartons Lometto will give half a million, maybe, and say: return at your expense to Italy all the other merchandise that justifies a higher disbursement, then we'll see . . . Do you follow me?"

"Perfectly" Belart says enraptured and with an ironic smile in her gray-brown eyes. Enraptured by the fact that Angelo, without even immediately realizing it, has preceded her and placed a hand over hers, immobile on Hans's backrest and beyond the field of vision of the lover-gorilla-partner-pimp-lackey.

"If I really manage to get you the three and a half million you want instead of the two that Lometto is willing to shell out at the most, in that case will you give me two hundred thousand lire for my favors and fifty thousand for the half day's work you promised?"

"Okay" Belart said immediately, interrupting Hans, who had not yet opened his mouth but was about to do so. "We agree. I trust you, Dr. Bazarovi, implicitly. I like you."

"Good, that's a deal. So let's have the two hundred and fifty thousand lire. Schillings or francs, it doesn't matter."

It didn't even cross Angelo's mind that Belart might not travel with two hundred and fifty thousand lire in foreign currency, and certainly she would not take them from Lometto's wad and count them out in front of everybody and neither would she send them by postal money order: Angelo would have put his hand in the fire that Belart never traveled with less than four, five million in cash for cigarettes and coffee, and that she kept the bank notes there, in between, or just below the three beauty spots. If one listened to her, she always had sudden chores to settle at the various customs stations on the border—for one thing or another. And she too must slip cash disguised as chocolate bars into the various ledgers she handed over at the booths.

"No, first we get the three million and a half, then you get the two hundred and fifty thousand lire in lire" Hans broke in, with perhaps the first decisional sentence pronounced by him during all those meetings.

"Oh, in lire!" Angelo exclaimed. How could she ever give it to a type like that? Why did she drag him along with her? Just imagine a Jasmine Belart–Angelo Bazarovi couple? The end of the world, and of all frontiers.

Only at this point did Angelo realize that under his hand he held the smooth parchment of fingers embossed with rings, with traces of roughness from detergent.

"On your word?"

"On my word" Belart confirmed, opening two fingers like claws and sucking one of his in between. "But make sure it's four, not three and a half. Three and a half net and half a million for you."

The gold canines glittered like two spendthrift croupiers around a pink table. Belart pushed forward the rake of her tongue and poured an *en plein* of saliva on both lips. One could tell she was woman at home in a gambling house.

And yet Angelo sensed that this gypsy-ex-vamp of the roulette cared only for one thing: read a hand, pocket the dough allowing a glimpse of a thigh or breast, and shut behind her quickly as possible the door of her *roulotte*. She cared nothing for anyone, strange to say: only for her official gallant, her Hans, and money.

Angelo lingered a moment, pretending he was disconcerted and then nodded yes with his chin and got out of the car: he was sure he had drawn a blank, that he would never see that half million. And he had even put his hand in hers out of carelessness! Who knows what Belart had thought of him! That he needed a mother, or that on the subconscious level he was a cuntomaniac? And how could one trust that half-assed guy who perhaps was the true boss, Actors' Studio at its best he was so bland, a *straight man*?

He walked very slowly toward the two partners, he had always liked the cold. This availability of his to corruption consoled him after all, even though he derived from it only a mocking smile from under Hans's little hairs and those under Belart's nose, indeed, this new quality of his exalted him. He caught himself rubbing his hands and skipping—while Lometto signed to him to hurry up and get there—cheerful as after overcoming the fear that had gripped him the first time he had dived from a five-meter board: he didn't know how to swim very well or how to dive from the side, so just imagine—but he had wanted to test himself and the water had welcomed him as it did everyone else. In order not to reduce all the terror to stretched-out arms/closed legs, he had told himself that, having overcome the fear of the five meters, he must now overcome the vanity of six and must confine himself to diving from four. Descending, overcoming the forward thrust, one day he would be able to dive perfectly from the side of the swimming pool.

He got into Lometto's car, told a completely different and for him gratifying story, and the two cars began to move to the encounter. Which was gossipy, cordial, and there was absolutely no talk of money, only the back door of the van was opened and out came hundreds of torn, balled-up pantyhose. Lometto and partner recognized their product (from the colored thread in the elastic, put there so as to recognize the sizes at the packaging stage—this recognizing was bullshit too, since it wasn't their merchandise at all but put together hastily by the most peripheral workshops in the area), nor did Lometto demand a guarantee that it was actually a matter of a forty to fifty percent of rejects, he took their word, and the partner kept saying "Oh yes," and it was even hard to tell why Lometto had brought him along, since Lometto did and decided it all without even consulting him. Certainly he was anxious to erase as soon as possible from the face of the blackmailing firmament the echo of that *or else*, which, Angelo would have sworn, Lometto had curled around Ilario, out of maternal instinct. Angelo, having translated Belart's *or else* literally, now realized for the first time that perhaps he had been too heavy-handed: he had been too direct, impersonal, objective. Was this the secret dynamite which transformed frankness into allusiveness and allusiveness into *falsity*? *Saying things as they are?*

They decided to go for a snack at an inn a few kilometers away. The van was given a signal to follow. Lometto insisted that Angelo get back into the car with the two Austrian-German-Swiss, he a bit Polish and she perhaps a bit Turkish or Afghan, in order to convince her to lower her demands. Angelo simulated a sigh and joined the two in the mauve-colored automobile.

"Things are going the way they should. Let's have the half million, kids."

"No" Hans said, smiling; was it the smile of someone who has figured things out and was proposing an exchange against nature before a lady so as to render the humiliation of the denatured person more stinging? "Later."

At the inn the money was passed from an overnight bag to the big suitcase. Lometto, in the car, had removed from his the surplus Angelo had managed to save him. Both parties, while complaining, declared themselves satisfied.

Belart now pressed her hand on the back of one of Lometto's, spilling tears with brio over the loss of image, etc., of profit gone up in smoke, etc. Lometto said, "But it's impossible, it's because I trust you, but . . ." etc. Lometto had paid less than he would have been willing to pay, Belart had taken in a trifle more than in her heart of hearts she must have expected; that half million in between seemed not to count, not to belong to anyone, the fruit only of Angelo's ability and nothing else. Angelo, to make fully felt the weight of the golden bridge he had been, naturally kept apart for as long as it took to impress on the four the illusion that he was irrelevant, that it was all their doing. Then, after the agreement was concluded and finalized, he got up, asked to be excused, went down to the toilet. He peed unhurriedly, shook off the drops with a grand gesture, dallied while washing his hands, dried them very slowly under the hot air. Hans wasn't showing, neither was Belart. They had screwed him. He heard steps coming down the stairs. It was only the Mire partner, still gasping, still a fish out of water. Angelo was so downcast that he pretended he didn't know him.

He went back up by himself, threw a glance which was reproachful but not too much so at Hans, immediately put on his previous smile, and sat down again next to Belart. People were closing umbrellas and folders with bills of lading, descending to the toilet, now a second *Kanne* of coffee was asked for Frau Belart, who had not taken off her white mink coat, but had unfastened it by one tape in front and loosened it over her shoulders. Underneath was seen a somewhat grandmotherly blouse with a lot of cream-colored lace embroidered with beads and small leaves of gilded metal. But on that blouse already such a cross between Old Vienna and the Ottoman Empire she must have added a Parisian touch, removed perhaps a double layer of Bemberg, because she now was letting the fur slip all the way along her hips and one became aware that the blouse was made of a silk thin as a cobweb, thin and transparent, a transparency of which the whole room of truckers took possession in a flash, reflecting in it an entire project.

The man from Parma, having paid what had to be paid, and at any rate destined to tachycardia, lost himself in the enumeration of the horizontal beauty spots on the right breast of Belart, who, Angelo noticed after counting on the walls all the deer antlers on display, also had two pretty tits which shot a bit outward, ensapphirined by two large and dark nipples of a truly champion length and porosity when soft. Lometto continued to go *pip-peep* with his calculator.

Angelo was brooding over the con of the half million, calling her all the so-called filthy words he knew by heart: big whore, prick eater, déjà vu. And all the while she thanked him for his precious collaboration, said goodbye to Lometto, inquired and asked for information as to future collaboration—"only pantyhose"—and Lometto had him translate curt sentences like: "I don't believe there will ever be another collaboration, my dear girl," and Belart in the end shrugged her shoulders, the two parties suddenly indignant with each other, the farce over. The motors were turned on, their customs separating forever.

"They're gangsters, did you see?" Lometto said to the partner in a singsong that came from the pit of the stomach. "The people you run into. But it went off all right anyway. Account closed."

"You really could pay me for a full day . . ."

"Yeah, don't hold your breath, I've already taken enough of a loss."

"I shouldn't have a loss with you. I don't have any capital invested" Angelo said quietly. "You have to have some gall, palming off that sort of merchandise . . ."

"But in Hungary they're all the rage!" Lometto said, quite cheerful.

"Well, I'm really glad it's over. This is the first and last time that I act as the bumper between two gangster cars."

"What do you mean *two*?" Lometto cried resentfully: was Angelo forgetting that there was a stranger with them, a partner?

"You're just as good as they are. To give them those pantyhose you've got to be . . . Well, anyway, what do I care?" Angelo adjusted his aim, mindful of his unhappy attempt at making himself into a gangster. "They're the pirates of our times. You saw the two little fellows on the van. Two hundred pounds each."

"I weigh more than that" Lometto said, and he and his partner burst out laughing while Angelo, resigned, pulled out his cigarette pack and, running into a consistency of watermarked paper with his fingertips and then flicking the thin blades of edges held together by a paper clip, flushed and began to cough to stop himself from laughing too, to not betray himself. He felt that something like a fishbone worth half a million had stuck in his throat.

Adorable Belart, blessed Jasmine. Putative Mother, Jasmine Belart. To her he dedicated his last exam, to her canines that could sink into flesh with indefinite generosity, to the grease stain she always had somewhere, to the three beauty spots—horizontal, vertical, disposed like the eye of a goddess?

Women, indeed, were punctual, they arrived late out of delicacy to allow you to call them whores and to lighten the burden of their definitive loyalty, the concreteness of their coquettishness unendurable for a man . . .

Angelo's social episodes or adventures always reached Lometto in waves, never as they took place. Angelo did not want to be distracted by advice of any kind, even a nasty *moral of the fable* was preferable. Even if afterwards Lometto embroidered it with taunts and comments for months on end. Lometto remembered everything vividly and he had nothing to lose by not forgetting. From all this he drew pretexts, always negative, with which to turn against Angelo the typical presumptuousness of the failed man devoted to good works. Lometto asked for information on the persons who benefited from such bounty—that is, the *characters*—the subject of by now distant narratives, and could never properly grasp one essential thing in the life of his travel companion: that he no longer saw anyone, not only that but that he had to make a certain effort to re-remember or, if he still remembered at a distance of months, it cost him an effort to re-narrate. The persons, the subjects of his attention and conflicting feelings at one time, had evaporated *en bloc* no less than the characters in which he had for an instant solidified them *to kill time*, and certain things that the instant had contained. He had to search for them among the folds of a past that seemed neither remote nor recent but never existed. Angelo forgot. Lometto could not understand this, because he was afraid for himself.

"So, if you and I should no longer work together, and you no longer come to see me, I disappear, never even existed for you."

"What are you talking about? It's probable, yes, I don't know. As long as you're there, you're there, then afterwards no more. No more even in my mind, in my stories. No more. I don't do it on purpose. That's how I am."

"Some friend."

"Try to be my friend now."

Angelo was always very satisfied when he was able to give such profoundly reasonable and sincere answers: he felt that Lometto, in the end, was only one of the many corporeal apparitions that men bestow on each other, strolling down the street with their shoes on their feet before taking them off at night, not an umbilical cord, not a point of reference in the present-past of his life, which did not have one. But this sensation was momentary. Most of the time, or often, it seemed to him that Lometto had become indispensable to him, that he was pouring over him some sort of steady affection that would extend in time, into old age, even against his will, as with Giuditta, a little Sardinian girl who was five years old and whom he had seen grow up. Or at least he hoped it would be like this, but he knew that it was not, that nothing withstands the test of time, its capacity to macerate relationships, any relationship, even the most true. Besides, Lometto was too distracted by himself to care about a love not guaranteed *in itself* like a stock-market share. He demanded eternity in exchange for clichés. The past did not count, had no power over Angelo: he wanted the proof of the power of things from the present and in the present. The waking state of love and affections must be pathologically insomniac and reciprocal, or insomniac and unilateral, but insomniac. A little nap was enough to crush several idyllic years. In any case, all he needed was his small quotidian mythology to fill the void left by breakups, misunderstandings, disillusionments, by all that which had slowly mired into a corner the small heap of dust sprinkled with the water of his accidie.

Angelo would as soon as possible go away elsewhere, immediately after his degree, he would not even find *time* to kill *it*, to lick his wounds. He hated pain, no less than regret and rancor. And ended by despising those who inflicted it on him. He first despised them, then ignored them. Forever. Phosphenes which at night echoed in the brain, from time to time.

Angelo knew perfectly well that he had adjusted his sights when he said "forever," "never again forever." *Forever* was really forever, such a thing really existed, he, in his corner, was the living proof of it. This as far as people were concerned. As for characters, he could play with them as he liked, consciously unfaithful to the *reality* enacted in his existential radius. Through the brain they entered as nervous systems and from the memory they issued as puppets. It was even preferable to forget about them. For example, he would have liked to tell Lometto how he had arrived at that request for the poison pill or pills, but Lometto had immediately pricked his ears at the possibility of inheriting his house. Tell him the horrible sentence, the horrible truth-hypothesis that had been imposed on him over the telephone by that faggot from Anguillara. But he couldn't, he could only tell him stories about friendships that had ended badly without admitting to him that he had embarked on the search for affections that he knew to be impossible, in order to escape loves that at least *in words* were possible only for him. It had seemed to him that touching lightly with his friendly affection could not arouse suspicion, that his disinterestedness would be obvious; he must throw off those incandescent chains which marked him with the most infamous of verdicts, that of *falsity*:

false because desirous of achieving a goal by a double cross, false because he expressed the truth of his feelings directly without taking into account those of others (including their absence), false because he was able to love while remaining alone, false because he demanded everything with the air of someone who wants nothing, false because he was false, false because he had falsified himself by dint of taking care not to become false. Oh, there was enough to go crazy, that answer hammered away in his head day and night and in the morning it was still there, an anvil on which nothing was being forged, and which nevertheless would again emit blow after blow, scream after scream.

There were two things which he had until now hidden from Lometto, both very recent: the first, on the subject of his bad luck with the German girl, a drug addict whom he had put up in his house and who had walked off with the whole bundle of those hundred thousand lire bank notes slipped into his pocket by Belart, paper clip included; the second, that over the phone Belart had told him that she was "Jasmine Belart, not *die kleine heilige Stottererin*," and God only knows what that meant, perhaps gangster jargon, because not even Jürgen had heard such a locution as "the little stammering saint." By now it was too late to tell him about this, everything was over between Belart and Lometto, officially over. And as for the absentminded uncut half a million, Angelo had actually been on the point of telling Lometto a moral fable about "the devil's flour," but in the end he had muddied the waters, in view of the fact that only Angelo's devilish flour unfailingly turned into chaff, while Celestino's yielded exponential Californian harvests. He certainly did know all about the right guano that is needed, and which nourishment the earth sucks up most avidly.

Angelo at Christmas gave presents to Celestino and Edda: two Bohemian crystal vases, the heritage of purchases made at Gallinone, two absolutely beautiful pieces. Those two demanded presents; in a certain sense, it gave them the certainty that they were paying him more than his due and that Angelo was simply giving them presents that they had previously paid for. They applied the same reasoning to the Christmas gift boxes that they sent to important customers. Angelo's presents were not followed by even a thank-you, they had not even learned that they should unwrap them. Angelo unwrapped them, to spare them the trouble.

Lometto looked at the two vases of burnished crystal, two unique masterpieces in which streaks of enamel floated, and grimaced.

"They're no big deal."

"The gifts you gave me *are* a big deal" Angelo retorted.

Only after two years of collaboration had Lometto agreed to give him a dozen with double gussets for Mother's Day. And he had held it against him, as if it were an immoral act, what an impertinence to ask for free pantyhose! taking advantage. Angelo had told him to go to hell and stopped asking him for them. He asked Edda or the girls in the office, who did not dare ask for details. Those with small gussets amounted to a few dozen pairs a month and seeing that he asked for them in three different sizes they thought of him as a Don Juan of appreciable standing. Angelo loved to arrive at the publishers' for whom he did translations waving the pantyhose he was offering to the women editors who were more amusing and endowed with common sense, and under the eyes of those he excluded. None of the chosen had ever received a token of respect so amply feminine and useful while sitting behind an editorial desk.

Since the presents preceding the two vases had been followed by a request for a loan of two million because the notary's document for the house cost more than expected, Lometto in fact granted him the loan, but with a thirty percent interest charge. Angelo had been shaken by this favor so similar to a noose around his neck, and granted moreover with the sorrowful eyes of someone who has taken the bread out of his own and his family's mouth for a friend and has decided not to ask again to do him any favors, and Angelo decided not to ask again, but had reversed his decision due to the *dishonestly* earned and naïvely lost half million. And besides, he was a trifle ashamed that people like Pfefferman, when they came to dinner at their house, could never rest their eyes on something that wasn't vulgar and cheap.

Lometto got Edda to wrap the two vases again and went into the other room, where the Christmas boxes were stacked. He returned with a panettone in one hand and in the other a box of three . . . Angelo fulminated him with a glance, grabbed the stuff without deigning to look at it, went outside, and dumped it in the car. He knew it would stay there only temporarily.

"Don't you even say thank you?"

"Did you ever say thank you to me?"

"Three bottles of champagne and not even a thank-you."

Angelo let it go; he only said: "I'm not a connoisseur, I couldn't tell the difference between it and apple juice with carbon dioxide."

Since he had to hurry and deliver the last boxes to people there in the area and Angelo did not feel like keeping him company, Lometto told him to stay for lunch, climbed into the van, and left. He looked like the abominable snowman in a beige, plush-lined windbreaker, with a stain of coffee or wine or sauce or blood running from the elbow down, and then a muffler, gloves, leggings . . . Imagine showing up in such an outfit at the houses of shippers and piecework contractors!

Angelo remained alone with Edda in that kitchen heated to the bare minimum, like all the other rooms, although it had the advantage of being a trifle warmer because of the steam from the pot of boiling meat. Angelo saw too many things all at once: that Edda, for example, had a too satisfied and therefore taciturn air, and that the dark marks under her eyes could compete with Ilario's, a splendid fifteen-year-old who by now had the vigor and energy of a mature man; and then when Belisario appeared, the middle one, holding a skein of string in one hand and in the other a small piece of paper with a schematic drawing of a puppy—he definitely knew how to straighten the legs of a dog!—Angelo saw all the bruised signs of some great secret activity.

And this involved even Berengario, the third, by now twelve years old, who in the brief space of a year had from a child become an adult like his brothers. All three of them were tall, had broad shoulders, long thighs, strong necks, and thick, shiny hair, all of them very beautiful and predisposed to conquer a good part of the world.

They went up and down from the tower and, in turn, came to give a kiss to their mother, who roughly chased them away. This, however, Angelo noted, had never happened when the father was present, and the kiss, much more hasty, almost dutiful, was given to him, in the wedge of skin closest to the tip of the ear. Not to the mother: the mouths departed, true enough, from the center of the cheek but they slipped toward the corner of her mouth and would have reached it if she, bawling happily and calling them mama's boys, had not pushed them away with a shove of her open hand. Angelo was fascinated by this, could not make up his mind to leave, and the four of them acted as if he did not exist or did not count or added a touch of exclusiveness to the manifestations of their somewhat morbid tenderness. But for Angelo, who had never given or received any, every tenderness was morbid and inwardly he excused himself for having thought this.

There, as they stood, the usual lively gabble that Angelo and Edda managed to burble out over the phone, sometimes laughing heartily, was absent. And indeed, it had been over the phone exactly a week before that she had given him an impression—how to put it?—of exaltation, that's it, of an animal at the mercy of uncontrollable, out-of-season heat. Now he no longer remembered anything of those words that had so perturbed him. She must even have confided something intimate but Angelo, foreseeing it, had moved the receiver away from his ear. When he had brought it back he heard in the space of a few instants vocal dips, raucous sounds, throaty, a nasal sigh. He shivered, thinking back on it. What was cooking?

With a long fork she pulled out the boiled meat and then, as if this were only an operation following the one before, opened the drawer of the kitchen table and popped a pill out of a rectangle of tinfoil and turned on the tap at the sink. A bit of water in a ladle, the neck stretched slightly backward, and she swallowed.

"Don't you feel well?" Angelo asked.

"Oh no, just like that, you know, sometimes I too get a headache."

"How did the piglet end up?" he continued, just to say something.

"The same as all the others, in the mass grave behind the stable." And she laughed. An ugly laugh that made her belly wobble. Angelo imagined the navel adjusting and twisting in a frenetic grimace of rage and gaiety swollen beneath the top layer of skin. Angelo hoped that she would stop laughing, stop talking, and yet it wasn't true that he stayed there only because he wanted to settle the bill for the phone calls as soon as Lometto got back. He stayed there because he breathed her, and annexed to the little he knew the tacit version of Edda's life.

Edda had known love rather late, she had come with her family to settle in the Mantua area when she was already twelve years old, she had passed directly through the hands of three men—from the grandfather's fields to the father's furniture glue, to the husband's pantyhose—and Lometto had seen to fitting together the pieces as one can do with a closet or a shelf: to his own measure, that is, filing, sawing, planing down here and adding there until the ideal shape had been attained . . . and she had been delivered into the hands of three more males, the sons. Of course, he had not been able to strip her completely of her southern inflection or even all superstitions and magics of a "straw-stuffed" childhood. And as a matter of fact her three sons had all been delivered at home, because she had always refused not only to let a doctor touch her, before and after, but even to go to the hospital. She had always summoned from down there—from Caserta—her mother's midwife—a Sicilian—the same midwife who had brought her into the world and every time the first thing this midwife had asked for had not been towels and hot and cold water and fire, but a bundle of straw. To stop up the holes in the windows and the drafts of the doors, keyholes, various fissures, chimney hood included if there was one. To prevent from entering a certain baleful wind which would have brought misfortune to the woman in childbed and the newborn. Lometto had turned red as a pepper on that Sunday when all five of them had gone for a swim at Desenzano and he, a bit to one side, had been forced to answer Angelo's offhand remark: "What strange navels your boys have. They look homemade, like ravioli."

So Lometto had confided in him, begging him to keep his mouth shut but happy to unburden himself of something that each time irked him to death—him and his mother and everyone on his side. But there was nothing they could do because Edda and her father had demanded it in writing in front of the notary before the wedding, the notary being none other than Edda's own brother . . .

Since males go to school and females in any event get married, the man and wife were happy together, and Edda had been left the only possible initiative, to disguise her southern submission as northern alacrity. Any sign of gratification on the husband's part when for instance there were guests seemed to her a wifely investiture bestowed by a patriarch, and after so many years she blushed at some of his salacious remarks—though less and less; she blushed out of necessity if only so that, gratified at entrapping a by now damaged timidity, he could point out to the guests: "Look how she blushes!" They were lovers and partners and accomplices and every bond that united them in this trinity of roles was impenetrable to any other, complementary but avulsed. Theirs was a harmony that functioned because scanned at fixed intervals, there were no changes of register or admixtures of type. The general baton was clutched in his fist, quite tightly: it was baton, whip, and goose feather, and always recognizable in its changes because always only one thing at a time. As happens with all contrived, well-made beings, one could never say to what extent Edda was herself or to what extent she was following instructions.

For quite some time Angelo had noticed how many efforts she made to second the husbandly praise that would have her all home and workshop, but many lies and imprecisions had soon become evident: it was not true that for her sons she cooked in terms of vitamins and calories, carbohydrates and proteins, she opened cans and fixed the spaghetti with paste like so many other mamas, and she used corn oil—something inconceivable to Angelo—and she never had anything really fresh in the house aside from milk straight from the cow. Everything was frozen: it was almost impossible to sink one's teeth into one of those steer steaks about which Lometto sang paeans, bred "especially" for the family. It had to be booked the day before, and since Angelo was always called at the last moment either to Mire, Inc., or by Edda, he too ate like everyone else, customers included: bread and salami, grana cheese and bread, frozen trout fried up in a hurry. Edda, in the impossibility of living up to the culinary pedestal on which her husband's domestic megalomania had placed her, lied shamelessly, resorted to deceptions: one could still feel the slivers of ice under the scales, but there she was swearing that they had been brought to her "alive" an hour before, "expressly." And so at Angelo's remonstrance because of the greasy and insipid salad, she called as her witness an unknown saint and chanted "This is super-virgin olive oil." Angelo urged her in words not to feel guilty about it, but his palate was no fool. And she, unperturbed, went on smiling and swindling people's taste buds and olfactory senses. She had introjected everything of her husband's, even the babyish pleasure in denying the obvious.

No one but those two, Angelo now thought—while Ilario reappeared and furtively, perhaps annoyed by his presence, opened the drawer in the same kitchen table—could ever have the right on his side. And if the two of them did not have it, it meant that right was on the wrong side because it was not on theirs—perhaps it was something one took before meals, a tonic based on vitamin C—that is, it was a right that must be eliminated. Their wrongs were ineffectual, that's it, because there was a whole implicit and external system, overturning all that was right, which propped them up so well that only a fanatic could have gotten the idea that there was something to straighten out. When it was not possible to be right—and here now it's Belisario's turn at the gurgling kitchen sink, the American mania for vitamins has even caught on here—they knew how to lie shamelessly, that is, naturally, aware that they must act in such a way that everything would continue to be permitted to them, and that the *ultimate* right was *superior* to the insignificant contingency of its being or not being on their side in each instance.

Angelo, alone in the kitchen, stirred the risotto: the number of their enemies must be the same as these precooked grains, enemies like Bananone, but who knows how many others. The Lomettos' arrogant indifference to every principle and norm that did not entail a profit for the Family—theirs—must have created enormous obstacles for them in the bosom of the small town, but they were also nonexistent obstacles interposed by the same *species* of families who, not being equally powerful, could set up only surmountable obstacles. They could be dismantled, like those in a horse show: where ecclesiastical acquaintances were not sufficient—for the purchase at fire-sale prices of plots of land donated to the Curia by lonely little old ladies: it was Lometto who had told him this—the party acquaintances would intervene: Lometto boasted that he had several men with the Christian Democrats and at least one in every other party and that "ideology is there only to be bought." For the sake of vendettas he had roads deflected on the province's urban plans, also water canals, or had caused the expropriation of land belonging to *disagreeable* people for the construction of public facilities, such as the gym or soccer field or town incinerator, or he first bought them at bargain prices to resell them at a price one hundred times higher. Angelo thought that, while he out of courtesy was stirring a risotto, Lometto was somewhere putting on the *pressure*—that is, getting things cooked in much less time. And now here comes Berengario with an awl in his hand from which dangle loose Band-Aids and gauze bandages, and he too opens the drawer without even his brothers' glance of embarrassment, gulps without water, and leaves, remarking absently: "You're still here?"

Edda had returned: Angelo noticed that she held her eyes high and well opened, perhaps a trifle fixed: it was incredible how mother and son had the same black eyes, a black at times pellucid, at times of pompous senselessness.

She began to set the table in the other room.

"Always late. Who knows where he went. So are you staying?"

Then she said that she must run upstairs to her room for a moment, she had a kind of sudden dry impulse to vomit, it always was like this when she had her period.

Angelo lifted the lid from the by now overcooked risotto, strained his ears, went around the table, opened the table drawer. There was the small box, white and blue, although perhaps that *Pausinystalia yohimbe* was printed in slightly heavier characters than the original which had passed through his hands. Quite an organization! What speed! But did Lometto know about these processions from the underground to here, from the butchering of the dog Gelo all the way here? Or had the four of them waited for his witnessing presence to lay a trap for him and induce him to have a certain reaction, to confess he had guessed, perhaps in order to corner him in that involvement from which he had so skillfully disentangled himself? Must he be the one to tell them it ought to be sucked and not swallowed? He shut the drawer again as if he had never opened it. He stayed for lunch, watched the boys lift their forks as if in their fingertips they felt shocks at contact with the metal, saw them eat frenetically and laugh frenetically, with Lometto glued to the television screen. They did not say anything of note, they wished him a Merry Christmas, he reciprocated, the relatives also came. At the turn near the elementary school at three o'clock the fog was already so thick that he had to get out of the car to make sure that he was in front of the poultice of reed mace and that he was accurately hitting the pond with the triple champagne box, Jasmine Belart brand.

Angelo felt ecstatic about himself, because of this strange new ability (acquired who knows how or when) *not* to express an opinion, *not* to reveal the extent of his deductions. He concluded that being constrained by it, being constrained to do something in the sense of the three monkeys who don't see, hear, or speak, could indeed render life a bit more zoological, but in recompense what general relief if, as a habit in others and a bizarreness in himself, one was able not to feel rancor toward oneself. He smiled to himself in the face of the cinereous fog, in that calvary of Mantuan roads without traffic lines: he had learned to size up troubles and delights at a glance, late but better than never. Solidarity was quite a wonderful thing but a minimum of negotiation improved it: he could even continue at other times to hasten to the help of the person who collapses under a burden disproportionate to his strength, but, seeing all those colored little trees through the windows and neon comets over the doors, he told himself that from here to Easter there was plenty of time to convince Christ to drop in on the carpenter and urge Simon the Cyrenian to go by the public weighing station to find out beforehand.

Rarely had he thought anything so vulgar, he immediately admitted. If he should listen at all to the spellbinding calls arising from that path of thought, pick out their realistic aesthetic whose uproar is equal only to the intensity of absolute complicity, let himself be pleasantly tempted by a mirage of degradation by now even within his reach, yet it must remain a wholly reliable game in his solitude which had shouted heard said or put forth an effort. And if this remained within the confines of a game, he must expel the Lomettian reflex which had crept into him: turn and re-turn it over at his pleasure, but in the end shatter it. And that is what Angelo did. He got home all in one piece despite the fog sucking at the sides, at every side, it seemed that the wheels of the car had a sixth sense for what was on this or that side along the neutral asphalt surface. Angelo said to himself that this time too, by a hair, he had escaped the risk of becoming *normal*, a driver smashed at the bottom of an escarpment who is bending over backwards to tell you which is the correct road.

"Did you see Armando? . . ."

Friday.

"Did you see Armando? He just came up" the fellow with the toupee says to Angelo.

"No." Angelo has descended by a shortcut farther ahead. It seems that it would be an exaggeration to climb back up and say, "I'm here." Chance does not want them to meet today? Fine, at this point he too could wait, his balls are properly emptied, even though yesterday every time he tried to concentrate on snapshots of pleasure, all that the brain set before him as an erotic take were two buses of blind children on an outing to Manerba.

"If you hurry, you're sure to see him, he's with the other two. A minute ago, a matter of a minute."

"Never mind. Thank you."

And Angelo proceeds in the opposite direction, to avoid giving the impression that he is nevertheless in pursuit. Angelo sets great store by his public image, and in this sense there is not a single person, albeit with a toupee, who is not important. Talk of not giving a damn about people, as they say in his hometown: everything that concerns his not-giving-a-damnism is still always dependent on an image of himself that he would like to install in others. Conversely, he would not mind running after him if this were what he wanted. Since this is not the case, best to let a few minutes go by before going back over the path so that not even a guy with a toupee will get the wrong idea about the intensity with which he restrains his lack of hypocrisy.

Angelo is vexed: can it be that Armando last night felt not the slightest impulse to dial his number? why wait so long? why didn't he show up at his house at no matter what hour, why leave him so much time to reflect and cut things down to size?

"It's not worth the candle" says Larousse, sitting between Moschina and Carmencita, and he fills in the small squares.

They talk about travel, while the audience waits for Angelo and Carmencita to begin picking on each other. Angelo lets himself be dragged into a pestiferous topic: the image of the homosexual preferred by the press and cinema. How about going there and blowing up city rooms, production companies, and whole movie audiences of smirkers?

"Miss Panama!" Moschina puts the last touch to the puzzle and all arms drop down again.

Then a circle is formed around the towels and they play cards, five-handed briscola with discards, two never seen before also participate, one plumpish and half bald, the other hairy and well made. They teach them the rules, in Milan the game is played differently.

"For example"—Larousse plots the course—"in pinochle you cannot close without having forty points in hand and you have to use the other player's cards and jokers."

"What time is it?" says Carmencita.

Larousse becomes irradiated with nose-dial meteorology when anyone asks him the time, they all do it on purpose: he points his head at the zenith and now he declares: "Five after five."

He never gets it right.

Zizi plays too, he has three hairs on his head and yet won't pass up the fashion of having them curled. He throws down his cards, resuming his vacation stories—at a wedding in Tunisia he and the Contessa had to service everyone, under the tables, beginning with the groom. The women were kept separate from the men—one hundred and twenty, plus the priest, Coptic.

"Ah, Africa loves!"

"What are you waiting for, drop that card, Angelina, what are you thinking about?"

On the two of swords there is the drawing of a small angel crowned with myrtle and sweetheart roses. Angelo, asking himself which of them might have it among his cards, conjures up its features: the plump little arms, the nose a bit snubbed. This is the fragment of dream he's been pursuing all day: a crystal casket of the Sleeping Beauty variety, but newborn size, let us say forty by twenty centimeters tops, lifted from a grave by the Seven Dwarfs, of course, and the grave is situated in the untended garden of the villa over there; inside, however, there is not Giorgina Washington, but a very alive and plumpish little boy who suddenly pushes up the lid and runs up the church steps, all smeared with blood.

"What are you waiting for, pay attention!" says Zizi. "It's your turn. Stay here with us, don't get lost!"

The game over, after a swim in deep water, among the usual catamarans of gawkers, they all decide to go and have a pizza.

"Oh, if we'd only known" says the older and balder of the two men from Milan. "We have to have dinner at Pino's, some other time."

"But who are those two from Milan?" Angelo asks, since nothing is happening at the pizzeria. "Two friends?"

"You bet they are! Together for nineteen years."

"He's Pinuccia's brother, the handsome one."

"They don't look at all alike" Angelo says, mortally wounded, because he rather liked the *brother* and now he becomes aware of the twinlike resemblance. He cannot become related.

In the evening Angelo stays at home, in the vague expectation of a telephone call. Armando's? Lometto's? He would like to pick up the dream where he left it, or from where he does not remember anything else. He tries to complete it by adding something of his own: the boy, risen from the coffin-casket, has familiar features and an affable air; he is not fat, on the contrary he is slender, he bends down on the steps and brings his mouth close to a rivulet which in the fog shines forth with a scarlet glitter. He suckles on blood. Then a hearse passes, on it a very small enameled white coffin, an arm seizes the little boy and erases him from sight. Destination unknown—the end.

But following a bier there must be a priest, a priest's *perpetua*, Angelo murmurs. The night is full of stars, but the sky is narrow, there's no longer room for anyone, not even for the old-time phrases with the words "night" and "star." Then the sky cleanses itself for an instant of all earlier glitter, Giorgina Washington furrows through the blue night with the perfect almond of her celestial eyes like a dawn, opened and extinguished. A few piercing hours like this, without being able to blot out the visionary quality of the nerve cells of the man alone on his terrace, instigated by darkness to look in his life at everything he will never be able to see.

Today he decided to pop over . . .

Saturday.

Sunday.

Monday.

Tuesday.

Today he decided to pop over to Sirmione even though, after the tragedy of the resuscitated-drowned man of last year, he no longer likes to go there.

Here Angelo's fame began on a day many years ago when he was still working in Milan. That day he had come to the defense of a naval scullion on vacation who thought he was on the Hawaiian islands and ran around with a tiny piece of cloth between his buttocks and the father of a Bergamo family had rushed to the management of the Grotte demanding that a squad car be sent. Two carabinieri had arrived and wanted to take away the bare-ass. Angelo had jumped in and they wanted to take him away too. At that he had begun haranguing the bathers, no fewer than about seventy derelicts from the boulevard, from design, hairdressing, ballet, travel agencies, and fashion. He had yelled about the stupidity of the government financed by them, which instead of making good use of the taxes with which it was kept—the carabinieri began to look around, staring at their employers—by chasing the tax evaders so superabundant in the Bergamo area and the big-shot dealers from whom they received hefty envelopes, spent their working days worrying about uncovered buttocks and keyhole scandals. It ended up that at least a dozen of the unemployed, happy to do something, surrounded the two cops and the two reckless citizens, prevented their being taken away, and the two southerners in uniform left, dazed at realizing from what sort of dregs they had until then squeezed the wax with which they shined their shoes, so dazed and shamefaced as not to do him the kindness of asking for his identification.

The young man, the mutineer of von Gloeden, never stopped thanking his paladin and invited him to dinner, not that evening, because he couldn't, but the next day in Milan.

Angelo always gladly accepted a dinner invitation, it was a change for him who stuffed himself with sandwiches to pay for a bed in a room with two other Italian immigrants. The appointment was made, to simplify matters, in the Galleria, and he had a stroke when he saw those two amnestied buttocks sitting at a table in Motta's get up now and come to meet him bounding out of skimpy long-thighed shorts similar to a raffia skirt. He suffered impassively the embrace of a white blouse redundant with laces and embroideries of bananas and pine-apples and tiny parrots perched on palm fronds. He wore a pair of small wedgie sandals and down to the buckle from the neckline rippled a kerchief of purple silk with rhinestones. These were dangerous people, people who no longer had anything to learn and who exposed simpletons like himself to unnecessary risks, Angelo thought in a definitive way. He wished he would end his days in a ship's hold full of rats, in chains. He had brought for him, as a sign of his gratitude, a brown parchment with exotic birds on it. Thanks to the sea, he was weighing anchor that same night from Genoa. This is the sort of crap that cut short the brilliant career of a Don Quixote.

Today there is not much room between the slabs of rock that slope down to the lake. This year there have been torrential rains all through July and the water had not yet receded because the fields did not need to be watered. Many bathers must be content to lie stretched out under the olive trees because there is not enough room for everyone in the sun. Whenever Angelo comes here he has the impression of having been shut up in an open-air museum, of being held there against his will, of not having been able to reach the exit in time before the doors were closed forever.

In the middle of the lake not a single yacht.

As soon as he sees him, he experiences the same blow in the stomach, a knotted tangle of tendons liver spleen comes home to roost. Unlikely that also today he'll go and drown a bit. To approach him again, see him swallow water and terror, sink, rise, and look at him with that grin of a witch's cat he had learned last year.

He picks up his tote and, with great caution, without looking back, very attentive about setting his feet on dry ground—a couple of years ago here, slipping on the slabs, he broke his leg—climbs back over the fence under the kiosk ("Hey, this is the first time we've seen you this year!" the soda vendor yells at him) and leaves. Better the Terrazzine.

No small cheerful mouth wreathed in corkscrew curls has descended from any yacht, no small hand to deposit in his a fraternal pledge, the prize for a revenge that has hit its mark and has not been turned back against him by the last-ditch survival of dudes in white or red shorts.

In the car he had this fixed idea about lilies: today Giorgina Washington, Aurora, would be three months old. With her alive, with her irreducible presence alone, all his vendetta would have hit the mark, fitted into the bow one after the other with perfect synchronicity desire/realization. Giorgina would have been his living October Revolution, a sharpened peg driven into those masters of the normal, masterful Aryan race. A progressive revenge, constant, definitive, and never concluded, sent him by the inscrutable heaven of chromosomes to shake at its foundation, and without his or her moving a finger, the arrogant empire of one of the many czars in circulation. There was no need to have a strong arm for this sort of revenge. It was in every sense within his reach.

At the middle of last January, after Angelo, locked in Mire, Inc.'s conference room, had already coordinated schedules and geographic distances and customer availability for the nth prospecting trip in Europe, at eleven-thirty he was informed by Lometto himself that the trip was canceled and that he had been removed by a majority from the position of head of the company. Bananone had won. The new director appeared with a triumphant and more than ever brilliantined banana curl on his forehead and went straight to place himself in front of the lobby pier glass, to adjust his tie and smooth down his jacket with its thin gray and blue stripes. Lometto said goodbye to the girls as if he were going to stay away for an hour due to a contretemps of trifling significance. It seemed that everything seemed unreal because that's how he wanted it. He only said: "Give it three days and he'll be calling you names."

Sluts, that is.

Not even a month after this event Angelo went to Penzana—

famous among other things because an old Michelin guide listed a Mantegna crucifixion in the local eighteenth-century church and now famous only because Lometto resided there since in the meanwhile the crucifixion had been spirited away—to settle some phone bills and resigned at this point to discontinue his occasional services. Having entered the farmyard, he noticed immediately that next to it, indeed attached to the stable, foundations had been excavated at the height of the frost and that the workers and laborers took advantage of that sunny fog to erect walls here and continue moving the earth over there.

Since Edda was busy in the dwarf pit and Lometto was at the Town Hall, Angelo circumnavigated the area under the suspicious eyes of the bricklayers, who had never seen him and were all dying to know who he was, because he probably had the demeanor of an assessor, a troublemaker. Poor deluded creatures! Angelo had asked one of them, who looked like the foreman: "What are you doing here?"

"Ask Signor Lometto. Who are you?"

Angelo understood that there was no point in giving explanations to alarm them and went into the kitchen, encased in the warmth of his own jacket. On the desk in the office, to which he had moved to make a personal telephone call to a lady editor to find out if he has guessed the correct size of pantyhose, he found two packages wrapped in brown paper, on top of each was glued a sheet of letter paper with the heading: "DEN, Ltd.—Classic and Novelty Pantyhose," plus street, telephone, fiscal code number, Value Added Tax account; so apparently Lometto had thought well to legalize the cellar stuffed with handicapped and was beginning on his own a new activity of production and trading, after having lost control of Mire, Inc., and without wasting time, in fact getting ahead of it. Angelo thought that he recognized in this explanation a hint of Lometto's on the necessity of always knowing a few months in advance about the arrival of an amnesty, a government tax pardon. In fact, from the little Angelo knew, Penzana was categorically excluded from the production—legal, that is—of pantyhose.

Angelo continued to look out the big kitchen window in the direction of the cement mixer, which was operating, indeed almost too fast. Wonder how many gears that machine has.

Edda came in to prepare the midmorning coffee for herself, her sister-in-law and mother-in-law—Angelo could not help thinking about those smiling monster women who, through their semi-frozen nostrils, inhaled that warm aroma destined for the bellies of the three boss ladies who, every so often, on the excuse of going to the toilet, came upstairs to put their hands between the radiators' elements in the house of Lometto's sister, since all the others were turned off.

"But what is it you're building?"

"We're extending the stables" Edda said, smiling at that regional official formulation behind which Angelo could see a special low-cost loan even before her teeth were bared. "With the coming administrative elections your comrades will get their comeuppance, we will get into the driver's seat again. What's the fun of doing things on the sly when you know that they can be done just the same in broad daylight?"

The Christian Democrats had lost the previous administrative elections and Penzana was now governed by a junta of the Left.

"It's because of that assessor of public works, a tough nut, a fanatic, he probably accepts a tip from someone else to turn down ours. What a son of a . . ."

"I don't see where the stable comes in . . ."

"It comes in, it comes in. You'll see . . . Meanwhile we build the stable . . . Did you see the nice plan?"

She unfolded it for him on the dining-room table. Really a strange stable: to begin with, it had two floors. An elevator. Three toilets. A waiting room.

"I want it to be all made of travertine. White. And then we'll see who has the guts to come and tear it down!" she said, going to turn off the gas flame under the coffeepot. "Did you see the new letterhead?"

She ran to get it. *Den*, thought Angelo: undoubtedly working for it was the same as attracting the evil eye for the whole year.

"Do you know what it means?" She had a certain penchant for intrigues.

"Distributions . . ."

"Edda Napaglia. The firm is in my name. Do you like the paper?"

"I like the idea. About the den, the denizens."

But Angelo was thinking about something else, not so much about the fact that almost all the possessions of this side of the Lometto family were in her name and that she was an all-purpose *woman of straw*: he kept looking impatiently at the drawer of the kitchen table, who knows whether Edda would open it, whether it had become a habit, especially in his presence. There was something so crazy about her, in the sudden wrinkling of her brow, making the black of her eyes rise from inside the bags as it were, like suns of incandescent pitch within the white teeming with the red worms of broken capillaries. The light in them flickered on and off like a neon sign announcing vendetta. "I would really like to have another male . . ."

"What do you mean another male? You mean another child."

"No, no. Male. And I have an idea about it . . . But it is still too soon."

"An idea about what?"

"About that one" she sighed, as usual both serious and facetious "he could even make him a President of the Republic."

"And why not a female?"

Angelo followed the hand spoiled by dishes and moving cartons as it pushed through a hundred automatic gestures toward the most violent, clutching the handle and pulling out the drawer. She turned her back and over the kitchen sink she swallowed.

"Females! Me, if I'm born again I want to be male. Just look at inheritance: my father is leaving me only twenty percent of his business, because that is our custom. My brother gets the rest. And he also got to study."

To Angelo these seemed sacrosanct reasons but in Edda they were only the mnemonic part of the last lesson she had received from her husband, who did not care in the least whether she had gotten to study or not, just the opposite. A conclusion arrived at without great difficulty was that, at any rate, Edda by now was making constant use of the "pick-me-up."

The end of that February was very dry, a great number of building sites sprang up along the provincial highway to Mantua, everyone was in a great hurry to build, as if they had all been informed in advance of a new pardon for building violations and did not want to risk not receiving that supreme act of grace from a government resigned to everything because of the ballot boxes.

There was a large, creamy sun which took the frost off the cranes and the beards of the bricklayers. Spring must be forced, not only in the strawberry hothouses but also between brick and brick, between roof tile and roof tile, and, in view of Lometto's resistance to making another son, between spermatozoon and spermatozoon. Everything was coerced at the end of winter, torn with brute strength from an adolescent earth, from a still awkward and torpid general situation. It was with this sensation, in the middle of March, that Angelo turned into the small dirt road that led to Lometto's farm: now one no longer bounced between holes and puddles, there was an affinity between the convexed flatness of that whipped-cream sun and the roadbed covered by a most beautiful, still very black layer of tar. He was immediately told everything.

Lometto, to challenge those who had put obstacles in the way of his project for a new pantyhose factory in the area—with loans from the Agricultural Department and without the authorization by Industry—had dared what could not be dared: at the expense not only of the junta but of the entire commune of Penzana.

The Communist surveyor of the small commune with its two thousand five hundred inhabitants—so rich as to have almost all services neither more nor less than Toigo—this assessor of public works, a sworn enemy of Lometto's, had instructed a firm which worked under the aegis of the province to come and lay down asphalt on Penzana's three main streets. The firm, subsidized by the state as regards both machinery and the supply of already prepared tar—a few kilometers away—was composed of three workers and a kind of foreman. The province had granted three working days plus truck and roller and all the necessary cubic meters of tar plus a small excess over the applied-for length and volume.

Now Lometto, who for the first time in his life was not part of the junta—that is, the first in the last twenty years—had the imposing presence of a neo-realist mayor and knew how to inspire fear with the simple suggestion of propping his hands on his hips. Around ten o'clock in the morning of the first day of work, when operations had already begun with the first truckful of tar poured onto the entrance near the arcades, up there, near the registrar's office and the church with a small cemetery next to it—almost completely abandoned today because everybody goes to Toigo—Lometto had shown up and placed one foot on the first step of the churchyard.

As happens in such cases of public works, once vague instructions have been imparted over the phone, nobody any longer takes an interest because nobody knows who exactly should take an interest and, the weather being fine, the assessor's yes-men and the two firemen were even more irresistibly drawn to the wood stoves or fishing for catfish in the small adjacent lake.

Then Lometto had lifted his foot and headed for the arcade, a few steps away, where the commune's offices were, and from there he had waved to the foreman. It must have been a gesture of such unbounded suggestion that the man had raised his cap and made his deductions unaided: "Good morning, Mr. Mayor. So this is where we start."

"Yes, do this stretch up to the gate of the cemetery" said the distinguished gentleman with the fake marmoset overcoat collar "and then follow me."

Lometto must have had a lot of respect for this Don Galetta, in whom Interpol had also taken an interest in the past because of the theft of the crucifixion—Lometto had said this in passing, laughing to himself, as if it were some harmless nonsense invented on the spot to add color to the priest. According to Edda, however, because of the slights he inflicted on her regarding the first-row pew in church, "he did not deserve even that much tar."

"But aren't we supposed to continue down this way?" the tar man had said.

"There's a small change, you have to finish the large square and immediately begin work on the other road past the houses. Anyway, come with me right now and I'll show you."

Taking a short ride in the Mercedes, the foreman had gone with that very affable and authoritative gentleman, they had turned in skirting the "kindergarten" building on Lometto's Private Road (Lometto's and Den, Ltd.'s, of course). An hour later, having left behind sufficient traces of their passage in the middle of town so that no one should doubt that they had begun and would also continue there, roller and tar spreader were directed toward the dirt road and the tar truck was waved ahead to go all the way down there, no, after the farmhouse, not there, farther down, to the right—there was a subsidiary stable there—then turn to the left and unload in front of the manure heap, where the path broke off. That afternoon and all the next day and the morning of the third day, paths, little paths, little bridges, the farm's small inner road, everything was tarred with great care, under the amiable eye of that man "who must also suffer from the cold, standing there watching," as the foreman told him, what a humane mayor, sending a woman morning and afternoon with a bottle of Amarone!

So the roads of public concern still had their old winter pockmarks, and Via Privata—which had now become the obligatory artery for the loading and unloading of Den, Ltd.—was beautifully polished and smooth, with all its zigzags, in and out of the fields, drawn with precision, with those petulant finishing touches possible only when something is for free. Only late in the evening, in the fog, when the small group of workers reported to the commune's offices to announce they had finished and before leaving wished to thank the mayor for all his attentions and salami sandwiches, the assessor rose up from his chair and rushed to see Lometto, his hands now in his pockets now in his hair now up in the air, as if he were learning his part in the imminent "Christian Democraxi" drama. There in the farmyard, where one couldn't see the end of one's nose, threats of lawsuits flew about and that he would have to pay for that prank ten times over. But apparently Lometto only said that if he were in his place he would not do so and the assessor opened his mouth wide for an nth time but nothing came out of it. Then the real mayor arrived, a very rich Communist who was a peddler and knew how to barter and barter himself, and he tried to convince Lometto to pay what he owed to the commune's coffers, not one lira more nor one less—that is, with a net fifty percent profit over the actual cost of the service rendered by the province to a private citizen. Lometto willingly agreed to pay, because that's what the law said, and declared himself ready to pay five percent, actually let's make it ten, of twenty million over four years, because one must not set a bad example. In the end mayor and assessor decided to be satisfied with being amazed and they themselves put a lot of tar on top of the affair to immediately stop it from spreading.

"Mine are roads too, aren't they?" Lometto had ended his tale, staring at Angelo and licking his imaginary whiskers till they almost fell out. Then, after having bent every one to his arrogance—a true and proper test of strength, according to universal morality—when no one expected anything in exchange, he had sent here a gold pen ("not all gold, the nib"), there a year's subscription to *Famiglia Christiana* for the wife, a round of grana cheese to one councilman, a demijohn of Chianti (local) to another, a ham (boiled). Nothing was ever, out of contempt, returned to the sender. Not that Angelo thought those people were so naïve as to enjoy sinking their teeth into these wholesale delicacies: probably they had all concluded that sending them back would have been even worse. They let themselves be corrupted by so little out of despair, exactly. And besides, Angelo did not even believe that Lometto had the time to differentiate between the gifts he boasted he had made, was making. He could have sworn that what was involved was the standard box of three bottles of stuttering champagne, Jasmine Belart brand—by the way: how many times was she Veuve?

• • •

Today Armando is farther down than usual. Is he alone? Angelo can't see exactly, it seems he is. He begins to walk in his direction, Armando is looking toward him and does not seem to recognize him. So then in full light one can have the same optical illusions as in full darkness.

He goes past the villa and the ashes of the bonfire, always in the same spot; it's probably lit at the first light of dawn or late at night, some solitary romantic who cannot tolerate the sight of water without associating it with fire. Millions of dry tellins crumble under his gym shoes, mini liquor bottles, the carcass of a rat at least thirty centimeters long. Now he sees two tiny white legs rise from behind Armando's back and no head. He's with his son, Angelo thinks, here we go, the structuralist worries begin.

Instead it's a little blond, pale man peeking from behind the bearded neck of this two-headed creature. He's embarrassed, he didn't want to be a spoilsport or seem curious.

"*Ciao*, I did not mean to disturb, I didn't see you had company."

"Sit down, I want to introduce my friend from Rome."

Angelo introduces himself without reaching out his hand. He is not interested in touching that lemon-colored little body, so effeminate and disdainful, which from the first moment has looked at him with a superior air.

"Don't I know you, haven't I seen you somewhere?" Angelo says, just to say something, ready to leave them alone again.

"He's an actor, he works for television" Armando prompts.

"I don't think I ever saw you" says the little blondie with the tiny wrinkles of a little old lady announcer, with a well-placed voice and an affected manner.

"Oh, I didn't mean commercials, I meant in some railroad station turning tricks. After all, it's a small railroad. Well, goodbye to you."

Angelo knows he had a disturbing effect on the couple, for they remained speechless, but he did not intend to spoil anyone's afternoon, much less his own. He could have phoned him, offered him that intimacy, but no, he settles down even farther away than usual with someone displaying all the symptoms of hysteria, ready to run wild. How close they were, they might even be embracing. He must go somewhere else to hate right away.

"I'll join you in a little while, all right?" Armando shouts.

Angelo twists his mouth inside, profoundly disgusted, it's the usual thing of having your cake and eating it, the fear of losing something.

"It's up to you. We can meet past the villa when you're ready" Angelo answers without turning.

But he goes beyond the villa and reaches the central section of the Terrazzine and then even farther down, mumbling hellos between clenched teeth. He takes the towel from his tote bag and for about three hours sends curses to all Armandos full of promises and devoid of substance.

Now Magra dei Veleni is singing something from *Francesca da Rimini*, so they say, but she clearly can't handle it. Tonight many of them are going to the Arena in Verona, that's why they're leaving so early.

Angelo gets up and walks to the path below the farthest point of the escarpment; it is so long since he last set foot in the camboge copse above the highway. After he reaches the top of the first rise he turns and sees that the hairy man, Pinuccia's brother, is following him and attempts an uncertain, crooked smile. What a beautiful man, a pity he's a brother.

Angelo quickens his step as he ascends, he does not want to stop with him. There is this fantasy of finding at last a corpse among the thickets of the undergrowth which accompanies him like a conditioned reflex. With his eyes he searches down the incline, in among the tall grass and the bushes: nothing today either.

If Armando had really had the intention or desire of seeing him, if his encounter with the little dolly had been accidental, he would have brought along the photographs to show him and would have insisted on his staying, would not have let him leave like that. Instead, he had not brought the photographs and had forgotten all about him. Angelo knows now that he's being followed, he turns into a path that leads to the top of the hill, he can't wait to slip out of the wood and make it clear to the "brother" that he mustn't get out of breath for him. And he does not want to offend him or hurt his feelings; how can he make him understand that, under different circumstances, in a meeting of speleologists, in the most remote caves of the Gargnano, for example, he would really have liked to pick him out with his flashlight from the surrounding darkness and discover that he, a total stranger, was *he* and nobody else? But like this, to be pursued in a copse at his age by a friend with a receding hairline and a paunch and a brother down on the beach, he feels he is under the surveillance of twenty years' worth of gourmet dishes that peep out here and there amid the fronds, by the lullabies of when outside it rains and the wind blows and inside in the fireplace burn the logs of life *à deux*, the hysterical solicitude of cohabitation between males, the fear that everything lacks salt, or is overdone. One ought to make love also with everything that one doesn't see and which clings by the very fact of breathing. It is preferable to switch off the flashlight at a depth of one thousand meters, close one's eyes, and hope it's not a dinosaur.

Angelo descends again on the opposite side of the hill, lengthens his stride whenever someone stops—runs to his car, after having elegantly shaken off the brother/lover, and starts the motor.

Sunday he sleeps, so to speak.

Monday he goes to Milan by train to hand in the translation at the publisher's. As always, he must look for an excuse to justify the sudden absence of pantyhose, which here are called collants, with a nasal sound. They all think that no longer giving these presents is just another one of his bright ideas and that, in any case, he had always bought them at the notions store on the corner. The tax on royalties has increased, that's all he needed. The promised advance, he points out, never arrived. A check in accounting: what do you mean, of course it did, it's because of the banks, they too must skim something off his miserable earnings.

In the evening, at home, he draws the curtains in his room, lies down on the bed, listens to the buzz of mosquitoes ready for the nocturnal attack, manages to concentrate only after a long time. It is the presence in the other room that disturbs him. For her a man who has not made children is someone who has come into the world for nothing. Through the wall obsessively penetrates this mute unstoppable gabble of a woman who has given birth in pain *for nothing*.

No more Terrazzine, he does not want to see Armando ever again—nor the hairy "brother," the evoker of virility and woolen slippers for whom he feels a growing attraction. He halted immobile among the locusts of the first knoll, Saturday, watching Angelo start the car, and did not dare make the slightest gesture to him, while Bombarola, out of breath, ran after him and asked him for a match. From him, in a bathing suit.

In the evening the phone rings.

"Angelo?"

"Yes."

"*Ciao*, it's Armando. I looked for you all day. Was that your mother?" The voice is rich and self-satisfied. Angelo, by instinct, answers in dialect, to put him straight.

"I've been out all day, I went to . . ." But where is it he went? He doesn't remember. "Oh yes, I went to Milan for work."

"I wanted to tell you that there's nothing between me and that actor. Why did you disappear Saturday? I couldn't find you."

"You most likely didn't look carefully. And I got up on the wrong side. And what do I care, what there is or isn't with that guy? It's just that with me you've got to watch your step."

"You're right. What a relief to hear you."

How strange, there's not a single word that confirms his behavior. Apparently he likes to express himself this way, above the lines.

"Are you coming to the lake Thursday?" Armando asks. Today is Monday, why only Thursday?

"If the sun's out, yes. If it's not . . ." But Angelo would like to ask: And if it's not and I don't come, what are you willing to do?

"It will be, you'll see. Try to come. I want to talk to you. I knew that business bothered you. I'll bring the photographs. I'm sure you'll find them interesting. Do you like children?"

"In what way?"

"Oh, in general."

"In general, yes."

If it were up to him, all photographers would starve to death, you can bet on that, and also those who sing or paint or write or make films or act. Forever there in a perennial darkroom, on canvas, on a stage, a tape recorder, a printed book, and from there they always believe that the world owes them something . . . A tape recorder . . . At the crucial moment Edda had cried out.

"O Ilario, O Belisario, O Berengario!" It was so difficult to understand it, even from the reel, listened to only once because of the duplicates, and then put away together with that obscene lump of money. Southern interjections are always so ambivalent, always mean so many things all at the same time, if you're not from those parts for two thousand years at least you don't catch all the nuances of everything they acutely encompass and of all the rest they so gravely exclude.

". . . bothered? I found it repulsive. There was such complicity between the two of you, I looked like a dried fish in a store window full of sweets. How could I suspect that besides the wife, the pizzeria, the kid's vacation, etc., I also had to stand in line because of a little dolly with teeny white legs. Disgusting!"

"You're right. I'm sorry."

Armando said he was right because that's not the point, he thinks, mortified.

"Thursday at what time?"

"Quarter past one. She's about to leave, we're almost there. I must stay with them. Then tidy up the house, the mess of the packing. We'll be alone."

Yes, and he might even bring home salted sardines to clean, or three thousand portraits of naked children to study in "solitude"! Armando has definitely not understood a thing, he believes that it is absolutely necessary to prepare a frame—the bed, whiskey within reach, musical background, a photographer's studio with spotlights in the right place, the typical good taste of someone with a completely posterior conception of modesty. The thought of entering his house and finding himself, by tragic fatality, smack in the middle of a wedding day or first communion poster turns his stomach. And perhaps all the walls are papered with particularly successful souvenirs. How can he make him understand that he prefers the static stimulation of a meadow or a pebbly riverbank or the bark of a tree, if possible without carved hearts?

"All right, Thursday then. And thanks for calling me. If it rains, I'll drop by the pizzeria sooner or later."

"Sooner."

On the first of April this year psychosomatic leukemia has put an end to Jürgen, his body, which was becoming a wave of evaporated water. He has died for the idea of a caress which, since it could not be *true*, had become *ideal*. Because all that Jürgen wanted from this surgeon friend of his was a caress, and it did not come. He had died for the idea of a caress. Yes, various utensils were stuffed up him, and ever new ones and in great quantities, but that was not exactly what he had in mind, he who was an incurable decadent romantic. He expected that after the routine of the vibrators this caress, once his lover—by dint of using them—had worn out his militaristic sexual ghosts, would have come to make him happy forever, to reward him. But that wasn't happening. And year after year the desire for a caress—

for which he had denied or given up everything in his personality which did not please his lover—had been replaced by the idea of the caress, the fatal compromise with a hostile reality which little by little had hollowed him out, breaking down the last defenses of his organism already auto-undermined for so long out of gallantry and always resurrected by a miracle. Jürgen had died because of the most horrible adjustment of sentiment when, unlived, it becomes sentimentality—that is, the idea of the sentiment that *must* come, that will come *tomorrow* when compliance with his friend would be as perfect as that of a dog with his owner and there would no longer be any diaphragm, any exorcism to rise between him and this friend of his taken in the heat of "pure instinctiveness" which foresees, strangely, the subjection of one of the two partners. When Angelo, in February, sent him the German translation of letter 81 from *Les Liaisons dangereuses*—from the Marquise de Merteuil to the Vicomte de Valmont—and, in the middle of March, Jürgen had still not recovered, he understood that it was hopeless and that where literature fails not even life-force therapy can succeed. Jürgen's brain had begun to leak and so had his veins and his bones, and it was useless, indeed outrageous for Jürgen to telephone his lover and suggest to him what he had not understood by himself, and Angelo could not betray the secret Jürgen had confided in him, the opprobrious secret of his trivial sentimentalism. In fact, even in March, the surgeon had continued to propose to him ersatz caresses: of rubber, of polystyrene. Jürgen would have liked to hear him say, "I love you," perhaps while a hand touched his cheek and not his buttock, and this idea obsessed him, and the more it obsessed him, the more he became willfully obtuse in the matter, pushing his lover always further from such an expression of love, words and gestures so typical of a lost century and among *species* by now extinct. This Jürgen had admitted to Angelo and for the first time Angelo had seen him blush. And he must have died while inside him grew this desire which no one except Angelo, in that swamp of plastic and leather pricks and pins threaded through nipples, knew, died without ever having fulfilled it, died for having transformed it into an increasingly abstract idea increasingly cut off from those fingertips which held its realization. Certainly to die for the idea of a caress is the highest fulfillment, just as continuing to live for the idea of an idea without realizing it.

Swimming.

Oh, if one could only stop embracing fossil men in the dark, in the full light of one's salt caverns.

Angelo looks around. If he were sure of being alone he would start to scream. He comes out of the water, dresses in a hurry, gets into his car, and wanders through a couple of spots that he thinks are isolated, his vocal cords already vibrating in the imminence of his outburst. But there are picnics everywhere tonight which definitely look as though they're going to last until midnight. Like evening meals on the grass given by Pasqua, the sister of Gino and her husband, she always newly pregnant, and each time an interruption or the nth small coffin on the third day of life. She too ashes, by now. Ashes Jürgen. Ashes Giorgina Washington, and the special ashes that sit behind the steering wheel and have prompt reflexes.

Still in April—but last year—there began to be talk about the need to make a trip in order to introduce Den, Ltd., officially, and that it was necessary—by the end of May—to reach Oslo and then from there go over all the prospects again on the way back. Angelo, after that funeral, had become a more serene orphan.

Since Lometto wanted to economize, he refused to go by plane on the way out and come back by train, stage by stage. At the same time, however, he wanted to do things in a hurry because time is money. There were always these dashes against space coming into conflict with time which clashed with money and the whole thing collided with Angelo, who had to reconcile the various empirico-philosophical reluctances with Lometto's purely practical desires. The upshot was always definitive in relation to the precariousness of all parts with one another. That is: one was always at the point of departure.

Angelo refused to go by car—Lometto was perfectly capable, as on other occasions, of making it a single haul all the way to Copenhagen, every two hundred kilometers saying, "Come on, come on, another fifty and then we'll stop to sleep, what's fifty more or less," then they would stop to sleep, to piss, to stretch their legs. No, not by car. And the time had also come to change the conditions of their trips.

Meanwhile Angelo received an offer from Jeff Sayre for a tentative early-winter collection before final bankruptcy, and since Lometto wouldn't make up his mind and the dates coincided, Angelo left for Paris without even warning him but leaving an address with Edda.

Lometto phoned ten minutes after he set foot in the office and told him there was a change, a number of customers must be seen first in Belgium, in Brussels and Charleroi, then he must go on all the way to Dortmund and then to Berlin. And then Oslo. By car? Angelo asked, already injecting the rumble of refusal. We'll see what's more convenient. We'll see, my ass, you won't get me to go all the way to Oslo by car. Et cetera.

Just as he was about to leave, Lometto was seized by driver's block: he complained about having to make the trip alone, that this was not correct behavior on Angelo's part. Well, you don't expect me to return all the way from Paris just to pick you up! Why, what would be so strange about that? But you really have something missing up there. But what will I say to customs, how can they understand me? What about all the others who don't know the first thing about foreign languages? They show their documents and go through, you don't have to tell them the story of your life in the army. And what if they take off my mudguards like that other time? Now listen, Lometto, it's your problem, since you don't pay me on the way out you might as well take the trip by yourself, even if I was over there. But no, he protested, I pay you on the way out, it's for the return trip I don't pay you. Whereas if you go to the station right now and catch the first train to Brescia . . .

With quibbles and demands of this kind Lometto could consume hours even on the phone—he kept on and on endlessly, so that Angelo sometimes thought that he was not the one who paid the phone bill or that he had tampered with the lines, because he certainly liked to use the phone. Not like Angelo, who, faced by the Paris dilemma, had used up only five units to establish the fact that for him too "time is money." This was the only way to gain respect in the working world: tell them to go take a crap and pass on to other shithouses, without flushing.

Without compromising his stands—the meeting in Brussels, the commitment to fly to Oslo at least from Copenhagen—he tried to come up with something to meet Lometto and his excessive hesitation about driving alone halfway. Angelo knew that in order to have a decent trip by car from Penzana to Brussels they had to leave on Saturday, sleep over in Frankfurt or even sooner, in Heidelberg if it were up to him, leave again at their leisure Sunday morning, or not leave from Penzana on Sunday. Lometto came up with a thousand excuses to remain in the warmth of his *Aryan* nest until the last possible moment and then kill himself and others with hauls of one thousand five hundred kilometers by night, save on hotels, on food, on paydays. And there never was an accident to teach him a lesson. Angelo now felt all the more responsible, strange to say, fearing that Lometto, alone, falling asleep at the wheel, would indeed have that accident, but a real bad one. And here was Lometto calling him again on Friday to complain that he should return to Italy so they could take the trip together, that he would have him on his conscience if anything happened to him. And Angelo called Demetrio.

So that Lometto would pay for hotel and meals for Demetrio, Angelo told him that Demetrio would even wear a peaked cap, but wanted fifty thousand a day plus expenses, a mere nothing and only because he was a friend of his.

"Even if I have to drive with my eyes blindfolded or propped open by toothpicks, no!" Lometto answered. The usual discussions. Fifty thousand wasn't anything for this sort of inconvenience, leaving a whole post office in the hands of . . . NO. So stop bothering me, look, as far as I'm concerned don't take the trip, I'm not going to travel eleven hours by train to pick up his lordship. Really? No, you'll have to manage, you should have thought of it before, if the trip was postponed it's your fault, I would not have come here to Paris if you'd stuck to the plan. After three or four phone calls of this kind, Lometto, on his own, went so far as to offer, huffing and puffing, that at the very most he would give him meals and a bed.

And so Lometto, relieved by this no longer solitary drive and Demetrio enthusiastic, set off for Brussels. On Sunday afternoon, late.

The two did not hit it off, they drove and drove and drove without finding a single subject or conversation throughout the hundreds upon hundreds of kilometers.

Angelo found them collapsed on the beds in the room he had booked, annihilated by reciprocal boredom, unable to get out a word, their faces contorted and purplish, Lometto in undershorts snoring with his eyes open, Demetrio fully dressed, his arms twined around that tiny aged adolescent's body of his, his little face contracted into a fist of damp little wrinkles and resigned humility. They managed to confirm that they had stopped "only to go." And to eat; so that's why Demetrio was clutching his belly, trying not to show that he felt "a bit sick." Indigestion from hard-boiled eggs, he rarely ate them. Lometto, with his usual joviality, had convinced him to gulp down ten of them. As many as Demetrio ate in an entire year.

Demetrio had not put up any resistance, he'd eaten them, if a person eats anything it's because he likes it, or else why would he? It was his problem if he felt sick now. Had he complained? No, so what's his gripe now? All this in a whisper, while Lometto was shitting on the bowl and Demetrio next door writhed on his little bed. He only said "He'll get over it, it's not serious." Angelo burst out laughing, not out of sadism, he was thinking about completely different eggs.

Lometto got up, his arms dangling, and said, covering his voice with the gush of the water:

"Listen, couldn't we ship him home?"

"Look" Angelo said in a slightly louder voice, making it clear that he was ready to get even louder. "He goes back, I go back. I'm not about to look like a shit for your sake, and besides, remember: he's a friend of mine, before I ever knew you, get it? So don't you dare bring it up again."

Angelo had completely broken with Tirlindana because he had been unacceptably rude with Gino, who at the beginning of April had accompanied him to the Versilia and Tirlindana, seeing him at the gate, had not let him in and, pulling Angelo aside, had said to him, "Leave him by the door, God forbid, don't let him in, he's bad luck. Look at the face on him! You mustn't be seen with him anymore, you'll contaminate me too with the evil eye."

"He isn't worth the air he breathes, do you realize?" Lometto whispered as they went downstairs to see whether the pantry could get them some coffee at that hour, which was neither night nor day nor dawn.

"But what do you want him to be worth, what do you want him to be worth, let's hear. He did you a favor, he made it possible for you to stay a day longer with your wife and your boys. He's driven you for fourteen hours at an average speed of one hundred and fifty, fitting in a piss and a gulletful of eggs, he's lying there, broken in two, and now, since you've made it here and you've achieved your goal and now you have no more use for him, you would like . . . Stop all this, you're disgusting."

Lometto got on his high horse, in the deserted lobby their sentences became formal, as if between strangers. Lometto said only:

"One can't trust you, you always want to do things your way. Trust me, let's get rid of him. He's bad luck."

"Oh no! You too! Let's change the subject, actually go to sleep. You have three hours left before the first appointment."

"I'm not tired. I'm not a softie like you."

"Suit yourself."

Lometto spread his legs wide on the rug, and let his elbows fall limp on the armrest, prepared to stay there until he managed to convince Angelo to wrap Demetrio, tie him up, and deliver him to a Belgian post office. Angelo was thinking about the favor Tirlindana had done him by helping him get rid of Gino! But that was not the way to behave. Now Angelo, with cautious malice, just as he had done with Tirlindana's abnormal speciousness, tried in silence to grant a few sacrosanct reasons to Lometto too, to see whether there was any possibility at all of justifying his deep antipathy for Demetrio and sending him off to hell, that is, back to Italy. Angelo in a flash succeeded so well that he was ashamed of it. To punish himself, he resumed defending his cause and Demetrio's by bringing up examples of friendship beautiful enough to be framed, examples not about Demetrio himself—he did not want to put Lometto on the qui vive—but about Gino, just as characterless, ballbreaking, and faithful as this one here. In the lobby arrived the first metallic sounds of the awakening hotel, cups and dishes softly clashing during the preparations for *petit déjeuner*. Lometto, who drinks in every one of Angelo's words and refreshes himself from the direct source of that Neapolitan coffeepot which blends poisonous aromas and incredible apotheoses of the friendship of friends *like that*—Imer, Gino, Demetrio, people who sucked your marrow without ever losing that air of sacrificial cherubs, renouncers, resigned to the best of the worst. How good it had been for him too, going to Paris or away with Lometto, taking a work-vacation far from them, who enveloped his existence like flypaper, and from Gino in particular because he was the most assiduous, the most obstinate, the most "enamored," and came to his university apartments with crates of fruit, and vegetables, heavens! when Angelo perhaps might or might not have been interested in a kilo of oranges, two grapefruits, a few tangerines. And Angelo was unable to get his point across, to convince him in a nice way to restrain his horticultural expansiveness. And how was his mother, was she taking her insulin regularly? and his sister, was she practicing new scales on that tuba there, what's it called, oh yes, the Fallopian? In short, impossible to even get near him by now, Angelo saw diabetic placentas everywhere.

And Lometto now was commenting: "What about this bucket of coffee, how long do we have to wait? . . . Come on, let's ship him back . . ."

Angelo pretended he did not hear and continued on about Gino, soothing Lometto with a fifth glass of freshly squeezed orange juice.

. . . and, on returning to Verona from the Versilia, because of Tirlindana's inconsiderate act, all the insults that Angelo had taken from Gino for years had been completely forgotten, and it was again he who owed apologies to the persecutor. Who took advantage of it to ask him immediately to go with him to Greece the next morning by car. Angelo protested. All of a sudden he had caught an extra nuance in Gino's behavior, a light of madness that pulsed in his gray eyes. There he was, gorillaesque and hairy, with that mellifluous perspiration of his, that turkey or chicken farm exudation. He held his gaze askew, like a madman absorbed in meditation, he fiddled with a small knife long and sharp beyond words and the way he cut that melon—Zionist of course: in April—so slowly, more slowly than necessary . . . did it smack of "forewarned is forearmed"? Angelo did not want trouble, he accepted the Greek shafting. He sent Edda an incitement to parthenogenesis.

"But then that postcard . . . with the marble prick . . . and in the back written: 'Do it by yourself!' . . . without a signature . . ." Lometto said, fulminating him after being fulminated in turn by the revelation.

. . . he was so upset, and now it was he who felt like inflicting harm, like killing Gino and making an end of it in a lake of melon rinds. But where would he get with his watermelons? Certainly he would get to the gay wedding in Amsterdam, and then again here, at the mayor's, and then later on he would present appeals to the Vatican Court indulging in offers of lentils and plenary fava beans. Angelo made the trip all the way to Brindisi outraged, as though he had been forced to show himself in the streets in a dress of white furbelows, with pannier and many little bows on the hips. The railroad vegetable vendors did not stop at anything, their trade called for burrowing at one hundred and twenty kilometers an hour into the darkness of a tunnel munching on an apple. All that was left to him now was to get his doctorate in escape/research. Angelo explained to Lometto that

Gino was like a chick which, hatched by a bitch, had mistaken her for its mother and could not resign itself to leaving her and not learning how to bark. He was an all-purpose mother, precisely.

"That is, a bitch" Lometto remarked. "And then?"

Sometimes Angelo returned to Verona and, since no one in his absence had been so free as to take advantage of it, fruit and vegetables lay rotten on his balcony. But Gino didn't care, the essential was that his presence should manifest itself in all its stench from the very first instant that Angelo set foot in the house. Was it clear now why he could not allow such an appropriate gesture as Tirlindana's to free him from a tie of this kind? And why for four days he could not be found at Verona or at home? Because there wasn't a shorter path to get rid of him than going with him to Greece! That's how it was, period. He wouldn't let anyone treat his friends badly, to be the cause of his immediate break with them. Same thing with Demetrio. Was that clear?

"But he doesn't even give you potatoes, that would be different. Certainly with the price of vegetables . . . Come on, let's load him on the train."

Angelo had risen from the table and thrown his napkin in Lometto's face and gone outside into the fresh air. But not even this act stopped Lometto, who pursued him now among the parched flower beds and swore that nobody had ever thrown a paper napkin into his face.

The next morning, just as they were leaving the hotel, while Demetrio was doing his apprenticeship in his new role as personal porter, Lometto started again: "Listen, before it's too late, since we must pull up our anchors here . . . Why are we dragging him along? We can't even chat with each other. I've got a project here, something my father asked me to do. But you mustn't laugh, you hear?"

"No. Demetrio stays. You're wrong, with Demetrio present we can talk about everything."

"Come, let's take him to the station . . ."

"I'm not a petty louse like you and Demetrio isn't a petty louse like you either. The sooner you drop it, the better. What's this project about? A mausoleum?"

"A family chapel. What do you mean, mouse-oleum?"

"The same thing, more or less."

"How did you know?" Lometto asked, worried.

"Like that. You know I can read your thoughts, don't you?"

". . ."

"Now don't make that face, it's a coincidence. Are you planning to inaugurate it yourself?"

"You wish! You're going to die before me, my fairy godmother . . ."

"Provided you stop breaking my balls with this business of sending back a small postal parcel after having opened it. First he wants to enjoy his Saturday and Sunday mornings at home playing the satrap . . . Satrap is a kind of . . ."—the explanation followed—"then he drives me crazy asking me to inconvenience a government employee to whom he doesn't give a lira, and now he finds the cost of a mattress and a brioche too much to handle. You really are some shit of a sock maker from way back. The family cell! Now we know what the neo-rich waste their money on!"

Incredible, but Lometto did not know the meaning of neo-rich.

"Look here, the shit with the neo has got to be you. And I won't even let you see it . . . A bargain . . . You know what a square meter in that cemetery costs? Come on, give me a figure . . . We'll pay for his train ticket, half each, we can even afford to send him first-class. We'll even look classy . . . You've got some friends!"

"Look, Lometto, if it comes to that, as a friend a thousand times Demetrio rather than you" Angelo lied. "My fingers are itching, this is the time I'll flatten you like a dried cod. How dare you, people aren't at your service, they aren't Kleenex!"

This was a sentence that had been flung at Angelo many times, but they are Kleenex, Angelo thought, and they like it. Then one day they will all get together and unroll in a procession. A procession of Kleenex. Used.

Demetrio realized that something was wrong, and he maintained a low profile, kept busy as best he could, carrying suitcases and jackets and shoes in his hands, still with that look of acute indigestion. He was so clumsy in everything, so jerky, so tense that he became confused, stumbled, apologized without cause, took ages, couldn't even lift Angelo's suitcase, full of jackets, sweaters, and slacks brought from Paris. They left for Dortmund and there it was discovered that they had an extra suitcase in the trunk, put there, Angelo remembered quite well, by Lometto. Angelo said, never mind—he wanted to excuse Demetrio's carelessness; he obviously had grabbed and dragged along at random whatever was in the lobby—we'll send it to the owner COD. Lometto, for the first time, had a smile for Demetrio. All the clothes were size 60, large extra-large. Lometto looked at Angelo with his head tilted a bit to one side, his eyes beseeching. A tortoiseshell toilet set. Perfumes, colognes, silk ties, Italian wool jackets, a double-breasted between-season gabardine suit that looked as though it had been sewn on him it fit him so perfectly. Angelo turned his head away several times, shaking it. They continued on to Berlin. Lometto's cheerfulness toward Demetrio lasted exactly the time it took to call him a thief and try on all the clothes—that is, one day and one night. Then Lometto closed up again, as though authorized by a majestic elegance which required a contemptuous though polite tone with the help. Demetrio became even more downcast, more befuddled . . . and yet he never opened his mouth in the boss's presence—and he sat there in the back like a stowaway on board. Although Angelo talked to him, he emitted his little cackling laugh and remained silent, and then, the wretch, twice he dared insist, saying that he definitely did not remember taking that suitcase, what a careless cuss. Lometto sighed and said that he had run the risk of being terribly embarrassed . . .

The evening they arrived in Berlin, they left Lometto to his calculations and walked to a nightclub, and Angelo kept reassuring him, telling him that now the fun would begin and that it was a great convenience, for the modest price of a beer, to run into hundreds of men who took turns in the hop cask set up for the purpose. Demetrio was being particular, shook his tiny head and hee-hawed, incredulous at the thought of bellyfuls of famous cocks of anonymous males. Demetrio still managed to blush at Angelo's choice of words, he was shocked with delight, spoke about God and, still not having digested the drive, about the Dantesque "great circles." But there really was something that troubled him, it was clear that he was pawing the ground to shake off a yoke.

"But didn't you talk about anything, anything all through the trip?" Angelo tried to draw him out.

"No, nothing. You know, concentrating . . ." And Demetrio was so laconic by nature that he did not feel like describing what kind of *nothing* had not been said.

"Listen, you little plaster saint, you can't always be so passive, wait to be spoon-fed, people get tired of it. You're always the princess on the pea who waits to be awakened by a bean. Snap out of it this time. Lometto is terribly stingy, you must at least give him the impression you exist. Don't be so tense, he won't bite you."

"No, that's not it, it's that . . . oh, forget it."

"What?"

Angelo immediately caught on, something incalculable must have happened between the two of them, either during the trip or as soon as they got into the hotel room.

"Come on, let's hear. I can tell already anyway."

". . . without even bothering what I . . . that I am your friend . . . there, in his underwear. He starts to . . . at two feet from my face . . ."

". . . all the while talking about this and that, right?"

"Yes-s, who could have imagined, but it was hot in Belgium too. I pretended that I didn't see anything and turned to the other side. Then you arrived."

He hadn't even locked the door, because there's no need to lock the door just to take an aspirin for a headache. He looked at the small live ball bobbing on the jet of air.

"Don't take it to heart, he'd do the same also with a dog, after throwing him a bone. But with somebody he doesn't know . . . completely irresponsible! But not because he likes you, only to find out whether, just like with the eggs, you would have the gall to refuse. Or he saw in you a cock eater, some blessed bitch who pounces on everything that's the right shape. Gums free of charge."

"But he . . ."

"Not at all, he likes . . . he would like women if they didn't cost money. It's not because he likes you, you understand? It's because you're included in the expense account. With the same indifference he'd fill you up with hot water and use you for a foot warmer. I could procure little boys and little girls for him galore, at one hundred marks, and what's fifty thousand for him? A spit. But nothing. Never. But if an amoeba goes by and opens its mouth and . . ."

Angelo was very disturbed by this extravagant act of Lometto's, and didn't say a word about it. Let him slowly ripen his needs, such as they were, let him struggle by himself with his whims included in the price, he was not interested in talking about them unsolicited. If there was anything more than that, sooner or later he would have to admit it, at least to himself. Lometto admired male prowess and praised it openly to Angelo: he liked robust, athletic males like his sons, he detested effeminates, so his pass at Demetrio was as perverse as the attraction of an enlarging lens for a louse. Demetrio must have seemed to him a protozoan incapable of understanding and willing, a restless *perpetua* full of tics but ultimately obsequious to all the priest's caprices. The essential thing about a hole was that it shouldn't cost anything.

So Demetrio was left behind in Copenhagen, Lometto and Angelo flew to Oslo, from there to Göteborg, then they took care of two Jews in Malmö, and ferried across. On the ferry, it's hard to say how, talk turned to that family chapel in Toigo Lometto had mentioned again, shouting "Carrara marble" and its price—the same as building a house with bricks—as well as the fact that father and father-in-law had gone down to choose the blocks and see to their shipment (marble and steel and brass, Lometto had emphasized; but the subject did not interest Angelo, and Lometto, instead of impressing him with his burial niches, made him yawn; already his mother was giving him a headache because she didn't want to depend on anyone, not even when she was dead, so she had already bought everything for herself, even the photograph for the oval . . .); then they went on to the trip's mutual debits and credits, standing in line with trays at the counter. Lometto, when the moment came to figure out who owed what, always pretended: either that he had no memory or that he had mistaken memories, depending. He never acted in good faith. Angelo was sure of it. Three times in a row he had forgotten gloves, scarfs, and umbrella at his house, and if one day he hadn't remembered that he had forgotten them precisely there, Lometto and family would have continued to use them and put them away in the closet upstairs. That time Lometto had said was it his fault if Angelo forgot his things all over the place? there they were, what was he supposed to do? throw them out? The thought of returning them hadn't even flitted through his head. And anyway, he had added, if he didn't take advantage of this opportunity, when would he ever have a pair of marbled pigskin gloves? All these stories, all and many others, came back to Angelo when money was the subject, issuing in single file from the hold of his rancors set aside for better occasions.

Now this new nonsense popped up about a phantom advance that Lometto had supposedly given him in Berlin and Angelo had never received.

"But try to think back, it's not that you didn't get it, you've forgotten. If instead of always running around and getting it up your . . ."

"But when, goddamnit, when?"

"I told you, the time before last that we were in Berlin. Two months ago, I gave you three hundred marks, before you got off the car, yes, and then you went back by train."

"But I had plenty of marks of my own, so why should I have asked you for them? And besides, two months ago? In Berlin?"

"How do I know what you do with your money! But I'm sure I gave it to you."

Now Angelo, figures, chits, slips, and notebooks in hand, forcing his memory to recall a buried balance, buried because resolved, held himself ready to show what was involved in the new total that with a conjuror's adroitness Lometto would plunk down on the table the moment he'd torn up his and dropped it into the ashtray.

Lometto began to waver. It was clear why he insisted so much on those three hundred marks: because he had never given them to him and, not wanting to admit he was mistaken, he now tried to widen the opening of his arrogant top hat so as to pluck out of it ever more closely laid traps and entangle Angelo in a confusion of data and places and figures and days in order to contort the initial situation worn down by now by the black on white of a fusillade of indisputable computations. Lometto, lifting to his mouth teaspoonfuls of tiny shrimp in pink sauce, came up with more small amounts given and not noted, a previous mistake in the calculation of days on a trip four months earlier. Angelo, immovable, dredged his mind and, not discovering in it any fault of his and not feeling guilty because of it, continued to come upon one argument after another and watched Lometto, who withdrew gasping and then sallied forth on the attack again. Angelo was precise, he always wrote down everything and immediately, never overcharged, so as not to give Lometto the satisfaction of his becoming gradually like him. Lometto, cornered like this, besides having a heartfelt interest in saving, in stealing three hundred marks, pursued a further purpose, much vaster and far-reaching: he fished around in Angelo's "bad faith" to regale him with an atomized inquisition on the overall honesty and faithfulness that was owed him. Angelo, in that mire of half-accusations and half-suspicions and half-insinuations, while attempting to defend himself often fell into contradiction, because he did not concentrate on the object of the contention—the hundred or two hundred thousand contested lire—but set out on the wrong foot, getting bogged down in ideology, in the phenomenology of memory as a weak category and, therefore, merely existential and personalistic. Lometto, clinging to his figure with a few zeros, immensely enjoyed exasperating him, always in order to find out whether Angelo within him nurtured some aspiration for revenge, such as giving away the names of customers and prices to the competition, or, who knows, to ascertain whether Angelo, in the turmoil of the wrangle, would reveal he knew things he should not know. Arousing his anger was the quickest way to look into his mouth. Once Lometto realized that there was nothing recondite in Angelo and that his clumsy contradictions were merely the fruit of an honesty as exemplary as it was perfidious, he limited himself to saying, "Maybe." With that "maybe" he did not intend to admit his mistake but to say that, not being able to be right "immediately," he conceded his munificent suspension of judgment.

These were sums that, when added up, were insignificant, those two did not have much of a cash flow between them: so many days so much money, a few advances in currency for personal expenses, and that's it. At the moment of adding them up, you would have said it was the double-entry accounting of some protoarchaic Germanic indemnity for murder.

Lometto, calmly, dug into the third shrimp cocktail, listening to Angelo as he continued pedantically to justify his total and suspect innocence.

So, between one confutation and the next concerning lire and florins, meals and advances, never paid for and never given, Angelo told Lometto that he was so much better when he tried so shamelessly to prevaricate, lashing out left and right in the hope of landing a blow, better this crossing of scimitars in the light of day than the mellifluous bite of the scorpion concealed under the pillow. He said it to him in other words but he said it to him. Ah, this perennial translating of Italian into dialect! When would he ever, when would he have the opportunity of not being obliged to descend into vulgarization, at least during these duels to the death? And Angelo had a stroke of genius: why indeed make the effort of defending oneself and never attack in all the splendor of one's own rhetorical vestments? Who did Lometto think he was, always forcing him to renounce every literary pleasure in order to indulge in the necessity of homiletics? Certainly, however, what a relief to be faced by someone who forced you, true enough, to the pettiness of translating aulic into rustic, but who then did not yield to refinements, turning you into a sponger for the rest of your days. It was stimulating, even though enervating, to hold your own against the competitiveness of Lometto's "if so much gives me so much": his weapons, unlike all others, were displayed, hence they availed themselves of an extra reflex, an impure solar beauty of their own.

Angelo now got a whiff of some thoughts in the mind of Lometto, who was bent over his sixth shrimp cocktail—he could pack away the sea. Angelo immediately stifled these supposed thoughts, reminding him immediately of the profound diversity of their two strength-capitals: Angelo socially was nobody, but what he was *he was*, the same as saying he was he, he was everything he had and he was everything he carried with him in life, besides a change of underwear in his bag. Lometto had billions in personal possessions and real estate, he determined the fate of dozens of families, he had sons of his own, a wife just as spiritual about the dogma of property, and he was continually gratified by a social hatred and envy which stimulated him to obtain always more, and sow always more *enemies* and drag along always more every time he had the wish to say "I." But on his own he would not have had the capacity to *be*. Absurd though it might seem, he was not an individual but a system, in which Celestino alone was but a small pawn. Lometto was an entity more abstract and collective than he thought he was when he received his bank statements. A point of reference in the investment of money, not of life. And probably he would have become that also for his *treasures*, indeed perhaps he already was what he boasted he had: a number, a big number that had sired small numbers worthy of him in all and everything.

"That's exactly the way it ought to be!" he said, smirking an instant with ruthless pride.

"And anyhow, to get back to this sum that's supposed to prove that I have received this money . . ." Angelo resumed, because this is where he wanted to get.

But Lometto, absolutely furious because of the earlier tirade, cut him off and said: "You're the one who's full of complexes, because you have no power and with all your culture and degree you're nobody, you're not even working for a politician, a party, since you haven't the talent to be an entrepreneur. You're a great big zero. And you thought up all these fine speeches to fool people . . . And anyway, you said it yourself that you're a failure, didn't you?"

As usual, Lometto had pretended he did not understood the sentimental nuance with which that sentence had been used before; or was it precisely because of this nuance, in fact because of a basic sentimentality repressed with difficulty, that it was proven that Angelo was a failure, period?

"You forgot to include the thirty-four marks in Ulm" Lometto interjected. "Now go ahead and add it up again, you'll see it's correct and who's right."

"I've got another one here where I wrote that I returned it to you. Properly dated and signed by you . . . And to stop all this useless talk, look, I don't have a bunch of hungry kids to feed, I don't even have this alibi or pressure, and I don't even need to believe that procreation is a social task to feel in good standing with God and country. Procreation does not ennoble anything that is not already noble in itself. Animals making other animals . . ."

"I am not an animal! I'm a Christian. And my sons too. You're blaspheming."

"Shit, Lometto, all shit. Go look for something else. It isn't by going up cunt or ass that one is in good standing with one's conscience, with one's definitive mortality . . . I look at the stars and they always tell me that I've understood everything, and they wink at me. After me, nothing and everything the same as before or in a different way. I like it so much I could die. You look at the stars and wonder whether perhaps you could harness the energy of the black holes. But these are two different contemplations, one of which has, however, the wrongheadedness and arrogance of calling itself progress. What use is that progress you make if the result then is men like you and not like me? It is an apparent progress, which has not shifted the caveman's psychic quality one micron. You sit there, in a suit that isn't yours, a silk shirt and tie, Lometto my ass, and as you lean against the backrest of your chair, it is as if you were holding a big stone club. And as for those forty-eight francs . . ."

"A future like yours sends shivers up my back only to think about it. There, soured, alone, without anybody to take care of you . . . without a lira . . . but perhaps you are the shrewd one, you've probably got plenty of lire. I know your kind of mummer! Lots of lovely populist talk and then, like the Communists in Penzana . . . once you've got it made . . ."

Now Angelo hurled a bolt of lightning from a clear sky, whispering bent over the small tray: "Sure. But just consider where you stash it, all your money, if some accident happened to your oldest. Some irreparable mishap to your manpower of the future, to your little saints with their gift of gab."

Angelo hadn't touched his shrimps, which now swam in their limp sauce. The two stared at each for quite a while, Lometto with his eyes popping. Angelo pretended indifference, rearranged on the table the scraps of a slip already put in the ashtray. Ilario was his alter ego, the marvelous thoroughbred envelope he had never been, the man whom women and men—he had noticed—turned around on the street to look at with deep emotion.

"Do me a favor, change the subject. No, I don't even want to talk about it."

"But . . ."

"No. I'd rather you got on the train and went back right away by yourself . . ."

"You're blocked now, eh? When it's convenient for you, you're ready to spend, aren't you?" Angelo said, smiling maliciously. "And besides, how can one have such a vision of life, you're trying to say. Mine is a present, not a future. It suits me fine . . . Anybody can die, I don't die with him, I leave him all the pertinence of his passing. You've got three, perhaps four, such pertinences: you would follow them into the coffin a bit each time. You: I mean to say your capital invested until the year three thousand . . ."

"Until two thousand and eight . . ."

"But you should be glad I'm like this, not only because you have one less competitor in general, but because if, for instance, I had Nicola's head I would be your agent, I would go to Luxembourg for you, would gang up with your customers, over certain discounts for instance, and when your merchandise no longer goes, zack! I replace it with the cheaper stuff of one of your competitors. You know you're giving me spittle for my services and my commercial nose. You ought to kiss the ground I walk on that I am so . . ." Angelo had learned many things: every so often, into these vast fields of gratuitous, loudly enunciated philosophy he sowed here and there a few small therefores and so reached the nitty-gritty.

Outside there was a quarrel among sea gulls which covered even the noise from the engine room.

"Yeah, you have another think coming, it's the product that

counts"—it was his favorite refrain—"if you haven't got that, with your nose you can sniff up . . ."

"Oh, there we go again. Balls! If you know how to go about it you can even sell the phlegm out of an old people's home. All old people know how to produce it, it's selling it to young people that's difficult. Unless you have connections* with the Vatican . . ."

"Is there a lot more coming? Come on, there's no point in your insisting. I already paid you. You're not going to confuse me."

"Commercially speaking, you're worth nothing, Lometto. And from this here, black on white, it's clear instead that you didn't pay me, that you dreamt it at night."

"Because you're worth a lot!"

"But that's the way it ought to be, right? You produce and manage, I trade. It isn't even a matter of knowing languages. Look: you wouldn't be able to sell me even five lire worth of merchandise. You're forever whining, you have no talent at all. You'd get nowhere. You still have the face of a peasant who when the Angelus sounds talks about hail. You do not have the gift of credibility and synthesis. You are an ugly open notebook."

"What do you mean?"

"That when, for instance, I must give a message over the phone with date and price and terms and best regards in German, I do it adeptly in three minutes. You, in Italian, need twenty because you spend ten crying the blues and you dupe the customers, and then they must be called again because, between one sob and the next, it's never clear what you have agreed on. That's all. Synthesis. Condense"—and Angelo held up his clenched fist. He didn't say that "synthesis" was also the quality of saying with ten thousand words arousing enthusiasm what others said with ten words causing people to yawn.

"Why do you mean, it's not clear? What is decided is decided by me, obviously! All you have to do is ask me, what need is there to get on the phone again?"

Lometto listened to these repetitions of old conversations, evidence for the defense, impassive, spooning away, while Angelo, his voice gone by now, tried to make him understand the *genetic* reason for the impossibility of his having received that total of one hundred and seventy thousand lire at the rate of exchange without having made

* *English in original.*

a note of it in his diary, counting, as Lometto had insinuated, on the fact that Lometto would forget about it and that he, Angelo, was not the type of person to do such a thing, and that all the evidence the other came up with was blatantly false. At this point, exhausted, Angelo, still with his first and last pinkish cocktail before him, knew that he was about to give in this time too, that, to bring an end to it, he would make him a present also of that small owed fee, and that then, for days, he would accuse himself of stupidity and curse himself for his foolishness, with suicidal self-hatred. Instead, belching, Lometto said: "Maybe." Without even raising his eyes, blinking his lashes once with skepticism, and passing a hand over his belly.

Angelo thought that his own must be half closed because he couldn't see anything; only small cobalt-blue spots in a gray mist of plastic backrests and stone clubs, a porthole-shaped stain full of the dark matter of sea gulls with splatters of anthrax where the wings had touched. He picked up the cocktail and threw it into his face, lunged over the table, and landed a portentous smack, knocking Lometto head over heels into two young Nordic ladies who collapsed on their small trays of tea and buttered biscuits.

"What are you doing?" howled Lometto. "He's crazy, help!"

And with a great crash he fell onto the planks, still saying: "I'll press charges, I'll press charges, I'll send you to jail!"

Angelo was about to go around the table to help him up and perhaps kick him in the ribs when he was stopped by a waiter with a white fez who had to ask the gentlemen whether, please, they'd mind continuing this on the pier, since they were docking.

Once on land they became reconciled over the necessity of finding spot remover at the hotel. Both had gotten what they wanted. Lometto had managed to provoke Angelo to a reaction which proclaimed his complete good faith and his ignorance about things which, one could deduce, were very close to Lometto's heart, and Angelo had obtained the meager satisfaction of a deflation similar to the last bubble of a hysterical pregnancy. At the hotel Lometto changed and gave his jacket to the floor waiter, actually the room waiter—that is, to Demetrio, who began removing spots, happy to be doing something after so much inane strolling about Tivoli, where nobody had slipped an arm under his, imploring him to give in. Then he had been in a sauna near the station and all he had seen were some old fjord wolves with their eyes glued to the entrance door for two hours, they too waiting for somebody to arrive. The small shrimp stuck in the buttonhole of his lapel was the first true event in that chaste and Hamletic city.

Back in Italy, Demetrio was unloaded with every precaution in front of his house. The next day, late in the morning, Lometto calls and says: "You know what happened to me this morning? Half an hour ago? That friend of yours phones and . . ."

Lometto came to a pause in which one clearly heard his tongue immersed in a mephitic salivation more abundant than usual.

"And . . . ?" Angelo really didn't know what Demetrio could still have to say to Lometto after so much silence.

"And he says: couldn't you lend me ten million? Just like that."

"What?"

"Yes, ten million, like a neighbor asking for a cup of sugar. Ten million."

"No!"

"It's not for me, says he, but for my cousin. He wants to enlarge his workshop. Like that."

"But that's absurd!"

"Exactly."

Angelo was poured plaster, he'd had the time to harden, crumble, never to be pasted together again. In the coffered ceiling of his knowledge of Demetrio this was a round-headed corner he would never have expected. Ten million. Like that. So Demetrio was flying.

"Do you know anything about it?" Lometto said, offhand, sucking air through his molars.

"Nothing. May I drop dead. It's as if you told me you're having tea with Frankenstein."

"Not one or two, and discussing interest first. Ten."

"And you?"

"And me. I told him I was busy elsewhere, I pretended he hadn't said a thing."

"And he?"

"He said thank you and that he'd call back later . . ."

Angelo was afraid. Could Demetrio have confided in some criminal relative? Was blackmail on the horizon?

"Can you figure it out? What would you do in my place if he calls?"

"Me . . . I can't figure it out at all."

Lometto wanted to know whether Angelo was informed about the reason for the blackmail, which he himself was already assessing in all its plausibility. Angelo, unheard of, turned a deaf ear. But if there was anything about which Lometto had been generous all the way it was his inalienable serenity in relation to sex, and that his buggering workers shouldn't dress up like women on the job, so as not to slow down production, and that's all. And that they must punch the clock on time. And that the women workers—subjected to actual interrogations by a trusted *Kapo* of his—were not pregnant at the moment of being hired and that, indeed, they would denouce each other if among the newcomers smoldered the destabilizing Red activism of maternity; only for these did he have a mortal hatred. So you can imagine, a squad of only lesbians and buggerers would have been his dream: no pre- and post-maternity, no family contributions, infrequent menstruations.

"Listen, Celestino, don't pay any attention. If he turns up again, you call me. Leave things as they are. I'm not going to say a word about it to him either. In fact, for me Demetrio dies this very instant. Thanks for getting rid of him for me. It's simply a question of style."

"Yes, but what do I get out of it?"

It wasn't even necessary to get rid of Demetrio, who, after so many years of assiduousness, from the moment in which he was dropped at his door, disappeared into the nothingness from which he had come. Angelo heard nothing more about the business and concluded that there was nothing to hear. He gave a sigh of relief which perhaps concerned only him and he didn't care to prod some lazy curiosity on the subject. Lometto hadn't called him back, and this could mean everything as it could mean nothing. He took the silence at its word. It was enough for him and more. Let everyone, if at all, think about his guardian angels in due time. He had no need for them. He saw to his own blackmailing.

In the continuation of his thought dream, the ashes of Giorgina Washington have a compactness which gives the lie to the commonplace about what the dead are made of. And those Oriental eyes even then seemed made of black glass, with a soluble silica of a question that swam out and drowned you in the answer you were unable to give. Fake pupils cannot be ashes. In the coffin they must lie intact in the forehead waiting for someone who will assume the burden of their hammering horror. And then Angelo clearly sees that the little dresses of the tiny dead girl are lifted, the flesh still supported by the small slats of the intact skeleton, the small folded hands a bit parchmented, but not much. But how can he see if the coffin is made of wood? From what side does his gaze penetrate? And why has he mentally raised the lid? The mind's eye is insinuating itself from where? From nowhere, because it looks like a bier of glass, a casket of crystal, in fact of polystyrene resins. To save money.

On a beautiful day in June, Angelo got into the car, used a lick-lick as big as a house, lured Giuditta into the meshes of his love, not, however, without a slight shove from the small Sardinian mother. It was a Saturday afternoon, Lometto's family all onstage, distributed over farmyard and crenellated mansard and cellars (by this time almost completely dismantled and from which the last tools and old looms were being removed) and the new headquarters of Den. The trip they had just finished had resulted in a downpour of orders, and Den, hampered by the necessity of looking like a modern stable (bales of straw and hay piled up to the ceiling occupied the rear shed, delicately placed on white marble on which here and there wax tests had been made: a mirror!) and the need to fulfill its real purpose with the installation of new equipment—from the twister of raw thread to the latest double-drop loom—prospered both inside and out. By now also the roofs had been put in place and Lometto was experiencing the thrill of competing with Mire, Inc.—that is, with the seventy percent of shares that were not his. And he gnawed his nails over the remaining thirty controlled by Bananone.

Giuditta had been, as always, reluctant to leave with Angelo, then she had accepted with the all-wise expression of someone who is doing a favor that can no longer be avoided. She was really fat and pink like an "animal cartoon" piglet, as Angelo's mother said. In her long, thick, and vaporous hair, she wore a profusion of red barrettes. Her hair was chestnut, as though irritatingly smoothed to silk by the continuous caresses she received when she least expected them. Otherwise she shrank away. She had become the consolation of all the spinsters and all the bachelors in Piazzetta del Teatro, after having been the same for the neighborhood near the Ospedale Nuovo where her mother had settled down when she first arrived from Sardinia. Angelo and his parents at that time still lived with the brother-son. The mother had appeared from the insular void five years before, had said that she was seven months pregnant, and assisted by Angelo's mother, who had taken her to heart, had given birth to this fatherless Sardo-Italian child. When the Bazarovis moved to the center of town, Angelo's mother had convinced the unwed mother to move there too, into a small apartment. It was incredible how the old mother had convinced the young one to move, saying that this way she would not have to worry about entrusting Giuditta to strangers. Only Angelo knew that for her the stranger was none other than the young unwed mother. The small and confused Sardinian mommy—dominated by a desire for redress, repressed and contained, from which she drew all the energy to face the troubles of emigration into the land of Brescia with a big illegitimate belly—had begun to earn her living, cleaning here and there, and willing to do anything, provided they let her drag along the little girl. But from the very first month Angelo's mother had considered it unseemly that she should show up at work with a change of diapers, baby and all, and, sighing over young wives who don't know how to do anything, not even get themselves married, had offered to look after her. Giuditta had spent happy days fussed over by the two old people, who, since they lived scowling at each other, had certainly been repaid by the sweet and bothersome chore of raising a child properly as a means of communication. And they also slept very little, like all old people, and at night there was a continuous display of loud complaints for having been awakened by the whimpering which, for hours, they had expected with four perked ears. Because the Sardinian mother worked also at night—in a restaurant on the lake . . . Well, in any case, a further reason, if anything, to keep the child away from bad influences. "We all know, Sardinians, and women, nowadays are all eels" Angelo's mother had once sighed out. But she had never frankly looked into it, knowing more about it did not interest her. Angelo's mother, recently, had come up with another theory about death: that her husband, if it hadn't been for Giuditta, would have let himself be tempted by snails (absolutely forbidden) much earlier, at the least. Certainly, she was a lovely child, but God forbid she should have come into the world, let us say, three years later.

The old father woke up at dawn starved for affection and made a tour of all the houses where, around seven o'clock, Giuditta put in an appearance, counting the minutes when he or his wife would be able to go and pick her up. Angelo recognized the old fox who marked you forever with his solicitous claws when you were small and beat it when you were grown up.

Nevertheless, it was a pretty little picture to see the old hypocrite with a tear in the corner of his eye and a packet of Charms—always the same!—in his open palm, waiting for Giuditta to appear and embrace him around that belly of his which all night long had deambulated around the refrigerator. Giuditta, placid and matronly though she was, even then had none of the docility typical of chubby little girls. She was obstinate and disdainful and bestowed her favors with an eyedropper. But she had impulses to which she abandoned herself, even though they became rarer as she grew. She was vivacious but never incontinent, and proud of her rotundities and her tiny ass, which she gladly showed to everyone. Once a girl the same age had yelled after her, "You're from hunger!" because of her mother who had to do housecleaning and God knows what else, and since then Giuditta smilingly showed that no one went hungry and that, on the contrary, she was quite plump.

With her mother away at work, Giuditta came and went in all houses as she pleased, welcomed by trumpet peals from within. In every kitchen cabinet she knew the shelf where the bachelors, widowers, widows, the poor things in general, kept candies and chocolates wrapped in tinfoil which are given instead of change. Besides, in the freezer compartment it was now the accepted custom to keep Popsicles and ice-cream sandwiches. And she was insatiable. At age five she looked two years old, but she wasn't or she did not want people to think that she was completely dependent, even though she already knew how to ride a two-wheel bicycle.

She ran small errands up the hill, to the baker's, and one stopped to watch her with her shopping bag dangling all the way to the last stone on the small road, waiting for her to turn her head and laugh. She got on line, with the shopping bag hidden in the folds of her little dress, and her hands clutching its handles, and she diligently waited her turn, and she did not mind if someone pushed ahead of her. She was intimidated by people in a hurry. She gazed at the shelves, spellbound, forgetful of the number of rolls she was supposed to buy. Finally someone reached a hand inside the showcase and picked out a cream puff and she returned to her senses, twirling the tip of her tongue in the gold of the cream and announcing the correct number of rolls to be bought. She was never satiated and she never asked for anything: the cream puffs rained down from above to reward her frowning indifference. If anyone, in exchange, asked her for a kiss, she said, "Kisses are coming tomorrow," and she stuffed into her pocket any sort of thing with cocoa and honey and almond and sugar. The corners of her mouth were pollinated with ocher yellows and a dusty spume. She liked Marsala custards, biscuits dunked in sweet wine, liqueur-filled chocolates. Angelo was in love with this egotistic and rebellious little girl who snickered straight in his face whenever he tried to caress her and who writhed in his loose or even mimed embraces. Who knows whether his father then, as he now, felt guilty about that passionate love for a child, the easiest to experience because rarely thwarted and of little cost.

But Giuditta was already an adult, she contested and rejected his love; those one-track effusions of Angelo's, without any need of exchange, did not interest her. Being loved left her indifferent, it seemed to be a nuisance typical of her sex, and that's all. Too many already did it for lack of something else to feel alive, because they could not rely twenty-four hours out of twenty-four on oleander trees, a stray cat, the blackbird in its cage. Giuditta seemed to have grasped all this, the lack of imagination of those who have a need to love. She understood, bouncing her hair with a "no," that there was an absence of freedom in this devotion she received from the barber's childless widow, the custodian of the Risorgimento Museum who lived in red overalls watering flowers and dusting memorabilia, the mad electrician in odor of sanctity, a recluse in a dark attic, and from at least four more singles who hystericized the air thereabouts and spied on her legs to find out to whom she was heading. She sensed she had created around her an atmosphere of jealousy, and she alimentarily exploited this situation of solitary tensions which did not concern her and vanished in a place called the "past" by her decrepit wooers: there she had never been. Her mother was her true, only love and she saw so little of her; she concentrated on her when she finally reappeared on her moped—now in her small Alfa Romeo.

Their embraces were long, they lasted interminable instants, both again embraced by sounds from their native island that no one else heard. The windowpanes from which they were watched on the small square were clockfaces that said: hours and hours and hours of embraces. A thing like that must be good for one's health. And the wrinkled, pious, feline, jellyfishlike, cataractic, hebetudinous, buffoonesque eyes were excluded from it. The singles dare not breathe and so the panes do not mist over.

There was such a hunger for affection in the old men and women and the lonely middle-aged persons, about whose lives nothing is known, that Giuditta, despite her few years, had instinctively assimilated it to a form of cannibalism. Cordiality was a civilized form of bloodthirstiness. Perhaps that is why she ate so much and never said thank you for cream puffs or pies or ice creams, because there were too many hands reaching out for her very fine hair, her fresh, polished cheeks, her bare, so well-turned little arms. Perhaps she was afraid that they would wear her out.

At times Angelo felt entitled to count on Giuditta's emotional compliance because he had been the first to watch her sleep in diapers and he felt outraged by that increasingly harsh rejection, the same outrage he had felt once writing to an acquaintance in jail . . . and thus, he thought, unable *not* to correspond—and the man had returned the letter to the sender. Angelo had picked her up hundreds of times from the third- or fourth-hand crib, telling the Sardinian mommy it was all right to go, that he would take her to his relatives, if he decided to return to Verona. In contrast to her usual prickly manner, she could never thank him enough, and she trustingly went away to work for whole days, to iron and wash—at the beginning. He, very nonchalantly, told her to prepare the bottle, that he would give it to her, and this is what he did for several months. It was exciting to see something grow within the confines of one's highway with neither start nor finish.

Once the house was bought there in Piazzetta, every now and then Angelo got up from his translations and went to look at Giuditta as she slept. He lay down next to her, took her hand, because she let him have it only when she could not pull it away. He felt regenerated no less than an old man and was certain that he was not harming the child. Awake, she pushed him away as though his discretion were a kind of supreme invasiveness. He always felt this terror of contaminating her with his breath, he always kept at a proper distance from her, resisted every desire for physical contact. Angelo, in life's decisive difficulties, did not love himself enough.

He liked the thought of an amorous effusion, but not the effusion itself. He was satisfied with the gesture, knowing that the possibility existed of transforming the intention of happiness. His caress, his kiss, his embrace without caress, nor kiss, nor embrace must have put the child on the qui vive. He was not like all those other weirdos on the Piazzetta. Awake, Giuditta refused to be exclusively his since she suspected that that mimicry of love was the most dangerous trap. She immediately began to demand other homes, brought up the names of competitors. Angelo took her now here now there as soon as he saw that with him she wilted and everyone said, "Oh, don't worry, I'll keep her here with me; no, it's not necessary for you to fetch her, it's all right; yes, I know what she eats." Each one expressed his yearning for Giuditta as best he could, transforming it into avid solicitude, something that grew within the confines of each person's sterility.

She was very beautiful. Her eyes, not from these parts, it goes without saying, dark, turquoise, emanated a sheaf of lunar penumbra upon nocturnal tides. They issued from a crossing of races spasmodically intense in their blood, bringing together in one instant in those pupils the fact of being alive and unique and unrepeatable and of not having to say thank you to anyone, gods unto themselves.

Fortunately, Giuditta liked everything that wore pants and a shirt opened to display the first hairs. She liked boys much older than herself. From behind small walls and iron grilles she watched their dribbles and goals, and God forbid if an adult came to disturb her, she repudiated everyone. She knew who would share the world with her and who was cut out of it. When one of the boys addressed her she blushed and found it rather difficult to regain her poise. On all males not yet worn out by wood stoves, by the cloths with which to cover small cages in the evening, by that fifth corner of square objects that is seen only at a certain age and at a certain degree of bewilderment, she poured a jagged passion similar perhaps to the exclusive, compact passion for her mother.

Giuditta had also learned how to be waited on. The small bicycle had become for her the means to this would-be knighthood aspired to by pants around the age of ten. Angelo once had suspected that she herself had punctured her tire with a nail and on another occasion on the terrace had used a screwdriver to fiddle with the brakes. Then she went out on the street with an already prepared sulky look and stood there between the two soccer teams until one of the small boys, preferably the aphasic one, left center field and got busy doing the repairs against the small wall of the Suffragio Church. He was her favorite: a kid who gave no hint of growing up, with diseased vocal cords, and who addressed her in a hoarse voice briskly and with infinite patience. The two of them chattered for hours through the gates—Giuditta liked it very much that between herself and the boy, when there was no broken bike, there should be some obstacle, the conversation then seemed more interesting. They talked about tires and rubber patches and wheel spokes and carriers on motor scooters and about getting a driver's license right after confirmation, the lexicon of true love.

Giuditta had her handmaidens, whom she tyrannized: four girls older than herself who never stopped looking for her to play with, in truth to be introduced into the encampment of the distracted knights who played among themselves and seemed to interrupt their forays up the stairs and under the arcades only at a gesture from Giuditta and from no other female.

She was mercurial and precious merchandise!

Giuditta was shy with Angelo, but she also reserved solely for him her most beautiful impulses, provided she saw him rarely: she ran to meet him, dropping her small bike, opened her arms wide at the last instant and he lifted her up and made her spin in the air, always holding her firmly at arm's length. Then, with the due distance, he hugged her and smacked her a kiss, kissing the air which in that instant grazed her cheek. He too was just like those other solicitous bats, with the difference, though, that he had the advantage of being the youngest and, besides being able to look like a father, he had the illusion he could communicate more spontaneously with her, the wild, unpredictable creature, capable of changing visiting itineraries for weeks on end, without giving a reason for it. How much he suffered from it; it is not possible to say except by saying it straight out. He went home and said to himself "I must tear her out of my heart," for he actually used these very words with himself. And he imagined that, at the same instant, at least another five people were in vain resolving on behaviors and attitudes that would cave in as soon as she asked, "May I come in?" appearing on the threshold, triumphant over every decision to break away.

So this outing in the car had all the prerogatives of a momentous occasion and Angelo's chuckling delight was ineffable. From the corner of his eye he watched the child, who, in absolute silence, looked at the countryside full of men standing around sluice gates in their underpants. She rose, stretching a bit, but did not ask what they were doing. The yellow leaned against the green and the green against the water's sparkling black. All of them must certainly be looking for a soccer ball that had fallen into several ditches.

Giuditta lengthened her neck against the window, which was not turned down despite the heat, and unbuttoned the first small button of her small dress of red percale. Angelo drove very slowly, inebriated by the faculty he had acquired, together with the weirdness of having completely become Dr. Angelo Bazarovi, of lighting a cigarette without stopping on the verge of the road as he had been doing for a year and a half. Now he could drive with one hand, strike the match against the box, letting go of the wheel—steering it, however, with an elbow—light a cigarette and look at Giuditta almost simultaneously. His life as *Homo sapiens* never ceased to surprise him.

He dreamed of definitive tests that would have allowed him to put his life on the line in case she were in danger, so that he could die for a noble cause, such as bringing Giuditta back safe and sound to her aphasic suitor.

The little dress was already becoming tight for her and the shoulder straps cut a bit into her shoulder blades. These were all things that had belonged to other little girls, her mother collected them from house to house—she no longer needed to do this and Angelo did not at all believe that they were personal secondhand dresses; they were an unknown and impersonal hand and she probably bought them at the flea market in Brescia, where she went to work in her little Alfa. For single gentlemen, he could have sworn, who do not have this kind of clothing around the house.

Only the little shoes were brand-new, small blue closed sandals, and Angelo was somewhat remorseful because he had not thought of them and had been beaten to it by the museum custodian. But the small gold bracelet and the silver chain were his. Her mother had slipped them on her after a struggle.

Giuditta kept her lips just barely apart, so red and swollen, so unaware of the breath of vitality they expired every time inside the car's body. Angelo smoked with the window half rolled down, to let out some of that energy which he did not want to do without. Everything was so absurd: his propensity for that little girl who did not love him enough, he, in his existence thus conceived and suffered, aloof, without affection, a few postcards, a few phone calls from Imer, whom he saw less and less, the "*ciaos*" on the street, the quickies—what a resonant word for muffled dawdlings!—with their energy and beauty, what a waste all the time spent waiting in the analysis lab and the lady doctor who, at the suspicion of chlamydia, had said: "This will take a while, we might as well drop the formalities." It was always the women who saved him in the nick of time from his complications with men.

So, having come to the end of the dirt road and ascended to the asphalted street, Angelo parked in the completely barren yard—only in one corner some rocks had been arranged with, inside, ten different species of flowers filched here and there, and they all had struck root. Nobody would have the time to look after flowers and plants except on the level of micro-propagation. There was building machinery being dismantled and, above all, pieces of the crane that were being wedged together on a truck. The boys ran out and began to use the Volkswagen for a seesaw with Giuditta still inside. He noticed her laughter in crescendo. Edda stood on the threshold and was dressed with a certain care, perhaps she was getting her husband to accompany her to look—only look—at the shop windows in Mantua. Giuditta had passed from laughter to a sedan-chair poise. It did not escape Angelo that between Belisario, a slim giant by now, and Giuditta flowed a silent attraction fanned also by the two brothers. Definitely, they desired a little sister, even if Edda had a propensity only for males.

She said that Lometto had gone to the bank.

"Obviously. On a Saturday afternoon. Then he complains if when I get gasoline here in Penzana there's always some employee who comes and tells me that nobody can stand the sight of him."

"But what's the fun of going on working days? You know what he's like."

"You bet I do. Who knows what satisfaction he gets out of interrupting the manager's day off and forcing him to open. When did he say he'd be back?"

"Oh, who knows? We've been seeing so little of each other recently. What with Mire and Den and Padua and those parts over there, halfway through the week he's never home. Only for the *bare* necessary *minimum*. And now he's also gone into men."

"Men?"

"Yes, men's socks, didn't you know?"

"Hmm . . . no."

"Why, yes, down your way. He's got a partner. A certain Demetrio . . ."

"Oh."

Inside the house there was a camphored silence. Angelo looked around to see some of the new, freshly stuffed carrion. The boys had gone who knows where with Giuditta. To see the calves, probably, or a mounting in the stable. The middle Lometto must have wanted to teach her something, to hook her up and get her to carry out an order. He was always teaching everyone.

"You know, I'd like to have another child by him, but he . . ." Edda resumed.

"But you told me that he also wanted it."

Angelo looked at the drawer of the kitchen table.

"Well, yes, not really . . . Some days yes and some days no, it depends on how he feels. Sometimes he uses it, sometimes he doesn't. He says that first they must all be used up."

"But how many of them did you buy?"

"Family size for one year. I can't get him to stop using them in the act."

"One can feel the lack of a female here, a little sister."

"Not on your life! I'd rather have an abortion. Another male, yes."

Angelo did not understand right away what Edda was alluding to, but he understood that it signified one thing only: the legitimation of an illustrious dynasty, its beginnings. Four, how to put it, like the Borgias, let us say, or the Medici, or the Savoys, the Agnellis, the Sindonas, the Gellis, or five or three or six like the D'Orléans. Few ideas but heraldic. And yet Angelo was convinced that, despite all appearances, behind this lay the long hand of Lometto, who saddled his wife with either madness or ridicule, depending on the situation.

The idea could not be only Edda's, who had none or did not have the right to express them. Once, perhaps distorting a misunderstood maxim of her brother the notary, she had said to him, "Trouble not about them but watch the sparrows": besides the restraint of indifference she could only count on contemplation. He probably arranged things in such a way that she would assume the risk of that dynastic enormity. He probably made an offhand suggestion, then another, she developed it, he would have felt it his duty to call her crazy, she must have deduced that it was her task now to become obstinate, and the trick was accomplished: she wanted a fourth boy. Now he could decide as he pleased, hiding behind his wife's subordinate extravagance.

"But I do have some bait to convince him to let me make it" Edda said, pouring hot water into the coffee cups. This too had become soluble. Was Edda's lure for Lometto another one of Lometto's lures to involve him? Edda had such implacable flashes in her eyes, like someone who has elaborated a desire for vengeance before it is necessary, just to be safe. Angelo, strangely, heard a little sprite tell him that he must drop the subject and that it was not in his interest to know more. And that nothing was ever spontaneous either in her or in Lometto, and that if it was a matter here of confession about some existential melodrama, it must have been premeditated down to the last comma, and therefore dangerous. It is not true that it is costly to confess, it is more costly to listen. Angelo had removed every grate between himself and the world, he meant to die either by his own hand or by a natural death, if possible, not because of someone else's confession. He was changing for the better, that is, for the worse, he sensed it.

In the house, perhaps because of the coffee's licorice aroma, the odor of phenol acid had disappeared: in recent times the taxidermic technique must have attained the desired perfection. He imagined Gelo, legs splayed like a newborn calf. The memory of that subtle odor coursed through his nostrils. He jumped up from the chair and could not stop himself in time and yelled:

"Giuditta! Where's Giuditta?"

No answer.

"Why, with the children, how she's grown since your father's funeral."

Angelo ran to the stairs and reaching the winding staircase of the Tower, twisting an ankle against the banister of the first step, then crashing against the railing with his left hip. He imagined they had locked the door, laid her out on the wooden bench, put her to sleep with an injection, and quartered with expertise along the dotted lines where the sutures would later be least visible: under the feet, around the wrists, the three of them gnashing their teeth because, for the sake of display, they must give up the jugular vein which solves everything in the blink of an eye.

With a kick he flung open the door: he felt transfixed by eight hostile eyes. Giuditta, completely naked, with her hands behind her back, did not know too well whether she should look at Angelo for some reason or other, or continue to admire the red crayon marks that crisscrossed her small body. Lometto III had put below her feet the customary pedestal used for the chicken and all the other more or less important ones, and which was recycled as soon as the current embalming had found its way to the mass grave behind the stable. Lometto II held in his right hand the red marker and was almost finished circumscribing the various anatomical sections on the back. Lometto I delicately brandished between thumb and index finger a small scalpel, with a vaguely professorial gesture. Giuditta's increasingly hostile look passed from Angelo to Ilario and Berengario and Belisario as if to say: "Throw him out."

Angelo had the sensation of flying and bumping his head on the rafters that stopped him. Belisario held in his hand a very large needle threaded with a meter and more of jute.

"What's there to scream about so much?" the dictator, Lometto II, said peremptorily. But Angelo did not at all remember having screamed, he took this for an impertinence.

"Have you gone crazy? Don't you see we're playing?" Ilario added.

"You shut up, or I'll give you a kick in the ass that'll leave a mark. Get dressed, Giuditta, we're leaving."

"Some manners!"

Angelo grabbed Lometto II by an ear:

"You, you idiot, you're the first I'm going to throw off the Tower into the yard if you say another word. And then the two of you. And let's have the bracelet and chain."

Angelo was afraid he would begin to cry, he was moved as by a recognition scene. On the shelf at eye level stood the pedestal with its trough where he had once seen the piglet. Now there was Gelo, the puppy, but for an instant he saw Giuditta, her smile vitreous, neatly combed, naked and glabrous, with her little snout hovering over the plywood basin. He saw the seam under her belly, from there she had been emptied of all her innards, from the hole opened in her navel. On the floor there was a long and skinny squirrel with a tiny drop of blood near its small ear. Giuditta was slowly dressing, while Angelo circled around her and with a cotton ball dipped in alcohol tried to remove the spots, he used up half a bottle and as a result spread the Mercurochrome color all over her skin. He picked her up, he had put her dress on backwards, the child bit the back of his hand, he gave her a good smack, she responded with a kick below the belt; Angelo shoved Ilario aside and went out toward the stairs. Screams, and the tips of her sandals jabbed him frenziedly here and there and her hands pulled his hair.

"A court case! Criminals!" He had already reached the bottom of the winding staircase.

"Go take a crap, maniac! It's gotten so you can't even play anymore" Lometto II retorted from above.

Now Giuditta went at it with her nails, mortally offended, and she dragged them over his neck and face. He laughed like someone possessed, he reacted as best he could, not even he knew what he was doing. Maybe it was a faux pas. Maniacs. Lunatics. Or was he the lunatic with his untrammeled imagination? Maybe he had exaggerated, maybe it was he who did not understand the new seductions of childhood, more technological and clinical than when he was a child.

He opened the car door and pushed Giuditta inside. Ran to say goodbye to Edda from the window.

"But aren't you going to wait for him?" she said. "At four o'clock I have an appointment with a gynecologist, so he's got to come."

"No, look, I can't." Angelo was sweating. "Your sons . . ."

"Sure, I know, you look all upset, why? They do it with all their pals."

"Do they? All animals as far as they're concerned. Look, let's not talk about it. *Ciao*."

"But you know, children are children. Come inside, come on, I want to finish what I was saying."

"*Ciao*, I'm not up to it."

Angelo started the car and disappeared. Now he was sweating even more. Giuditta kept her head low, her eyebrows creased.

"They were showing me how you empty out a girl" the child then said, achieving after only ten kilometers a certain boldness about her tattooed nakedness.

"A squirrel, Giuditta, a squirrel, the small animal on the floor."

"A big girl" she insisted, offended.

Angelo noticed two small blood spots on her wrist.

"And what did you do to yourself there?" At the side of the road he slammed on the brakes. The girl slipped her wrist into the neck of her dress. Angelo grabbed it forcefully.

"But what did they do to you?" He opened the door and pulled in a big mouthful of air.

"They stuck in the needles but I didn't feel anything. Now we are blood brothers."

Angelo passed a hand over his eyes, then over his hair, wiped and shook the sweat from his brow with one finger, he had no more cigarettes. Lighting up on the side of the road, if he'd had one, would have been the same as nostalgically digging up his past as a hopeless smoker at the wheel. Go back, set fire to the fief and roast Lometto and all of his ilk in it. He started the car again, trying not to exasperate the child. At the first café he stopped and asked for a tincture of iodine or something like it, but they didn't have any, where was the pharmacy? At last he was able to disinfect the two initiatic little dots. Giuditta, taken back to her mother, who was all ready to leave and entrust the child to him, as soon as she got out of the car said to him loud and clear: "I'm never going to go with you again. You are a he-whore."

And from her tiny pocket she took the small jewels and flung them at him. Angelo told her mother that it was nothing, picked them up, and handed them to her. He was sorry, but that evening he could not stay with the girl and his mother too was away at work.

Angelo went home and began to move about chairs and pots in the throes of a mechanical panic. He felt the need for an inner change, either here or there: where he was he no longer felt at ease. He stretched out on the bed, closed his eyes, and was confronted by the chart in the butcher shop on the square: joints, flank, loin. He said to himself that with Lometto, with the Lomettos, he was through forever. And who knows where she had got that word, he-whore.

Early on Wednesday morning . . .

Wednesday.

Early on Wednesday morning Angelo leaves for the lake; the car seems flooded to him, it puffs and at the stop sign it does not idle. After a few kilometers he is forced to give up the idea of going over last night's dream, in which a priest resembling a porcupine explains the whole situation from the height of a solid-ivory pulpit, hundreds of people watch and comment in religious silence; a man arrives with an Indian turban on his head, explains in his tongue what he knows, there then arrive some lay sisters, sort of heavyset white nurses, and behind them a procession of children with pennants and crutches, all blind.

The priest and the Indian have clarified their position as official witnesses for the defense, speaking a tongue that nobody in the hall understood, and yet it has occurred to no one to ask for an explanation. Every time that Angelo would have liked to do this, there was something which, purposely it seemed, distracted him: the image of a small German saint, who began to stammer out of her little cardboard picture, all blue and gold. The populace opens its umbrellas, fastens again the buttons of its raincoats, and returns home, dissatisfied but sheltered by the universal jubilation that clarifies everything and yet leaves things as they are.

End of dream.

He smells the stench of burning from below the seat, through the rear window he sees black smoke rising; so that's why behind him they kept honking their horns. Should he turn back? continue? He doesn't have far to go.

Just before Lido di Lonato, after turning into a small side road, the car stalls and stops definitively, not even idling. It won't start. On a piece of paper Angelo writes "Broken down" and reaches the Terrazzine on foot. To have it picked up by the tow truck will cost a fortune, and only tomorrow will it be possible to find out whether the publisher's check has gotten to the bank. Asking his mother for a loan only means plunging her into the most inconsolable spleen. For her it is shameful to have a son with a college degree who takes trips to Egypt and then does not have fifty thousand lire in his pocket to take a trip to the supermarket.

Angelo swims in the water, which is already too warm, he likes it ice-cold, as in mountain streams. There, in the deep water, he hears the voices of the first ones who arrive from the escarpment to chase away once and for all the rats and snakes, the fauna of co-tenants descending from the hill to the water hole. The first to appear in the water is Clemente, the "brother," the "friend." They look at each other surprised. They wave one hand simultaneously, swim toward each other. Angelo is grateful to the car, which provides him with a down-to-earth approach from the enchantment of nuanced messages. Here comes Clemente's companion, who waves to him from shore: wets his hands and face and goes back, past the reeds. Then it is the turn of Pinuccia, who sets a number of soda cans among the stones of the shore. They've had an abundant lunch, maybe the engine is fused, or it's the battery, or the ignition, it's the last day of the holidays, call the tow truck, tonight they're leaving for their real vacation, he's got to find somebody, in fact somebody with a cable, and in fact somebody with a cable willing to tow it for him.

"Beautiful sun" they both say as they come out of the water.

Stretched out on towels and cots, the three of them begin to talk—Pinuccia stays apart, reads *Repubblica*, which he alternates with *Novella 2000*. Clemente says little, it's always the other one who speaks for him, Clemente is absorbed in a half smile dedicated elsewhere, Angelo resumes with the car's tantrums, he really didn't need that. The *ciaos* multiply, they arrive in threes, fours, with baskets, bottles, transistors, even deck chairs. Also Dutch tourists from last season. For hours. Clemente suggests that probably the best thing is to tow the car, that he has a cable and everything and would be glad to help. Favors received redeem the flatness of their chronicle.

After a few shoves the bug starts up: the miracle buzzes supersonically enveloped in a cloud of atomic proportions. Clemente yells at him to go, that he will follow as long as the motor keeps going. Without stopping at the stop signs or at a red traffic light, the car makes a beeline at eighty kilometers an hour for Montichiari and at the traffic light before the provincial highway for Mantua the motor dies and refuses to start again. Clemente hooks on the cable and that is how they cover the remaining five hundred meters. Angelo is moved by this very efficient solidarity; nervous, he continues to laugh, twirling the steering wheel. They park the wreck in Piazzetta del Teatro Sociale and Angelo decides to go back to the Terrazzine with Clemente and bring along cold white wine from his apartment for everyone.

"Come, I live here."

Inside the house Angelo embraces Clemente and kisses him on the mouth, trembling *like a leaf*; this formulation makes him shiver and pleases him.

Clemente says: "How come this change?"

"I don't know. Let's go to my room."

In the bedroom they begin to collide physically, frenziedly, but Angelo is worried: there's always his mother working at her crocheting on the threshold with the other women of the neighborhood. It seems to Angelo that he can hear their homogeneous conversations, voices that never are startled: with eyes bent over their knitting they talk about ulcers, sciaticas, slipped disks, prolapse. He is overcome by nausea.

"Let's go" he says, pushing everything back in. "We'll stop somewhere else."

He doesn't like Clemente's prick: it's white like a relative's, the glans the gillyflower color of Belart's roadster, two very red veins like city streets on night-scene postcards. A "Do Not Enter" sign.

They go back to the beach, pass side path after side path; Angelo never gives any sign of wanting to turn in somewhere. From the plastic bag he pulls out two bottles of white wine, grana cheese, and bread. Straight from the bottles the wine is gone in a flash: there must be more than twenty throats waiting. A punctual glance, and Clemente starts up the escarpment. Angelo continues to chat, talks and talks especially now that he knows he's expected in the grove. When a whole bunch of them go to the water, he gets up and absently ambles to the wild fig tree, and disappears up the slope.

He already knows everything, like a host with duties toward his guests that he cannot avoid. He walks ahead, running away. In this Angelo never stops being surprised at himself; he wants to run away in an orderly manner, he must not confine himself to running away mentally, otherwise he will never get out of this troublesome story of Giorgina Washington, it is she who lays siege to his life and renders his everyday thoughts a burden, who prohibits any deviation which does not have her for its goal. And now a sexual encounter, no less. The performance that is waiting for him will find him totally absent and consenting, impotent and participant, because Aurora invades his mind with the shadow of the two prongs of an oneiric ladder against the porthole of the Tower, to spy on those three as they empty out and sew up. And in the moments in which he is about to forget about her for a while, she sucks up all of virility, injecting, with her unpunished death, a surplus of oxytocin into the pelvic area of his commitments.

Still at the end of June last year, he received a phone call from Edda, so happy because Den was doing so well that it couldn't do better. Even though with a certain delay, she was also informed about the business of the shrimp cocktail: in her eyes Angelo and Lometto were the two only true men left in the world, incomparable. She had a boundless esteem for both of them, this eternal quarrel between the two friends gave her the measure of her husband's invincibility and the faithfulness of his collaborator.

"May I have the pleasure, the honor of inviting you to dinner? I have a duck that's not doing anything out there in the yard. You've got to hurry, or else I'll serve it up to you embalmed. And so, while you're at it, you can prepare the schedule for the end of the summer. I want the Berlin market organized right."

"You know how to cook it in orange sauce?"

"No. But I can look for the recipe."

"Just as well that you admit it. Just roast it stuffed, the way you've been taught."

"Anyway, are you coming or aren't you . . .? You know he has started to use those things again."

"So you're saying that you've got your business this time too?"

"Yes, well, I . . ."

She was revved up: the gulping habit was beginning to have its effect. Was he perhaps supposed to convince Lometto to let her make another male child? and to put the condoms back into the cupboard for a while together with the stock of safety matches? or even to . . .

"I mean one time with and two without. He says it's like Russian roulette. We try, as a gamble. I hate the Russians, and he does too, you . . ."

"As a first dish you can make me tortelloni with ricotta, since this isn't the season for pumpkin."

"I can find a thousand and three males if he . . ."

". . . And remember, I want a clean tablecloth and glasses that aren't chipped."

"Do you know that we start as soon as I put them to bed . . .?" Edda must suddenly have realized that not only did the boys go to bed by themselves now, but probably equipped with milking gloves. ". . . Anyway, when the boys sleep, you know, the walls, the noise, ah well: until dawn. We've also tried to do it in the bathtub, Celestino banged his back, he slipped. He looked so funny . . . But there's no way he'll take them off. And . . ."

". . . there must be two glasses, pretend I'm an important dinner guest, a customer, one for water and one for wine. And buy some olive oil to dress the salad, the seed oil you use tastes like horse lard . . ."

". . . God, it's too beautiful! What a wonderful thing the Lord has invented! It really picks you up, and besides I realize, with the trips you take, I can't let him run around like that with his thing standing up. You know how he is in the morning . . . He says I'm never satisfied . . ."

She laughed full-throatedly after much childish giggling, perhaps without even looking to see whether one of the sons was there. Angelo was embarrassed for her. Was it possible that Lometto hadn't noticed that his wife's behavior in recent times had become rather high-pitched? Or had he been so insane as to encourage those ingestions, just to impart new élan to sex that was becoming threadbare? Were there secret maledictions in her that must be nebulized from time to time?

"Agreed then, as long as it isn't broiled . . ." And he was waiting for an answer when Edda turned to someone, certainly a son, and in clipped southern dialect said something that sounded like an imprecation. He didn't know that she bestowed her secret language on her sons when her husband wasn't home.

"Yes, agreed, tomorrow evening . . . Hey, you who know all about what's high-class stuff, did you ever hear about big tail?"

Angelo again feared a trap: had Lometto also told her about *his* sexual tastes?

"Why, it depends . . ." he answered, clinging to the memory of Demetrio's answers.

"I really want to get one. It's a nice fur. Distinguished. I'll pay for it with my own money."

"Try and repeat that name if you don't mind."

"They're having a summer fur sale in Mantua. Big tail."

"Oh, you mean broadtail."

"Yes, that's it."

"Sure, you're right to buy it. After all, another tail can always come in handy."

They said goodbye laughing, which after all was what she wanted, since she repeated the name without taking Angelo's correction into account. A fur coat like that, with that kind of name, represented a *status symbol* of Adamitic grandeur.

The next day Lometto was there, roaming around inside the "stable" equipped with an industrial elevator and majolica tiles in the lobby, and Angelo asked him sarcastically whether Demetrio had gotten in touch with him in order not to ask him what he expected: whether everything was proceeding smoothly with Belart. Lometto shook his head and said nothing, shrugging his shoulders. How could one tell if he was preoccupied? Now he cohabited with very dark sunglasses, which until that moment Angelo had not noticed but must certainly go back several months and were worn also in dim places where they couldn't be necessary, and a recently imported Sicilian beret. Many things covered him from the forehead down also at sunset. But he was an expert at pretending preoccupations, depression, demoralization due to the degradation of civilized life, at fixed intervals he desperately wanted to make it clear that the world was so very unjust to the just men who keep it going. Angelo had learned to drop the ball each time and he exposed himself to remarks or personal opinions only on the condition that Lometto came out into the open first. Now, if anything, it was he who must say that little word whirling in his head: Jasmine

Belart. (Angelo had leafed through all his *Duden* because of that little stuttering saint: in vain.) Seeing that Lometto did not make up his mind, Angelo kept quiet about everything and nothing.

The two of them had in recent past often gone in for little games like this: Now I'm going to take paper and pen and write down what you're thinking at this precise instant. Both of them always guessed correctly, and so often were they thinking the same thing that they only had to glance at each other fleetingly to understand nuances not grasped by others even after hours of conversation. The only advantage that Angelo had over Lometto in this regard was that Angelo when he wanted to remain inpenetrable, if not on the subject of his thought, at least in its formulations, decided psychically to use a hermetic language, not accessible to Lometto's vocabulary; Lometto, instead, was completely in the open: the vernacular essentiality of a linguistic dualism balanced between "good people" and "bad people" made telepathy for Angelo easy and swift like a whimsical stop on a park slide. He sensed that Lometto had begun to be afraid of this There were days when he did not want to see him at all for fear of betraying something, then he made him deal with Edda, who presented instructions so contradictory received from her husband and no plausible explanation, that Angelo concluded that this was inevitable so as not to reveal the double aims and warty little roots that gave the instructions meaning. "Celestino said you've got to do it exactly like this" and Angelo executed to the letter, without even knowing what he was to do with this or that customer or shipper. According to Lometto, the less he knew the better things fell into place. "Which place?" Angelo dared to ask after the operation was accomplished. "No concern of yours" Lometto answered. If that's what he wanted, fine . . .

They went into the house, while the boys and the brother-in-law were setting the table under the portico. The dinner promised to be succulent and the guests many—the family, the entire cast onstage. Angelo was ready to hit, in the kitchen he realized that the aroma had an extra dimension as if he saw and heard them slither out of the pans to form the ghosts of that moral redemption he was passionately seeking for two, perhaps three years. He felt keener even in his shoulder blades; his looks, his humorous little remarks lured husband and wife toward the abyss and the trap which this time was his, not theirs: they would fall into it, he would jump away. With an extravagant gesture of which he was rarely capable: shrugging his shoulders. Now with irritation he watches Edda as she cuts slices of polenta, squeezed out by her fingers on the plastic pouch. He had really hoped for a nice homemade polenta. Lometto pecks in the pickle and salami dishes. The perfume of the roast obliterates the smell of fresh varnish left behind by the painter, who is also their professional milker cum truck driver cum night watchman. Lometto, totally enthralled by his gluttony which shuts off his mind, only now removes his skullcap and glasses.

"The end of spring would be the most suitable season to become pregnant, and also the beginning of summer . . ." Edda sighs, distractedly.

"Can't you get off the subject? Children cost money."

"Yes, but just one more . . ."

The two peck at each other with studied irony, Edda says how lovely it would be to see those three sculpted in a mountain when the two of them are old and that one piece of the Dolomites would be enough to fit in four. Angelo lets them delve deeply into the fetus of the multi-presidential-mountaineering-Michelangelesque topic, then at a moment in which, if casually, the eyes of both founders are turned to him, he says, peeling the skin off a slice of salami: "Why, instead of making it, don't you adopt one? The baby of that southern girl who killed herself in Penzana, for instance."

Lometto, wife and husband, sit paralyzed in a supreme effort at nonchalance; he feels them turn rigid, as he concentrates unswervingly on the scrap of gut that detaches itself from the slice. Varied sounds of spoons stirring things in the background, the oven door opening and closing, not a word.

"I don't want bastard ovaries from some whore!" Edda shrieks, perhaps a bit beside herself, but she's always just as excited about nothing. "And besides, I want a male, not a female. *Mine, mine, mine.*"

The atmosphere is suddenly so tragic, for reasons unknown to Angelo or for some other nonexistent reasons, that the taillight of his sentence, "so you'll be able to salve your conscience," goes off.

Edda, leaving the kitchen, says to her husband: "You take care of the polenta. You can all go to hell."

Angelo watches Lometto as he tries to reach the burner with the sizzling grill, holding his head in a very unnatural position as though he were trying not to be seen. And from the chair he grabs his skullcap, sticks it on his head, pushes it down low over his forehead.

He fiddles with the yellow slices, recoiling somewhat at every turn, sucking his scorched fingers. Angelo doesn't say a word. Objective attained: to detach himself with a clean cut from all that the Lomettos are and have been and will be and reproportion the role of accomplice that they wanted him to be, to become.

"Who knows how these ideas get into your head? Where do you get them from?" Lometto says in neutral tones, still with his back turned.

"Now, listen, I don't think I said anything so unusual. Adoptions are on the order of the day. It's true your wife can't stand women, but what a reaction! *Bastard ovaries!* Of some poor soul, some vagrant who, it seems to me, has paid quite dearly, wouldn't you say?"

That "wouldn't you say" is even heavier, a real challenge, it would require an answer. Lometto doesn't say anything, he slides the scorched yellow-and-black-striped slices onto a napkin.

"You didn't tell me it was a girl."

"Didn't I? I thought I did. Let's sit down. Dinner is ready!"

And all of them come running: father, mother, sister, brother-in-law, nephews, sons, the relatives dressed in black, the milker, his wife. The two ducks come out of the prototype oven (a bargain supplied by his brother-in-law, a unique sample never reproduced for commercial reasons and which he has gotten for little or nothing), the bottles are uncorked, and Edda, who appears smiling under the portico, has even powdered herself a bit around the eyes, wears a light black, vaguely Japanese dressing gown, and looks at Angelo, only after stretching the fold of her eyes and lips into a knife edge filed by a line of cyclamen-colored makeup.

"Go wash that mug of yours, go" Lometto says, huffing.

"Just a bit of makeup . . . Come on, let's pretend we're in Montecatini, taking the waters!" Edda says—and ready, set, go, they dive into their plates.

They all have a great appetite for meat and jokes, epics and alcoves, table and bed, why not! an extra glass, an extra chunk, the barrel full, the wife drunk, the cretinous aunt with money, the once-removed cousin, oh well! these children, God bless them!—Magra dei Veleni should be here now: "*Benvenuto, signore mio cognato,*" all off-key. Lometto is very solicitous with Angelo, and his plate is continually being filled up and that bad little head of Lometto II, forgetful of the promised kicks, and in this perfectly instructed, pokes fun at him, says "Are you still inversed?" and calls him a glutton while protecting his own plate with one arm. And then from inside arrives the sound of Ravel's "Bolero" and Lometto I bursts out: "Again? We hear it three times a day! What's this urge, this dirge!"

"Yes, always the 'Bolero' " Lometto III adds. "First it was Fred Buongusto, then 'The Boat Goes' and now the 'Bolero' . . ."

And the adults laugh, because they think that the boys are not connecting the music with the accompaniment of something else. Of course they do! One time when Lometto, in who knows what town, had asked Angelo to phone Edda, and one of the three had answered "What is it?"—there was no way to get them to understand that they must say "Hello?"; Lometto II even answered "What do you want?"—at that unusual hour of the night there was a background sound of the "Bolero" and when Lometto had finally come out of the hotel bathroom and picked up the receiver the background had suddenly disappeared before Lometto XY put on his mother. But at Lometto's house there were only two phones: one in the office downstairs, the other in the bedroom. So someone in the office, undisturbed, was using Ravel to shake his castanets without keeping the entire bedroom floor awake. This false naïveté of believing that children are always the last born!

So they ate with all due gaiety, and everything was smoothed out because not touched upon again: neither the offensive business of adoption nor that little Austro-Turkish word Coptafuk.

Then the mother too had something to say: "And what about my house, won't you come to see it?"

As if he were a public health doctor neglecting another house call. "I've got a lot of beautiful furniture too, you know. Oh, but what a card this Dr. Bazarovi. Come, I'll show you, so you too can tell me that it's beautiful."

He went up a few steps and was in the apartment of the two old folks: narrow rooms taken up by walls and floors full of "modern" carpentry, neat and orderly like a room in a mortuary, full of candy dishes with ribbons and almonds in initialed cotton hankies. This immediately made him feel at home.

Stuck in the frame of a picture of a small copse, brook, hut, sheep, shepherdess and shepherd, there were three or four old photographs. While the woman with her eyes gleaming with a particular light blue followed Angelo's mercifully encomiastic journey from the old bed of "when she got married" to the new but "antique" bedside tables—properly sprayed with buckshot and then polished with tallow—Angelo, in search of new striking adjectives, slipped out the childhood photos and asked who Celestino was and who the others were.

"This one, don't you see? Look, he's got the same mug as now."

"So skinny?"

"Oh, as children they were both thin as nails. And blond hair. He began to put on weight in the army: and then when he got married . . . Look: the same flapping ears."

"Yes, yes, it's he, precisely. But if you hadn't told me . . ."

"And look at the eyes! He got them from me. Boys take after their mothers. He doesn't even seem to have any in the photo, it's two holes all white. My Bruna, instead, you see how black they are? And now I'm going to give you a nice cognac!"

Angelo gulped, while all the others waited at the bottom of the stairs for him to finish polishing his eyes.

As he returned from the banquet under the cement arbor, Angelo thought about Edda's reaction as something already known and experienced previously: blood connections. It involved none other than Gino's brother-in-law, one day when Angelo had gone to pay a visit there, to those magnificent kilometric hothouses where the stinking-rich couple lived, simple, profoundly happy, and hospitable though secretly corroded by the lack of an heir. Pasqua had tried all avenues, or almost, and even Angelo had witnessed with trepidation two pregnancies that had gone bad, and finally also the contemplation of a small, premature being of a few ounces that labored transfixed by tubes and IVs beyond the protective double window in the Borgo Roma maternity ward in Verona. This too buried, Angelo felt entitled to enough familiarity to suggest during that regal luncheon: "But why don't you adopt one? I met a couple that . . ."

"No, I don't want anybody else's jism!" the man had blared, smacking the table with a blow that turned over two wineglasses and cut short any possible compromise concerning *his* blood.

Blood remained an absolute value, it came immediately after that of money and the two values compenetrated each other in the mystery of creation, they stood at the most biblical peak of mind and heart, fused in supernal symmetry.

And this value, one and indivisible, had been so all the more when Pasqua, good-hearted, energetic, in love, prone beneath her hemophobic man, had undertaken a radical treatment, going from specialist to specialist, ingurgitating everything, subjecting herself to two horrifying interventions which she described like so many extractions of already shaky molars, both aware that it was her life that was at stake. And for her husband it had remained an absolute value, irrefrangible, invulnerable, even afterwards, in his blind, muffled, and crude sorrow which could not permit itself regrets or scruples or extenuations even when confronted by her corpse which contained another.

From the hill to the foot of the field of stubble their two gazes cross without meeting. Clemente slips into the underbrush. Angelo begins climbing again. He turns around twice to throw a vicious look at a guy who has a transistor in his hand and has gotten it into his head to pretend he is listening in order to follow him absentmindedly but mercilessly. He takes a deep breath and dives in among the brambles. After a moment he hears the sports news behind him, turns around, and with a gesture tells the voyeur to beat it. Clemente and Angelo embrace. And there comes fatso again with his transistor, the two move apart. Angelo shouts, "Aren't you through breaking our balls yet? Get the hell out of the gonads!" And he waves an arm.

They go down along the slope, which is at least a kilometer. Clemente is a prodigious lover. Angelo can't wait for the moment when all this will be over. He feels like a special dessert given to the most faithful customers on the twentieth anniversary of a store's opening. His mind is blocked, so he sticks to all the prescribed positions. The thicket of ferns renders his anguish pruriginous and supple, the twig of nettle tickles his inadequacy, the minute thistle under one buttock stupefies his resignation. Clemente articulates at will his inexorable patience. He begins all over again. Angelo feels absolutely nothing, apart from a further discomfort: a grasshopper imprisoned under his right armpit. He must decide to make that visit to the cemetery if he wants to stifle this almost musical sentence within him: "*Ciao ciao* little sister little sister very good very good." It seems to him that the man with the transistor is the only one who somewhere draws enjoyment, together with Clemente, from the situation. Finally he has an ejaculation similar to shaving foam accompanied by a choked cry—the thistle! Clemente puts a hand over his mouth. He hears "Goal!" So that's over with.

"The most beautiful memory of Lake Garda" Clemente says, affectionately, so excited by this partner who has kept his eyes wide open for an interminable stretch of time, and laughed nervously because ashamed to be seen in the nakedness of his physical dislocation stung by a nest of termites. That forced abandon must not have escaped him, and the thing must have overexcited him. Did Clemente perhaps now understand what Angelo had meant with a sentence dropped nonchalantly about despair? the despair of not feeling anything? of no longer knowing how to communicate with oneself when a third person is involved? of no longer knowing from which gesture to begin in order to repeat the same gestures, passing them off as new? Had he glimpsed the small bactericidal monster of sexuality, the old sexophobia which again mounts its throne after years of having been chased from power? In Clemente predominates the serenity and earthly pleasure of having touched the core of a body dangling from a thread of madness whose end he cannot see. Angelo is laboriously *true*.

"If I happen to be around here, may I phone you?" Clemente asked him while cleaning his back.

"Of course. I'm in the book, it's easy."

Clemente rests an arm on his shoulder as they go back up the slope. Angelo is irritated by this familiar gesture of an unwished-for protectiveness. He endures it like a dead weight and hopes that the too narrow path will soon reduce the problem to a single file. Out of the wood he draws a breath of relief without releasing it.

"You've got a phenomenal ass."

Clemente proclaims the compliment with Thomas-like conviction, you must try in order to believe, the loin applied to a category of the spirit, the flesh that issues in quarters from love and travels in dotted lines on butcher-shop posters. A phenomenological ass, that's it. Why not? Angelo gives him a pat on the cheek, making an effort to share the division of sex into phenomenal asses and white pricks.

Clemente goes back to the beach by himself, Angelo stays for a while on the meadow to give him time. He collects a sample of every specimen with petals. At home he will catalogue them. From above he sees Zizi already about to leave.

"Wait for me, I need a ride" he yells, and runs down toward the highway, then straight to the beach to pick up his stuff.

He exchanges hasty goodbyes with Clemente and his friend, who runs after him with an invitation to Milan, races back up the escarpment. Zizi is waiting for him with the motor running.

"What pretty little flowers, are they for me?"

"Obviously."

"The usual cheapskate. You know that I only like American Beauties. Well anyway, come down to the Bordello tonight. Darfo's kids are there."

"But you know my car just broke down."

"I'll come and pick you up."

"No, look, make it some other time. *Ciao*."

Days which if you put them all together and squeezed hard wouldn't yield a drop of life. But that's life: massed together and dry, filled with sterile, repetitious events always the same, whose memory is lost. You squeeze, and out comes a dust of standard frustrations and a smell of phenol, a pulverizing of pharaonic gauzes.

From August through September there were as usual quick trips to Germany—Neustadt, one of the many small "new" cities with this name, Nuremberg, Schöngau.

And last November, Edda officially declared herself two months pregnant.

This seemed to have caught even Lometto by surprise. "They're selling them secondhand with holes in them" he had said. Pregnant with Ario, as she was going to call the fourth boy. Ario, period, the Aryan par excellence, the *Homo technicus* with superior gifts, another redeemer. He would be an absolute masterpiece, the *ne plus ultra* of the Lometto/Napaglia genes.

Edda so hated women that she supervised every new hiring, and Den—which was getting big—was occupied exclusively by women whose only female attribute was a presumed urinary apparatus buried beneath the ugliness of sometimes horrifying breasts and bellies and clumsy and skimpy clothes. These hirings had the further advantage of silencing the Communist junta, since they could be mistaken for a gesture of Christian charity.

The factory functioned beautifully: these horrors of nature—recruited in the surrounding areas and at certain times also elsewhere when production increased—came to join those six wonder women (issued from the basements of brothers- and sisters-in-law, in which they were immediately stored away again by their respective Nazarene hands at the day's end, and then there were also involved certain parish-house "attics") and they represented a two hundred percent guarantee that the technical times written on paper corresponded to those of the productive reality checked at any time during the working day. Even the micturition of these fortunate wretches had been regulated at specific intervals, just as headaches or complaints caused by peculiarly female cycles, or the kidney attacks of those who had had the gall to obtain a dispensation from inconsiderate bishops and get married with someone just as wretched and become pregnant. This had happened only twice over many years and the persuasive interventions of country priests and public health insurance doctors and the Lomettos themselves had convinced the wayward women to abort, since abortion "in certain cases" was sanctioned even by the health laws . . . of course, it wasn't something one should run around telling everyone, for in reality it still was half a sin . . . and the hapless creatures had shown up in the factory the next morning and, after the ritual offering of a small glass of Marsala, had resumed better than before slipping the pantyhose into the mechanical enveloper, under the vigilant eyes of Edda, and the mother-in-law and sister-in-law, and now also a full-fledged foreman, chosen, over Edda's wishes and resistance, by Lometto and not by her: a homunculus all cunning and deformity.

Angelo began to tank up regularly at the Penzana gas station: he only had to say "Fifteen thousand" and the old woman at the pump would begin to empty a secret tank of her own about the Lomettos. He listened while looking over the vegetables that the old woman grew behind her shack, the only questions he asked were about beans and zucchini and pumpkins, she answered a bit of everything. They understood each other perfectly.

With the same sensation of sleepiness . . .

BOOK TWO

Thursday.

With the same sensation of sleepiness and insomnia, Angelo, after having hastily eaten, leaves for that would-be appointment with Armando. An acquaintance takes him there on his motorcycle. It's the first time that he travels at almost two hundred kilometers an hour to arrive without hurry at so insipid a destination.

At the outer wall of the villa—a branch of purpureal bougainvillea has lunged during the night from the hidden rear of the garden—Angelo immediately sees the smile of the man whom he had entrusted with the message a week ago. His smiles could not be more expressive, they have nothing to do with him.

"Armando isn't here."

"Just as well" Angelo replies, ill at ease.

It has begun to drizzle. Angelo distributes ample smiles and jests to the scramble indolently picking the ripe blackberries. The surface of the lake becomes the spittoon of a storm that flits this way and that and does not know exactly where it will go to expectorate. He has always liked to swim under the rain, to feel hounded by the pressure that pushes you up and the other, pluvial, that pushes you down. And him there, the temporary man afloat.

Then close to Christmas had come Edda's nth strange phone call. Strange because, instead of telling him right off what they had found wrong with Lometto at the hospital—hospitalized at her insistence, because there, at least, they would force him to follow a diet and would take a look at his pressure, one hundred and eighty at a minimum—she said, full of exuberance: "So are you coming to pick up your case of champagne?"

"But wasn't he supposed to get out tomorrow? I'll come after Celestino gets out. Do they know anything?"

"He's not coming out tomorrow, he's got another think coming. He has to stay in there a few more days. It's better if he stays there now, with all the eating that goes on during the holidays. Just come, I can give it to you . . . the case! And the salami too . . . we just made it . . . It's so nice and big . . . so . . ."

"All right. I'll come; if he has to stay in so many days . . ."

There still weren't any obvious signs of her being with child, only her dress of prickly thin wool pulled a trifle on her hips and the navel was more defined than usual, but just a bit.

The boys were at their maternal grandparents', for their Christmas allowances. And suddenly, while wiping off the salami—without there being any need for it, she saw mold everywhere—Edda comes up with her matriarchal hyperbole: "Can you imagine how sore they'll be, the partners who have taken Mire away from us, if I were to bring into the world a son who's an American citizen? They'd die of envy . . ."

It is as though she were continuing a conversation accidentally interrupted a few minutes before.

Angelo was seized by a vague sense of vertigo: was this another trap-joke of Lometto's mediated by his wife.

When two days earlier he had gone to visit him at the hospital in Castiglione delle Stiviere, Lometto had not given him the slightest inkling of such bragging: he lay stretched out in his private room—it cost him the same as it would any insured patient installed in the corridor: that is, nothing—in those so-called pajamas of "his," huge with red and cream-colored stripes, the family pajamas used in similar circumstances by both his father and his brother-in-law. He was all pink and happy, something big was happening at Mire, Inc., some partner had begun to show up timidly at the house, to get the lay of the land, to see whether . . . And then Lometto had told him that, in cahoots with another hospitalized joker, he had waited for everybody, nurses and doctors, to be in the dining room and had put on a white smock and toured the place feeling the pulse of newcomers, laying his hands on appendices and livers, sticking thermometers in asses. He had asked one man, who was there because of an ingrown nail on his left big toe, after pretending to grow pale as he was fingering his wrist, whether he had taken care of his will, and had instructed the guy who acted as his straight man to call the chaplain. Oh, what a scene! The man had had a stroke and now they'd moved him downstairs to the cardiology section. But the chief physician had put a lid on it, fortunately there hadn't been any witnesses and nobody, he insisted, besides Edda and Angelo, knew about it. Loud and flushed, he expected Angelo to laugh but he had merely snorted, glanced at the chart at the foot of the bed, and left without saying goodbye. Lometto had run after him to the elevator door, embraced him. Angelo let himself be embraced, told him "*ciao,*" realized that no one apart from relatives had paid a visit during those ten days to all those billions under observation. From this Angelo deduced that Lometto's billions were only his, exclusively his, that he had no business associations of any kind. Otherwise, you can imagine the crowds.

Now he was looking at Edda, afraid of being duped: what else did they want to extort from him? had she too, like her husband, begun to think that Angelo knew too much? What presumption: as if in Angelo's life there weren't other people for him to worry about. At this point he had to put up a fight. He did so calmly, accepting everything at face value, playing the game, whatever it might be.

"He should be happy about it, don't you think? Where's the obstacle? A visa, and you're off."

"Of course he likes the idea! His son, President of the United States!"

"If Reagan made it . . ."

Edda was wrapping the salami in a grocery bag, rubbing with her thumb the small bumps marked by the string, one by one. Angelo did not lose heart, he could add a couple of general things of his own without committing himself.

"It certainly would be quite a coup for Penzana . . . To exhibit an American passport at the moment of baptism" but Angelo didn't really know quite what to say, and Edda laughed as if she had told him that she had seen a UFO and he had fallen for it out of politeness. But looking at her bluish gums he understood this wasn't a passing fancy, and that Edda laughed, stretching her lips like that, to get away with it as with any enormity she'd set her heart on. He was seized by true vertigo, and it was also cold there. The mania of false grandeur was the mania of true grandeur, because those were the authentic parameters of class distinction procured by money: not to keep even a single plant of cyclamen in the house, but to be able with a snap of the fingers to perform the genetic crossing of the Atlantic. Never to have learned how to swim but to bend the ocean to one's will.

Without a car any longer, and a broken-down bicycle, it must certainly be time to go back home on foot to his bend in the river . . .

Angelo kept his own counsel, he did not want to express opinions on the matter. But had the two of them discussed it between themselves? Whose initiative was it? hers, his, both of theirs? Angelo was traversed by impressions that could not easily be rationalized, and at least one thing was clear: it was Lometto's wish that Edda as a first move should explore Angelo's attitude in depth, then Lometto, according to need, would intervene in one way or another; or he would pull back, saying that it was all just nonsense, at which point Edda would offer her husband a helping hand, calling Angelo a simpleton who was always being taken in. It was with this tactic that Lometto used him as a secret adviser: without letting him know directly so as not to give him too much importance and then possibly have to pay him a bonus for those consultations all carefully *en passant*.

Angelo had proved that "he knew one more than Prime Minister Andreotti" on more than one occasion. You gave him the end of a thread, two, three, approximate data. He asked a few questions, and then told you gratis how the entire skein would unravel in the short or middle term—he did not believe in the long term. He had never been mistaken even once. For example, he had already foreseen that Lometto would recover the ownership of Mire within the space of a year, and the year was almost up. And in fact the first tangible signs of that "angelic spell," as Edda had called it, were beginning to appear.

But did Edda now want to be informed as to how elections take place in America? How a presidential campaign can be mounted approximately in the year 2030 and then laugh at him, Angelo, for months on end? The term was extremely long, even without taking into account nuclear-warhead intermezzos which would slow things down a bit.

It was absurd that the couple should invest Angelo with so much charisma on a subject so profoundly alien and odious to him—an operation of high gynecology on the Atlantic Pact level.

"It could be a sensible idea, no different than beginning to cultivate rice paddies in Tonkin because Vercelli has no cachet, that's all."

"I've already thought of the American name" Edda said, echoing herself. The case—the three-bottle item—was covered with dust, it had been there since last Christmas.

Angelo decided to find out how it feels to be shrewd: "If they taste of the cork I want a demijohn of the consortium wine, don't forget. You're three months gone, aren't you?"

"A bit longer."

"Did you do all your tests? But this is rosé, I'll cut my throat if it has kept."

"It's champagne, what a bore. Champagne lasts decades."

He puts the gift box on the seat of the car, there was not a snowflake anywhere and not even a cotton flake to create atmosphere. Cotton costs money.

"Yes, that is, no. But what do you know about women's problems?"

"Yes, no . . . that is . . . the echogram and all that . . ." But Angelo said the sentence through his teeth and Edda did not hear it, he was ready to leave, salami in hand, she with that sudden beseeching look spoiled by a forced clowning of the facial muscles exhausted by pretending they are pretending. Angelo exchanged a Christmas kiss, thinking exactly: her problem. And she was about to call him back inside, but he said that he must be off in a hurry, the fog, the damn curves, and he started the motor. He could have sworn that he had escaped one of those endless confessional bouts, corroborated during its pauses by the church bell, which continued to insist that hearts, souls, tongues, lungs should open up to the good tidings. As soon as he negotiated the first curve he felt a bit sorry for his rudeness: Edda was not a bad woman, perhaps he should have stayed to listen to her. But then he decided that he was glad he had not yielded to a compassion he did not feel. Now he slowed down and entered the main highway. Oh no, certainly not! He was really glad at not having contributed with any appreciable advice to Edda or indirectly to Lometto on that futurable Italo-American placental implant of theirs. He came to a full stop, opened the door, and flung the triple box into the pond to keep company with the one of the previous Christmas.

But also the bend of the poisoned river . . .

From Friday to Friday.

But also the bend of the poisoned river in its isolation has mithridatized him after two, three, four, five afternoons. And although he obtained his driver's licence only a couple of years before, it is no longer possible to think of replacing the car—a seized motor, too expensive to fix it—with a bicycle. In town it is very difficult for people to be seen in his company, especially young boys. Angelo has spent all these evenings at the bar on the piazza, outside, enjoying the breeze from the San Pancrazio hill, seated before groups of ecstatic Montichiari locals whom he has given ample lectures—on himself. They were perfect, all that they lacked was speech.

United, they got along so well with him and so gladly; they felt, if not strong, at least singly at ease, like plastic sponges accustomed to sinks and toilet bowls immersed for a second in the champagne of a dropped bottle.

Angelo does not ask them for anything, just to listen and be amused; there's not even a need for someone to play the straight man. Angelo proceeded by concentric circles and, night after night, he would send someone home with his head bewildered and the bones of his secondhand normality cracked. At least he thought he did. Meanwhile, let's have fun!

Not one of those boys who listened, fascinated, in the social anonymity that another twenty guaranteed would ever have dared to be seen alone with him strolling down the avenue or on the hill or even at a table drinking a coffee. Only a few rare eccentrics and ballbreakers, papa's sponges. Angelo spoke. And all he saw before him were human flies among curtains and he sublimated the instinct of his hand to open up in order to squash them and that of his eye to be satiated by reddish and blackish streaks of the air's pane, which, however, implied that there was blood in them—amiably rambling on about the concept of equality at all costs.

In the evening, especially when at the bar, he felt how tired he was of belonging to a *species* to which he did not belong. After afternoons of gray sun, after mornings spent in the library doing research for his translations on albinism or the condition of the Austro-Hungarian railroads immediately after the First World War, in the evening Angelo had to escape. In the evening his solitude without pretensions and his knowledge without quotations are of no help. He sits there in the piazza at the small café table and experiences the twinge that in some other place life is still palpitating and possible and that someone there is living, and that one must reach that someone. But how can you on a bicycle?

Ah, last year when Lometto came every now and then and they went to eat a pizza and then he took him cruising down the highway and settled down to wait—to sleep—for him to hook a trucker and climb up into the sultry heat of the cab. He waited, disappearing; the parking lot was enormous.

Angelo thinks about that today, Wednesday, as he presents a dissertation to his audience on the impossibility of delaying legislation against the heterocracy of the family and the foundation of a new *res pubica* based on work, singleness, test tubes, and sex bent like a dog's prick—any old way. The homogeneous gelatin of his non-paying listeners, all those indigenous freeloaders who colonized the world as soon as there were two of them, rebelled: they wanted a myth, an anecdote, a funny story, filth, not utopian passages from the civil code. Angelo is bored and struggles to pretend an interest and so arrives at ten-thirty, the best hour.

Now, it is not possible to continue spending the evenings like this, philosophizing about political equality and individual diversity when even the delegate of the Federation of Free Trade Unions diphthongs the hiatuses of his already limited vocabulary. Power is always attained by those who have not the slightest notion of prosody, better to go and turn tricks than sit there discussing.

So today, Thursday, late in the afternoon, Angelo showed up right in the middle of a dinner in the open and chose a car in the used dealer's lot, a Fiat 128, in a twelve-year-old muddy green. He took it for a test drive with the dealer, who left the table over his wife's weak protests: the gears are hard to shift, and what a stench of cow, but it doesn't cost much and he buys it. Beginning tomorrow morning, after the transfer of ownership, it will be at his disposal. Not much, actually it's a lot for him, who should have already been penniless for ages. He has worked for ten months on a translation and last Wednesday he found out that the last balance will be forty percent less than he expected because of a publishing trick called "stroke computation." After he pays for the consultations, buys food and gasoline, there'll be nothing left.

Would he accept a check postdated by fifteen days? he asked the dealer. "Why not?" is the answer, and the man sat down again under the porch to go on with his dinner. Angelo feels duty-bound to reassure him, the dealer says, "All right, all right" a trifle irritated: was he afraid perhaps that he would invite himself to dinner? He certainly doesn't have much to boast about, this parvenu mechanic, it must also have been quite a burden for him to keep on his lot that shitty contraption which pollutes the air over a radius of three hundred meters. He has probably given him credit more than anything else for his olfactory courage. "Yes, but I'd like to go back and eat now . . ." he told him. Angelo said goodbye, very embarrassed, polyglot college graduates who are broke always do make a certain impression.

But it wasn't specifically the fact of being almost broke—again the scarecrow of poverty with autumn at the door—that caused that afternoon depression at the river's bend, that spending of hundreds of minutes watching the disquietude of a solar calm bristling with mosquitoes and wasps. No, it's not because of the money he does not have—it is because of the money he has, that he might have, but come on now, that he has to all effects and purposes and that he dare not touch because in the silkiness and sheen of the traveler's checks he senses, sees dripping blood. This is why, since he put them in the bank three months ago, he never even went to look at them again, feel them under his fingers, nurture again the Brazilian dream of a beautiful escape and an absolute shoulder shrug. And the recorded tape: never again listened to, what clues can he derive from it, since the only thing he should do is hand it over to a magistrate? He has promised never to use it if . . . But precisely that *if* has not been respected, or did it just lapse? An absolutely stalled situation, blocked, glass-covered, taxidermized. Murder by poisoning or an actual fulminating meningitis?

And tomorrow, when he'll have a car, what will he do with it? He'll go back to the Terrazzine or Sirmone. Or the Bordello. Twenty lire, not twenty thousand dollars, the destination.

Friday morning the car, washed and deodorized with sylvan pine—"magic water," which brings out the until then clandestine nuances of cowhide—is ready and Angelo can take it away. He contemplates it, mastodontic in the corner, against the railing of the stairway that leads to the old mill. It has wheels, windows, a motor inside, it is an automobile and can move a person. Excited, he goes up to the library, he does not feel like taking the usual stroll to the market. He finds it more congenial to invent for himself a curiosity for Marino than to lead himself into the temptation of making his mother the disproportionate gift of a spider stockfish. She keeps asking him "And now why don't you eat Egypt, why don't you pay the light bill with your money from never-never land?" Faced by death, with over their heads a recently repaired roof, a minimum pension, a cemetery crypt paid for, old women get a swollen head and never stop pestering with the recklessness of trapeze artists equipped with a safety net also in heaven. So, no stockfish, but Marino *tout court*:

> *A flower, a flower breaks its skin and gives birth,*
> *And blond, flowing hair is born,*
> *Two serene eyebrows after the hair,*
> *Now a forehead and with it a face.*

And between a locomotive of "Group 685 state railroads; (some) ex-680 state railroads, ex-686 SR; ex-681 SR (maximum boiler pressure: 12 kg. per sq. cm.)" and a "sight refraction," one always feels like poking around in the most local depths of village libraries. For example, it was at the town library in Cremona that Angelo discovered *The Listener*, edited by Joe Ackerley, for several decades, it was there in all of its years, a collection richer than the one in the British Museum. At first he had thought of writing his thesis around it, then he had opted for John Ashbery because of an ancient vendetta which had dragged on since the latter had said in New York, "Oh, these Italian queens," when he didn't want to fuck with him. The initials were the same, and Angelo already had the folder printed, the color of cat diarrhea. The title had been the most difficult thing to conceive, because it had to fit into just a few lines.

And here, very surprised, he comes out from the back of the reception room and says to the librarian: "Would you please explain to me how it is that there is a whole century of the *Gazzetta di San Luigi Gonzaga* up to and including yesterday?"

"It's simple: every library here in the outlying towns collects, besides the provincial dailies, at least one other not national Italian daily from another province. Montichiari has been assigned the *Gazzetta di San Luigi Gonzaga*. In Carpenedolo maybe they have all of *Il Giorno* and *Il Resto del Carlino*." Angelo rushes back to the rear and begins to turn the pages in a great hurry: so it must have been toward the end of 1978. He still remembers well the detail of the cold, the fog. Proceeding by exclusion: October or November or December. Such an event must have been reported, after all it doesn't happen every day. He feels a shudder pass through his head and in his left eardrum: it peals, as though a phonic mine, very minute and triune, were exploding brilliantly. All this has been too quick, he has not had the time to catch the flash that ignited between mercy and analogy. A flash in code. Too bad. He begins leafing through the enormous rough binding of the year 1978: all those DC and MSI and Rotary meetings, all those knights and presidents on podiums, all those double-breasted suits with fingers stuck in the last buttonhole. Groups of schoolboys, veterans with flags, all those close-ups of pear-shaped heads (Lometto: "And the barber asks them, 'Should I wash it or peel it?' ") adorned with ties, while they are signing something fundamental, all those beautiful red-light movies, all those "idlers" and "disturbers of the peace" in October. Greater calm, however, during the first week of November: smiling dentures of assessors, monsignors, professors, executives, at a charity banquet, a few women, few but good, and again priests caressing children lifted high to do it more quickly, blessings from behind barriers, a bit of Mantegna, and all the purse snatchings, one by one. The Christmas holidays approach, who is in is in, who is out is out. "THE GREAT, TRAGIC PROBLEM OF DRUGS." "EDUCATING CHILDREN IN BEL CANTO." "MAFIA: REALITY OR COLLECTIVE MYTH?"

Already many times Angelo suspected that the most ancient things, in order to escape the deterioration of a by now ineffectual glory, have taken the best road to eternity: remain ancient by becoming cretinous.

And here it is, it had to be there after all, but it is a very slim item at the bottom of the fifth page on Saturday:

"Penzana: Between Wednesday night and Thursday morning Santina Tartaglione, age 19, poliomyelitic, originally from Casaria in the province of Naples, orphaned at an early age, she herself an unwed mother, committed suicide by cutting the veins on both wrists with a razor blade. The unfortunate woman, considered by many to be leading a loose life and addicted to reefers, appeared in our small town a year ago and was welcomed with Christian charity in the bosom of a parochial association which provides work and lodging to handicapped people. Her ill-advised act should perhaps be imputed to the difficulties encountered in trying to reconcile her maternal duties with an occupation. Found bloodless at dawn at the entrance to the churchyard, the young woman has seriously endangered the life of her two-month-old infant, who was discovered half frozen on the side of the provincial highway. The local authorities have made arrangements for the return of the body to her native town, where the unfortunate woman had lived in an orphanage, first as an inmate and later as a cook. The baby girl, promptly entrusted to the care of the Mantua Hospital, is now completely out of danger and will as soon as possible be transferred to the same institution in her mother's town. There are already a great number of applications for adoption." It was not signed Charles Dickens but N.B.

There are very few items by this N.B. throughout January: the inauguration of a monument, the crisis of the junta, a head-on collision between a jeep of the customs police and a truck loaded with pantyhose. Who's going to sing at the Al Mirante Club. A tankful of gasoline spilled by unidentified persons endangers the life of the Communist assessor and his family. All normal. Extremely laborious prose, pieces written over and over, the words doled out.

"Ciao!" Angelo shouts exultantly to the librarian, then he plunges down the stairs with a photocopy of the article in his hand and from the bottom of the stairs down the slope toward home. Hurray! he has found a way to put the twenty thousand dollars to use and how amusing these merchants and industrialists and politicians, these pirates of our time who investigate each other to *know* more, to have, if need be, one more instrument for blackmail! and so it is with this Belart and her *"kleine heilige Stotterin,"* the German for "small stammering saint," or indeed the Italian name Santina Tartaglione, and what is an instru-

ment for blackmail if you are divided becomes, when united, one more guarantee to count on your adversary who by now is your business partner.

His mother shows him a square parcel on the kitchen table.

"Just brought by the mailman. I had to pay five thousand lire postage due."

It is small but heavy. He opens it. Wood shavings, a letter lying on a white neck that peeks through: "Jürgen wanted to leave you the angel which belonged to my aunt's grave. I thank you for your kind letter. You were a dear friend to my son and I will always be grateful to you for this. He was a cross for me, but it is difficult to resign oneself. Unfortunately I did not understand very well what I was supposed to do with the reel you sent me, I don't even own a tape recorder and a special one is needed for this. At any rate it is safe and I will simply follow your instructions should the need arise—and I really hope it won't, that you too will not leave us. Most affectionately, Veronika Oelberg."

He takes out the angel which he has always looked at with covetous eyes: it is carved from very white, uniform marble, it does not have a single crack, and the fact of having been exposed for one doesn't know how many decades to the inclemency of the weather has given it a velvety smoothness which cameos its gracefulness. It does not at all recall anything funereal, but rather the optimistic bizarreness flung out by a baroque altar panel. It is very beautiful and it is his, as it has always intimately been from the very first moment he saw it in Jürgen's studio apartment.

"That's what we needed—angels, it's already impossible to walk through your room with that stuff all over the place. Angels, oh Lord! And don't forget the five thousand lire, I don't find it in the street."

"All right." She has threatened to live until the age of ninety, so he might as well not contradict her.

He continues late into the afternoon to contemplate the angel from all angles: he closes and opens door and shutters, tries out half darkness, the full light of day, in profile, three-quarters, with the lampshade directed at the face, and from above. It is ever more beautiful, more alive. And each time on its surface he meets Jürgen's smooth glance, he too incredulous that then, after so much death, there should follow another death, different, which a matter of fractions of instants would prevent him from knowing while alive . . .

Looking at it from the back, with the folds of its gown and the flowing corolla of the barely inclined head, does it not look like a lily? A lily for Giorgina Washington.

He picks up the angel and gets into the car. Oh, the effort it will cost him to detach himself from this object which is so alive, the most precious thing he ever possessed. But he must be capable of it: nothing else could ever prove worthy of being an homage to Giorgina Washington. It is right that this gift should somewhat drain his blood and slow down its vital course, that he should feel lacerated by the thought that in one hour he will have forever renounced the yearning, the gaiety that this angel inspires in him . . .

. . . Angelo once had a flash that he himself defined as a flash of genius: that is, that the Lomettos did not at all enjoy the vaunted if vague political protection, but that they were good tightrope walkers on the make-believe high wire, that their tactics had been so successful that the very politicians considered themselves protected by them. Otherwise it was impossible to understand how, of all the promises that Lometto said he made, not one of them was ever kept. His art of corruption was fed more by the knowledge of men than by true and proper payoffs. The Lomettos accumulated money and power without ever disbursing anything but the golden suggestiveness of the words "carrot" and "stick." And, at the moment of the final promised reckoning, they were very adept at making it clear that much greater proof of "faithfulness" and "morality" was required . . . To Angelo it seemed that many must be the victims who fell under the ax of the hazy vanity of such indescribably insignificant words. Who could impart concrete resonance to the word "morality," for example, if not the one who wields and establishes the law and by coining sugary dogmas is always ready to distribute punishments? Whether one liked it or not, Lometto was the Father of Penzana and its surroundings, and every time the left-wing junta met, his spirit was silently evoked and, at the moment of making a decision, all the deliberations ended by having the unmistakable flavor of the Center-Left on the Right's mentholated camphor.

Perhaps because guided by this local legend, tribally danced by *chorum populi*, Edda wanted a fourth male, a super-male, as soon as possible—she no longer had the time for another diabolical fox-trot. Someone who would be the tangible incarnation of a relationship with the celestial spheres, someone who, announced beforehand by cattle breeding, cheeses, land, houses, pantyhose, and roads covered with asphalt at the town's expense, would bring a new, definitive comet-star over Penzana, Toigo, Mantua—in other words: over Italy. An Italo-American male.

Lometto, seized by the neck of a forty-year-old uterus that knew where its fetus was at, had at the start complained to her about the period of intensive work to fill the summer deliveries, but now it was done: impossible even for him, omnipotent Lometto, to postpone the happy, sensational event to August, to the holidays. This May parturition really did not find him jubilant, and he certainly was not going to go there to assist her. Wasn't it possible to deliver the baby at the U.S. Consulate in Milan? Would they allow the midwife from Caserta to stick her little skeins of straw into the air conditioner? But what folly anyway! Amusing but expensive. And, by all means, he must maintain the most absolute reserve with everyone, they must all be dumbfounded by this affair, Edda had said, bestowing on Angelo in Lometto's presence a classically vulpine look.

She had put the presidential flea into her husband's ear—he had shrugged his shoulders but one could see that this perspective opened up practically infinite political horizons, for himself, for his sons, and also the pride of a certain type of teacher's pet along the lines of: "I put it up your ass smooth as oil" as regards all of Penzana, Bananone, and those turds and incompetent partners who were wrecking Mire, which had piled debt upon debt and charged fire-sale prices and had an inventory that was exploding and in eleven months had lost what he had given to distribute (. . .) in an entire year: a billion and a half. A company that was no longer worth anything, just walls and scrap iron, filled only with the echoes of smacks on the asses of female workers and clerks. One must resign oneself to one's own thirty percent. The same old song: knowing how to lose right away was the best profit and investment. And immediately go on the attack on fronts not foreseen by the "chumps." This son would boost his morale, giving him new energies, new entrepreneurial ideas. Why didn't Angelo take a look at the *Gazzetta*: the question had now come up of putting through a superhighway with American investments, beginning at Castiglione and cutting down toward Penzana, all the way to the sea. And he already had half a deal with the Vatican, for a certain packet of privileged shares, because, just imagine, whoever heard of a superhighway not making a profit? And everybody wanted to get their hands on it. All the more because, in order to do this, they would give him a loan . . . in short, he would work with other people's money at a five percent interest rate. And he would put it in another bank at eighteen . . .

Angelo was bewildered, he could neither follow nor figure out the tare. Too much information, and all at once: it wasn't like Lometto. Ah yes, and he would have him baptized by Wojtyla.

In February, they resumed traveling up and down Europe. After an accident in Innsbruck in which Angelo, because of Lometto's inattention, followed by braking suddenly, had gone through the windshield with his head, it was decided they would go only by train. The business of the windshield—*wraparound!*—the regrets Lometto continued to harp on because this time the insurance had not reimbursed him, lasted for months until New York—the insurance paid him for the thefts of the substandard transistors and even the broken side-door windows: that's why they were always so cheap and he parked anyplace! because every time he had suffered a theft he made a net profit of two hundred thousand lire. The fact that he had not been able to manipulate matters in such a way as to be reimbursed had made a greater impression on him than the dynamics of the accident: the huge, sudden star rippling across the glass, the glitter of shards inside, and, perhaps, in front a man under the wheels, Angelo lifting his hands to his bleeding face and exclaiming, happy: "Luckily, I just took off my glasses!" and then running out toward the tragedy, but the victim was just a brown bathrobe which popped out of the trunk of the shafted car, thank God, and Angelo going to the guardrail and pressing handfuls of snow on his head and forehead. Lometto didn't even have a scratch—he had simply bounced against the steering wheel with his belly and had not suffered any fracture or dislocation. Angelo watched him as best he could through the blood and snow, and saw him open his arms wide and examine the damage, while the squeezed but unharmed occupants of the gypsylike vehicle in front poured out shouting, children, Turkish women, and Lometto looking at the pushed-in muzzle of his car's body, the broken headlights, and nothing else on his mind, Angelo thought with hatred, and not even an internal hemorrhage. His real hemorrhage must have been the thought that the fellow behind is always at fault.

Edda all by herself was taking an English course on records. After two months she knew how to say "good morning" and "good evening" assisted by some prompting . . . and she had already spent three hundred thousand lire on monthly booklets on glossy paper and in a leather binding, and was not going to make any further progress. But she had inherited together with her notary brother an advance share of the family estate, peanuts in comparison with what the illustrious relative was gobbling up. Without consulting anyone, she had bought the same maternity dresses that any of her workers, ecclesiastical circumstances permitting, could have afforded. To her this seemed a great luxury and she'd gone overboard: now she was not only parading her big-tail fur, but at a sale she had bought two sweaters and skirts by a famous designer. Lometto had said she must be out of her mind, she had fluttered her eyelashes, flattered by the coquettish compliment.

Angelo had witnessed the scene, which, however, came to a strange conclusion as soon as Lometto left the room to go to a Mire board meeting: Edda had sat down on the edge of the kitchen table and clutched her head between her hands, her face seemed wrapped in a wrinkled rag, suddenly old, southern-Hamitic, and then smoothed out in all its triangularity. The eyes gradually opened wide with a panic-stricken look, the cheekbones were drawn back and shimmered, the slightly parted lips stretched thinner than usual. Why did Edda play these tricks on him the minute they were alone? what did she mean to tell him? oh, Angelo became anxious to get out of there, he did not like to remain alone with that woman who seemed to mock him, changing moods as soon as Lometto got out of the way. What was it she wanted to communicate to him without resorting to the officiality of words? But in this was she or was she not in agreement with her husband? No, Angelo decided, in this performance she was the only actress and he the only spectator. But Angelo tried every time to reach the closest emergency exit and he too was always seized by panic; the draperies on the true stage were so thick and heavy and somehow smelling of incense, the fissure between the curtains could not be found, and it was completely dark. Angelo's brief delay in opening the door was enough for Edda to transform her face into a screen ruthlessly *herself* which denounced something bared. Then the sound of steps on the outside and she, as if in an intermission, began to speak about orders or the weather. Should he tell Lometto about it? was his wife sick? had she ever suffered from nervous breakdown? and what about the Sicilian mother, always in and out of neurology? why did she suddenly behave as if she had lost all light of reason? And all those Coptafuk pills, all those gossamer wings of cantharides, or Spanish fly, that must have been fluttering in her mind for more than a year now? what did her gynecologist think about that?

No, Angelo would never be able to put the question in real terms, it seemed to him he was already exaggerating, giving free rein to his love for the romantic and his intimate need for unnatural catastrophes. Nothing is better than remaining silent, especially with her. Quite capable of saying to him, "But what are you talking about, are you going crazy?"

Lometto was going through a period of great success: not only were his own Den maneuvers proceeding quickly but with a putsch in the middle of March he had taken over Mire completely, one hundred percent, making a profit of billions of lire with a simple paper chase through banks and bankruptcy judges—everybody gave him credit, all he had to do was lift a finger and the creditors' periods of grace were extended full of trust and joviality. His unquestionable ability and financial talents attracted a hatred that one could smell even at Penzana's gates, while Angelo filled up at the old gasoline vendor's, who had an unrefined tongue. Hatred made him grow all the fatter. All those who'd been thrown on the pavement came one by one to pound the asphalt of his Private Road. It seemed that the Italo-American fetus, as it was gradually taking shape, lavished all around itself lucky hors d'oeuvres. Everything went marvelously for Lometto, even the only credit given up for lost was recovered—against this customer Angelo had applied just in time one of Lometto's teachings: lubricate one's rank telephonic politeness with undertones of blackmail. Because of this, because of this unhoped-for money which had reentered the cash register thanks exclusively to him and his oratorical gifts, Angelo counted on that trip to New York, and without discount, to act as Edda's companion. Trustworthy people did not exist for Lometto—with the exception of Angelo, who, it is true, was "exorbitant" in his demands, but was also the only one who, after being paid, did not come up with unpleasant surprises. That is, he did not double-cross, knew how to hermetically keep all professional secrets, although Lometto had never given away much, confining himself to certain hints about certain financial matters on behalf of a certain clan made possible by a certain fiscal law on its way to parliamentary approval, a certain short-term amnesty. Lometto knew ahead of time some things that common mortals would never even know afterwards—that is, all things of interest to him—and by now he could no longer resist the temptation of regaling Angelo with confidences of a Mafia-financial-Masonic type on the privatization of the state. Lometto had blind trust. At those levels of bank, administrative, fiscal, notarial, and political perdition, Angelo, at any rate, no longer understood a thing and would not even have been able to summarize what the logorrheic vanity of the shrewder one had lavished on the simpler one during the trip.

Edda was already taking treatments for her milk, unwillingly—but Lometto had demanded it in the presence of the notary—that is, his brother-in-law—before marrying her. That she would nurse her children until they were six months old and not do anything to interrupt the nursing, with the penalty of possible claims on the Napaglia estate—but this seemed to have been more than anything else a way of getting back at the father-in-law, who, when it came to patrimonial guarantees, had been just as tough with the Lomettos before the same notary.

What amazed Angelo was that now, suddenly, the two of them needed to have him underfoot in order to come up with such private matters, and that they were insolent enough to set him up as judge, there, with his back against the wall. Every time at the second month Edda had desperately suffered from mastitis but Celestino had been adamant, he quoted the Bible, "you will nurse in pain," the children must grow "strong and healthy" and only mother's milk could do that, to hell with the aesthetics of the breast and the discomfort of mastitis, that's what tits are made for, right? and besides, whom was she supposed to please, him or somebody else? all right then, her tits could stretch all the way to her persimmon because he liked her anyway. But the pain, Edda had interjected weakly; the pain the pain! it'll help you get even more attached to your children, then I'll help you get over the pain. And the three of them—Angelo by now felt he was part of this matrimony even though excluded from the patrimony—burst out laughing. A President of the United States raised on mush from jars! Never! They both had a great time with this joke about the presidency, they kidded each other, seriously.

Angelo, instead, looked at them and did some figuring: the orphan child of a mother who committed suicide and an unknown father must now be more than four years old, probably she had already been adopted, possibly more than once, or perhaps she was still in the orphanage . . . and here they thought in terms of the White House.

So at the seventh month—that is, in March—Lometto began to

feel out Angelo, to estimate his money demands for a couple of weeks or thereabouts in America. To act as interpreter for Edda and take care of all the formalities with the consulates. He personally, apart from the fact that he could not desert his two companies, and even less Mire in the midst of its process of reappropriation or expropriation, certainly wouldn't go, because he too would have needed an interpreter. Lometto tried to blackmail Angelo morally, presenting the opportunity to him as a gift he was making him after so many years of collaboration profitable for both of them: he had a wonderful trip ahead of him, a unique occasion, he would pay for his ticket and overnight expenses. Angelo asked him if he was crazy, he had already lived in New York for three months, and going there did not interest him at all. On the other hand, what would he say to a Brazilian son? or Nepalese? In that case, it would definitely be possible to come to an agreement over a ticket and expenses for the stay, and no more. Lometto thought about Brazilian inflation and the likelihood that someone would ever get it into his head to politically desire an Italo-Amazonian son, and turned up his nose. So, with continued halts and resumptions, the exhausting negotiations began.

Angelo: that for him this would be a job like any other, that he was not granting discounts, on the contrary by now his daily fee must be regarded as automatically increased for trips in Europe, that for a year and a half there had been no adjustments, wasn't it true that he had adjusted his price list because of inflation and complained every time to the customers about increases in labor costs and industrial electrical power in Italy? Besides, how was it possible to say how many days Edda's stay in a hospital would last? Certainly, with her strong physique, she could deliver the child and give him barely enough time to run among the various embassies and call a priest before catching the first plane back. But what if there were complications? If Edda had to remain bedridden, what do I know, for a month? If it was a podalic delivery, if . . . yes, feet first, the infant presents itself feet first and it is necessary to perform a cesarean if they don't want to let him croak, in America they do everything with the feet, don't worry they must be used to it, they even live with their feet in their mouths . . . "But what are you trying to insinuate?" Lometto asked. "Let's agree on a lump sum" Angelo continued. "Whether it lasts fifteen days, twenty, or a month. Eight thousand dollars plus expenses."

Lometto had mimed a brief but intense collapse, flopping limply into his armchair onto a boxful of colored balls, tried to change the subject, rehashed the story of the wraparound windshield and said that, in short, since the insurance . . . in short: had he or hadn't he broken it with his head? and so why didn't he at least have the good taste to offer to share the damages? No, he was going to look for another interpreter. Angelo laughed to stop himself from crying over that proposal about the windshield. He helped him get rid of the fragments of that thin glass, silvered inside and colored outside, and meanwhile, persuasively, to stop himself from kicking his ass, told him that yes, it was best for both of them, and that the Mantuan Sock Manufacturers' Association would get him plenty of interpreters, all of them equally incapable of affixing the correct prefix and good only at giving orders and never taking care of even a trifling request for information, they would have some time with a temperament like Edda's. He should think about it; in any case, to engage him now for May he must pay him half the amount immediately and half at departure. Lometto accompanied him to the door of his car, amusing himself by puffing into the wind to see the small nuclear mushrooms of his halitosis in the gelid springtime morning. He didn't say a single word. Angelo left, neither of the two said goodbye to the other. A good sign.

For fifteen days they did not call each other once. Angelo had signed a contract for a new translation, which, this time, would be paid in full. Lometto was no longer indispensable for quite a while. He would not come down a dollar, ready to come down two thousand—the extra two thousand he had had the foresight to include in his calculations.

Then it was Edda's turn to break ranks: "Do it for me . . ." and despite the big belly, which must have infinitely enlarged her navel and, as a sexual trap, rendered it unfrictionable like an open parachute, she made certain clicks of the tongue, and Angelo tried to picture her.

"But if I must act as godmother to the mother of a future President of the United States, what are eight thousand dollars plus expenses in the face of history? If I did it for less I would be considered a cretin for at least two centuries."

"But can't you meet me halfway?" And Ravel's "Bolero" had begun to blunt the flattery. "I'm the one who wants your assistance, don't make my life even more difficult with Lometto. Did I ever ask you for anything? Well, this time . . ."

"I'm not asking for anything more than I get from other companies . . ." But there was no other company, and in order to earn eight thousand dollars net in publishing he would have had to get bedsores on his buttocks for two years. There, for one month, he could even come down to seven thousand.

"Seven is still too much" Edda complained over the phone: was she scratching her belly? had she slipped her hand inside her maternity dress?

"Not even a cent less. By the way, how are you?"

"Fine. Not one of my sons has ever given me a hard time in delivery, and now you are giving me the trouble all at once."

From certain background rustles Angelo understood that the "Bolero" was not dedicated to him, thank heavens. She and he, at the other end, were giving the final touches to the masterpiece.

At the eighth month—that is, four months ago, in April—that secret had leaked out to the sound of trumpets: the whole town knew about this enterprise, and Edda gave herself the airs of a capricious high-class lady who went to deliver in America as others would go for dinner to the Bersagliere. By now Edda was unreachable, no one could beat her to the finishing line of Neo Orkese birth pangs.

"So what are you going to do?" Lometto asked again. They were headed for the train down along the underpass at Hanover. This was going to be their last trip together.

"About what?" Angelo had said, but he knew that Lometto was dying to negotiate the American sojourn once and for all, an affair to which Angelo, with a great effort, had not alluded during all that time. They no longer had the need to talk, by now they read each other's thoughts reciprocally and completely. Now in Lometto's he read "tickets," tickets swimming without apparent meaning between "seven thousand" and "six thousand" dollars. To speak in order to deny this evidence of reciprocal telepathic reading was even more wearing now, more complex were the preliminaries to convey the idea that there was no premeditation and that everything was spontaneous, more labored were the turns of phrase in order to erase in one or the other this mental X ray already developed and viewed.

They instantly understood all that was necessary to understand: the men, the situations, the possibilities, the commercial reliability of the companies they visited, the trust to grant, the type of payment to demand, and even the restaurant to go to (Chinese or Mexican or Spanish or German), what to drink at specific hours of the day and night, the remarks to make in the presence of others and those not to make, the anecdotes to trot out in order to give them a polish and an additional pinch of spice for the family's glee when they returned to Penzana. They both could slide along on a carpet of telepathic conventions communicated with one-fourth of a glance: half a glance was enough to sum up the states of mind and reflections of an entire month.

Lometto no longer succeeded in hiding anything from Angelo, and this annoyed him—even with those mirror-lens sunglasses. He certainly did not want Angelo to stick his nose in things that did not concern him, especially him, always so cutting and offensive. As in that business with Belart, Angelo had read perfectly that Belart must have told him about the matter of the half million to settle the pantyhose complaint, since he was anyway forever excluded from their intrigues. And he had also read that Lometto was dying to shout after him that he was a pimp, that he was double-crossing him, except for the fact that, by doing so, he would have given away other plans—one the Coptafuk, two the champagne. Angelo had even managed to turn the page that was under this one—that is, to read that Belart's little blackmail and the van and the excuse of the torn pantyhose and the three and a half million and the partner with tachycardia, all of it had been staged by Lometto and her to seal officially with witnesses "the last time" and be able in all tranquillity to go at it, away from the indiscreet eyes of bedeviled and by now all too vigilant partners—at that time—and from Angelo himself—by his own choice—with deals of hundreds of millions which would be all the more substantial the more Lometto and Belart could distract people from the connection they had had until then with Mire. Then Angelo, without effort, had turned over also a third page: he could always tell him that he, by phoning Belart even before going to Vipiteno, had understood all of this so well that in order to facilitate for both parties the making of a tabula rasa of the past with Mire, and be himself radically scraped away from the possibility of being irritated by further attempts at persuasion, had asked Belart for two hundred and fifty thousand lire—which had then become half a million thanks to her good heart—to give the two of them as well as the partner who also accepted it as obvious the definitive break between Belart and Lometto/Mire. He even turned another ten. In one of them he read Demetrio's stuffed body with Lometto on top using and abusing it, complaining that he wasn't worth even the rope he had cost him.

Program: approximately ten days before the happy event she would be shipped to New York by plane, and there enter the private clinic O Paisiello directed by Professor Witzleben, a German Jew of great obstetric and gynecological renown who had left Münster—not during Nazism but immediately after—to start a new career among the rich Italians of Brooklyn.

For the first time Edda herself renounced being assisted by her private midwife. This is what Angelo had been allowed to know four days before departure. As for Angelo, Lometto said not a word. Angelo very vaguely and threateningly stated that in all probability he would accept a substitute job in French at the Hotel Institute of Desenzano . . . What suspense for the three of them! Lometto again began to pour out malicious details on the gas chambers, to throw him off the track. He must certainly have before him the fanciful mountain carved with the faces of three Presidents to guide him through the labyrinth of his megalomania, a thread so definitely presidential as to transcend, in its significance of good omens and faith in the future, the very notion of Ariadne's thread.

Here in Penzana after the return crossing, Ario would be baptized again, it would not be possible to get Wojtyla to come to him, but a cardinal had already guaranteed a very punctual papal bull, and he, with his connections, would certainly be able to get the American Ambassador and his missus from Rome and Andreotti, or, at the least, Donat Cattin to come to his front yard. At any rate, Lometto said, trying to be witty, hadn't Prime Minister Andreotti been photographed with the best names of the biggest scandals and trials and Italian-style thieveries of the postwar period? He could come and get a flash photo at his place too . . . A small, updated Yalta there at his home among model stables and selected cows and pantyhose, in an atmosphere of Washingtonian immortality hard as rock . . .

"I'll show them who gives the orders here . . ." was the last sentence impressed by Lometto in the sealing wax of his universal optimism.

And Edda and Angelo passed through the transom of passport control.

This was the very first time that Edda had flown. During the eight hours of the flight from Malpensa airport to Kennedy she hadn't closed an eye. Every detail of life on board excited her. She had eaten with a good appetite and bought cologne for three generations to come. She'd insisted on getting the company's silk kerchief. She shared with Angelo the frightful vibration of the landing and they decided to escape together, as soon as they could, to the roller coaster at the Luna Park in Brescia. Their enthusiasm was such that it seemed to become a political transgression. The moment she got off at the Immigration Office, she no sooner said that she "felt lighter" than she was immediately seized by heavy nausea. And from that instant on it was hell.

The formalities were soon taken care of—it was enough to open their respective wallets, as in all English-speaking and Finno-Ugric nations. Nothing surprised her because, once she was out in the open air, her mind seemed to be turned to the splotch of vomit she had left behind in the arrival lobby. It was insistent vomit, from whose unchanging colors one might have said it was already old before having been thrown up. Now she was giving him her arm and, at intervals, she exerted small pressures on the inside of his elbow, as if wanting to call him to order. Was she afraid that if he were to be distracted, it would all be over for her too?

From the airport to the clinic they took a taxi instead of the bus. There was no reason to begin saving right away, Angelo thought. For all that, seven years before, out of pure ignorance, he had taken a taxi and followed the meter with bated breath. He still remembered the amount he had paid: forty-four dollars, one tenth and more of what he possessed.

The reception at the clinic, that late Sunday afternoon, had been amiable and discreet—Angelo had with him a copy of the bank telex sent from Mantua to the National Bank, Branch No. 3, in Manhattan, not too far from the clinic and the East River along which they had just driven. An employee named Concetta Macaluso said she spoke Italian and for an instant Angelo felt lost; when she opened her mouth out came certain Calabro-Apulian stridencies so close and Neolithic that Edda apologized and said to Angelo that he must immediately tell them that she did not understand a word of English.

A small suite with all comforts had been reserved for her; it was dark by now and for that night Angelo would sleep on the convertible couch in the small living room that opened on the room proper; tomorrow he would look for a place to stay in the neighborhood.

At home he had already given instructions for the roof to be fixed and a new floor to be laid in the small bathroom, urgent work because of the many infiltrations of water and cockroaches. His mother's sunken eye was the best guarantee that the men would work just as they pleased in his absence. Lometto had finally given him all the money, and in dollars, since by his choice the negotiations had begun based on this currency—that is, six thousand five hundred instead of eight thousand, but on the nail. He had taken with him about a thousand dollars, a tidal wave of money come to think of it, since Edda would pay out of her pocket the day-to-day expenses (twenty dollars for the room, and twenty for food, at fixed sums). Angelo had calculated that with yogurt and fruit and hamburgers he would live in style, spending half of it. Egypt was waiting for him immediately afterwards. And he ate a few meals in the clinic, there was no need to be shy considering what Professor Witzleben or someone in his behalf had demanded in advance as a basic daily rate. Angelo gave himself the task of further burrowing his way into Edda's heart, of making her feel well and at her ease: he would be close to her at every necessary moment, and if he were to go out on his own while she was sleeping or if she gave him permission to do so (the agreement said: twenty-five hours of assistance out of twenty-four), he would call her every hour. Nevertheless, from the very first, he did not have the impression that Edda wanted him to feel important and indispensable. She seemed already realized in herself and in her secret autonomy, as if she were putting or had already put the final touches to a plan whose realization by now concerned only her, exclusively her. Precisely because only three hours after landing Angelo felt like a marionette without art or part, he made an effort to create for himself ad hoc the sensation that Edda was left to his care like a wide-eyed timorous little girl. Edda passed from the gentleness of a new mother, pleased at having a gentleman interpreter as companion, to a sort of Praetorian animosity directed at a common servant too well paid not to feel a servant to the depths, and so servilely independent in his manifestations of solicitude, thanks to the money safely tucked in his pocket, as to set aside the servant/master relationship and to expect treatment as an equal. But Edda immediately disabused him on this score. What had brought them close together in the air—a flight, a goal—separated them once on the ground. In Edda there immediately became manifest a will for destruction that took shape in her minute by minute. Nevertheless, as hysterics will, she tried to suppress thought and assume artificial attitudes contrary to what she felt or what she tried not to feel. Angelo saw several battles take place in her, without being able to say for what good or for what purpose. Now as he watched her back, as she turned to the garden, he understood that he knew nothing about her. She was an unknown woman, like a tug-of-war in herself, split to struggle with equal strength against that part of herself which had fled to the two extremes only to wind up in what was the middle.

But Angelo needed to believe in her in order not to sink immediately into the ecological depression which gripped him when he too approached the window and looked at the garden. He decided that the manifestations of irritation and aversion in his regard—an aversion so impersonal, with him as status symbol of a world which nothing now prevented her from hating with her entire being—testified to a deep attachment, almost visceral, even though malicious. Angelo understood that it was too late to speak and that now it was she who rejected all confidences. Alone she prepared for a leap into the vow which she had never fulfilled for who knows how long and which she carried within her hard as an inorganic calculus of a vendetta by now accomplished but never manifested completely. That first evening, while she was unpacking the suitcases, Angelo heard a crepitation coming from a small cellophane bag and saw that, with a deferential air as if it were the most delicate relic, she placed it with great care on the closet shelf. He would have sworn that in it there was some simple, atavistic straw. They chatted quietly about this and that; Angelo said that, if the doctors permitted it, he would take her to the theater to see a comedy she would certainly like, *The Wizard of Oz*. "Hoo" she said "I'd like to go very much, we don't need any doctor's permission, if you say so it must be good."

He couldn't understand whether she was making fun of him or what; they had discovered the "Bolero" precisely thanks to him, and what a job it had been to convince them to leave the movie house, and not see that sentimental pap all over again.

A nurse arrived, a very tall, bony matron, peroxide blond, an inhumanly professional smile, and immediately Edda froze and said simply: "Send her away."

Certainly the nurse must have immediately understood that so long as Angelo was there, she would be completely superfluous, and she was annoyed by the equally professional amiability of Angelo, who repaid her solicitude with a smile à la Heidi. She came back a couple of times, not easily routed. Each time he told her that, really, Mrs. Lometto did not need anything but sleep, and the next time she came in, along about half past nine, that Mrs. Lometto had enough stamina to face immediately another ocean crossing and give birth while unloading on an empty stomach the luggage from the plane's belly.

While Angelo was dialing Penzana's area code and the number, the nurse, with a touch of hostility for having been set aside so impertinently, informed him that the next day Mrs. Lometto would be examined by Professor Witzleben, and finally, not receiving any answer but only a motion of Angelo's chin, said good night for the last time.

"Hoo, all the airs they put on just because they can give an enema" Edda said. It seemed that hating all other women was a method to spare herself.

There was a small refrigerator bar in the room, at a moderate temperature and with non-carbonated drinks in bottles and not in cans, the peak of exclusivity according to the management of Paisiello for Mamas, of course: orange, pineapple, maracuja and grapefruit juices. They were not hungry, they looked at the two semi-steaming trays brought in during one of the matron's penultimate attacks and Angelo took only the small bowls of cooked fruit and pushed the cart out into the white corridor.

At midnight Edda was still not sleepy. On the telephone she said for a second time that everything had gone well. Lometto asked her if he—Angelo—could not bargain a bit, get a bit of discount from the clinic. Angelo sent him the usual curse. He suddenly felt more of a servant than ever. It was too late to curse.

Edda got up every ten minutes and raised by another bit the blinds she had just let down by as many slats and widened a trifle more the crack in the window she had just narrowed. Neither of them had wanted air conditioning, they preferred the heat to a sore throat, and now there was this ambiguous breeze coming from the park, where, Angelo had noticed with horror, certain Mediterranean trees—dwarf magnolias, two olive trees, a cypress, and four palm trees—were made of plastic.

She wore a night dress that was antique, to say the least, of white-on-white eyelet-embroidered linen, like certain sheets or curtains which have cost decades of embroidery needles and a woman's wasted life; she'd had her hair trimmed just before their departure, and her face with its puerperal spots beneath the bangs was strangely almost pretty above the squat funnel of her torso. Angelo, stretched out on only a sheet in the small contiguous room, watched her, watched the indentation and hump at whose sides rested the diaphanous hands with their chewed nails, and he thought: what might she be thinking about? As much as he was able to read Lometto's thoughts and emotions, even his plans, everything about her eluded him. Edda remained completely armored against any investigatory gaze of his. At times it seemed to him he had reached the final wall which separated Edda—who was on its other side—from the rest of the world, and once there he could not help but think about something that troubled him deeply: it did not matter at all to her, in the most absolute manner, whether it would be male or female, President or garbage collector, American or Italian, human or Martian, alive or dead. That she had borrowed that belly from the circumstances and had adjusted to it, growing around it. At other times he believed he understood that in that belly Edda had accumulated a sack of poison, although he could not tell against whom—perhaps not even she herself could tell.

There was an instant during the night when, in the dim light of a small eternal flame, their eyes met for the fraction of a second: Angelo had the impression they were the eyes of a blind man, so open and opaque, the less they saw, the more fixedly they looked in the right direction.

The next morning, when at ten o'clock on the dot Professor Witzleben arrived, she created the first real unexpected problems for him.

"Tell him to take his hands off me" she said in a peremptory voice. She did not want anyone, anyone, not even Professor Witzleben, to touch her. To Angelo's request to be reasonable and the curt reply of the doctor and two nurses present (translating the replies, curt besides all else, for Edda, who was not used to such translations, was quite a problem: she cursed only Angelo because he alone was the only recognized interlocutor), she shot back just as definitive a refusal: she was perfectly well, she did not want any kind of new examinations, the ones done in Italy and handed over the very evening of their arrival would have to do.

"But the amnio test is missing here" Professor Witzleben objected. "It's nothing at all, signora."

Nothing doing. That little Vandyke did not impress her in the least. She said she wasn't a debutante after all, that she'd made another three males, healthy and with sturdy constitutions, and she had no desire to begin discovering new techniques now, of all times—they advised her to do pre-delivery exercises. The ones she knew and had learned from her mother were fine: wait, scream with all her might, and give a good push.

"But precisely, signora: it was possible before because you were not even forty years old. It's a delicate age, certain tests are routine after a certain age . . ." The Professor smiled, and this rendered horrible the impact that Edda's glance must make on that tiny Vandyke-shaped mouth into which dipped an infinite drop-shaped nose.

Angelo blunted the translation of this pointed remark; the Professor realized that he was cheating, politely asked him to see him in his office, and he and the team left the room with a stern "goodbye," which Edda answered by turning to the other side of the bed.

Angelo tried immediately to talk to her, he felt very concerned about her. She turned around again and said:

"I'm tired. Let me sleep. Go for a walk."

"Are you sure?"

"Yes, go! Who's keeping you?"

No, he was told, Professor Witzleben was still in the wards, Angelo should come back a little later.

He left the clinic like a kite imprisoned too long by strings not its own. He no longer even thought about looking for a room, and even less about calling on John Ashbery to spit in his eye—too late, he had read somewhere that because of certain troubles he too wore glasses: for one reason or another everybody in the end wished the world would go blind.

He took a taxi and went directly to Fifth Avenue to buy himself a device he'd wanted for some time—that is, ever since he had received strange anonymous phone calls and a couple of death threats, even though in his heart of hearts he always thought that they had gotten the wrong number. One time a voice altered surely by the filter of a handkerchief or by closed nostrils had whispered into the barely lifted receiver, "We're going to do away with you, you big Marxist faggot" and he would have liked to say "Look, you got the wrong number" but they hadn't given him the chance. Another time, at the same hour of the night, he had lifted the receiver and said all in one breath "Get on the waiting list, you're not the only ones." Ten minutes later there was another call but he didn't answer. He had often thought that by a tragic coincidence of fate perhaps that had been the first and last time that Italo had called him from Anguillara . . .

It was, in short, a small device which, attached anywhere on the receiver, recorded the voices of both speakers. In Germany he'd heard that in America they cost half as much and in fact all he spent was three hundred dollars. The small machine was no larger than a matchbox with adhesive rubber at the base; it had marvelous power and was much more refined than the one he had once seen in Munich. They let him try it out. He called Edda, just to see how she was.

"Come back right away, where on earth did you end up?"

"But . . ."

"I don't know how to call Italy . . ."

"It's . . ."

"No, you come here. I want to talk to Lometto right away. I'll tell him everything."

". . . ?"

In his heart he sent her to hell. He just had time to listen to ". . . I'll tell him everything" and to get them to explain the adjustments necessary for the regular taping at a distance—up to seven meters, a prodigy—and rushed off.

Edda, after rejecting the nurse who offered to take her for a walk in the park—to do so she would certainly have to "put her hands on her," at least on her arm—heaved a sigh of relief at seeing him. She was crying. Angelo was shaken by this weeping full of anguish which he could not explain and she said nothing, sitting with her head bowed on the edge of the bed. Angelo went to the bedside table where the telephone was. The only thing to do, and also the only thing that diplomatically would have come to him spontaneously, would have been to start crying along with her. He feared it might be misunderstood as something included in the price. He lifted the receiver, Edda dried her tears, said not to dial the number anymore, and that she was hot and sweating. Really not a whole lot. Again the blond, tall nurse from the previous evening appeared, he expected her to say that he could not see the Professor. It seemed they had already been there for an eternity, so much did Edda's impenetrable silence deafen him with her elusive confidences that did not confide anything in particular. The head nurse wanted to know whether Mrs. Lometto really did not want to try half an hour of pre-delivery exercises. The translation made,

Edda's gaze filled with flashes of a furious cheerfulness, she began to laugh in sobs and covered her mouth with one hand.

"Just look how long she is, she looks like a shit pump."

The nurse, without even going to the trouble of smiling professionally, understood that there was nothing she could do and withdrew, forcefully slamming shut her lashes, since she could not do this with the door, which closed automatically.

Angelo and Edda after a while went out into the post-atomic garden. Now the only thing Edda wanted to know was when would they go to the theater to see the Wizard. Angelo kept silent, how irresponsible he had been to make such a proposal. He only wished that the sack would burst open as soon as possible into the light of day, so they could book the return flight.

What she had not phoned before, she phoned afterwards. But only incongruous mommy twitterings to the expectant daddy. Nothing about everything. Gesticulating, Angelo tried to make her understand that here it wasn't as in Italy, that after eight o'clock there was a discount and that, sometimes, she would turn the household in Penzana upside down in the middle of the night. He too spoke to Lometto: little about America and much about money. He could hear sleepy sighs, almost swoons, as when one decants from one dream into another and realizes too late that it is a nightmare, and resignation in dollars which, perhaps because of its course along the cables, arrived on this side weary and rising in brief swells. The basic rate for the clinic paid in advance, a lump sum of eight million lire which in the end would certainly be multiplied by three. Lometto's feelings had been terribly hurt at having to subject himself for the first time in his life to an irrevocable letter of credit and another fixed due date for an open amount guaranteed by two banks. His American myth, faced by a usurious inflexibility equal only to his own, was somewhat shaken. But nothing could be done to change Edda's mind about her intentions, since Lometto aimed at convincing her firmly by trying to dissuade her: that son must be American, must be called George Ario, cost what it may. If, on the other hand, it was just a female, never mind, Lometto had whispered to him, with time she too would become attached to her. And Edda had financed the enterprise, exactly fifty percent, with the money of her advance inheritance, as between two equal partners. At any rate, Edda had saved wherever possible: for example, on the small baby bonnets and bloomers, all of it the legacy of her three previous children, everything scrupulously blue—the only new thing she had was a small yellow set, in case fate were to prove otherwise, as though for her yellow were the only acceptable gradation of pink.

At half past nine on the third or fourth day Angelo was sent for by Professor Witzleben; Edda was still having her milk and coffee with bread and hadn't said a word since she had awakened. In the hallway the office girl had explained to him that it wasn't part of the agreement that he should sleep there every night . . .

From door to door—nobody was to be seen out in the corridor—Angelo followed bleatings and, at a certain point, he had the impression that they became yelps.

"Push that button" the girl said.

There was a full-fledged bark, the door opened automatically. The Professor was talking to a monstrous little dog, ugly, yellowish, with orangeade fur, squat and with a squashed muzzle and a frightful, gaping mouth. One would have said that it had been put together from four or five breeds sawed up here and there and sewed back together at whim, careful that the various parts were put back in the right place. There had been many slips. And she yelped, spinning around herself on the rug, and jumping—not too well.

"Down, Dawn!" the Professor was saying to her without bothering to greet him or turn toward him. "Dawn, down! Oh, hello! Come, come, sit down. She's a bit nervous, she's still convalescing."

Angelo sat down. The dog watched him with an expression of natural disgust, dripping slobber. Her small covetous glints she reserved exclusively for her master. There wasn't much to say. Professor Witzleben seemed much more interested in saying "Dawn, down" and "Down, Dawn" to that obscene monster than in paying attention to him. Angelo thought that he didn't know what to ask him either and, at any rate, Angelo was not going to hazard any hypothesis about Edda, respectful of her silence and her fractiousness. From a small steel basin, bean-shaped like those one sees in operating rooms, the Professor was now lifting filaments of meat and offering them to his darling because she'd begun to snarl, not liking the interruption of their games caused by the stranger. Angelo had the impression that the Professor was leading the dog down the garden path, and one could clearly see his effort to create this sort of family-life parenthesis in order to broach a specific theme.

Angelo rejected the procedure as a lack of respect for him and promptly got up and was about to say goodbye when the Professor returned to his senses—that is, to him, Angelo—and sat down again, not without telling the dog, which was now prancing all over the stuffed chairs, for the nth time: "Dawn, down! She barks in five tongues, you know, a bit in Yiddish too." That is: down, Dawn/Dawn, down. Her name was Dawn and, obviously, she was a bitch. Angelo felt like asking him whether it was true that he, a Jew, had left Germany after the Holocaust because with the Liberation, "the air had become unbreathable," as Lometto had insinuated. Professor Witzleben was one of those little fellows who not only take it for granted that they can get away with things in any situation and bring their skins home, preferably remaining inside them for quite a while, but emigrate for reasons of triumph, never survival. It was in any case the first time that Angelo had heard talk of a Jewish collaborator who had suffered a career upset with the opening—American—of the concentration camps, that is, their closing (and who knows for how long), and who undisturbed, almost out of snobbism, wrinkling his nose and slamming the door of the hut, goes to God's country because already in 1950 in the German Federal Republic he smelled a "stench of burning as never before." Perhaps here he had found the appropriate terrain to refresh his sadomasochistic nostalgia in some Sicilian-American clan which guarantees for originals an oligarchic protection and privileged solidarity within a putrescent city or the miserable neighborhoods under its control. In short, he was someone who had been able to recreate for himself the desired atmosphere. Certainly weirdos, also called renegades or snipers, exist everywhere within any allied *morality*, and who knows whether history's invisible façade is not written precisely by people fed up with clichés who do all manner of unusual things in an attempt to rebel against an education in *eternal values*. So now he absentmindedly looked at Professor Witzleben, or rather, at his legend, elaborated by that joke-monger Lometto who perhaps invented such things at night if only to ingratiate himself with a customer and obtain a discount of another five hundred dollars, and he saw the gold frames of his glasses paired with Eichmann's steel frames in dark synagogues observing Yom Kippur and meanwhile counting the scapegoats and then in large tiled rooms, under a livid light, manipulating live guinea pig-brothers on marble slabs and all around every possible technico-sanitary little object to confer scientific objectivity and status on the scene, then back to the synagogue to pray before an expanse of candles that resembled a fire—all bought out of his own pocket—and finally in Palermo-Mondello for the baths, the dainty twinkle of his glasses and the bronze-colored Vandyke in an armchair at the Grand Hotel Des Palmes . . . And now here he is in New York, right in front of him, owner of a chain of clinics for mommies and a horrible dog that gave you goose pimples just to look at it.

"Cigarette?" asked Professor Witzleben. From a case he extracted an ivory cigarette holder. "This is the fifth time, eh, Dawn?"

Angelo frustrated the other's expectation of being faced by a curious person. A professor who has been everything while having only one thing in his head, one of those who have turned it into a reality and now are, let us say, famous surgeons and have cut and sewed up thousands of people and then it is discovered that originally they had barely reached the sixth grade, were housepainters or sold shoe polish from door to door, had made a name for themselves on the flour and gasoline black market, and the last time they were seen in a particular country were impeccably dressed, had a suitcase, and waited for a bus: Angelo understood that he had before him a banal and inscrutable being, just a dandy, nothing more.

Angelo took the cigarette—mentholated—from a leather case with gold edges and at that point the Professor began to ask him strange questions, whether it was true that he also spoke five languages and whether he had ever thought of having himself circumcised.

Angelo did not know what to say and whether to say, what kind of distances to keep, and whether, as usual, he had already created for himself a whole insurmountable prejudice against a harmless little old man who wanted to do his best. He was at any rate very polite and said that, in regard to Edda and the missing tests, he knew nothing, and that about medicine, aside from bacteria and microbiology in general and this in a very superficial manner, he knew nothing at all, and then that he knew absolutely nothing, was not informed about possible treatments or injections or pills or drugs—and here he got a slight jolt and mumbled—taken by Mrs. Lometto during her pregnancy. He only explained to him the business about the southern midwife and the straw she put into locks and drafts, etc., and the expectant mother's desire that it should be a boy. Angelo wanted to reassure him, instead he manged to alarm him even more—perhaps he was simply delighted. But what did it matter? The doctor could ask Mrs. Lometto all these questions himself, because anyway he would be there in the room to translate, it was up to her whether to answer or not. The dog now was uncontrollable, with one leap she jumped into Angelo's lap and began looking at him askance after sinking her claws into his belly and one of his thighs . . .

"Please . . ." Angelo murmured. The cesspool snarled. The Professor did not intervene. They remained like that face to face for an interminable minute. Dawn's eyes were a yellow he had already seen somewhere else.

"You're not telling me much, Mr. Baz . . . Baz . . . ?"

"Bazarovi. Does she bite?"

"It depends. Anyway, thank you. Dawn, down . . . She acts like this with everybody. *Auf Wiedersehen*" and Angelo saw him take out an investigatory monocle: also the Professor had eyes that he thought he had contributed within the limits of his possibilities to the well-being of the malaise that Edda had decided to carry by herself all the way to the end and in the manner she had set for herself. He was covered with Dawn's hoary yellow hairs; the foul bitch now jumped down while Angelo got up, preparing to heave a sigh of relief immediately after turning his back. But Dawn flung herself against his right foot and bit him just above the heel. Giving her a kick and sending her rolling over three times to crash against the desk was a single movement, just a thump and a yelp.

"Damn you!" Witzleben cried, rushing around the desk. "Oh, Dawn, Dawn!" The old man picked her up in his arms, undecided whether to curse immediately or concentrate exclusively on her. He palped her under the tail with a frenetic hand. Angelo was paralyzed by the scene and he did not know whether he should immediately take off his shoe and sock or whether he should be sorry about the kick or give another one to the tanned, perfumed old dandy. On the Professor's fingers a thin thread of blood. "You'll be a virgin again, Dawn, you'll be a virgin again, my most human baby, I promise you. Get out!" he shrieked, pressing a bell. "And don't show your face around here unless it's strictly necessary! Down, dear Dawn, darling . . ." he kept soothing the once again broken idol.

The wounded pride of Dawn, the many times virgin who would never get down and now of course did, and the offended pride of Professor Witzleben gazed up from below with a look of stupefied common martyrdom. Angelo barely managed to see that both had the same interrogatory-yellow eyes of those who go looking for trouble and find it. The secretary knocked and entered. A small commotion.

And in any case the color of the bitch-master's pupils were too identical for at least one of them not to wear contact lenses . . .

He went to tell Edda that he would go look for a room and that if they came she should say "good morning" politely and for everything else do as she pleased.

At the night sauna on First Avenue there were only fifty-year-olds playing baccarat and not many of them either; it was thought that only the over-forty-year-olds were immune to AIDS. He chatted with a couple of Embassy attachés and presented his theory on the subject (he had one for just about everything): that the virus was a lovely and secret laboratory invention ordered by the CIA to slow down the political and commercial success which was making American homosexuals the chief protagonists of their country and that at the proper moment the vaccine, which absolutely had no need to be discovered because it was created in a test tube alongside the corresponding illness, would pop up.

Nobody had ever heard this one.

The first week went by, then on Wednesday of the second week Professor Witzleben—Angelo, out of regard for Edda, had once let himself be seen in the garden petting the bitch—during his customary morning visit and after asking whether Angelo had come back from the YMCA (money saved, as many showers as one wanted to relieve the mugginess, and sometimes also a bed for the night), says: "Today is your two hundred and seventy-third day, right, Signora Lometto?"

"Take one or leave one" Edda answers calmly.

"No particular symptom?" the Professor asks, picking up the chart at the foot of the bed at the same time that several hands with nails covered with neutral polish lunged to get there first.

"No. Hungry" Edda answers.

"Nothing else?" insists the ex-wanderer. He delicately smooths his Vandyke as if it were a very precious heirloom.

"Ask him what he wants from me? If the time hasn't come, it hasn't come" Edda bawls. To ward off trouble Angelo immediately raises his hand and, pressing on her right hand, silently implores her not to repeat the usual scenes, scenics, scenarios of all the preceding days.

"No, Professor Witzleben, Mrs. Lometto is not feeling any pressure" Angelo offers. The pressures of her charge are of a different nature and all held in tightly.

"I'd really like to know why you keep me on nothing but warm water. It's been two days since you've given me anything to eat!" Edda now shrieks. The warm water must be the consommé.

"Very well, there's no push? Take her immediately to the delivery room" Professor Witzleben orders peremptorily, and turns on heels no less than seven centimeters high.

Edda looks at Angelo without understanding: as soon as the stretcher on wheels comes through the door, he is forced to translate.

"Nooo!" Edda yells, foreseeing a sacrificial anti-nature rite.

"Would you be kind enough to ask the lady whether she wants this child alive or dead?" says the peroxide-blond matron with cesarean written all over her, while she prepares gloves, Vaseline, and enema.

Angelo sighs and summons up the courage to translate the enormity which does not allow one to foresee any natural birth pangs and leaves. On his heels, Professor Witzleben reappears along the corridor.

"Starting from this moment the child to be born is in great danger of life. This, thinks Angelo, is a Freudian slip by a Jewish obstetrician. We're the ones responsible. She will be given an injection to stimulate her." He flings out through the door of the operating room followed by two nurses and a young doctor who ordinarily takes Dawn for walks.

And so, while on her wheeled stretcher, Edda is headed for something that resembles an abuse, she wails and yells:

"Angelo, my dear Angelo, the straw!"

"All right, don't worry. I'm rushing to get it. I know where it is."

"It's in the closet."

"I told you, I know. You'll see, not even the slightest breath of wind will come through."

Angelo hurriedly gets the crackling little bag and, since he must be on hand, also the small recorder from his bag, which he does not like to leave around at the YMCA—oh, the scream that new humans are said to make! the very first "Aaaa" that distinguishes them from all other beings and will take them on a beeline to Z! And now there are four of them surrounding an already injected Edda, but above their small masks all their momentary attention is for Angelo, who, slightly crimson in the face, with a thief's stealthy manner, jumps here and there and puts stalks of straw into nonexistent fissures and locks since everything is glass and steel and wall without a chink.

No tension for all the rest. Edda, who till the last of her still conscious strength refuses to collaborate; Professor Witzleben, who from behind his mask—Angelo has one too—makes a grimace of pleasure, and this is enough of a signal for the entire team to proceed. Another injection. Edda screams as if they were raping her or could not make up their minds: everything recorded. Then: *"Dearest Angelo, a Coptafuk!"*

Now she was losing control of herself. Witzleben, at that word, opens wide his tiny phosphorescent eyes and stops for an instant with his scalpel in midair. Angelo looks away and continues to inspect the room and place stalks of straw like the fairy-tale stork so as to prepare the nest for this one here who doesn't want to hear about sticking out his head—or feet—on his own. God, what torment. Edda held down by four hands, imploring in southern dialect that they let her go . . .

And immediately afterwards those famous words so neutrally listed: "O Ilario" (exclamation mark?), "O Belisario, O Berengario," these so ambiguous vocatives: before losing consciousness she presented the encomiastic summary of her uterus's history.

. . . it is a tiny black thing, dirty with black blood, horrifying, saffron yellow underneath.

"Everything okay?" Angelo whispers timidly, prepared for the worst.

"Technically yes" Professor Witzleben says. "It's the second case this week. Apart from the hyperbilirubin."

And Angelo is too fascinated with what is now happening before his eyes. They are sewing hand over fist. The desecrated beauty of that navel, inside which from now on the cut-and-saw of the cesarean will prevent the triangular eye from flashing uncontaminated its terrible appeals . . . Instant after instant, following the dotted line of the stitches, the eye migrates elsewhere, liquefying in a zigzag its canonic iris until it disappears altogether, swabbed gradually by gauzes, and where there was that ferocious prehensile god there is now a tiny knot which closes a gigantic rhomboid, flabby and encased. To make this profanation more total and businesslike all that is lacking is for someone to approach the thread and break it with his teeth as his mother does with stuffed chicken. Living is supposedly this: to translate mythical ethical-aesthetic-erotic trinities into basted chitlings, without even hoping that a gash leaves at least a scar, because usually it is a stretch mark.

But where is the child? The child has already been taken elsewhere, to the incubator.

"But is it a boy or a girl?" Angelo asks the young assistant in a low voice; Professor Witzleben has already vanished.

"To tell the truth, I didn't notice."

"But that's not poss . . . But was it all right?"

"Hmmmm . . ."

Angelo has wasted so many precious seconds admiring such a display of sartorial arts that he has forgotten about the sex. He rushes through the door and looks to see where Professor Witzleben might have gone. There! He catches up with him.

"Oh, that was very sweet of you to pet Dawn . . ." he says without slowing down.

Angelo senses that his thoughts are already with the little yellow urine-drenched clump, and is shocked by it. He makes an effort to remain calm since now he has partly made up for the sixth defloration he has caused the dog—and the other five? could they all be kicks in the ass? But stay away from this note. He wants to know whether to call him George as Lometto wants, or what.

"By George,* didn't you see it?" asks Professor Witzleben, who is still walking at a considerable pace: curse the pronoun "it"! and what impudence neutrally calling a newborn "it" instead of "she" or "he" as he would with a dog. "In any case, I could have sworn to it. And probably Mrs. Lometto knew all about it. Women always know everything, that's why it's best to keep them at a distance." He sketches an elegant little smirk: at his age! "She knew perfectly well what amniocentesis is, all I had to do was watch her as she answered. Probably she did it without anyone knowing, including her husband. You know, there are so many strange motivations . . ."

The bitch must have gotten the scent of his approach, the barking began at a distance of one hundred meters.

"She's crazy for innards . . ."

Angelo found the Professor's remark somewhat banal: everyone knows that obstetricians feed their pups with what's left over.

". . . on one hand because they want to have it at all costs just as it is, on the other hand because they wish to eliminate it as soon as they find out . . . When it comes to our dear Mrs. Lometto, we might

* *English in original.*

say that . . . Here I am! Oh, Dawn! No, no, don't be afraid . . . yes, anyway, that she wanted at the same time to do a thing and its opposite."

Angelo is very confused. First: he still doesn't know whether it's male or female; second: what the fuck is the Professor talking about, what language is he using?

"But, Professor Witzleben, to tell the truth I . . ."

"In short, dear Mr. Baz . . . ?"

"Bazarovi."

"Mr. Bazarovi . . . unlike me, you know how to pronounce my name! Down's syndrome, don't you know?"

And Angelo sees the syndrome there at his feet, yellow, snarling, revolting. What inhumanity linking something human to a bitch almost as if to pay her a compliment or do her homage. How viscid this Witzleben: Down's syndrome, no less! Angelo had an impulse of rebellion, and from that instant, since it seemed to him less brutal even though the bitch was still involved, intimately he called it Dawn's syndrome. It was more poetic, and it would never have occurred to anyone that she was an ugly, nasty, and malodorous bitch; perhaps, in time, not even to him.

"Come to my office later, at your leisure. We'll have to take care of all the formalities with your consulate and the office of records. And all *the others*."

Instead, with the word "down" the virgin Dawn risked planting herself in his head like a nail and bringing bad luck to the newcomer. He was becoming linguistically superstitious. The effect of the straw, he told himself. And so with enormous steps he covers the entire corridor, turns left, another very long corridor, a few patients about, papas, relatives, all going in the same direction, he follows them, his mind works on its own and curses itself, its inability to grasp the simplest notions, such as Down, no! such as dawn, which is just rising in this meridian epilogue of late morning, this dawn which cannot be a common dawn, this dawn which produces a syndrome.

Certainly the Professor meant to say something properly expressed at random, an innuendo, an association of ideas: which? But he is definitely dismayed every time he sees this man, he has not even been able to ask him whether the child is male or female: he feels physically exterminated in the face of the vastness of his pompous and triumphant animal-loving nullity. It is old Mantua . . .

In front of the incubator a piece of tape stuck to the glass box-casket: "? Lometto," where the question mark probably stands for the first name not told in time to the nurse who fled with a full basin.

Tubes, not many, the child turns its back. Angelo huffs, impatiently, he's had enough of all this fake suspense. And it's not that he can't step around and look at the child from the other side. The small head moves slowly and also the tube somewhere underneath sways in the ultraviolet incubator, but it is only so to speak a head: it has the same conformation and features as Dawn's muzzle. The tape also says "5 pounds 10 ounces," not quite three kilos of new stuff. Not much. And the small yellowish body moves a lower limb all the way: it's a female. There she is, the future first Italo-American Presidentessa, the unbreathable and inconceivable Aria for everyone, aside from Edda . . . Now, first thing, stifle giggles and pity and phone right away. And prevent oneself from preparing speeches. Let it come as it will, it's just as well. And yet Professor Witzleben must have some good reason to associate her with Down's syndrome, Giorgina's fate will be precisely this, continuously being ordered about in one way or another. "Now, come, be a good girl, stay down." Edda has been temporarily moved into another room, where she will remain under observation for a couple of hours. But *she* is all right, nothing unusual, only a bit dazed by the sedatives or something. Angelo gets the key from the lobby, the Osco-Calabro-Apulian receptionist attempts a well-wishing sentence in "Italian," he returns to Edda's suite and the gismo goes *clowck* as it adheres to the telephone's receiver, with the instinctiveness of a bombed millipede. He can go ahead and call Mire at seven, half past seven in the evening, they're all there, they begin from the first hours doing overtime under the counter.

"Hello? *Ciao.* It's a girl."

"All right, we'll keep her" says Lometto in a quavering gay voice, and then he shouts, probably toward the main office, "Are you happy now? It's a girl!" and then: "So we'll call her . . . a nice American name for good luck . . ."

"There's more . . ."

"Did anything happen to anybody?" The voice becomes a little less trepidant, more relaxed.

"No, the mother is fine. But they had to give her a cesarean at the last moment. Edda is still sleeping. The girl is a bit delicate."

"Oh, if that's all. When are you coming back? At Mire we're all in the shit up to . . ."

"There's something else."

"Yes? What else is there?"

"Yes . . ."

". . ."

"She's mongoloid."

". . ." Throat clearing, an armchair squeaking. "Stay on the line." Shuffling, door closing, shuffling, armchair squeaking. A voice being cleared: "Mongoloid, you said?"

"Yes."

". . ." Long pause: sculpted mountains collapse, highways crumble, Italo-American-Vatican banquets fold into gelatin under a sudden storm, the mocking grin of Bananone and Co., defenestrated but avenged, and all those women in the underground den in this instant passed in review one by one, deformity by deformity, and the devastating outcome: "Blood of my blood . . . it can't be!" Then, imperious:

"She must disappear."

". . ." Angelo's head recoils as if he had received a blow on the temple. "Excuse me, what did you say?"

"Disappear, you've understood me perfectly. She must be eliminated. Is that all right? She must not touch ground here."

"Celestino . . ."

"But do you realize what *we* will have to suffer . . . she . . . will experience in life?" he says in a low voice already saturated with all that which, as a foretaste, will be his due from this precise moment on.

"So what?" says Angelo, loosening the lump in his throat. "And so what?" He could continue for hours nuancing that "And so what?" He could, for instance, tell the story of his own life if it were interesting enough to justify Giorgina Washington's life such as it is and for what it is, alien to all normative expectations, and nonetheless itself, unique, unrepeatable, she, the Miss Universe of herself, which is in the end what counts. But it is too much, and this pause fallen between two voices is an implied echo of the struggle that the pros at one end of the cable and the cons at the other are flinging at this "And so what?"

"Don't give me so-whats. It's easy for you, she isn't your daughter. Angelo . . ."

". . ."

". . . I'm in your hands . . ."

"Not true, you're in the hands of what's convenient for you."

"I don't want to see her. She must never get here, understand? neither alive nor dead, understand?"

"How, then?"

"In no way. You take care of it."

"Sure, why not!" and meanwhile Angelo is stroking with one finger the small technological millipede. Lometto had repeated ad nauseam: when there's nothing else you can do, losing right away is the best profit.

"But don't you realize . . . my family . . . here at Penzana . . . Help me."

"I'll see. I'll call you back as soon as I can" he said, and said by him it already seemed a moral involvement, a form of spontaneous alliance, superior, credible; one must never use certain weapons if one wishes to find them well honed and resplendent when the right moment arrives and, above all, if one wishes to defeat an adversary much shrewder and better prepared than oneself; not leave him with the impression that a secret, somehow miraculous stroke is involved, or he'll think that you're as much of a master as he is and, therefore, highly unpredictable; not give him the opportunity of having something similar to an unexpected vision of the idea he has formed about you, but act in such a way that what one declares oneself ready to do is the mere consequentiality of your usual thought, while the only thought that you are pursuing is his, nothing but his.

"Hello? Can you hear me?" Lometto asks, worried by this second-long pause.

"Very little now" Angelo said, barely whispering.

"Speak louder. Where are you?"

"I'm yelling. Can you hear me?"

It was definitely an advantage having frequented a theater company in one's youth.

"Yes . . . very little . . . Speak to the director of the clinic. Explain it to him."

"But do you realize?" Angelo said, turning his own previous anguish against him. "Hello!"

"Hello! Hello?"

"Hello!"

Angelo heard him perfectly.

"Hello, can you hear me? Angelo!"

"Hello!" he repeated for the last time and then hung up. He needed to reflect from that very instant, to bounce on the euthanasic waves of that tiny whimpering voice, that final squeak of a rabbit caught in a trap. He thought about Professor Witzleben and saw Lometto superimpose himself and merge into the tiny wrinkled face with its golden Vandyke, the dyed-blond hair, the small yellow-blue eyes. The Professor was also waiting for him to settle accounts, he too seemed in a hurry to get rid of those two nuisances. Perhaps with a dollarish little word also get rid of the latest arrival. Quite capable of feeding her to Dawn or perhaps Dawn herself was but the slow surgical transformation of a mongoloid entrusted to his discretion. But no more fantasizing: he asked first of all how much longer they would have to stay there, the answer was one week because of the stitches, ten days if the infant did not begin to nurse, she was a bit weak, and Angelo gave orders that Mrs. Lometto should not, for any reason whatsoever, be left in the room alone with the infant, these were orders from Italy—that is, from the husband—neither at the moment of the first feeding nor, above all, at night. That every measure or pretext must be taken for the infant—the name? no one knew it, they must wait for the mother to wake up, she had never mentioned it, she had wanted a boy—to remain as long as possible in her incubator, incubator so to speak, or glass deposit box, a pure formality, the child was perfectly healthy, so to speak, only her bilirubin was a trifle high and a *little hepatitis*—poor little thing, staying *in there*, with the mother's psychopathic condition, a healthy bearer who had already given her a liver this big even before she was born. This over the room phone to the office of Professor Witzleben, who said that he was in perfect agreement, obviously a reckless act of the mother . . . and besides: a mother like that . . . never a blood test . . . But he would call him later to the office, meanwhile he was going to connect him with administration. They told him with immense joviality that they were already in a position to set a fee of three thousand two hundred dollars more due to the complication of the cesarean, "thank you very much,"* which prolonged, you understand, the sojourn covered by the lump sum, and if he wanted to come to the office to sign—"to pick up for Mrs. Lometto to sign," he corrected—the bills involved, since afterwards with the

* *English in original.*

banks . . . Lometto be damned too, since with that story of the big-tail fur he had refused to get a credit card for his wife! Now it fell to him to pick apart with Edda the various items of her calvary—so many thorns, so much money. All this was unserious indeed, clearing mines from a stretch of land while pretending to be in a barrel trampling grapes and a vintage feast is in full swing.

An hour later, Angelo was again calling Mire, Inc., from the booth in the corridor.

"So listen: Edda has just awakened and hasn't been told yet. For the moment I've chosen to tell her that it's a little girl and that's all. You know, the new stitches . . . it's best to avoid fits . . ." And he thought: as if she had expected anything but a mongoloid female! "I spoke to *your* Professor Witzleben . . ."

"I don't even know who he is."

"But you knew a whole lot of things about him. I'm not the one who picked the clinic."

"Come on, keep going."

"It hasn't been a conversation like my name is so-and-so and yours? . . . I tried to test the ground . . ."

"And so?"

"So. I think I can say that he has understood what I was aiming at . . . on your behalf."

"So there are possibilities. He's German . . ."

Angelo held back a laugh: Lometto's National Socialist convictions about Germans and the cult of the race right in the middle of the 1980s were unshakable. It also suited him to make believe now that he had never been grazed by the thought that a German could do away with someone impure except for motives of idealism. To say "He's Jewish" would have been equivalent to confessing that he was *also* willing to pay up because the *impure* do not do each other in out of idealism.

"Yes."

"That's good. He's a man who understands."

"He too in his own way."

"Meaning?" Lometto said, and Angelo saw him go *pip-peep* with his little calculator: how much did it cost to understand in one's way?

"I can't tell you now. I'll call you back as soon as I know something definite."

"Definite what?"

"Bye."

Angelo waited for another hour, not in Edda's room, outside in the park. Skyscrapers, cars seven meters long, a small steamboat displacing kilometers of cubic meters coming down the East River, an even sky, plastic vegetation: New York. He only hoped that he wouldn't get diarrhea like the last time.

"Twenty thousand dollars."

A Marconian fading away: the dot-dash-dot of a prolonged whistle, tiny frog thighs that sizzle transporting over the copper a small gold ingot *on the nail.*

"Have you gone crazy? Do you know how many million lire that is?"

"You're not giving them to me. Look, as far as I'm concerned, I won't even touch your daughter."

"But it's immoral!"

"Because you're so moral. And anyway, listen, why don't you get help from your connections who gave you this address? Your Professor is up for sale in twenty-seven languages. Or perhaps if you come up with a Colombo, he might do it free of charge."

Angelo could have sworn: he had not gotten the name of the clinic from the Sicilians, but from the lame typist of the Sock Makers' Association or the messenger of the Chamber of Commerce. But Lometto gave himself airs, worse for him. Anyone who wants to have a mountain vacation must pay for the air.

"But you, you, what do you think about it?"

"Me? Look, if I think of what you and your family have put those frights in the basement through, it might even be better for you to do her in."

"But we treat them with kid gloves . . ."

"No, iron gloves, like currying horses."

Angelo puts a hand over his teeth: he can't take it any longer, he must end the phone call as soon as possible. The technological millipede, morality, murder for money, America, oh God what a laugh! here it is, the North Atlantic Axis, treaty or trick!

"Listen, Lometto, see what you can do."

"Call me back later. See if you can do anything. Perhaps disconnect a tube somewhere by mistake . . . But is she really so healthy that . . . didn't you say that . . . ?"

"Yes, a bit of jaundice, her weight, but I'm afraid she's completely healthy. This isn't a business that will take care of itself. *Ciao.*"

And all this receiving the calls not at home, where Angelo in his place would have run to find a minimum of quiet in which to think things over, but at Mire, Inc., occupied between one phone call and the next with floss and telex and agreements with creditors.

Angelo returned to Edda's room just as on the four-wheeled crystal platter that bandaged entree was being displayed, the small green mask removed for an instant, the lid replaced, the green light lit again over the lemon-yellow flesh: Madame was served, and fainted at the same time. No tit test.

Angelo stayed with her to watch over that presumed faint, her face half hidden by the sheet. The humidity was becoming unbearable: it was only possible to die from it, not faint like this, without considering that one might melt away by mistake if one left the salts to the discretion of others.

In Angelo's opinion, Edda was not opening her eyes because she had not yet found the "spontaneous" reaction to have as soon as she was called back to the reality she must face. But he did not speak. He dried her forehead with a linen cloth and caressed her hands, immobile on the sheet. Then, as soon as the matron of the evening shift came to force him to accept being replaced and insisted with looks on the necessity of his allowing her to justify her salary, Angelo headed for the incubator. Giorgina was peaceful, she was not just struggling to stay alive: one of the tubes in her tiny arms brought acid and glucose, the other served to provide a certain measure of purification, gamma globulin, etc.; to detoxify her from the Coptafuk which Edda had taken until the very end, Professor Witzleben had said, digging up old memories of postwar depression. She would live, with a vengeance, and Angelo would protect her, indeed was already about to give her the dowry necessary for life: high-class blackmail. He smiled at the small contracted immobile face, turned completely toward him in a very direct message, newsworthy, in its way romantic, which not even the small green mask over the eyes and the glass inside the glass could blur: "Don't torture yourself, call me Dawn and stop worrying, but love me, I want to live." Angelo smiled at her, he looked around, nobody was there: he wiggled two fingers. They had, so to speak, found each other. No syndrome would convince them to resist *looking each other in the face*, before being swallowed by the *shame* of their own faces. With him at her side she would live, he would help her find consolation in the monstrosity of the faces of others: just to begin with, those of her relatives. He knew how to take off the blindfold which has become the necessary shroud in which to hide oneself so that the healthy, the pure, the conforming might allow such creatures to survive. And if not even she would be allowed to play with life's dolly, he would teach her to take it apart piece by piece and break the spell which had excluded her. He hated the word but whispered to her: "Trust me, you're in the hands of an *expert* in the breaking of ready-made spells." He felt gathered into the protective womb of a faith he had never before experienced, warm, easy, *just*: a political faith in life. He also felt more expanded spiritually, as if he had touched something tangible, not dangerously universal and hence not liable to bend like taffy to the interests and tastes of the first insolent person to appear with a mouthful of absolute values with which to ignore the relative values that make up the shopping list. Political faith in life was one step higher than faith in life, and that's it. Living, not surviving, was life's highest political revenge against those who proclaimed the sacredness of some to underscore the profanity of others. Angelo never stopped teaching himself something more, and this sharpened in him the sensation of some sort of one-track love, naïve, tragic, and aware. "*Ciao ciao* little sister little sister very good very good" he whispered to her.

"Look, Lometto" he told him the next day "we're not talking about discounts here. We're talking about jail, risk. And besides, I assure you: you know well enough that pockets to be lined never show up one by one . . ."

"How's the weather there?" Lometto said, just to be able to concentrate on the present business which ravaged him because so close to his heart. Perhaps this was the prescription centenarians never reveal during interviews: when a hand grenade whizzes by, ask whether it's hailing.

"Don't you want to know how your wife is?" Angelo broke in, shocked.

"Yes, you know . . . How is Edda?"

"She fainted at the sight of her. It will be some problem to convince her to nurse. God, what a mess, Lometto . . . It would have been better if you had held on to your six thousand dollars . . ."

"Six thousand five hundred, if you don't mind."

". . . yes, whatever it is, and if you'd let me stay home . . . the responsibility . . . and now this thing . . ."

Angelo lied very naturally and he felt good, as never before. For him it was an unusual experience, he must be careful not to be carried away by the feeling of tenderness and deliquescence he experienced so intensely at the mention of the word "corruption." Was that which in men is first nature being granted also to him at least as second? Now he counted on the fact that Lometto—who for years had remained ready for the "I suspected as much!"—would fall into the trap of considering it his *first* nature, better concealed than in others, but nothing special when confronted by the test of new opportunities. And it was also to be expected that Lometto, in order not to attract attention and perhaps be the cause of sudden resentment with catastrophic consequences for himself, should pretend not to attach any importance to this new facet in the character of the until then incorruptible, touchy, maniacally "honest" collaborator. Angelo touched—barely grazed—keys which to him were completely unknown and miraculously from this issued a symphony that seemed to have been conceived and constructed over years and years of natural discipline and predisposition. Angelo, in short, felt he had dug up from himself the unhoped-for, bad faith's song of songs: credibility. He felt he was suddenly being catapulted into a net of psychosocial references in which it was restful to be caught and confined himself to doing nothing, letting himself be transported by the warm human current for which evil exists and must be fluidified by an even worse evil of which no trace should remain because we all know that in the end good must triumph and the righteous will be rewarded. He felt he was on a podium. This complicity in the great simpatico-mafioso manner suddenly transformed bundles of wood ready for the pyre into so many magic wands anxious to twirl in the air for a select audience unmoved by mass spectacles such as burning the heretic. Rarely are those who understand men and heresies interested in a heretic in the early manner, fire and all; they prefer by far a convert—that is, a heretic but doubly so, one who finally by coming to his senses espouses the true cause of causes, theirs. Sanguinary spectacles never please sensitive hearts, who organize them only when they are forced to by the rare madmen who will not listen to reason and insist on having faith in their own. Angelo thought of all this during the few instants of the phone call, he felt within a sudden burst of claws tearing down and away, but he did not feel pain: at stake was Giorgina Washington, he must act in such a way that Lometto would trust him blindly, he must not even for one moment entertain the idea of actually having recourse to other emissaries or intermediaries, this idea must not even graze him except to convince him that he already had the ideal person within reach, somebody who unexpectedly, who knows for what profound conviction as regards ideal life, adhered morally to his intention to do in the monster. Admitting the bad and the worse and calling good the part made visible by the mythical prejudice about the serpent, it followed that Angelo officially, definitively gave it to be understood that, the era of "yes" and "no" being ended, the monster existed and had to be eliminated. With the blessing of some sage or expert, in this case Angelo Bazarovi, high priest of Superior Causes, the business became a matter of routine within the bureaucratic procedures of the Department of Legitimate Legitimations.

"But how would they . . . proceed?" Lometto wanted to know.

"Look, that's their business, pneumonia, meningitis, hepatitis B, their problem. I've got other worries: the consulate, the passport, the bank, Edda, all this mess to take care of . . ."

"Twenty thousand dollars! Just like that!"

"It's up to you. With all the people you know can't you . . . ?"

"I don't know anybody."

"Well, in any case, in the meantime I must act as if everything were normal. Settle what can be settled, do my job anyway, right? There's an Italian parish priest who comes here, what do I call her? Certainly not Giorgina." Giorgina was out since Giorgio in dialect meant "slut" and Giorgina meant the same thing in diminutive because of temporary considerations of age.

"Anything you want, what do I care! Call her . . ."

"Look, let's give her a name above suspicion: Fortunata."

Lometto remained for a good thirty seconds without uttering a word. It seemed that Angelo had flung a poison dart into his eardrum.

"Are you jerking me around? Look, cut the crap. If you've got something to say, say it right away."

Angelo didn't understand his reaction.

"What the fuck are you talking about? Did you or didn't you say to give her a lucky name? What could be more fortunate than this!"

"Now you just listen to me . . ." Lometto was trying to say something completely different, Angelo could tell that he was struggling but that this silly business of what name to choose, for somebody one was planning to bump off, was suddenly becoming too entangled an affair to concern him.

"Lometto, will you tell me what the fuck you are thinking about? Anyway, what do I care whether you call her this or that? Hello! You like Aurora?"

"Yes, Aurora is fine . . ."

He seemed to calm down, heave a sigh of relief, certainly he was upset, everything seemed to sharpen his nefarious despair. Then, *en passant*, almost glad to change to such an innocent subject, he repeated:

"Twenty thousand dollars! It won't be easy to explain that to the Bank of Italy."

Angelo made no comment, neither now nor later—on the tape the exclamatory words "twenty thousand dollars!" must have been recorded at least a hundred times, luckily it could run for three hours and was double-track. He let him writhe in the procedural bulkheads he invented in order to expatriate twenty thousand dollars from Italy. But to begin with, he had a bank account in Switzerland. That was Lometto for you, exactly: he pretended, even after having given himself away out of vainglory with his mania for money stashed abroad, that the difficulty—phony—was of an insurmountable nature because bureaucratic—that is, *legal*.

During those days of assiduous phone calls without respite Angelo acquired some aristocratic ways with which to refine his upright position in the telephone booth. For example, he stretched out his fingers when he was holding a lit cigarette just to measure the passing of time—a cigarette was an irreversible hourglass lasting three minutes and twenty seconds, filter included. The concept of time, of smoke, of nails, in imagination deposited in the expert hands of a manicurist-courtesan, conveyed a sensation of distinction which distracted him from the necessity of listening to murderous nonsense and mischievous complaints. He stood there with the nonchalance with which queens go to kiss for the second time in life the ring of the selfsame Pope. It was—how should one say?—a bluff.

He appreciated all the more—in this state of relaxation and ennui indispensable to his daily dose of playacted hesitation—the hot flushes which raged at the other end of the wire among the open pores of Lometto's well-tested lard. Angelo was convinced he had—for anyone who might see him gazing vaguely into the distance beyond the glass door—the cherubic features of someone being briefed about the aurora borealis in the stock market.

"Hello, Celestino, are you still there?"

"Yes, where do you expect me to run to."

"Well, you know, don't you, that you are still the one who pays for the phone calls?"

"Cut the crap. Twenty thousand dollars and he talks about message units! What guarantees do I have? And how's her health now?"

"She's rallying, slowly, but she's bound to recover and be well. She's suckling now, today for the first time she's given her the breast."

"Yes, she told me. But it's still in the incubator."

"Yes, but not for long."

"Twenty thousand dollars! Guarantees . . . what are they . . . ?"

"Stop talking rubbish! Guarantees! The Professor knows his business, the more time goes by, the worse it is. Look, I'm fed up. In no time we'll have a slaughter of the innocents, every day, every time, all we talk about is getting rid of one of them. It's always the same. It's your business, yours and your wife's. Tell her to choke her and get it over with. Or drop her on the floor by mistake. I've done my duty, you can't expect me to get in this with both hands. A finger, yes, but no more."

"And to think that just a tiny injection, pushing some button there in the incubator . . ." .

"Why don't you negotiate directly? I already told you to. Or you could take the first plane and pop over here. He might even give you a discount."

"Oh, cut the crap. You're no friend."

"Go fuck yourself, Lometto. See what you can do on your own."

And this time too he slammed down the receiver, purposely. He hastened his steps to Edda's room, and sure enough, before the bend in the white corridor toward the stairs for the mezzanine the telephone operator leaned over and called him.

"Mister Beserouvi!"

Just as calmly he returned to the booth.

"Hello!"

"Do you think this is the moment to slam down the receiver? to go in for your prima-donna antics?"

"Listen, you have no choice here, and neither have I. In a week at most we vacate. Either the thing is done properly and as soon as possible or zilch, get it? There's no point in your going on and on about it, I'm not going to do in that little girl with my own hands."

The small auricular device seemed to push out and draw in tiny, perfectly animal-like legs whenever it emitted its squeak of total adherence.

"What time is it there?"

"Listen, first how's the weather and now you start with time zones? I know that to you yours seems the worst, but put yourself for an instant in my place."

"Yes, but you won't put yourself in mine."

"I'm already in your place, Lometto, unfortunately, the place I fill here *is* your place, not mine at all. I've been paid for this, and you know that out of dignity I never cry into the plate I'm eating from."

Pause. He obviously liked this one.

"It'll take a few days . . ."

"All you have to do is tell me that you've deposited the money over there, and I'll take care of things here."

"Meanwhile, couldn't you see if . . . you, I mean . . . I'll give you five thousand . . ."

"*Ciao*, Celestino, have a good sleep on it, because you need it."

"But Professor . . ."

"The Professor doesn't give a shit for your twenty thousand dollars! You know, here dollars come in the millions. If he does it, it'll be because he doesn't want to disappoint the customer, certainly not because he drools at the thought of your money. Who knows how many . . ."

"I'll call you again tomorrow, same time."

"But . . . won't you call Edda at least to find out what she thinks about it? You never mentioned it to her, did you?"

"I don't give a damn what she thinks. This is my business."

"Thanks for not saying 'our.' "

"Go screw yourself."

"All right. So I shouldn't even prepare her? Nothing at all?"

"No, nothing at all, but how does she act with the thing?"

"It's hard to say how she acts with the *thing*. Indifferent, she holds her to her breast without even looking at her, she takes her when they hand her to her and hands her back when she's finished."

"Nothing, a bit of shock . . ."

"*Ciao*."

"*Ciao*"

Two days later the last of the traps for Angelo and Aurora arrived, the most difficult to neutralize.

"But the money, just in case, to whom should the twenty thousand dollars . . . ?"

A too direct answer would have been enough to queer the whole deal. There was the sublime pleasure of intelligence when it bends to the dictates of shrewdness as a pastime and routs, to great advantage, all unaccompanied shrewdness. Angelo sensed, carnally, that he had one more guardian *self*. He made him flutter his wings obliquely and just barely:

"Professor Witzleben, I think—here at the clinic, I imagine. I'll find out, in fact I'll go right now."

"No, that's not necessary, I give them to you. They're in your hands."

"That's a load of shit, Lometto."

That's why, after a lot of haggling, a remittance of twenty thousand dollars arrived at the Manhattan Bank in the name of Angelo Bazarovi, passport no. D 124512.

Angelo withdrew the entire amount in cash, went around the corner and deposited the pile—what a *pile*! the pruriginous intoxication of certain terms which are taboo in the higher spheres of thought!—at the Rockefeller Bank, getting from them the equivalent in traveler's checks and sending the warranty to his home address in case of theft or loss. From there he called the airport, he wanted to find out if it was necessary to go on the waiting list in order to leave the same day. He gave the names, call back in an hour. He explained that there was a young mother with offspring. Sutures and bills, everything had been opportunely arranged for in advance. He took a cab to go to Fifth Avenue, where he had bought the acoustic millipede. There was no reason to stay a day longer in the clinic and besides Aurora had acquired the lovely pretty pink complexion of someone who has definitely taken the right road to see a rainbow here and there in a personal way, setting aside the common fate of seeing all manner of colors. He had four copies made of the recorded tape, on the copies he got them to erase what Edda had said—he didn't think it very refined: she had cursed, pleaded for Coptafuk, a mess of a mother—and he mailed them off with accompanying letters of instruction prepared the evening before on the receptionist's typewriter, one to a lawyer, one to a notary, one to Jürgen's mother, and the unedited original to himself, also with the letter of instruction in case he never returned. He took the opportunity to repeat his condolences to the world that was losing him.

The first flight was at 2:50 p.m., he still had two and a half hours left and if he confirmed immediately he didn't have to go on the waiting list. He confirmed and right away in the clinic there was an unprecedented turmoil of orders and counter-orders. He immediately demanded an ambulance, with what Mrs. Lometto had shelled out she could have visited all the states with sirens at full blast. Edda received the news of the sudden departure with joy: she raised her eyelids a little less slowly than usual. But then she immediately began to pack. Angelo ran into Professor Witzleben in the park and the latter, although he had given his authorization, looked at him in a strange way, as if now that request—which he had expected would come up in one way or another—remained pending and therefore he had the right to display greater distrust than usual. Was the Professor also a mind reader and his bitch Dawn his indispensable medium? He deigned to look at him with a superior air, it was absurd to put an entire ambulance at his disposal just to go to the airport. All the more since the signora, considering her age, would never be a steady customer. Dawn trotted with divaricated legs, half bandaged on the posterior, still with that muzzle of hers as if disgusted by the deflowered putrefaction of a world that never seeks remedies. The light canvas hat on the Professor's brow, his white bush jacket, his Vandyke sparkling with tallow, and his gold monocle, which appeared and disappeared amid the fronds, followed or heralded by the yellowish beast, made him think of misfortune about to strike. With his fingers Professor Witzleben was sprinkling magnolia scent on the plastic magnolias from a small crystal pitcher. When their eyes met, Angelo understood that, impossible to say how, Witzleben knew everything. Angelo waved to him, the other turned his back to him, set the pitcher on the ground, and extracted from the pocket of his bush jacket a small flagon with a gold-tasseled atomizer. He headed for the pittosporum hedge. Dawn turned her muzzle toward Angelo and stared at him with the watery yellow of a hyena facing a missed meal. The Professor watched Dawn as though he had prearranged a human destiny for her and no longer knew what to do.

At the airport he phoned Lometto a second time for fear that he might call the clinic and be warned. He told him that everything would be settled within the next forty-eight hours and to call as little as possible, in fact not to call at all. That he should get a good night's sleep on it, as usual, and that he had been able to convince the Professor not to complicate his life by charging separately for the obsequies, they'd be on the house.

Then he called Bertolli.

Bertolli was a very dear friend of his to whom he never turned for help even in the most serious moments because he did not want to disturb the composure of their relationship, which always seemed barely just salvaged by a Hapsburg excavation along the lines of the Crypt of the Capuchins. It was a fragile and precious non-friendship, on the razor's edge for fifteen years now, made up of the all and nothing which distinguishes the ineffable matter of the Prime Mover. Angelo took the liberty of calling on Bertolli only when faced by authentically cosmogonic cases that had not even the remotest suspicion of a "problem" or a "reality." Bertolli was so gentlemanlike in his manners and delinquentlike in his gaze—full of the mandarin irony of someone who has read Japanese and Chinese on the sly, displaying on his shelves only novels by Pitigrilli—that Lometto would certainly mistake him for anyone but never for what he was: simple, decent, conservative. He could be taken for a killer at the least, a pimp on the average, or a Communist-Trotskyist magistrate at the most. Angelo asked him to please come to the Malpensa airport, to stay close to him with all his silent eloquence and for the time necessary to construct a "witness," even though more suggestive than effective. No, no messes, neither now nor later, that's a promise. No, no broken leg or rib, no leper imported clandestinely from Africa to be treated at his expense. Yes, an English tie was fine. Could he, at least for once, opt for pants that weren't knickerbockers?

During the flight Edda stared straight ahead into the void and at the cart with drinks and cigarettes that passed up and down. Aurora Lometto, the failed George Washington II, had remained almost all the time in the arms of Angelo, who continually whispered little words to her, which, however, had no relaxing effect on the mother, hard and insensitive, emptied into an unhappiness from which every desire had evaporated. No less than three times it was he who, with the help of the gentlest flight attendant, sent as if from heaven, changed her diapers. She asked him if he was the father, obviously.

"Yes" he had replied with maternal spontaneity.

"She has your eyes."

It wasn't at all true. He had to squeeze Edda's elbow several times to convince her to do her duty and uncover her breast and nurse her. She did so automatically, looking obliquely at the ocean without hatred or love. Angelo was never to know whether, finally, she knew about her husband's intentions and realized she had a Cain at her side. If that were the case, she didn't care at all.

It was hot also in Milan, despite the fact that the sun was just barely there somewhere. This is the dawn of the Italian syndrome, he thought as soon as he set foot on the ground. While they waited for their luggage, still holding Aurora in his arms, Angelo went to the nearest telephone and dialed all the numbers of the Lometto residence, minus the last. But why should he warn him now? why should he get Lometto to come and pick them up there, while they were having breakfast, and so perhaps give him the time to organize a couple of gorillas? He hung up. He'd go by taxi to Montichiari, and from there he'd call him to come and get them. The important thing was that Bertolli should be there and see that he was holding a hale and hearty little girl, the rest was unimportant.

And there is Bertolli, outside the barrier, stiff, as if he were inside a sentry box at Buckingham Palace. Smiling, his polished cheekbones reflecting the theogonic light from the eyes of one who knows a place where you can eat warm brioche in the early-morning hours and the pale lips, shut tight over the far-ranging discourse of one who never will tell you where.

And just behind, Lometto, in shorts and a greasy undershirt.

Angelo, swaying between Giorgina and two suitcases, first of all puts the daughter into the father's arms.

"Let me introduce Dr. Bertolli."

Lometto and Bertolli turn simultaneously toward each other. Bertolli's smile, always very open, seems to say: finally! I'm so happy, how did your last haymaking go? even though he had never heard a single word about Lometto until that moment. Because of this Angelo is certain that the smile will have the effect of a mine floating into the insidious guilt feeling of Lometto, who in that diaphanous outstretched hand will see the professional satisfaction of an incorruptible financier or a ruthless hit man who has nothing to fear, sure of himself to the point of indulging in cordial greetings before frowning.

"Pleased to meet you" says Lometto, lowering his glasses over the infant. Then he raises them to Edda, they embrace, keeping at a distance. Edda begins weeping quietly, looking inside her sleeve for a handkerchief that she does not have. Lometto's glasses move in brief orbits between Angelo and Bertolli. Angelo knows what he is thinking: that this Bertolli is not the one who makes the olive oil. The flight captain, who has come several times to look at the baby and compliment the mother, passes nearby in the lobby and goes "coo-coo" inside the small yellow bundle at the height of Lometto's belly and greets everyone with great joviality. And this is the Italian syndrome: that nobody ever is aware of anything and treats other people's tragedies with undergraduate cuteness. Lometto holds Aurora against his bosom like an armful of twigs.

"Watch out, she's slipping down on you" Angelo says, starting off at the head of the small procession, toward the side parking lot. Lometto sidles up to him, points with his hand to a convertible.

"Yes—but the guy who makes olive oil—watch out!" Angelo says.

"You'll pay for this" Lometto hisses.

"I advise you to be very careful, Lometto, or else. I've got enough on you to put you away for twenty years. Even if you factor in a couple of amnesties to solve the nation's problems, you'll still do at least ten. May I give you a piece of advice, before you go ahead and talk nonsense?"

"Advice from you? from a thief? a blackmailer?" He stops and waits for Edda. "You hold her for a moment . . . and get going . . ."

Edda obeys, gathers the bundle of twigs, while Bertolli amiably accepts the suitcase of that silent lady, who is stifling in her big-tail coat. Angelo and Lometto walk away again.

"Well" Angelo says, putting his hand into his cotton canvas jacket, "this is your tape with our chats. One of the five existing in this world."

Lometto opens his hand, closes it again, instinctively looking around.

"And the twenty thousand dollars?"

"You know me, don't you? even though it was convenient for you to think you didn't know me well enough. In your opinion, what could I do with them?"

"Brazil."

"Whether you believe it or not, they're still yours. Of course, on one condition."

"Which?" Lometto asks, ready for anything.

"Let's talk about something else first. First of all, I should tell you that I have given orders to hand over tapes and the accompanying memorandum letter about what I have witnessed whether I die a natural death, by accident, or by violence. That is: with me dead, for you there's no way out whatsoever. But the thing is not as personal as you might think, it isn't that I want to get back at you at all costs. Basically, because I hope you'll croak before me, and so I'll spare you all inconvenience. Second: you'll lose the interest on the money, and that's true, perhaps, as a matter of fact, it'll be reduced by expenses for safekeeping by a number of lawyers—safekeeping of the tapes, I mean, in short: peanuts—but those twenty thousand dollars, your price for the murder, you'll get them all back."

"Oh, really? I knew it was a joke! those tapes are something you made up . . ." Lometto says, beginning to laugh, with droplets of sweat rising on his forehead.

"Shut up. I return them to you on two conditions: that Aurora is treated with all the care and honor she's entitled to. On her third birthday you'll get your dollars back, you shit."

"Look, I give you my word, I'll keep her, I'll take care of her, I'll do everything that you want for her, but first give me back all the tapes" Lometto implores.

"Those, never. Not even after she's three years old. Or who knows . . . I'm giving you my word as far as the dollars are concerned. And that's all. I don't want to risk cutting short my life by your hand either, this immense human event which is called Angelo Bazarovi, I consider you unworthy of injuring me. You're vulgar, stupid, arrogant, on the political plane you're everything I hate most. But, let us say, on the human plane I can't even pretend I hate you, not even if I try, I can't. We've been together too many years. I'd like to have you executed in a public square, but the doors to my house will remain open to you until your fate is decided . . . And since ninety-five percent of Italy is made up of people like you and I'm the one who runs the greater risks . . . well . . . if it's convenient I might even invite you to dinner sometime."

"What are you driving at?" Meanwhile they reached the car. The luggage was loaded. Edda got in, bowed her head and, of her own spontaneous will, now uncovered her breast and drew her daughter to her. Bertolli, rapt, surveyed the scene, taking in its monstrous beauty: the woman's expression of resigned revulsion, the swollen cheek of the infant who sucked with wide-open eyes and oriented herself among stretch marks and freckles cascading from shoulder and neck.

"And who's he?" Lometto said in a low voice.

"Don't worry. A simple witness of completed delivery, period. To tell the truth, not exactly and not only. But for now let's drop it."

The mad gaze of Lometto's sunglasses at the dangerous serenity which Bertolli emanated from his vast ivory-colored receding hairline showed the extent of the terror engendered by false impressions. Everything went off splendidly, better than planned: the constellation of suggestions that Bertolli spread around him, his discreet demeanor, the absolute absence of *bon ton* prejudices and therefore the lack of concessions to the schizophrenia of the enriched proletariat, together with inherited economic privilege which had never put him in a situation of doing good in order to improve his position, his humble faith in the Tudors, with particular regard to Elizabeth, everything contributed to the jagged but encircling fascination of a *pure* delinquent. And it was with this mutable impression of dealing—who knows?—either with an agent of the Military Security Information Service or with an owner of brothels and gambling dens that Lometto observed Bertolli out of the corner of his eye. When he saw him avidly aiming his gaze at the bared breast, Lometto must have thought that Edda was lost. And perhaps also the mongoloid. It was obvious that Bertolli was ready for anything, besides being a sexual maniac.

"Aren't you finished nursing her yet? Close up shop!" Lometto yelled, staring nastily at Bertolli, who was absorbed in his Renaissance references of Madonna with Child retouched by Bosch and exhibited at a dog show. Glasses or not, by now it was all the same to Angelo.

They said goodbye through the window, Bertolli headed for his car waving his hand and smiling just as he had come.

Angelo leaned over the car window, Lometto was inserting the ignition key.

"Have a good trip. You'll see that with time you'll get attached to her."

The window rose slowly, Lometto kept pushing the button and looking ahead. With the window closed, he saw Lometto's answer take shape on his sharp-edged mouth:

"B a s t a r d."

This was all that Edda had heard of the noise of tongues between

Angelo and Lometto. As always and for all things, enough to understand, enough not to understand at all, to be curious or indifferent, tell one's share in everything one knows or keep silent about it forever. Angelo asked Bertolli to accompany him upstairs again, he wanted to watch the takeoffs for Cairo.

"Who are they?" Bertolli asked.

"Employers" Angelo answered, slipping his arm under his.

This was the first time that someone else came to welcome him on his return, it had never happened before, for any reason. The ideal was to ask for it expressly.

After keeping to generalities, Angelo remarked, sighing because of the weariness brought on by that other, almost concluded nightmare:

"It's a shame for the little girl." Even he didn't understand why with Bertolli he always said things he didn't feel, perhaps because Bertolli was so much better than he at correcting the aim of those he truly felt. This is what at the time of psychoanalytical romanticism was called "plagiarism."

"Why, what's the matter with her?" Bertolli asked. So there he was, beginning with his typical answers followed by a question mark.

"No, I was saying, you know . . ."

"The little girl! But did you take a good look at the mother and father? Down's syndrome is certainly a quality leap from the genetic point of view."

Angelo was spellbound, with a cup of cappuccino in midair, and he shook his head: he was in Milan, and the man in front of him was not Professor Witzleben. A conspiracy, this "get down" syndrome. How far did Bertolli's plagiarizing power reach?

"You too . . ." Angelo threw him a suspicious look.

"I too what?"

"The syndrome. But what is this, jargon? I mean, why this 'get down' syndrome at all costs?"

As he accompanied Angelo to the station, he summarily explained to him who Professor Down was, what chromosomic alteration meant—Angelo listened with terror, unable to go and hide, he was so ashamed. Psychomotor retardation aside, almost all the symptoms of mongolism and chromosomic theory had more than once been used to give a *scientific* explanation of homosexuality . . . he felt he loved Aurora all the more because she bore all alone and by now irrefutably the burden of such a diagnosis decided among pranksters. He continually fingered the traveler's checks in the pocket of his jacket, where there was also the small recorded reel: this was the guarantee that he and she would live. Bertolli shook his hand.

"One really ought to do that child a favor: get rid of the parents by euthanasia, don't you agree?" Bertolli said, slightly dreamy over the picture he was enclosing in the frame of his inscrutable and exact vision of the entire affair.

Angelo would have liked to embrace him, but he knew he shouldn't. Bertolli seemed somewhat vexed by the legislative impracticability which continually impeded his impulses or proposals for remedies of authentic generosity and human empathy. Angelo waited for him to move down the flight of steps before embracing him unseen. Under the arch Bertolli seemed to seek out a more suitable beam of light, one whose color was closer to the chrome of sulphur than to that powder color of the marble struck head-on by the dawn. Then he disappeared.

The Toigo cemetery is deserted. The living are on vacation, and despite the prolonged schedules of daylight saving time it will be difficult to call them back from lakes and swimming pools until the day after tomorrow when the count of the dead of the exodus casualties has been completed. There's not even a custodian, not even a little old woman to tell him quarrelsomely how many young and strong she has seen move on to a better life with her always there with her trudge-trudge of sciatica and more undeserved days.

There, the "Lometto Family": and one immediately has the impression of having entered Piazza Vittoria in Brescia. And certainly someone has entered because from the small wrought-iron-and-beveled-glass gate—lilies of incandescent steel and a few ears of wheat, decorations already seen somewhere else—half the lock is missing. Not even a flower anywhere, nor a little wreath nor a melted-down candle stub. Nothing. Nothing of the gilded or carved letters that one expects. Nothing of Giorgina Washington either.

This time too he'd been screwed by Lometto. Angelo had thought of everything but not of the essential: the little girl's safety. He should have told him at the airport that for her the same condition applied as to himself, and that he would have legally used the tape whether she died by accident or illness or murder. But Lometto had neglected confronting him with a fait accompli: among businessmen the law reigns that what is valid for contracts is valid for blackmails, and you can't go back on them. Too bad for the suckers who omit the negligible details. Angelo hugs the angel to his chest: for a little while longer it will still be his. The funerary temple was never inaugurated. Or spoiled, considering the little monster with the smiling mouth and the magnetic black eyes. Nobody made a debut in the crypts. Angelo pushes the small gate and rushes out, unable to explain the mystery: Where have they put Aurora Lometto?

The house there in the back must be the custodian's, there's a huge rotating crucifix antenna, it must pick up thirty-three channels plus the Holy Spirit, to say the least. He rings the bell, a dragging sound of slippers, summery, and a very curvaceous woman looks out, her hair a scorched red, a chicken leg seasoned with garlic and parsley in one hand.

"What is it? Did they turn off the water at the faucet again?"

"Good morning, signora . . ." Angelo is a bit uncertain. "Can you give me some information? . . . Oh yes, don't worry about it; it's mine, I didn't take it from here."

"From where, then?" she says, with a lazy bite into a tendon.

"But don't you see? You're not thinking that . . . But don't you see, this isn't something made from a mold?"

"What do you want? You're making me miss the whole episode."

And with a hand that isn't greasy she straightens her housedress, tries to answer Angelo's polite smile, and reveals the complaisance which is typical of Mantuan women married to gravediggers but married after a youth of witches' sabbaths.

"I wanted to bring this angel to the grave, the crypt of Aurora Lometto. I wonder if you know. A little girl . . ."

"Why, of course" and she raises her hand to her mouth to hide the beginning of a giggle. "Excuse me, you see, I don't know who you are but once in a while . . . I don't mince words: with all due respect for the little dead girl, but they had it coming, those people . . ."

"But she's not here in the family chapel" says Angelo, pointing his arm at the monumental absence beyond the big wall.

"You bet! You bet! She isn't here, all that money for a mongoloid! She's in Penzana, in the old cemetery. Behind the church. Do you know where it is?"

"Yes. Strange . . ."

"They thought it would be a waste of time to bring her here—for the chapel, I mean. You know, we've done plenty of jobs for them, my husband and I, and here and there, the bricklayers, the carter, the phone calls. Never a five-lire tip, promises . . . 'at the first opportunity you'll see this, you'll see that.' And then the first opportunity ended up in Penzana, not here."

"Maybe the chapel wasn't finished, perhaps they're still at work on it."

"Not at all. There's even the eternal light already, but they always keep it turned off. Well, after all, there's nobody there yet. No, I don't think so, you would have to ask my husband."

"There's no need."

"You know, he went fishing . . ."

"Oh . . ."

"He's not here. You like catfish?"

"Thank you very much, and excuse me. Yes, stewed with peas. I've eaten it. Goodbye."

As he turns to leave he hears: "If you like it, I'm making it right now . . . Do you want to have a taste of it? If you like peas, you're not the only one, you know?"

Angelo turns toward the callused hand and those strong teeth sprinkled with chopped parsley. He looks at her kindly, chastely, with the deference owed to any woman who shovels in accordance with national statistical averages.

"So . . . my husband will be fishing until midnight, you know, it's the weekend and we don't work . . ." the woman says in a seductive voice, shifting the femur on which she leaned against the door and staring at him with wide-open eyes. Angelo lowers his to a layer of compressed gravel and scrapes it with the tip of his sandal. Exactly like a horse pawing the ground before taking off.

"Actually I'm in a hurry now."

"Okay. Another time, then. I'm always here, you handsome hunk. Stay on the ball, eh." And she goes back inside to her soapy devotions.

Everything in cemeteries is so typical, from the guardians to the guarded. Giorgina who does not abide here and this one who will abide here forever and says "hunk" to the first person who rings her bell, all ready with sauce for the catfish kept sizzling. Everyone taking his revenge as best he can on his own death and that of others. Some disappearing, some screwing with widowers and visitors holding an empty pail in their hands, counting the tolls of the bell from the center of town so as to be there punctually when the new customer arrives, with the gray cotton housedress well smoothed out over the hips beneath the trade's mournful face. In Italy there will never be a scarcity of tourists . . .

How long since he has set foot in Penzana! Now all he needed was to see Celestino or Edda pop up somewhere. They never go on vacation, apart from her irrigations. He parks near the bank, four steps to the church, seven to skirt the steps of the churchyard, ten to enter the shadow of the side corridor which must lead both into the church and into the sacristy. The door is wide open. A woman is smoking as she folds a white surplice. Angelo observes her finger glide under the iron after picking up a bit of saliva from her tongue. Rather than dressed, one would say she was covered, not a centimeter of skin is exposed by the faded, rust-colored skirt, apart from a bit of the back of the heel because one of her stockings has a run and a bit of neck because it is very long and the hands—her fingernails are painted scarlet.

"Good afternoon, I would like to speak to the priest."

Once again Angelo, contracting his spinal column with a backward jerk, makes an effort to push down the surprise inspired in him by those profane nails. The woman, puffing smoke from her nostrils and squinting her small, close-set, owl-like eyes, stares at the white angel.

"Who, Don Galetta?"

"Yes, I think so. I don't know his name."

"I think I've seen you somewhere. Are you from the parish of Castelgoffredo? Do you take care of the charity raffles?"

"No, you probably saw me at the Lomettos' " he says curtly.

"Sure, I remember" the woman says, turning her back to him and starting to iron again.

"You are the priest's . . . housekeeper?"

"The *perpetua*, if you please" she says with a look of self-satisfied challenge. "What is it you want? You can tell me, if you wish."

"Nothing special. I would like to put this angel on the grave of Giorg . . . Aurora Lometto, you know the one who . . ."

"I know, I sure do, I know, I know. I was the one who closed her eyes . . ." she says, and Angelo keeps himself from asking for confirmation, whether she really did have eyelids, whether they closed, whether the eyes were not made of glass and she wasn't embalmed. "It's really a handsomely made little statue."

"I imagine the cemetery is still open, I'll just pop in."

"Certainly, ten more minutes. Go through this way, since you're already here, it'll be quicker."

"Thanks. Perhaps if you were to tell me where she is . . ."

"You are . . . the doctor . . . the foreign languages . . ." the woman says, looking at him obliquely.

"I'm a friend. Of Aurora Lometto's, I was a friend. I worked as interpreter for Lometto. I was the one who accompanied Signora Edda to America. I saw her give birth."

"Oh yes?" But there wasn't a trace of curiosity in her voice. "Eh, poor Aurora! You gave her the name, a beautiful name. But perhaps it's for the best like this. For everybody, I mean . . . they couldn't be reconciled to it. Neither before, nor afterwards either, when she died . . . poor people, what days" the woman comments, sucking in her cheeks a bit, without losing for a moment Angelo's expression, who mentally says: so everybody knows everything . . . the little that's granted them, naturally . . .

"But she seemed so healthy. Yes, there were some complications immediately after birth, but I would never have thought of fulminating meningitis . . . a few days after getting home . . . just like that . . . poor little girl . . ."

"Come, come, I'll show you the way. We'll all have our turn."

They set off under the high sun, which is unrelenting, they go down a narrow thirty-meter-long lane cut transversely by another approximately twice as long. That's the whole cemetery. The headstone is modest without a photograph. The name, the dates, and "rest in peace."

"When she died I was in Egypt. I heard about it from one of the office girls when I got back; she was already here. Were there a lot of people at the funeral?"

The woman seems to reflect.

"The close relatives. The announcement was made after the funeral. The notice must still be outside."

"I didn't see it."

"The kids probably ripped it down."

"Don't you think this angel looks very nice here?"

"It's even too beautiful . . . I mean that certainly, between you and me, this headstone here really . . . doesn't it look secondhand to you? I know I shouldn't say such things, but they have the whole town talking behind their backs. This business with America! They seem to exaggerate on purpose to show that they really don't give a damn . . ."

"Oh, the headstone! Surely they'll take the daughter to the family chapel in Toigo when it's finished, that's why."

Angelo looks around, exhumes the gesture that all must make before a headstone: he pulls up a blade of grass, levels the gravel . . . the woman emits a small smoker's cough. "But the chapel *is* finished."

Their eyes meet: gelid, as at the end of a performance completed and exposed. Angelo is sure that the woman—he cannot bring himself to call her *perpetua*, she is too much a creature of the moment, filled with the hostile lability of someone who makes it her duty to show a solidity of role which she does not have and about which, for all that, she does not care at all—made her nasty remark about the headstone by design, to give a touch of autonomy to her judgment and better disguise her total subjection to the Lomettos.

"Oh, you saw her when she was dead, in her coffin, I mean . . . how was she dressed?"

"Yes, never before. You know, they didn't care . . . a little yellow set, a white bonnet. She didn't even look like a two-and-a-half-week-old baby, she was nice and chubby, toward the end she ate a lot. Then . . . And such thick hair, some even in her ears, what eyes, how upsetting, they opened and closed, opened and closed. I was there just to keep them closed. Poor Edda, she had a breakdown."

"Oh, also after the first days, you should have seen how she suckled! I already forgot about the hair . . . Aurora had a will to live. I mean it, why are you looking at me like that?"

"I'm not looking at you at all like that."

"Fulminating meningitis . . ."

Now Angelo is scrabbling under the gravel, mechanically. The woman is silent and then she gives him a tap on the shoulder blade.

"What are you doing, digging? Fill that hole immediately. Come, now I must really close up. And besides, I also have to prepare dinner for Don Galetta."

"Well, thank you . . ."

"Not at all."

"Oh, now that I think of it . . . there's something else."

The woman starts off.

"That is?" she says, already beyond the steps, letting him go through first and closing from inside the sacristy the small door that opens on the cemetery. It is a very long "that is?"

"You remember, oh, I'm sure you must remember, Santina Tartaglione, she wasn't from these parts, she committed suicide . . ."

"You're pretty nosy, aren't you? What are you, a detective?" the skeletal woman says, resting her hands on her flat hips.

"And why should you, if you'll pardon me, think that I'm a detective?" Angelo retorts, staring at her amused. "She wasn't murdered, was she?"

"What are you talking about! I've got to go now, goodbye" and she waves a bunch of keys taken from her large side pocket.

"For all you know . . . I could even be a repentant unmarried father . . ."

"Who you? With a poliomyelitic . . . you? Who are you trying to fool? So then, that is?"

They had come out onto the dusty esplanade, not a tree around, a pavement of porphyry and the sheet metal of high-cylinder cars such as can be seen only in small agricultural centers. The car bodies are blinding in the sharp light which darts into the eyes—sunset's furibund beginning.

"Whether you believe it or not, I'm animated only by good intentions."

"And why don't you go and put your questions to Mr. Lometto himself?"

"I'm sorry, but where does Lometto come in now? In any case, if I really were interested, I'd already have somebody who could answer me. If you want to answer, fine; if not, it's all the same."

"She worked in his workshop along with the other wretches, right? What do you want to know? Look, we've always treated those poor women with Christian charity."

"That's not what I'm interested in, I would like to know where the little girl is now who was found there on those steps next to her mother who bled to death."

"First of all, you're making a mistake."

Above, a shiver of curtains behind a window.

"In what way?"

The *perpetua* again pulls out her bunch of keys and heads for the parish house directly opposite, which is attached to the bank, certainly in the past a wing of the old, gigantic sacristy.

"But what are these steps? The Tartaglione woman was found down there, at the entrance to the road you took to come here, on the provincial highway, and as for the baby, an icicle. A miracle that she was still alive."

"Here on the church steps."

"Yeah, the steps to the pyramids! halfway, on the highway, between the road to town and Private Road, where there's the 'kindergarten' on the corner."

"Where there's that car wreck?"

"Yes, exactly; obviously the mother left her there and then dragged herself all the way down to the end."

"That's not what the newspaper says."

"The newspaper . . . and what do you care? Insignificant details. The newspapers . . . It's just a way of putting things, right? It's a set phrase finding wretches on the church steps or at the convent's door" the woman remarks, purposely revealing a critical subtlety cautiously concealed to an unheard-of extent.

"At what time does Don Galetta get here?"

"Don Nocciolini, if you please. He already got here, he already went upstairs, that's his car."

Angelo turns his head and is somewhat startled: but that's Lometto's silver-gray car! Everything here emanates a celestine reflection, this tangle of religion and pantyhose, medicine and pantyhose, banks and pantyhose, charitable institutions and pantyhose, tearful stories of firings and pantyhose, pantyhose and its inalienable supreme rights. Only God is superior to pantyhose because he himself distributes them throughout the homes and, if God remains silent, you can imagine what the stylists do.

"May I see him? Tell him that Dr. Bazarovi is here and would like to speak to him for a moment."

"You like to give orders, don't you?" the woman says, entering an ample anteroom with a staircase of green-veined marble, a handsome red velvet runner over which the woman's long skirt immediately flutters. Could also this *perpetua*, this luxury, the scarlet-colored fingernails be typical of Mantua's parish houses?

The usual crucifix on the wall—but it is absolutely pure ivory!—a neoclassic chiffonier, a small Turkey rug with a monstrance woven into it that emanates golden rays; an evergreen plant in a corner rises to the ceiling, in an ancient terra-cotta with hand-painted lambs.

Don Galetta-Nocciolini is preceded down the stairs by his highly polished black shoes, just changed for the occasion, black socks, the black pipes of his trouser bottoms.

"You wish to speak with me?" asks a voice with a very heavy, almost unnatural dialectical inflection, before the mouth appears and stretches in a head smile beneath salt-and-pepper hair bristling like those of the porcupines in fables.

"Good evening, my name is Angelo Bazarovi . . ."

"I know, I know . . ."

"I'm here because of a case of conscience . . ."

"It is better to repent late than never. You've brought the tapes."

"No" Angelo says sharply, a singsong, provocative no.

Don Galetta could be the president of any local association where there is something to eat.

"So then it is not a case of conscience."

His purposeful lack of diplomacy calls to mind a cattle dealer who each time discusses the last figure without bringing up those that preceded it.

"I know who you are" he adds, rearranging the mental folds of his blackish smile. "I know you very well."

"I should imagine, you are Lometto's partner-confessor, aren't you?"

"How dare you?"

"Do you believe that conscience is only the appanage of those whom you or Lometto pick out?"

"Come into my study" the priest says, measuring him from behind his very bright glasses with a flash of distrust which does not escape Angelo, who could swear that those lenses are a gadget, a device for those who consider the *comme il faut* aspect of an authority, not for the one who inspires it.

The priest opens the door next to the chiffonier. They enter a large room with a bow window which looks out on a small garden with dusty rosebushes. As in the cemetery grown around the apse, here too there is something English in the architectural-religious arrangement. Will he be offered tea? On the sill of the bow window a mother-of-pearl schooner. Angelo sits down in a brown leather armchair with brass studs. It is always old, repentant women who make such bequests, undoubtedly, women who negotiate for the other world at so much a meter, paying in kind: a Maggiolini piece, a Stradivarius, a Louis XIV, a Chippendale. One ought to pay admission just for the furniture. Don Galetta sits down behind the leather-covered desk—and here too studs, but gold at the corners. He moves a solid-silver crucifix of obvious baroque craftsmanship. He crosses himself.

"I'm listening."

"Do you believe in the professional secrecy of confession? I'm looking for guarantees, if possible" Angelo asks, pulling a pack of cigarettes from his T-shirt. He does not ask for permission since the ashtray of beveled crystal overflows with Gitane stubs.

"But what sort of questions are these?" the man asks, adjusting his bulk on the chair's back and armrest.

The furnishings exude a dense taste for things which are antique but without a history, which have value inasmuch as they cost money, and that's that. It would be instructive to catalogue them in terms of the extreme unction which concludes their pedigree. Icons. Chalices set with gems. Several paintings with religious subjects. Pieces of carved ivory—the flagellation and other stations cut into an elephant tooth, the star comet, at the tip, the Magi, and so on, *à rebours*.

"I would like you to consider this conversation strictly private, like a confession" Angelo says without believing anything of what he is saying. He does not believe in private confessions but in public trials, guillotine and all.

"It is never too late to mend one's ways" the priest volunteers, taking a pack of cigarettes from his jacket of handsome gabardine. His gaze is very restrained on his side of the lenses, suddenly he must realize that he has begun with a repertory unworthy of those pneumogastric eyes which probe him ironically. Angelo answers with a clearly satiric dart of his eyes: come on, Galetta, you old fool, don't give me that!

"Listen, no theosophic dissertations between us, agreed?" Angelo proposes, as if to put at his ease someone who feels theologically inferior. "If you can guarantee me that what I'm asking remains between us, that's enough for me, otherwise I must *beg you* to confess me and give me your blessing."

"I do not hear confessions in my study."

"In that case, let's go to the confessional." But the atmosphere has already become irremediably gallowslike. Certainly Angelo has already injected an excessive desire for mockery, appraising the knick-knacks of the auctionary Curia: at least two hundred millions in Counter-Reformation works of art, more or less.

"I can't now. There are schedules. Come some other day. Tomorrow, for example."

"Do you first want to go to Mr. Lometto for advice?" Angelo asks, taking a bone-and-gold fountain pen from an amethyst penholder and scribbling on his cigarette pack to see if the nib works.

"Put that down and mind your manners in the house of the Lord! And besides, showing up like this in a T-shirt . . ."

"What *lord*? You or that other one of the pantyhose?"

Don Galetta jerks up from his chair and points his arm at the door.

"Out, or I'll call the police sergeant!"

"Who could he be, the third lord? Look, if you don't stop shouting, *I'll* call the police. Just sit down. Your conscience is bothering you, isn't it? And I was thinking that I was the only one to consider it a problem. And where do you think I heard certain insinuations about the *theft* of the Mantegna from your church, in the Michelin Guide?"

"How dare you, what are you trying to insinuate?" he bursts out, even more enraged, flaming purple.

"A priest who betrays himself by his own *confessions*! This is marvelous. One can tell you didn't study with the Jesuits."

"You're an oaf. What do you want from me?"

"That's a pretty little silver-gray car you've got out there! I know it so well, I've taken so many trips in it. Berlin, Amsterdam, Paris, Sommacampagna. I even broke my head in it."

"It's a secondhand car, regularly paid for."

"Oh, sure! and who knows what trouble you go to to place the handicapped without contribution in the cellars of family workshops. Who knows what expenditures of energy and gas you must have, what hassles with the families who rent them rotten rooms without water or toilet, and then you've got to convince them to abort because it's the Lord's will. And if one of them refuses, she is expelled from faith hope charity, right?"

"You're a moralist without morals. I know you well. Mr. Lometto told me about you, he told me what kind of a person you are. You make threats, you blackmail honest people, you think you know everything and you don't know the most elementary things about civilized coexistence. A hothead. Come to the point. Because in any case I know what you can and what you cannot do."

"Apparently you've already been instructed, ahead of time, or am I wrong? Of course, before other people one makes a point of refusing the first pew in church to the Lomettos if they arrive late, and then, on the sly, one gives one's blessing to the corpse of a mongoloid who died God knows how. Isn't that so?"

Don Galetta's mouse-colored eyes pop out, the lenses mist over, the clay of his Adam's apple crumbles. His throat has a nicotine rasp.

"Now do you still want to call the police? Let's say I make an official application for the body to be exhumed . . ."

"If that's it, then the local doctor, Dr. Pujahr, is more responsible than I am."

"The Indian?"

"Yes. He's the one who issues the death certificate and the burial authorization. The priest always arrives when things are over and done with. And Dr. Pujahr has returned to Bombay."

The same as saying: every branch of the *sacred* from medicine to funerals has its own bureaucracy, including the art of transfers.

"Done with how?"

Don Galetta gets up, straightens the belt over his prominent belly, moves toward the bow window, pulling in a longer, meditative puff.

"Done."

"A case of *conscience*, then?"

"What would you have done in my place?" the priest says in a whisper, as if he were going for broke, as if to risk a part of the whole which he knows without knowing how much Angelo knows. "I wasn't asked for an opinion, I certainly didn't say you have my blessing, let her die of meningitis. I blessed the dead body and amen."

And he stops, waiting. One instant is enough: and Angelo has nothing to add. So then Angelo does not know, not to the very bottom: this is what Don Galetta's brief sigh signifies.

"So she really died of meningitis?" Angelo says, astounded: then she was neither stuffed nor poisoned.

"But certainly! What did you think?" and the priest, satisfied, with an impulse of generosity adds with resigned bluster: "Not just so . . . fulminating, that's it. Helped along a little bit, let's say. But objectively lost and destined to die in a very short time after other useless sufferings."

Angelo feels like blinking his eyes, to prove to himself that they are not yet made of glass, and he sees that the other, lying somewhere else, is telling a perhaps irrefutable truth. He finds it hard to believe that everything has become so simple. No cyanide, no arsenic, no emptying out of innards and embalming: only the most brazen of the Lord's providences, a fulminating meningitis corroborated by clocks one has forgotten to rewind for a couple of days.

"Are you from around here?" Angelo asks.

"No."

"From where?—if I may ask."

"I am originally from Avellino."

"Oh, but you speak with a perfect Mantuan inflection."

"After all these years!"

"And you read the *Gazzetta di San Luigi Gonzaga*, I see."

"It is one of Italy's oldest daily newspapers."

"I know."

Don Galetta is still with his back turned. He lets the subject drop, for an instant holds his breath, turns to crush his butt on the small low Oriental table.

"Well, if that's all I'd like to have my dinner now."

"In any case, euthanasia is condemned by the Church. That in itself would be sufficient to get you bounced."

They both stand facing each other. They stare at each other politely.

"While I'm at it. You must certainly know the person who writes about local matters and signs them N.B."

Don Galetta exhales nitrogen-charged assent, admitting vexation.

"It's Napaglia Benito, the notary."

"No less. Mrs. Lometto's brother."

"Exactly."

"A fine circle. Really a fine circular siege. Difficult to enter and impossible to leave."

Don Galetta has a brainy smile and slams down his ace: "For you too, so far as I know."

"Oh, don't harbor any illusions. I come and go. I possess an extra elliptic dimension. I'm slippery and I'm not a collector, I'm not attached to things" he says, with an ample gesture of his arm at the antiquarian exhibition.

"This is part of the Church's patrimony, it is not my property, it is a universal patrimony."

"Tell that to somebody else!"

"You are good at looking into other people's wallets, aren't you?"

"Do you realize that your Church is about to go under, that it is already experiencing its Indian summer? There has to be a reason" Angelo says, looking around with an expert's eyes.

"You're raving, she has never been as strong as now."

"Indeed. The moment of lucidity that life grants to those who will lose consciousness completely and die the instant after."

"Good evening."

"Enjoy your dinner. And you may not believe it: but I'm not here for Aurora Lometto, aside from the small remembrance. I have no intention of any kind in that regard."

"Oh, that's not the reason?" Don Galetta asks, impulsively reaching into the pocket of his jacket. Another cigarette, standing there, at the door with the large pierced heart: silver and rubies and lapis lazuli.

"But do you have armored doors and an alarm system here?"

"And do you always walk around with a tape recorder under your . . . ?" But it's a hundred years now that he's realized that neither in tight shorts without pockets nor in the open sandals nor in the T-shirt nor in the cigarette pack would there be room for a tape recorder no matter how mini.

Angelo chuckles.

"You would not have said what you did say if you thought anything like that. The reel I have is enough for me. In fact, the two which make it up."

"Two?"

"Oh yes, so to speak, you have no way of knowing but I also own one made out in the name of Mrs. Lometto, of a, let's say, sentimental nature." Now Angelo is dying to glimpse the swirl of fantasies aroused in the priest. "But this certainly isn't something I want to linger on. Just assume it doesn't exist, I'm a gentleman when it comes to women."

"You, a . . ."

"A . . . ?"

"You know very well what I mean."

"No, if you don't tell me. A . . . ?"

Don Galetta shrugs his shoulders. "A Uranist!"

"Oh, my God, what a big word! Just say faggot or pig, like everybody else."

"A sodomite."

"I associate only with God Almighty. What about you?"

Don Galetta shudders through the dilated, obscene nostrils of someone who has secreted much of his sexuality in picking his nose upon wakening from sleep. The absence of a skullcap does not, however, exclude other possibilities of pastoral-sheepish works.

"Did you emigrate here with Mr. Napaglia, the man of the furniture factory?"

Tock-tock at the door.

"Don Nocciolini, dinner's on the table."

"I'm coming, Marta, I'm coming right away."

"Don't make me warm it up as usual, hurry."

Angelo smiles at him and lets his shoulders droop, a bit weary.

"Quite a woman, your *perpetua*. A perfect sentinel. She only says enough to hide all the rest and makes you believe she has said too much. Very clever."

"You have an intolerable way of expressing yourself. Marta has a college degree and is a lay sister."

"Oh, really, in what, nail polish?"

"The polish is a symbol of the blood of Our Lord Jesus Christ."

"For her alone, I imagine."

"There exists a dispensation by the bishop in this regard, if you wish to see it. Marta is a special case."

"A degree in what?"

"Guess" says Don Galetta, who is now again itching to play cat and mouse.

"She's probably a corporation lawyer" Angelo suggests, looking about with as much ostentation as possible.

"Oh, certainly not, she's a veterinarian."

"Why didn't I think of it sooner? Of course, the *dwarfs* . . ." Angelo exclaims, irritated by all these absurdities of reality accumulated during the last two and a half hours. "And she too is from around Naples, I imagine."

"No, she is a purebred Mantuan. But let us . . ."

"Provided your dinner does not get cold . . ."

"The reason for your visit, you were telling me . . ."

"And I was asking whether you had come up North together with Napaglia . . ."

"I don't see the connection."

"Yes, of course . . . Well, in some way, I too am responsible for having put a stone on Aurora Lometto: out of negligence and egotistic naïveté . . ."

"Would you like to stay? I'll have another place set" Don Galetta proposes, and dares to make the gesture of laying a hand on his shoulder. Angelo instinctively shrinks.

"No, thank you, I have no desire to see Lometto drop in for dessert, nor the need. And he neither, I believe."

"Oh, you are wrong. On the contrary, he is very anxious to talk to you."

"I do have a telephone. Here and now it is out of the question."

"As you wish."

His voice has become firm, irreducibly drowsy. Just as well, Angelo thinks, he was beginning to find him pleasant. And besides! that bow window! the mysteries deposited in that concave semicircle, synchronically in and out, in an irreconcilable contrivance of a fused appearance and reality, and thus incontrovertibly separate.

"And so?"

"I, you see, did not come at all for that little girl over there"—and he points to the cemetery on the side—"but for another, the daughter of Santina Tartaglione, does the name mean anything to you?"

Don Galetta jerks back his torso without moving the axis of his body.

"Now, listen, this is beyond all limits. I know nothing about this story. Talk about things over and done with! An accident. An obvious suicide."

"I hope you're not telling me that before things were over and done with, you didn't try to brainwash her, convince her to have an abortion."

"She was a fool, a reckless fool. She was very busy with the young men . . . out of town. I did my duty. I tried to bring her back on the right track. She was possessed. In her physical condition! She didn't realize that the boys were laughing at her. Sometimes she would come home hopelessly drunk. None of the men were from Penzana . . . here no one would dare . . ."

"Of course, the dirty ones are always outsiders."

"But in substance I have nothing to do with it. She insisted on having her own way and she paid."

Angelo does not understand how people so little gifted, let us say, in military dialectics can be so successful with God.

"Dearly."

"Dearly, yes."

"Certainly, if even your veterinarian is forced to say that she was found not on the church steps but on the provincial highway, it must be exactly because another version, the one presented by N.B. in the *Gazzetta*, for example, if one only starts scratching around, at the baker's or the woman at the gas station . . ."

"Oh, the woman at the gas station, that one! A lost soul, that one on Sunday walks past the church at ten o'clock singing the *International* . . ."

". . . a version that would not stand up for a minute. People always know more than one thinks, you know that, and gossip and lies and suspicions and fears and illusions form a large part of the truth . . ."

"What difference does it make?"

"And you ask me?"

"Yes, I ask you, if you don't mind" the priest says, bringing his hand to his hips, losing his patience.

"Oh, come, come. Aren't you the one who makes the lids for Lometto's pots? You are a full-fledged accomplice in this suicide, and who knows how many others, because of negligence, why think of all those bells between the provincial highway and out there that Tartaglione must have rung."

"But you are raving, my dear Dr. Bazarovi! Raving, I assure you. I, at any rate, can only be responsible for *my* bell. I never neglect assistance at that hour! here! She never rang."

"Not *afterwards*. Before. You've all of you in agreement committed her suicide. I know how these things go in a small town when there's someone who does not respect the rules: a polio victim who fucks around and drinks and gets pregnant and then has the nerve to ask for a job . . . and a southerner besides! And after all, Don Galetta, does it seem possible to you that a woman would go and commit suicide on the highway at that hour, with a child in her arms, in December?"

Marta's voice: "Well, then, my blessed Don Nocciolini?"

"I'm coming!" he shouts. "Well, now you've overstepped the

mark. I don't know anything about this story . . . lids, how dare you! Tartaglione never even had the time to ring my bell, admitting that she wanted to. Good evening."

"All right, I'll call you when you're not in a rush."

"Don't, if you can help it."

"Goodbye. Oh, do me a favor, tell Lometto that . . ." He was going to say: I'll give all of his filthy twenty thousand dollars to the little girl of the Tartaglione woman, but he stops.

"What?" the priest asks with weary curiosity, exhaling several prayers all at once.

"Nothing. That I hope he's hale and hearty and that . . ." Already from the threshold he sees halfway up the stairs the long skirt coming to a stop. "And that he mustn't take it to heart. But certainly you've already taken care of comforting him about the fact that the world is full of unpunished murderers and purloined Mantegnas. Don Nocciolini, Doctoressa: my deepest respects."

"The impertinence!" the priest says, closing the door with a shove of his hand.

Nodding his chin twice, Angelo exits into the twilight dusk of the cold Penzana light; oh God, the photocopied article in the side pocket of the car's door! he would like to ring, ask about that insignificant matter not even reported by the newspaper: the little girl's name. But never mind, he thinks, smiling to himself, and turning around completely, he raises his head. Before him, behind a windshield bathed in yellow-purplish light, Lometto and Edda. He is taking off his sunglasses. An invitation. The look in Angelo's eyes hardens as much as the look of the two spouse-partners tries to appear humble, distraught, vanquished. Angelo gets into his car, backs up, turns, cannot avoid crossing them for another instant, Lometto now seems reassured, vaguely reassured: certainly, the renegade's battered automobile is not such as to make one think that the twenty thousand dollars has already been partially spent. Lifting his finger from the wheel, Lometto points at something. Angelo drives off without looking in that direction.

He feels no loss at having given up the angel, and this surprises him, makes him happy. For every angel lost—and this does surprise him—a human being is found again. A bargain in flesh and blood. For the angel and for himself and, he hopes, for the daughter of Santina Tartaglione (but who knows what Belart knows on the subject!) if there is one, if she's still alive, if she can be adopted, if she can in some way be repaid for that ice-cold night. To transfer to her the love for Giorgina Washington, in memory of Aurora Lometto. Angelo can hear the tinkle of the links of these concatenated loves in the fading night.

The gasoline woman was about to close up and she immediately complains—about the storm, the rain, nothing has grown in her garden this year, and how long it's been that he hasn't shown up there. He no longer works for Lometto . . . oh, that little girl, yes, maybe she knows, the daughter of that lame girl . . . She knows everything. What's her name? Guess. But how can I guess, come on, don't be silly. Oh, she must have had her good reasons to call her that, what do you think? But how like that? To call her, her the fatherless child, the daughter of a wretch who had neither work nor family, and they didn't baptize her here, you know? I see, and where? In Castelgoffredo, and you know how? No, I already told you. Just look, I should have had tomatoes as big as this and instead . . . a bunch of little tinklers, rotten inside. You want me to check the oil? Yes. That over there is a whole bed of garlic. Calling her Fortunata. Oh, she had a head full of crazy ideas, that woman from Naples . . . Wonder who she thought she was? wonder what she imagined for her daughter, what . . . ? Fortunata! And the gasoline woman begins to laugh. Certainly heaven has punished those two, eh? May the mongoloid rest in peace, but the two of them had it coming. In America! There's a kilo lacking, do I put it in? Yes. You know, they say that Dr. Pujahr . . .

Angelo rushes home, phones a cousin of his who already has one child and at least Fortunata would be in good hands, a dressmaker and a dentist are per se adoptable parents, the important thing is that there be no obstacle of this kind, even though he knows that the process of adoption does not consider even the choice of sex: indeed, he would use all of the twenty thousand dollars not to adopt Fortunata but to corrupt in order to adopt her—have her adopted. Then another phone call to Galeazzo, the policeman in Naples with the anal condylomas—no, he still hasn't gone to be operated on, you know, people here at Torre Annunziata gossip, etc.—and he falls asleep happy, happy about his circle, so diversely round, so acentral. His is a light sleep which contemplates thought. Let us take this day, for instance: it isn't exactly a round circle, it resembles more an isosceles triangle blunted at the corners, three billiard balls—three beauty spots—three waves which contain the divine pulp of the day. From the stockfish he hasn't bought for his mother, to Marino, to a veterinarian's degree. *Fortune* which rewards the disinterestedness of those who never count on it. Angelo, now, has Fortunata, and he sleeps so well instant after instant, so profoundly and, from whichever side one might consider him, so delicately floating on the surface of everything.

What a good sleep! Everything was . . .

Saturday.

Sunday.

Dawn.

What a good sleep! Everything was so accurately preordained in that dream with half-open eyes, dreamed at dawn after the piss and coffee, his mother not yet in the kitchen. Then there was the tiny light gray mouse that has gnawed at all his ties: it strolled among his books and stared at him now from a shelf, now from the rim of the armoire, and he—the enormous white-black splotch resting on the yellow pillow-case—he who every so often completely opened an ocular slit on the animal which flashed about here and there and went, unseen, to spy on him from somewhere else. There was Lometto's van, which from the oneiric depths of the highway to Toigo and Mantua appeared first out of the fog and then out of darkness and entered the dirty wake of Penzana's streetlights, without noise approached slowly on the stage of his dream. The whimper from a bundle covered the nonexistent noise of the engine, not even the gurgle of the ditch can be heard because the water is frozen. And a calendar day with a corner of its small sheet curving back over the entire screen like a raised curtain: Wednesday, or Thursday, the nights of the alternate channels. Lometto at the wheel is returning from Padua, Mestre, Vicenza, or who knows where. It is three o'clock in the morning. This is the moment. The limping figure lunges to the center of the road, the razor blade slashes one, two times, decisively. A smooth braking, from a distance. Or an abrupt one, close by. The bundle already completely splattered with blood. She stands foursquare in front of the van. Lometto leans out of the window, his head swathed in caps and scarfs, starts to shift gears again in a hurry, swerves to the left, manages to slip away from the girl, turns into his Private Road and disappears bouncing like a madman between the asphalt and the road's shoulder. Or perhaps he had to get out of the car, with her clinging to the windshield wipers, he must have realized, bloodstains—not oil, not coffee—on the sleeves of his car coat, at which the woman is pulling violently while she howls things he does not hear, frightened to death, as he asks himself, does not understand how, what is happening, and why to him of all people, and the sight of the blackish sticky liquid on his hands, and he thinks of nothing else but to escape, he pulls away violently once, twice, she clings to him, another yank, the girl perhaps losing her balance and now on the ground, exhausted, not a strong, healthy girl, perhaps with an extra glass inside her for courage, or a joint, one of her legs smaller, weaker, and she drags herself toward the car's door, which slams shut, the panic that must have submerged him, the van bumping in the curve, and she realizes that she no longer has all that heat in her as before, that it is freezing there, that the ridges in the ground are like blades in her legs, and the thought of the small bundle, her daughter, and she tries to rise but falls, and several times makes this attempt toward the only possibility for salvation for both of them, all on her own she goes toward the mistake that will destroy her, toward the bank and the parish house, the people who are sleeping. But she doesn't have the strength. And also the incalculable time she spent waiting exhausted in the fog, hidden behind the reed mace along the ditch. Nobody, certainly she never had really thought that the desert is precisely in the center of town. Oh, if only she had turned into the opposite road, the one which for kilometers does not lead to any reliable house, she would surely have met somebody, some eccentric of whom no one is aware, some compassionate person, who at night goes to watch the stirring of shoots under the snow, a vagrant in a fur coat, a crazy old woman in a wheelchair who screams like a dog with rabies, or a romantic adolescent who wants for one night to suffer in the raw and open air. At a hundred meters from the Curia, perhaps she crashes down one last time, and it is the end. It has all spilled out, there is no more of it.

But then, Lometto, the poor man, he's not the one who invented social conventions and the law of profit and of priority in hiring, he has been pulled into this villainous business by the hair. Nevertheless it is still negligence *and* before *and* after. An ugly story, if one could prove it, even the unions would be forced to take a position on the illegal labor which floods in the North too throughout construction sites and factories and the magistrature in regard to the customs police which suggests alternative routes depending on the time of day and the condition of the roads. A field which, though not overturning anything, would involve half of Italy: charitable institutions, notaries, journalism, banks, priests, industries. And perhaps not even with the best of goodwill one would be able to remain silent about the anonymous pharmaceutical society which continues to grind out the panacea of the German-speaking victims of depression via Belart. One boom! Sharp, without stutterings. In the face of all this not even Justice could continue to turn a deaf ear.

Angelo dozes off again, smiling. He has never felt so safe as now, threatened as he is from many sides, besieged. He imagines the gorillas who shadow him and watch over his sleep on street corners, check who goes by, make great use of their walkie-talkies to be sure that nothing happens to him.

Then, halfway through the morning, he goes to the barber and has his head shaved to zero. As once upon a time, when he was a child, he follows the clipper up and down through the by now sparse curls, feels himself leaning toward an impulse of absolute practicality. Has the Neapolitan policeman already been to the Santa Maria Goretti orphanage? What difficulties must be overcome? Will he go in uniform? Surly mother superiors, their faces all bristles, every question answered by a question. Fortunata Tartaglione, already adopted—but that wouldn't be serious for Angelo, on the contrary, one less problem, he would pay out the dollars in installments to the adoptive parents—redelivered, retaken, readopted, where will she wake up? will she shut her eyes tightly against the sudden light of who knows what blinds raised in what haste? will she rub her blinded eyes and say which name first? Pick up three traveler's checks for one hundred dollars each and cash them, send a money order to the kind policeman for his expenses. He leaves the barber's and moves on.

This is the first time that he opens the safe-deposit box. With spit rubbed on his finger he reseals the envelope. Ill at ease, he follows the contours of the reel in a cellophane bag. How enjoyable it would be to cash all these dollars, one after the other, in a foreign country, in Australia or Brazil or China, scrabbling his fingertips on his pate.

It is incredible what a sensation of freshness it is possible to draw from oneself at eighty-five degrees in the shade while espousing the most cretinous of all theories, that of *pleasure*.

Into the envelope he has stuck a list of expenses conceived as follows: "August 1983, Withdrawn three hundred dollars, expenses for the usual Den of Mire—Fortunata Santa Maria Goretti Coxcombs Avoided Excursions to Naples."

A thin warm rain has just fallen and removed the dust from the things illuminated by the headlights, the asphalt is brilliant, the dark green fronds are laden with the glimmers of the red and yellow lamps of the melon stands in the fields. The Bordello must definitely be the fourth or fifth building on the left. But by dint of counting insignificant buildings, farmhouses and barracks which have no resemblance to a disco, Angelo has reached the center of the unknown village. He stops the car in front of a pastry shop, there is a girl at the door and she explains this to him with a vague smile of amusement on her lips. He thanks her, and since it's so early anyway, only nine-forty, he might as well go inside and have a coffee. From a table where the girl has gone to sit down a group of young men look up at him. And one of them suddenly says: "You must go back and take the road for Calvisano. After a while you'll see two luminous mushrooms in the grass. That's not the entrance, but from the back."

"Thank you" Angelo says, a bit annoyed. The tone he used to emphasize that "two luminous mushrooms." He drinks his coffee, now the target of the adjusted gaze of all the patrons, who certainly are not unaware of the Bordello's reputation. Angelo does not want to show that he is in a hurry, he lets them all bash their heads against his completely shaved skull. They must have followed his every move, how he tears the small sugar envelope, pouring out only one third, how he tightens his fingers on the cup's handle, the tension of his body, which was kept tightly together for fear of revealing an effeminacy that he might have absorbed by staying for so many days with the gays at the Terrazzine and which he might give away. Is he too affected in his immobility? too apparent in his nondescript shirt and trousers? And the voice which asks, "Pardon me, do you have cigarettes?"—doesn't it betray too great an inclination toward the petulant arrogance of the defenseless? He probably seems to be somebody giving himself airs. But he's not bad, the usual girl with a hand under her chin would say. For me, the guy next to her would add, he isn't a man, I swear, did you see how he looks at me? And together they would laugh, touching each other with their knees under the table, and she would remove her chin from her hand. And as soon as he was outside, the veiled voices would broaden and reach, blending, the tables of the neighbors, two couples of fiancés with their noses in huge glasses of ice cream topped by a small parasol. They would comment, judge, take a vote. Angelo, seeking shelter in his car, feels he is a trophy that no one wants to win.

When he arrives at the little "mushrooms," in the space reserved for parking there is no other car. He gets out, the gate is closed. And the two unlit mushrooms have definitely not been any help, he's been forced to back up twice, it's impossible that it's closed now, that it should have an off day on Saturday or that they are on vacation, little shrieks from inside. Two dogs lunge snarling against the metal mesh which encloses the large inner courtyard: one, the more dangerous, is on a chain, a panting belly that opens and closes like an accordion against the metal wire; the other is smallish with a tawny coat, a little mongrel which comes out of the gate and runs to meet him and give him a big welcome.

"Don't touch him" a voice that Angelo thinks he recognizes screams from inside the building. "He's got ticks."

What a way to start: the same as saying to someone who is at a cabaret show for the first time: don't touch the bar girl, she's got German measles. The huge beast which is tugging at the chain and growling, thirsting for human flesh, is a Neapolitan mastiff. Warnings which have come by express up from the South in those foaming fangs. Galeazzo was neither at home nor at headquarters.

"You'd better not get within reach of him" Messalina repeats, coming to meet him. "Oh, my dear girl, you here too? You too, you big intellectual? And shaved, besides, and with a mustache! But what are you up to, Angelina?"

Angelo has resolved to keep in check his flare-ups of rebellion, to play along, if possible, all the way to the semifinals. He does not feel like making scenes, he wants to silence the depression that has accompanied him since the pastry shop. He wants to know if life is possible there and what it is like, what flavor it has and if it is at all possible also for him to steal some by giving some. Force himself to practice D'Annunzianism, precisely.

Messalina introduces him to a couple of well-shaved clodhoppers who are talking about haymaking.

"This is a girlfriend of mine, a professor of *tongues*, a Mohican."

They look at him with indifference and suspicion, go on talking about agricultural machinery and leasing.

"Nobody's here yet" Angelo says, just to give something to say to the fear and shame that is rising up from the back of his heels. "This is a nice place. And where do you dance?"

Beyond the gate and at the sides of the metal fence and beyond the open space muddied by the rain, corn grows into the distance, the sound of canals comes from the open countryside. The crickets have resumed singing. Here in the courtyard hundred-year-old trees, oaks, beeches, and birches, which touch the roof of the former elementary school and rise above it. From the disco comes an oldish rock motif from a second-rate system.

"Oh, it's still early. First the men go to dance with the women in the normal places, then they take them home. It's after midnight they come here to get their bird piped by us. Yesterday, you know? Eleven. I was all by my lonesome, aha!"

Above the disco there's a wineshop; two concessions, and the people drink once downstairs and all the other times upstairs, in order to save. Downstairs in the deserted room Angelo orders a whiskey. Foam-rubber couches, tilted lights, a couple of posters of Marilyn Monroe, a small square dance floor. The toilets are upstairs. In the courtyard the white enameled iron chairs drip in the sultry air, and the mastiff still pulls at his chain. People arrive. Svergola, Raganella (because of his eyes), Cicciottella, Culaton-sur-ton, Evita, Palmira, Suor Sorriso, Four Plus Four, in an island of gaudy colors and scarfs blowing in the wind and liquid makeup, all of it sighted by a big ugly dog arched against the wire mesh like a mechanical figurehead which now wags its tail.

"Do I look nice? Am I all woman?" Svergola asks Angelo, spinning around.

"You're the end of the world" Angelo answers. Every faggot's dream is to be depicted on the altar under the Madonna's feet in place of the serpent.

The Bordello starts coming to life, a lot of cars arrive and a flock of scooters bearing thirteen- and fourteen-year-old boys call each other by the names of the villages hereabouts: Calvisano, Visano, Castelletto, etc., there are at least fifty of them, they are organizing to beat up somebody, later on somewhere else, Angelo understands, walking among them, it seems, unnoticed.

The "girls" have rushed to the powder room to touch up their makeup or roll a joint or slip on special lingerie. Now only the face of Suor Sorriso shines under the streetlamp with a natural tinted foundation. He holds his head slightly bent to the right as if he were ceaselessly at the side of a sickbed sadly listening, his hands joined on his small paunch.

"Only Zizi and I don't put anything on, *au naturel*, my dear girl, *au naturel*! Sure, keep busy, you painted decoys! They attract them, but we're the ones who shoot!" Messalina proclaims, patting fly after fly in the tide of young men that flows back and forth between gate and courtyard.

"Oh, shut up, Messalina, there's room for all of us!"

"But why on earth did you shave your head to the scalp? You looked so nice with your curls."

"Doesn't he look like a mustachioed Mongolian?"

"A hairy mongoloid!"

"This way I don't have to go to the barber's for at least six months" Angelo says, passing his hand over his head. A semicircle has now formed around them of adolescent jaws which laugh about everything and nothing: they all stand two meters back, as though in front of cages at a fair, and they shove each other, stick out index fingers, say theirs is like this, clutch their members in their fists inside their pants and make them bounce up and down.

"Take off your mustache too, while you're at it, or else you won't get anywhere here; get Evita to lend you her wig."

"And then?"

"Then nothing. A drop of perfume, a scarf, and you're set! You can bugger them all."

And now all the "girls" are back on the front lines, they yell about who is a bigger whore than the next, who has buggered more guys, who is more of a woman, they pretend to trip along the stairs falling over men who are going up to the tavern and pick them up and carry them inside, there are also a couple of wives in the flesh who play along and shout greetings like old acquaintances. Angelo knows that the questions he's asking himself are in their simplicity more mannered than any answer he could give himself. But they are also the only ones he manages to formulate. It's like this and that's that.

Cicciottella is presenting a disquisition to Four Plus Four (thus named because until two years ago he coughed up four thousand per blow job and, since now he doesn't want to admit that he has to cough up eight thousand, they've met him halfway, dividing by two and adding it up) about the difference between her eyes and those of Marilyn Monroe, whom he supposedly resembles.

Angelo finds it difficult even to smile, and hearing the coded sentences of this sexual complicity between proletarians and transvestites, he feels completely out of place. In this place everything fits together so well, everything is so well tested, everyone instantaneously finds his pleasure within reach, his normality and sexual and human functionality, one can feel that centuries and centuries of secret training have levigated something even more extraordinary and fitting than the *symbolon*: a convention. Angelo is already on his fourth whiskey. His is a mental site without precedents or sequels, if anything he is at the origin of a new training for something to come; like all things to come, it has no importance, nor does it have to live now. Used to drinking little, submerged by the general indifference and distrust, he's overcome by a push-button gaiety, asks around if anyone has a blade or a razor because he wants to cut off his mustache and put on lipstick. To sink into the part of a part of the others, desire for himself an oblivion that defeats the force of his convictions, return to the lost paradise of a pure faggotry, uncontaminated, abandon himself to the thing in itself established by the social clichés about sex. He clears his throat a couple of times, tries to speak in a falsetto tone before a mirror, the mustache falls, five hands are stretched out to make up his lashes, eyes, lips, nails. It is the cosmetic trick of the extinct Egyptian, the living servant who accompanies his dead master inside of his own free will.

More and more people are coming to the toilets, almost all of them men. Yes, well, men, with sexual organs made in a certain way rather than another.

"God, what a handsome bunch of tough-looking mugs, how macho they are! Those four over there have all been in jail, look at the scar on his cheek, and the tattoo on his biceps. They all know how it's done, and are full of surprises!" Messalina sizzles, squirming on the landing.

"If they go with you they must certainly be full of complexes" Angelo remarks.

What do these delinquents have that a decent man does not have? and this passion for jailbirds! all the clichés that surround prison, this blessed male con whom the penal baths supposedly give the final soaping to achieve a perfect divinity.

Messalina has started to act coquettish with one of them who has two missing incisors and a recidivist expression, long beard, dirty hair, filthy blue jeans. Gabry, Palmira, Svergola arrive to compete with him and they all cling to the ropes to scale this Everest of virility that Angelo wouldn't touch with so much as a paw, not even if he were a St. Bernard.

For the nth time he goes down to the disco and knocks back his seventh whiskey. He goes to the dance floor and begins to dance all by himself. Go all the way to the bottom of this bottom which is not his. Clapping hands of encouragement. As a child he danced in front of the glass panes of store doors. He used to go to a retired dance teacher together with a little girl and she forced them to learn certain set figures before allowing them to climb onto the jujube tree in the garden. But then that feeling for rhythm had entered his blood and every time he danced he thought he had become a bit better, more obedient to an inner need for discipline, and more athletic, his tendons acquired new psychic shadings. It wasn't true. Several times already he had twisted ankles or crashed to the floor on his ass, arousing laughter. One evening many years ago, in a fashionable disco, because of his brand-new shoes with their waxed soles, his legs had simply opened up under him and he had realized only after a good half hour that he had continued to dance *paralyzed*. They had to put both legs in a cast. And now he's going to attempt a pirouette in which he will risk the ankle of one foot and the opposite femur. One of the reasons that fill him with pride as he flings his leg up high and falls perpendicularly onto the floor is that he does not feel like and really is not the fruit preestablished by a compromise between demand and supply, but a product which engenders itself by itself and by itself attempts to impose itself in contrast with all the common sense of the current market. He arrives, adorned with many "zero" price tags which no one shares, and he continues without preestablished goals and without companion. One can dance to that until exhaustion. Dancing is a voluptuous pleasure similar to the theorizing of deafness presented by a mute to an audience of blind persons: only the theorizing exists, the dance in itself. Angelo twirls in a vortex, he knows that sixty seconds have gone by now, and another sixty and another sixty more and that he can make a spiral of himself without ever losing his balance for ten minutes in a row; he likes the dialectical determination which harmoniously spins from the root of his hair to the nails on his feet. And who knows, when he'll stop it'll be as if he had given a speech for hours on a deserted beach at three in the morning, in a café on the piazza, in the compartment empty or not of a train: everyone will in the meantime have vanished in silence, only he would remain, the witness of solidarity with himself and this time too it will be the first of a series of times all equally forgotten: the pain will not have become enfistulated, the wound will always remain open and fresh, and in the air there will be the echo of his human hum. The music increases in volume, and the small spotlights accelerate their intermittences. Angelo begins to strip. He is excited by the frankness of exhibitionism, not by the mystery of reticence. Mysteries do not exist as mysterious or as revealed, only a mythomaniac and imperfect mind can construct mysteries for itself and indulge in them and, in an alcove of linguistic superstitions, find the fascination of an exclusive desire. The rare times that he has been able to enjoy fully were after disemboweling all that he knows on the subject. How arched his desire has been, how intoxicating love in the full light of theories exposed and evaluated by overcoming the mutual terror. Angelo contorts himself with feline violence and his eyes see again the interview about homosexuals by a certain Pio Costante. Now with dancing karate moves he strikes out at those racist bestialities given widespread circulation. Now Angelo drums his feet, dreaming he is bouncing the chopped-off head of Pio Costante, severed because of certain Camorra intrigues, and he regrets, letting out a final howl, that this ax or Boy Scout pocketknife or electric saw did not descend in a time sufficiently close to the interview to give rise to the doubt that now a homosexual executioner was at large, a Robin Hood for those desirous of vengeance, someone tired of chatter who grabbed a tommy gun to be used above all against this mass of faggots who secretly gloat with pleasure at every reactionary intervention. To bump off quite a few of these asses milling in the wind, only good at being their own worst enemies. A hand politely stops him and Angelo hears a delighted voice that says "Not your shorts."

A burst of savage applause, men come forward, they compliment him, ask him how old he is and what make of car he has, what a pity, it would look so much better if he put on a wig! Angelo sweats and laughs, oh how sweet it must have been to see those corpses dangle in Piazza Loreto, a pity that they were so few and perhaps not even the most important. There are a few women at the bar, not beautiful, none of them beautiful. They are all very anxious to be seduced, one can tell from the way they chew gum. One of them has a childish smile supported by an obese American-style behind. She allows everybody to stick their fingers into her mobile pachyderm, hands disappear in the folds of flaccid flesh, and while they are palping her the men wink at Calcinculo, and sure enough Calcinculo goes up to the toilets, immediately followed by a couple of fatso's false suitors.

. . . Outside in the open air there's a great to-and-fro from the open lot to the corn rows, muddied shoes, running makeup, smeared lipstick. It's past midnight.

"Where's Zizi?" a two-meter-tall hunk asks Messalina.

"She left this morning for Sitges. She got herself a permanent. Thirty-three hairs thirty-three thousand. She called me two hours ago, she's already dying to get back, to come here. Hometown boys. She says that in Spain they're all she-asses, that they're all women, even more than she. Not everybody is a big he-man like you. Are we going?"

They go off. Angelo has clumsily made a few attempts at picking somebody up. His mask of tinted foundation, lipstick, eye pencil has fused into a patina pocked with sweat. He does not know how to go about it, and what line to use immediately after. A certain Mimmo rather likes chatting with Angelo. He is a collector of Fascist memorabilia and, seeing that Angelo knows German . . . Mimmo has a diffused, slightly raucous voice and a face grown disproportionately around a tiny knob of a nose. Angelo, who has picked up the slang password with which Messalina and the others go on the attack, at a certain point in order to hear the sound of it says, "Come on, I'll pipe your hose."

It seems to him he has quoted from memory an algebraic-Mussolinian formula of which he understands neither the meaning nor the possible development. Mimmo signals no no with his face.

Angelo is stinking drunk, disappointed, humiliated, the taste of lipstick in his mouth. Another whiskey. Then he goes to the sink in the toilet and washes away his face. He looks in the mirror: he's ridiculous in any case. He goes out into the courtyard, begins to walk.

It is late, almost half past two. The dogs have fallen asleep, one next to the other, under the car shed, and there's no longer a trace of the semi-transvestites.

His bones feel damp, the flesh no longer seems to stick to them, the sense of a body alien to itself, and not even a thread of anger. The pungency of revenge against everything and everybody including himself has been extinguished in him. He is capitulating. The world has no interest in him, an experimental man. Angelo would even have tried to kneel and worship the aspersorium of a male, a detached prick, but he is furious with himself: the thing would not have excited him, the object of his worship set out from too many indisputable premises. And what instinctiveness in these relations between men and queens, what an insipid ritual whose ideal vestal is someone like Messalina—with a dilapidated belly, a piggish leer, a repellent perspiration, and the stench of a couple of pisses they've taken on him—who, turkey-breasted and head held high, exhibits all the servility of the filthy sex, the sex of the beasts dear to the gods who have made them privileged by ordering them to scrabble in a domesticated barnyard called "differentness." This scratching and subjugated bestiality is nevertheless something, and Angelo does not even have that.

Cicciottella emerges from the cornfield, she is pulling up her denim overalls, Four Plus Four gets off the nth car of soccer players. Angelo does not catch any of the remarks they exchange saying good-bye. It is almost half past three. Only now, as he tries to throw up without succeeding, he realizes that there are whispered mutterings between the open windows of the cars which have remained in the dark under the streetlight turned off long ago. People who have a few last things to tell each other, future dinners to be framed by a private rendezvous or a promise. Tomorrow some will wake up able to think not about love but about the lover. This possibility of living such specific details at the beginning of another day, so precluded . . .

On the road back he tries to parrot aloud a couple of effeminate sentences, adjusting his facial expression as Cicciottella had done, closing an eyelid, shrugging his shoulders delicately . . . The darkest mystery.

He goes on driving, heads for the lake, with an imperishable sensation that sex is so very easy, so within reach for everyone but him. It was like dangling from a parachute that would never open in that direction but in no other either. And yet he too was falling, but without experiencing the intoxication of flight, already foreseeing the mortal impact against the empty bottom of the well-known. But it is lovely to drive at dawn with eyes warm with alcohol and sleep, gliding with one's body directly over the asphalt and dew. How long is it since he has witnessed an hour like this, the sun's big purple and pink rays behind Mount Adamello?

At the Terrazzine there is only one house trailer with a German plate, the second esplanade is deserted. Oh, to sleep! here the scent of the oleanders has the power of a bucket of icy water full in the face. Down the escarpment with a towel to spread out underneath. Here and there he bends down: wood anemones, maidenhair fern, dog's-tooth, a small Carthusian pink. Today he won't pick anything, he'll leave them in peace. The villa rests. But he cannot sleep, he gets up again immediately.

How delicate is the green sassafras, one would like to pull it up with a chunk of soil and transplant it in a pot at home. But Angelo lengthens his stride toward the slope while black, heavenly blue, yellow pupils dance before his eyes.

No longer within the gray lifeless pupils
The flash of youth smiles upon me.
O Halycon! Rain in the Pine Grove . . .

O companion of the lashless eyes, O the innocent, O the daughters of I—ario!

. . . Angelo is struck for an instant by the flash of the annunciation. Clusters of elusive presages and intuitions approach his sight, seem to slow down, give each other signs of recognition with enucleated irises of remote uniqueness. Then they dart away and disintegrate.

One fine day . . .

BOOK THREE

One fine day . . .

One fine day the phone rings. Sunday, the day for anonymous phone calls at discount prices. Angelo rushes from the entrance hall toward the terrace and the bedroom. If only it were the special messenger!

Day after day he's been waiting for this envelope which someone leaving from Naples who knows when was supposed to deliver in person. He himself had suggested to Galeazzo that the mail can't be trusted and that he would gladly pay for the messenger's trip, in fact he was immediately sending him another money order. He must get started as soon as possible. Because at last, and that was already two days ago, his policeman friend managed to get his hands on the negative of a photograph of Fortunata. Previously Angelo was not able to ascertain personally whether everything Galeazzo brought up on the telephone to drag things out and get him to send more money for expenses was true or not. But he had no other choice, he did not want to go to Naples at any cost. At any rate his investigations, Galeazzo said, perhaps to give himself some importance in such a little matter, apparently have unleashed a hellish uproar at the Santa Maria Goretti, and they didn't even let him in. And fortunately, he added, I didn't show them my badge but did things completely anonymously. Oh yes, and what are these things, seeing the point we're at? Angelo answered, piqued: I send you half a million and you're even afraid to use your badge. But why the hell do you think I turned to you? What the fuck do you think an ID badge counts for in these parts! Galeazzo said. Then further requests: another half million, no less, with an excuse to make your hair and your bristles stand up. There might be, yes, somebody in a position to photograph the little girl on the sly inside the orphanage, but it's expensive, you know the risk. To make it short, and only to find out what follows, the government employee would pay out two hundred thousand of the second five hundred thousand: (a) that the girl had not been adopted by any family, (b) that she was a normal girl of a healthy, strong constitution, even though thin as a rail, (c) that she is, so to speak, spoken for, and that it's absolutely impossible to adopt her. Period, that's all. Fortunata spoken for, but since when? When is this family going to pick her up? Impossible to get any answers, nobody knows anything. But come on now, they must at least know the name of this couple that want her! he should get in touch with them, and amen, everything becomes so much easier. Nothing. If Angelo went to Naples himself, he would solve the problem in a single morning: just as it is true that there are moments in which he is afraid of his own shadow, there are others in which he would break through even a line of *camorristi* thugs with sawed-off shotguns. He would present a petition to the magistrate in charge, just to begin with, or threaten to do so, which would be more in keeping with the aggressiveness of his conciliatory amateurishness, but he would get to where he wants to go. Isn't it around there, and a little bit everywhere else, that pious institutions are found with old people tied to their beds, children undernourished and bloodily beaten or broken in as prostitutes at the age of six? He would go all the way as if walking on water, without looking at anyone or any reason or superior lust. But by now the greater part is done, his cousin and her husband are agreed. Fortunata will leave the orphanage on a flying carpet, Angelo will pay what there is to pay for the corruption and the adoption and all the rest, if necessary he'll hand over the money gradually to the adoptive parents. Period. But it is also fair that the couple, before making a move, should at least get an idea of what the girl is like, what she looks like, after all one can't ask one's relatives if they would please adopt for your sake a little girl with frozen limbs. If she were handicapped Angelo would have to make commitments that go beyond the twenty thousand dollars at his disposal—nineteen and change by now. There are three photos, Galeazzo said, face, torso, and full length. Fortunata is in perfect health, she gesticulates and walks, to this the policeman can swear, but he did not see the child in person, aha! and there was no point in calling him back because he was leaving the next day for Tunisia on vacation . . .

Angelo has sighed more than once at the thought of those photographs: quite capable, down there in Naples, of grabbing the first urchin in the street, sticking a smock on her and a red bow on her head, putting her behind a gate and taking a photo of her for a packet of cookies, everything, what with one thing and another, for the modest sum of one million plus the hundred thousand lire mailed on Friday for the messenger, not to mention the cost of the money orders. And then, at his least possible remonstrance in the face of a first-class rip-off, he can already hear the Neapolitan cockerel fatalistically wag his combs and say "What am I supposed to know?" How can a train and a cab take so long? All right, take it easy, just as well, it may be a matter of another day or so. If he had gone down to Naples he would have only complicated matters with his false Saracen fury, armed with the empty thrill of an inept, inexperienced executioner, and it would have certainly become more difficult to tear Fortunata away from the charitable prison for which the state pays private persons for board and detention. Obviously these private persons in soutanes, habits, and double-breasted suits want to hold on to the raw material and so throw monkey wrenches and traps everywhere. In Naples children can be bought at auction, shipped here and there without return receipt, or else they are recycled, they can be ordered, why do people have to go and break balls in institutions? Let them use all alternative channels, that is, the most common ones: street corners, fish stands, the port, and blind alleys. This and more over the phone. Then Angelo asked some generic questions, one more incredible than the next, and he expected that to say the least the policeman would call him a visionary. Not at all: very Lomettishly and without laughing he said, "Everything is possible," though in a slightly more laconic tone.

Angelo was waving his hand, as if to chase away a bee from his bonnet and at the nth sigh the ring came to coincide with the hands of the clock: ten on the dot.

He is so in need of news, of last-minute contributions to shake and prune the useless branches of his imaginative efforts and electrify the so dry, stuffed present. If only it were the *perpetua*! he would dare to ask her too a surreal question, the same which has persecuted him ever since he met her: what color were Aurora's eyes?

On the phone somebody gives him the high-sounding name of a hotel and adds: "Stay on the line. Signora Belart."

"Hello, Dr. Bazarovi? How are you?"

It is a ringing voice, less hurried than usual, which conveys with small conviction an introductory cheerfulness kindled by the first cups of coffee.

"Dr. Bazarovi, I need your collaboration."

Actually it sounds like a cry for help.

"What for, do you need a good mechanic?"

"Please. Lometto."

Angelo conjures up a number of scenes, some details of what was for him the last encounter at the border of Italy, among little piles of dirty snow. He doesn't respond: Lometto? He doesn't say anything. He lets fall a pause, which must act as the *click* of the receiver when it is hung up after innumerable and vain hellos.

Belart continues: "I'm here at the Hotel Gran Gabriele, at Gardone Riviera, just below the Vittoriale. Can you come right away?"

"Listen, Frau Belart, I could pretend and act surprised, unfortunately both you and Lometto know very well that I'm informed about the main matter and, believe me, despite myself I don't want to know any more about it."

"But you *must* come."

"I don't know whether it's in my interest to come there. At any rate everything has its price. My relations with Lometto ended almost four months ago."

"Oh really? As to your fee, of course there's no discussion about that. I'm willing to pay well for your savoir-faire, not like Lometto."

God only knows why Belart has taken up residence there: is she perhaps trying to negotiate for the sea turtle which died of tuberous indigestion or the wooden statues or the ceramic and Art Nouveau lamps in the Vittoriale? Does she have a customer who wants an authentic altar from the funerary epic of taste?

"Frau Belart, that's not enough. I want to settle the fee right now. After all, if you kept me out of your most recent business, there must surely be a reason. The same reason should prevent you from dragging me into it now."

"You have not been kept out, you're the one who refused to collaborate with us, if you remember."

"So all right. And now more than ever."

"I am forced to beg you to come here. Try to understand, it's not my decision. You *must* come. The orders come from much higher up."

"Are you certain that you cannot do without me and that I really care from what height these orders come that I consider laughable?"

"Absolutely."

"Well, if that's the case, bye-bye and don't you ever call me again, for any reason. Goodbye, that is, I meant to say adieu."

"No, no! Wait a minute, I beg you . . ."

If he were to go, he could always ask her what she really knows about *die kleine heilige Stottererin*, Santina Tartaglione, the little holy stammerer.

"Dr. Bazarovi, it's about the Coptafuk. It's not easy to convince the *committee* that you have nothing to do with it. Only I personally believe that you're absolutely out of it. I am not *everybody*."

"Enough, Jasmine, with this farce of *being behind*. I don't want to get into it, I'm neither behind nor on the side of nor in front of anything or anyone. At any price. And thanks a lot for having made a fool of me with that business of the half million under the counter. Nice performance, a nice duo concertante between you and Lometto. I say goodbye once again, Frau Belart. This telephone conversation never took place. For any reason."

"You think so?"

"And besides, really, you make millions—of marks—on people's health and then you dare to say I must do things whether I like it or not? Adieu."

"If you don't want to do it for me, do it for your friend Lometto . . ."

"Lometto and I haven't been friends for a long time."

"He is in serious danger. If he doesn't accept our proposals there will be bloodshed for three hundred million. You know what life is worth today, don't you? Three hundred million *is* a lot of life, Dr. Bazarovi."

"Oh, he'll realize it by himself" Angelo cuts it short. Lometto, always Lometto, to hell with Lometto! And when will he, Angelo, ever be able to think again about Angelo Bazarovi in peace and about the defaults on his share of whims?

"No, you're wrong, the problem is that he doesn't realize it. *Wirklich*. He insists on positions that the organization cannot accept. And he is wrong and he knows it."

"Lometto is never wrong. Listen, Jasmine . . ."

"I like the way you pronounce my name, in the French style . . ."

"Listen, Frau Belart, say no more, I don't want to know anything. Get out of it by yourselves."

"And what if one of the three junior Lomettos should pay with his hide, for instance? One at a time, I mean . . ."

Angelo is irritated by this blackmail. Once more he sees Epaminonda over her bowl of soup in front of the TV, from a trapdoor in the cellar they are extracting the corpse of the ten-year-old son of a prominent person mixed up in shady peninsular dealings. The boy had been buried alive. Epaminonda smiled beautifully at the sight of those images which were excruciating for Angelo, they seemed to be the right soup for her stomach contracted by hatred. She might even have her good reasons against the "sons of swine" who have become the exact same "swine" as their fathers and whose innocence was merely a negligible transience. Epaminonda had all the wars behind her, and famines, and unemployment, and social humiliations. Plenty of hunger too. Plenty of exploitation. And a mill owner, exactly as in the songs, who had left her with an invincible disgust for "the facts of life" for her remaining fifty years. Angelo was dazzled by the purity of the hatred of the dear, generous, tender, human old woman, bewitched by the implacability of her thirst for vengeance which would stop at nothing, which perforated even Lucite screens and struck like a lightning bolt at the "sacred blameless lives."

But what about him, Angelo? Yes, him, too. One only had to scrape a bit beneath the skin to uncover a marsh of salt and anger, of a thirst for blood—his own which had been drained away. And certainly the supposition that those three taxidermists tanned also Giorgina Washington's hide increases the possibility that this could be a valid reason to deny Belart his "collaboration." If only some lives are sacred over others, none are sacred outside of *those*, and hence one could even do away with a couple of lives, sacred or not, shooting into the pile, and who gets it gets it. Why save Lometto, *healthy*, *Aryan*, and *normal*, and not a *sick*, *mongoloid*, and *different* little girl?

"Are you still on the phone, Dr. Bazarovi?"

"Yes. I have to think. The reasons you're giving me are not impelling ones for me."

"Take your time, I'll wait. But say yes, in the end. I have no other choice than to compel you to say yes."

"Otherwise you'll turn over the next card, the convincing one? You realize that I'm not really the pushover I seem to be, am I right? I have nothing to fear on the personal plane."

"Take your time, think about it. Also about this . . ."

Certainly, how interesting it would be to ask the phantom who makes rat shish kebabs to rent you the villa at the Terrazzine for the time necessary, long enough to hold here in seclusion the first of the junior Lomettos. And to begin with, get him to talk about his *sister's* end, and this already would be a sufficient motive to let himself be convinced by Belart's unreasons. She would pursue her aims—three hundred million? and why?—he that of knowing exactly how Aurora ended up. But it would be more fun to kidnap Lometto II, so conceited and sure of himself, the one who dreams of becoming a dictator and stuffing his teachers. To tear the truth out of him with pincers and tongs, and then sew up his mouth with jute, like a chicken's ass.

"I've thought about this too. I don't understand what you're driving at, my dear Belart."

"For example . . . Giuditta" Belart drops in the wire, like the tap of a file against a fingernail.

"Oh, I could tell you a lot of things on the subject, Signora Belart" but at the same time Angelo feels flattered: someone has gone to the trouble of doing research about him! about his feelings! "I hope one will be enough for you: Giuditta no longer means anything to me. My heart is dry as the bed of a vanished river."

"You are a poet . . ."

"It would be a useless folly for you and your partners, and it would not have any leverage on me, I assure you. With me, if I may give you some advice, you must argue with your most refined dialectics, let's say on political or speculative subjects more than about passions that I do not have."

"You are very clever."

"No less than you, Signora Belart. You have gone to the trouble of finding out some things about me, right? This and *more*. And you have wasted precious time, you should have concentrated more on Lometto, considering that you already know so much about him. *Die kleine heilige Stottererin* . . ."

"Do you have evidence proving that he did away with her, or had her done away with?" Belart asks peremptorily.

Angelo is glued to the phone:

"Frankly, I never even thought about it. Did you?"

"I didn't either. But his wife, a woman from the South . . ."

In front of Angelo opens up a showstopper: Santina Tartaglione, tied by the little Lometto brothers and razor-bladed, a unique specimen, a brand-new perch, Edda or Celestino becomes aware of the misdeed, these boys can't sit still for a moment, they load her with the baby and all at night and deposit her almost in the center of Penzana, and what a scolding the three budding executioners get!

"I know less about it than you" Angelo says, lying, because a detail from the gasoline woman is added to the picture: they say it's she, the wife, who procures all those handy cripples for him. Procures them for him to do what, besides working?

"So what's your answer?"

"No, no moral or amoral blackmail with me. I don't even believe there's anything special to find out about Santina Tartaglione; get the details you need from your original sources. Why don't you try and take a more honest approach with me, for instance?"

"That is?" Belart asks, suddenly raising her voice a tone higher.

"Think about it. I don't want to deprive you of the pleasure of getting there all by yourself."

Angelo wants her to get there semi-by-herself: he knows that there are tonalities which converge on a single idea without even grazing it openly. That idea always being: how much?

"I got it."

"You see? Let's hear, Signora Belart."

"A lump sum?"

"A lump sum only to come over there for a discussion. Make it a million. On the nail."

A million is proverbial, even though with inflation it risks really fitting on one nail.

"Don't you think you're exaggerating?"

"It's the only honest thing that comes to my mind right now, money. The neutrality it guarantees. If you agree, fine, or else do what you want. And with a million in cash, I must remind you, you still haven't guaranteed my collaboration"—he was about to say "complicity"—"you take your risks, since you want me to expose myself at all costs in a business that doesn't interest me, and I take my risks. Then we'll see."

"All right. One million. I expect you for lunch, that is, immediately."

"Shirt and tie?"

"Please."

Angelo senses for the first time an impertinent titter of happiness: doing things one isn't interested in is nevertheless still a diversion from doing nothing.

"I like you, Dr. Bazarovi."

"Despite all the information you have gathered about me?"

"Much more because of it . . ."

"Same here . . . I prefer powerful women over housewives, with housewives one can hardly talk about business, only about money" Angelo says, hoping he is sufficiently exhaustive about the meaning of that "liking." But it isn't so simple: he has never felt more true and more false at the same time in taking the usual precautions with a woman. But how can he explain to her, there, on two wires, about a third wire which, even though not excluding her completely, does not include her at all? Who knows if the beauty spots, in any case, are all in place?

"But on one condition, Signora Belart. That there is nobody else. Do I make myself clear? Hans, et cetera."

"Count on it. Hans! Who knows what happened to him! See you soon."

Angelo rushes to take a shower, which somehow supplants a blood test. He dabs on after-shave which he hasn't used for the longest time, his brain is pierced by the certainty of how he could ever have been so charming when he was young, how he liked to be liked, how this no longer interests him, how his narcissism has drowned in cultural anthropology. He dresses with care, does everything not to look like his father, a classical Italian male dressed for the feast to celebrate himself. But then he lets himself be tempted: combs back his stubble, uncovers his forehead, and in an instant finds not only his father, but also his grandfather: all there, looking at him with melancholy from the mirror. All those ruses for nothing! How excited he is before the armoire's glass: he's exactly the same as the last hundred years of Italian history. Can you believe that from an old Austro-Hungarian-Turkish oak this new lymph would come to titillate the nuts under the burnt-brown double-breasted suit. And the English shoes, which produce the blisters indispensable to a great occasion . . .

In the hotel's parking lot he immediately has a sensation of how well the burnished tints of his attire match the rose-colored gravel and the magnolias which hover languidly among the large dark green lacquered leaves yellowed by imminent autumn. Magnolias are such unpredictable plants, they always have a stored-up bud that will blossom and rot at any season. A crow seems to be following him right from the gate in the rear and now it alights on top of one of the pilasters flanking the wrought-iron entrance. All that is lacking is the discreet music for the tea or aperitif hour in the pavilion on the left, where the podium of inlaid wood set in the balustrade loses the glaze of its lilies and its cornucopias in azurine crackle. The crow emits a brief, sinister greeting.

In a flash the liveried doorman demonstrates all of his bent-over, off-season efficiency, he summons the bellboy—Angelo jumps: he is an adolescent dark of hair, and curly, tall and slim, with something simian but gentle in his features and his not very limber but interesting movements, he walks on rather flat feet, it seems he makes an effort to keep his toes pointed inward. His self split in a preceding epoch behind that figure which has grazed him with a skittish look, he glimpses at the height of the livery's collar a number of dreams dangling between present and future. He feels his blood stir, his hands which would like to reach out and remain rigid in his pockets. To be able to kiss himself and clasp himself with a touch of the hand on the shoulder of someone who stands before him and is already heading in directions that exclude him! He experiences the infinite sadness of being the shadow that another body accompanies toward the predictable goal of a winter veranda, not anywhere else. The bellboy backs up with a gesture of his extended hand. Frau Belart sits, her back ramrod straight, on a small sofa damascened in cream-pink velvet, the suit she is wearing is also cream-colored. Alone, apparently without a bodyguard. He contemplates her from a distance, absorbed in Middle Eastern thoughts. He is sorry that the suit's jacket, already by its cut, will leave in the creamy dusk of the lining every beauty spot reimagined, perhaps to gain courage during the drive in his thirdhand car, which did not hold the road along the *z*'s for Salò, the front axle was acting up and seemed to want to take off on its own, most likely down over the escarpment. At first he wanted to leave the death car along the lake, to avoid cutting a ridiculous figure when, after pocketing a million and bowing to her on his way out, he would have to call the dishwashers and porters to push it. But he started up again, walked directly into the hotel: one cannot always think that at the moment of apotheosis the muffler will fall off or the spark plugs get dirty or the pistons go limp.

Belart wears her hair at the nape of her neck, no longer in a spray, it is gathered in the back, unstylishly, the allure and grace of a Principality monasticizes the still very heavy makeup, two gold loops at her lobes bring into relief the gypsyesque origin or inclination of this woman whose disquieted and slightly weary luminosity summons up days of restless animal refulgence. All past rays of light are now lashing back and coagulate in impure spurious fragments on her lips, forehead, and nose, and, when she turns her glance toward him, also in the eyes and around them, a light which no longer puts up a resistance against the lost integrity of the past, so light, cinereous and violet and *starched.* They must now invent carambolesque focusings to be credible, since they want to be sad without being pathetic. Jasmine Belart has aged. Too ostentatious is the immutable freshness of the beautiful woman who from this precise moment will by now forever be older than the years she does not show.

Angelo is sorry that he will have to get down to the nitty-gritty with his first move and also that none of Belart's men, a century-old chapter worthy of the Orient Express, has taught her that a lady, even though a pirate of industry in distress, must never rise to greet, not even in the most serious circumstances.

"Alone?" Angelo asks, thinking: how silly, what a bad entrance line.

"Yes, alone. So to speak."

And indeed the doorman in person, looking into the greenhouse-hall at that very moment and from the door with the inevitable simulated Art Noveau stained glass, announces:

"Madame, telephone for you."

"You see?" Belart sighs, following the upward thrust of her loins and giving herself over to a race across the rugs and the central red runner. This competition with presences which control her from afar comes again to humiliate her thickened figure, disclosing the generosity of her hips and the beauty of the white nape of her neck which by right of age would aspire to the implicit laziness of someone who can afford not to be in a hurry. Jasmine Belart does not have much time. And her shoes with heels proportionate to her weight tell much about some recently suffered losses: they're not stiletto, but small, horseshoe-shaped shoes, good for sciatica or a hernia or a seduction on a holy pilgrimage. Love, Angelo thinks, love gone bad crossing borders and customs to be deposited in the common grave of some bank account and buy the certainty of its perpetuation or macabre preservation. Perhaps Belart is serving the last season of apparent grandeur imposed on her all her life long by her shadowy allies. *"Cherchez l'homme"*; perhaps an old age in relative poverty is awaiting her, and a number of thoughts obligatory in indigence when one has given as presents too many custom-made cars, or passbooks, or genuine brand-name watches to much younger and much less corrupt lovers: that it is not the money that is dirty, but love itself, dirty with dirt and abutting human sewage. And that it is always love which corrupts money, sucks it away, never the other way around.

As she reenters the hall mantled with tropical flowers, her complexion in its nonchalant manner is even paler and her lips vulcanize much more that so very Viennese fuchsia rose.

No blinking of eyelashes as she sits down, no sigh, no gesture of her ivory-bejeweled hand, a waiter approaching, she ordering for both of them and, almost absentmindedly, smiling in an exaggeratedly embarrassed way, so ill at ease, withdrawing into her sleeves, into her neckline, under the hem of her skirt as much sensorial surface as she can.

"It's getting very tight, Dr. Bazarovi, very tight."

To a friend or an enemy Angelo would reply, "Buy yourself a bigger size." But with Belart irony is not possible because due to the criminal hint made about Giuditta no revenge is possible: Belart resembles too much certain heroines of literature—Moll Flanders, Fanny Hill, and an aunt of Greene's, a gold digger à la James, etc.—for not being completely true and completely unable to do the evil to which out of inexperience of evil she alludes. Wholly woman, and wholly a friend, with a well-fixed and sporty goal in mind for all the rest, free from romantic aches and pains or erotico-epiphanic exploits at the crossroads of the second age. Angelo senses that that snow-white suit is shagreened paper and that behind the cloth there is the pulsating but crafty sex of a female offset which will not wait for the word from him or anyone else to have a *sense*. This is what always happens, that he becomes, in an already written text, a diacritical mark, the pleasure of a surplus of polishing—and from there to a polishing stroke the suspension dots are never more than three. It is probably because of his gaze without desire, but kind, interested, participant, that women rediscover when near him an unthought-of virginity, a small, hidden corner of hymen preserved through the confused disorders in the darkness of caves, and they have all the time to organize an indistinct letch for a man who is diligent and indifferent to their abuses, desirable because he has no revelations to make or elicit by fire or the rack.

Belart dismisses the waiter, grazing his hand, and raises her gin and tonic, the glasses touch. And from the neckline down there must be a body covered with beauty spots and paragraphs, waiting to be placed at the end of sentences all yet to be built, solid, material, weighty, and, above all, unassuming and aerial. When Angelo finally lifts his eyes from the rim of the glass and from the glacial italics of his splendid and inane imagination, he feels a distant tickling, very remote, like a phrasing rearisen from an extremely old echo, forestlike grunts, whispers in the ears of little girls in ditches and stables and haylofts. And then comes the gong, there, inside the fly of creased trousers—buttons of real mother-of-pearl. Who knows whether, faced by a verification of the so-called facts, everything would prove to be up to par. This is why one must not be hard from the very beginning, ask her nothing prematurely, for example: "And so what about this million?" The real hardness, if anything, must be reserved for the grand finale. Now he must infuse confidence in her if he wants to give it to himself. It is not a matter of generosity, but of rhythm, as in all matters of life or death. Angelo is certain that if he could make the negotiations trip along in endecasyllables with alternate rhymes, this opalescent flow would never be halted. The achievement of every human ideal of theory and practice: music written and played and its echo—that is, to compose harmoniously together money, sex, and prosody. To save face by unmasking oneself all the way, with every theatrical discretion. These are the things that Angelo and Belart, the one more, the other less, say to each other sipping gin and preliminaries. And Jasmine, who attracts him a lot, attracts him in her layout, chromolithographically, as among true forgers who share a common fund of goodness.

"You are too clean, Dr. Bazarovi. Dishonestly clean. As one no longer should be permitted to be. Being like this you oblige someone else to shoulder your share of dishonesty."

A perfectly Lomettian discourse, at least in substance: the sun is out but it rains. She's very beautiful and suited to the marbled light of this aperitif surrounded by draperies the color of fried sepia, over the leaves of the plants seem to run rivulets of water which make the deserted room pulsate. Belart's cautious moralism issues in breaths exactly at the center of the cone of debased spray that illuminates her profile.

"You don't hold it against me, do you, that I had you come here?"

"Oh, and why . . ." and with his gaze he seems to force her to rub together thumb and index finger in counting bills up to a million lire.

"Oh, the pantyhose, your complaints! I should have understood immediately that that was all a show to pretend you were burning all bridges completely with Mire and then resume negotiations with Lometto for the Coptafuk, with no danger of hostile partners, no Bazarovi. Lometto must really have laughed when he found out about that ridiculous figure I asked you for and that I found in my pocket doubled up. The candied cherry to top off your scheme . . ."

She avoids looking at him, her hands crossed over the glass which is clutched between her knees. Angelo goes on: "I had to, if I didn't want to look like an idiot to myself. He didn't want to pay my day's fee, he said that since he had to muddle through I should muddle through also. Talk like that. He also used me as a puppet even if in the end he did pay me for the day."

"Why do you continue justifying yourself for something so unimportant? How can I trust someone who justifies himself?"

"Don't trust, and it will be all the better. I'm leaving right now, I leave you the million and I also make you a present of the gas and time it cost me to come all the way here."

"Don't be so touchy . . . You were leaving us no other choice, I mean with the Coptafuk. Lometto was adamant and didn't want to take any more risks with you. He was sure of one thing: that you would categorically refuse. And as a matter of fact . . . So it was just as well to exclude you altogether without pointlessly turning it into a carefully guarded secret. You should thank him, everything considered. You know, it's dangerous to have useless secrets. Useless if the depositor had nothing to lose in taking them out when it suits him . . . Someone might get some nasty little idea in his head. Even you. A little bit of blackmail, for instance. And disagreeable consequences if one's back is not well protected."

"And is your back well protected?"

Belart looks at him from under her lashes, astonished. How could he doubt it? her eyes say.

"It certainly is. Too protected. Which is just as dangerous."

"No, I beg you, Frau Belart, you don't think that I feel under an obligation to believe all the crap that pops into your head . . ."

"But please . . ."

"Bullshit, turds, and crap I say. All that bothers me is that Lometto is having a good laugh at me and finds it convenient to believe that, strangely, out of stupidity or inexperience or pusillanimity, I'm corruptible for two hundred thousand lire just so that I can get my day's pay and not for twenty million, *for doing nothing*, only because there are people involved whom I don't know, *others*. But people are people and I have no illusions about the condition of their *health*."

"And yet, despite all this, you think one thing and do not do another—that is, you did not collaborate. In short, that's how you thought and we could not trust you."

"Oh, thanks a lot, you were perfectly right, that's exactly what I wanted."

"But listen, these pills have been commercially available since the end of the war, they have repopulated Germany with their stimulation . . . And now they have moved on to nightclubs and Eros Centers, immediately after the depression . . . They became a mass product, caught the eye of the Ministry of Health, etc., and have been prohibited, taken out of circulation, and do you know why, for ethical reasons, you think?"

"I don't care about all this. Governmental ethics make me laugh."

"And you've got plenty to laugh about: because they are highly competitive with cocaine, with which party and police officers fill their pockets in private. But because of this the value of Coptafuk has risen sky-high. And besides . . ."

She smiles, softly bites her lip, the tip of her tongue becomes smeared with lipstick.

"You don't trust me, do you? Otherwise I could tell you a thing, perhaps two."

"If it isn't some more nonsense or too subtle a truth . . ."

"Lometto knows nothing about the money you asked me for and that I put in your pocket. I swear to you on my two daughters' heads."

Angelo releases a subterranean sigh and can at his ease record the "*zwei Mädchen*" who sparkle in Belart's throat, exhale most tenderly, and detach themselves from her vocal cords and palate and lips, while she seems to grow melancholy as if she had vouchsafed one admission too many.

"If the lady and the gentleman would follow me" says the maître d'hôtel. Oh, these old-fashioned formulations that leave us enchanted and rob us of our appetite! "Luncheon is served."

There is the menu of the day with the usual choice between two entrées.

The sight of the food is attenuated by the chromatic uniformity that lacustrine atmospheres impart to everything when it rains outside, even to macaroni with tuna and tomatoes. They eat in silence, looking at each other politely. One thing is clear to Angelo, a thing full of bookmarks like so many stalactites and stalagmites up and down the pages: that the woman before him who holds her knife and fork like shipped oars and expresses herself in a most refined *Hochdeutsch* is a novel in two volumes and he will start directly with the second because the first is *vergriffen*.

No questions about the sold-out past. He doesn't care at all that someone on her behalf has taken the trouble of collecting information about him: what he truly does and whether the modesty of his life is real, whom he loves, if he loves, police record, etc. Not even that hundreds of people where he was born and has partly lived should be so eager to make believe that they know "how things stand." No less than two times in his life somebody has in foreign cities telephoned his employers to call him "a filthy Communist invert." Even phoned the old lady who had rented him a room in Milan. Now, if there are just people who go to so much trouble without being asked, just imagine if one gives them the courtesy of asking. Certainly, this business about Giuditta is horrible, because it definitely originates from a corner of the Piazzetta, from a single like himself.

Belart now seems to sense her guest's pardon and from that she draws a feeling of benevolence toward herself, relaxes imperceptibly in the upholstered damascened chair, in the purplish gray of her eyes cautiously slithers a dense vibration of pleasure which dilates in a somewhat foolish undulating expression.

"Is something on your mind?" Belart asks.

"I hope you'll first explain things to me."

"Come on, Dr. Bazarovi, you know everything. It can't be otherwise. If you knew how often Lometto mentions you."

"Oh yes? and what for?"

"Everything and nothing, just like that."

"Has Lometto sent you?" Angelo suddenly pursues an unthought-of route and stares at her questioningly.

"Oh, Dr. Bazarovi, Dr. Bazarovi!" Belart says, laughing. "You are too much!"

"Just thinking."

"No, no, and for what reason? . . . So then, you know of one reason, something that might have an effect . . ."

"Yes, in a very general way. But tell the truth, if you can, Signora Belart . . ."

"On the phone you called me Jasmine."

". . . perhaps I'm too presumptuous, or try too hard to put myself in your place, in the place of all of you, how shall I say? Really, couldn't it by chance be that you, deep down, continue to think that I am the gray eminence who stands behind all this business of the Coptafuk or what else, that, in short, Lometto himself has given you to believe something of the sort, or that you and Lometto are once again in cahoots to trap me?"

"To be sincere . . . one can never be sure of anything. But Lometto, no. He's not involved this time. Not with me. He is against me."

"The fact is that it has happened to me on other occasions, with regular pantyhose customers. I had quite a job trying to introduce Lometto as manager and owner and myself as factotum-interpreter. Even now there are people who . . ."

"Didn't Lometto ever mention it to you?" Belart asks, stroking herself under her string of pearls and shifting it with a fingertip outside the lapels of her jacket.

"Never. Even though he was dying to do so. Let us say I never gave him the chance."

"Should I really believe you? To be truthful, this is not what is being rumored in the organization . . ."

"Oh God, what a bastard! How can anyone go this far? But really, you, your problems with Lometto, the money you must have raked in, and now you want to involve me, a person who doesn't even have a job."

"You are so perfect, and at any rate you never leave behind any evidence to the contrary, that I will end up believing you really are."

"But I *am* unemployed! Please, don't make fun of me. Do you know why I came into the hotel through the back instead of the front? Do you know what kind of car I have?"

Digestion, afterwards, as they walk up the large staircase together with the wild-fruit salad, is decisively much better without nasty remarks at the foot of the steps. Belart leads, occasionally grazing a balustrade with the same fingertip she used to shift the necklace, then she lets her fingers trail upright over the marble, fans them out, closes them, separates two from the rest, flexes them, crosses them one over the other, and looks at him.

From a room comes a German lament at full blast, a lacerating *Lied*.

"Do you remember this?" Belart says on the landing, taking out along with her key a box of Coptafuk.

"You bet."

Eight blue letters against the white background of the unchanged name. The wrapping is entirely perfect, imitated with rigorous banality; for the rest, destined as it is for the black market and for what it is and nothing else, it certainly mustn't worry about appearing different, it would spell ruin. It has to be the good dear old Coptafuk of the corner drugstore when the nightmares of raids and an apocalypse in peacetime were still many, the same pill that gives tone to the women in the brothels set up in grand style, to their customers, to all those who impotently watch the Danube or the Rhine and no longer having the wish to die do not have the desire to live either. So take a Coptafuk and forget it. The door to Belart's suite opens.

"Something . . . something . . ." says Angelo, throwing his raincoat on the nth little armchair of creamy silk.

"Exactly: something no longer fits. In the composition, in fact. An initial business deal for two and a half million marks in less than two years, paid, as you say, in Italy? . . ."

"On the nail."

"Exactly. *On the nail*. Here's the merchandise, here's the money. Everything through the bank, obviously, this time, invoiced as a shipment of small hotel soap cakes."

Her nails are varnished with a disagreeable cyclamen red, her fingers covered as usual with rings of all shapes, one absolutely vulgar with a skull and tiny emerald-green eyes. They both now turn toward the leaden lake beyond the park's hard, solid vegetation. For Angelo there isn't much point in standing there, leaning against the railing of the small balcony, pretending to admire a landscape he doesn't see. For him the lake is the visual symbol of blindness: from every angle, in any weather and at any hour of day or night, he always sees the same faded blue cypress, somehow like a spear robbed of its balance by the wind without trajectory. Others make an effort to see boats there, small steamboats, shores, even sunsets. He sees only the *there*.

"Just to get to the point"—it is she who starts: and the point could be anything: Giorgina Washington, the junior Lomettos, Santina Tartaglione, Fortunata—"this is how things stand . . . Always provided you really don't know anything about it . . ." She tries again with a glittering smile from behind a window shade which she is pulling down because of the wind and drizzle. Who was the imbecile that convinced her to have her two stupendous gold canines extracted and replaced with conventional porcelain? And is that string of pearls for a girl of good family the souvenir of some aberration?

"Listen, Jasmine, get it in your head that I don't give a damn about convincing you one way or another. Don't waste your energy."

"What for? A belly dance? A belly dance accompanied by *Winterreise*? Why not?"

And she takes off her shoes, rushes to the bathroom, three minutes and she reappears with a kind of pareu twisted around her hips, bare feet, loose hair, no pearls, a very transparent, far from immaculate brassiere, and a tambourine in her right hand. Angelo would like to explain things but he doesn't succeed: he feels the dry throat and the difficulty in breathing which herald a collapse.

Jasmine shakes the tambourine and moves among table and *dormeuse* and armchairs and refrigerator-bar with adipose and restful slowness. If only she turned away that insistent gaze, but as she writhes she begins to speak:

"So then: half the shipment perfect. A huge success. It gives decent people the tranquillity of being able to drug themselves with the consent of a certain legality, I don't know if I'm making myself clear. Did you ever see a belly dance?"

"Yes. In Beirut. It was a business dinner. You know, commitments . . ."

"Oh, you're not very kind . . . Of course, they know perfectly well that it isn't all that legal any longer . . ."

The beauty spots, where are the beauty spots? Angelo's vision is a bit befogged, perhaps it would be polite to give her a tip at the end, give her a discount on the million. It's the least he can do!

". . . if only because of the new price, I should imagine" he says with an effort, exerting himself in following the adept movements of her arms, which follow the curves of her body above, below, and around. In such cases, one never knows what is the proper way to offer one's gaze, what type of participation is required to reassure the toiler who is sweating seven veils.

"Exactly. A tremendous success, I repeat. And no problems from anyone. No investigation, no denunciation, nothing. The request for a small contribution from the street cops in the districts with Eros Centers. Sweet as a liqueur."

In saying "liqueur" her hand slips between the knees and begins to rise in a frightful manner. And her lips: enchanting, narrating a realist magic that fades into every man's dream to create meaning from sentences which have none, trusting only in his own instinct of survival at all costs. The pareu or large kerchief opens and closes while with her hands she pulls down her pantyhose and mimes a very long caress over the carpet.

"Then catastrophe: the other half"—and following this German music which penetrates through walls and window: oh God, *Lieder* can last even an hour and twenty minutes—"potato starch with citrate, to produce the sizzling sensation on the palate. Ruined prospects, the market in turmoil. Lometto must understand that we have every reason to insist getting back half of the letter of credit he has already pocketed. Made out to a phantom company of his invention, naturally, the Savon Intime Hotel. Intime Hotel! And now he gives us the slip, hides behind this limited partnership of his, et cetera. The usual stuff." And the pantyhose sails limply through the air.

"Signora Belart, let's be precise: the usual stuff for you." Also the toenails have the same fuchsia polish, and it is probable that besides the pantyhose she has managed to take off unseen her underpants too; the shoe with its small hoe says "size 11," quite a foot. "I hope that . . ."

"What?"

How can he tell her that he hopes she's not getting too tired?

"That this *Lied* will never end. You are an exceptional dancer."

"You like my dancing?"

"Yes, it's incredible what two femurs and only one backbone can do."

"Dr. Bazarovi!"

Here, now, thank God, the music stops; and Jasmine stops too, with her bust on one side, her hips on the other, both hands arched over her belly. She is sweating but not much, proud of herself, vaguely wounded.

"I've danced for myself" she says, turning to the bathroom door, and she goes inside and the minutes that pass are more than three. If I were her I would cut my veins now, Angelo thinks. He also tries to think of some sort of mad act that could put her at her ease, how to make himself ridiculous in her eyes to restore a common balance between beings too overwhelmed by things dispatched and never arrived at any desired destination. He has decided that he will love her, satisfying her curiosity for that extra punctuation mark with which she has become infatuated and which can represent an exclamation mark between the menopause and all the other pauses yet to come. Who knows whether the thing is possible *platonically*. She reappears: her makeup is perfect, in a light silk dressing gown, not transparent, she smiles like a slightly crazy mother without complexes. Angelo does not care for this new attitude, he detests women who feel so defeated as to have recourse with him to maternity, he prefers them to crawl up the mirrors of their defeat, then he is more inclined to help them come down, to touch them.

"Coffee?" Bclart asks, and at a nod from Angelo she orders two coffees from room service. She puts on her shoes again.

"When I was a little girl I was always dancing, my mother taught me . . . I . . . are you interested?"

"No."

"I thank you for that. I'm not interested either in telling you that this is how I started. You know, you do irritate me, Angelo, and yet I could spend my life complimenting you."

"I too with you. We're a bit alike in character, we're a bit . . ."

". . . stateless, both of us?"

"That's it, precisely."

Angelo now begins hoping to see himself come in again, his eyes lowered, and leave the tray with two coffee cups on the table. What joy for a waiter never to look straight at the illegitimate couples who, in hotel rooms, expect nothing else.

"We're not *Banditen*, he's the bandit, and he doesn't even know. Lometto wants a test of strength" Belart says.

"Yes, I know him. He gives in, becomes reasonable only when confronted by the law of the strongest. And since he's used to always being the strongest . . . Even if you, let's make a hypothesis . . . it's so easy to do so, I mean to say here in Italy all families of a certain economic status do it . . . well, the hypothesis is: threaten to do in his kids one by one. Do you think it would help? No, not in the least. Before convincing him you would have to really do them in, and then, yes, then they will negotiate. But one wouldn't be enough, it takes at least two. The third the Lomettos could not give up."

"Luckily there are just three. We could begin with . . ."

"But what do you mean by we? I accept everything in good faith: the potato starch, the letter of credit, your reasons, everything, but you don't think that I . . ."

"Yes, I do. I don't have, we wouldn't have any other choice, they would strike. And hard. And you would be part of the pack by now."

"What do you mean 'by now'? And you think that I would lend myself to this sort of game?"

"Yes."

"And whyever?"

She rises, strikes a match—what happened to her pretty solid-gold lighter?—and says, exhaling the first puff: "Because you are now the depository of a secret, Dr. Bazarovi. Of a useless secret: my marching orders."

"And do you think that you're the first person who has forced me to be the depository of a secret I did not ask for? Come on! At least ten other people have pulled this trick on me. I should already have been gotten rid of many, many times, if it were so simple. And besides, don't forget one thing, Signora Belart, no matter how literary and unhealthy it may appear, unconfessed murderers like to have the possibility of a chronicler. They're vain, and their infamies must sooner or later be turned into 'exploits.' Aren't you vain?"

"You are incredible, I throw in the towel . . ." she says all in one breath, evidently the inexhaustible fount of convictions and the art of transmitting them. She has an infinite number of other cards to play. Angelo insists on probing her with his eyes, encourages her not to desist, to involve him, corner him, ruin him if she is able. A knock at the door, someone enters and exits. The floor maid with an unequivocally Friulian chin.

"Listen, Signora Belart . . ."

"You really have decided not to call me Jasmine?"

"All right then, Jasmine, how do I know you're telling the truth? that it's really so important that instead of the usual chemical components there is some healthy, improper potato starch? That that in fact *is true*? Besides: did you ever hear about homeopathy? The ideal cure for curing the potato spirits of us Westerners. And what would you expect me to do, without any objective data available to me?"

"Let us say you are under no obligation to verify. You must take some exigencies for granted. Nobody is asking for your opinion."

"And whyever should I take your side and not Lometto's, however things may stand?"

"I already told you. To avoid bloodshed. And it will happen. You are the only person who has power over Lometto, the only one who can talk to him."

"But that is no longer possible!"

Now also the wind is gusting more heavily. The shift in current changes the vibration of the mental image of the faded blue cypress beyond the windowpanes, transforms it into the glider that only a tourist anxious for good weather would be able to discern. Belart drinks her coffee, exhaling a sigh of medium profundity, medium loss of patience. Then she stretches out arms and hands on her chair's armrests.

"Listen, Angelo: something of vital importance for us has gone awry in this business because your friend Lometto has overestimated his true power of fraud. Or perhaps because . . ."

But Angelo thinks: you'll never know or find out the real reason for the potato starch: to detox his entire family.

". . . Or perhaps because something in Italy was about to block the possibility of continuing to produce Coptafuk and they or Lometto ripped us off on the last shipment a month and a half ago. Oh, it must be the fault of this government of yours which is still going after a couple of months, a lifetime . . . I'll grant you that."

Angelo tries to keep up with the relentless fire of Belart's intuitive associations, thinking at the same time that if she hadn't let that hair down over her shoulders he could see the beauty spots.

". . . On this subject you must believe me, Angelo. On this plane we must be agreed: that he has tried the rip-off and has succeeded. We never thought of anything like that, we have no interest in losing the business. Coptafuk is not a trendy product, a phase and that's it. We don't care to know whether Lometto is directly responsible for it or some third party went to the trouble of substituting potato starch for cantharidin and amphetamine. And it shouldn't matter to you either. This isn't aspirin, no one is going to swallow that . . ."

If Belart continues like this, she will make it impossible for him to make a fool of himself.

"We've already received several complaints, who knows if we'll be able to cover up the scandal. They reduce payments by seventy percent. Now we're supposed to put on the market three hundred millions' worth of potato starch in small one-centimeter cubes, changing outlets of sale, locations, purchasers, etc. Three hundred million paid instead of a few million for tubers and labor, do you understand? The loss that comes from this? . . ."

"How much is it, if I may ask?"

"Four hundred percent. One billion two hundred million lire lost because of Lometto's organization. And he must pay, reimburse at least the capital we invested on the letter of credit. You must show us *how.*"

"No less. I'm supposed to blackmail him."

"Yes, blackmail. You know your friend Lometto very well, a man who doesn't want to pay a day's wages and hints here and there that you have a finger in the pie; you must know his weak points very well. A target that he is sensitive about and which we do not know, and can hit accurately as soon as possible, before my organization aims at those others I mentioned to you. Besides, listen: I'm a mother too, I would like to avoid this sort of thing. And you too, I hope. Help us blackmail him the right way and for his own good. Give us a key that will turn all the way."

Angelo thinks about Epaminonda: does he really want to do something to spare Lometto one irreparable misfortune? two irreparable misfortunes? and what is this fire gnawing inside him against Lometto, against his ex-best friend? and this skin-deep desire for vengeance? for that way of his of accumulating money without ever spending more than the minimum necessary, holding on to all of it for ultimate purposes, because he wants to buy not things and services but human blood and so administer the world's justice. Wouldn't bleeding him a bit be good for him and the world?

"You're deluding yourself, Signora Belart . . ."

"Jasmine . . ."

"Jasmine. Lometto, I already told you, has only one weak point: his wallet. How to blackmail his wallet without having recourse to it is quite an enterprise."

"Aside from killing his sons . . . come now . . . try to make a mental effort for a moment. We all have something to hide."

"I don't."

"You don't."

"No, nothing. On the contrary, I'm even amused at the thought that that bloodhound of yours in the hall went on snapping photos with your pretty gold lighter. The only thing one might say is: see that Bazarovi, he goes for beautiful women of a certain age, but he never sucked me in! Nobody will believe that I came here to discuss money and Middle European financial intrigues. People would laugh if you tried to convince them to the contrary. At the most they would think that I'm here to copy the stitch on the valances of these curtains for my mother. You, Jasmine, consider me too important, all of you are wasting precious rolls of film. And time."

Belart laughs with all her heart, one feels she has one. And she's not insensitive to the compliment that exalts her certain age. But now it is Angelo who becomes distracted: what is happening to him is too, too exaggerated. Who knows if Belart now realizes that all Angelo would like to do is to order an *orzata* not from the Friulian waitress but to see whether before him will again appear his own youth in blue-black livery, that mixture of sky and blackberries in which to lose and intoxicate oneself, to undress the curly-headed bellboy and send Belart outside, forever, to operate the elevator.

Belart has the stolid-astonished look of just before, the halo of tartar on her upper teeth spares only the scintillating porcelain of the new canines, but the mechanism behind the two-tone yellow of the dental fence is broken, or pausing, and without words.

"*Gnädige Frau*, you must absolutely understand that I get off this story whenever I feel like it, even now at this instant if I want to. There's no point in taking security measures against me: I'm completely in the open by choice. I'm unique, a unit, and therefore I cannot be caught. It is much easier to capture Fantomas with all his identities than me who have only one and always the same. It's up to you. I'm sorry to have to repeat myself but how about talking money at last? What do you say?"

Belart stands up without further arguments or arrows to her bow and goes to the next room, the bedroom, disappearing behind the door.

Once he had the misfortune of spending a prolonged vacation due to circumstances beyond his control. They were on the Canary Islands, he and the woman with whom, for some years, on and off, he had had, as the saying goes, a morbidly platonic relationship. Forced to do the shopping himself because the woman, the squeamish virgin, threatened to kill herself thirty times a day and he must after all give her the possibility of doing so by leaving her alone, well, he had noticed that in the local supermarket there were mountains of huge packages of Valium, and that in every one of those Swedish, German, French, Danish, English, and Scandinavian shopping carts there lay nonchalantly among cheese and cans at least one of these green packages. They bought Valium with epidemic gluttony so as to be able to count on months and months of *guaranteed* tranquillity. So that's where the Coptafuk ended up: in those small families at the antipodes of those others who did not resign themselves to a dazed tedium by the fireside, the ones who wanted *movimiento*. With Coptafuk, the Eskimo peasants see even seals and reindeer as sequined dolls, creatures of sin, so you can imagine wives and husbands who have been freckled and washed out by the winters. And possibly, starting with three kilos of potato starch and more, they enjoyed a discount. This is the West: a boreal blend of euphoria and depression in the little Hollywood behind the closed doors of the hearths. Spanish flies with potato wings. An illusion, a fraud against themselves in which it becomes ever more difficult to believe in order to be able to survive, be it in depression or in euphoria.

"Money? Sure, let's talk about it" she says, reappearing before him and handing him an envelope. "One million lire."

With the other hand she removes a bobby pin from her temporary chignon and opens it by pressing it against a canine.

"Your money. And now let us get to the money Lometto owes to *me*."

"Let us talk for one moment more about the money of both, also about mine, first. Let us go by hypotheses, shall we? While I'm hypothesizing about Lometto's money, I wouldn't like you to forget that

I am at the same time hypothesizing about what would come into my pocket, assuming I will show up again. You knew you were risking a million for nothing . . ."

"Agreed."

"You will find it hard to believe me, but I doubt that as things are now Lometto can get together three hundred million in cash . . ."

"What do you mean?"

"He will certainly have reinvested the money in real estate. He never keeps more than thirty thousand lire in cash in his account."

"Well, that's his problem, he'll sell. And anyway . . ."

"A most arduous undertaking, convincing him to sell, even more arduous than that of getting him to hand over cash. But you were saying . . ."

"Yes, well, you see . . . do you know anything about paintings?" she says.

"A little."

"Did you ever hear of Mantegna's *Crucifixion*?" and Belart passes her tongue over her lower lip. "We know who's got it . . . in Penzana. We'd be satisfied with that."

"Oh, I don't doubt that the priest has it hidden somewhere for when he retires."

"Not exactly, not he: Lometto. Reliable information. But you really . . ."

"Jasmine, enough, please, let us not start that again. Lometto with the Mantegna! A work of art of inestimable value, surrounded by pantyhose, carrion of squirrels, piglets, owls, and chickens. This is as fantastic as . . ."

". . . as a simple truth, my dear Angelo. You're thinking, aren't you? thinking of how to blackmail him?" Belart asks, making for the first time an affectionate gesture with her hand on the back of Angelo's right hand. He leaves it there, pensive.

"Could be. Yes."

"I understand. You are fishing about in your secret pleasure of inventing possible blackmails that would not be possible for us. But I must beg you to stick to down-to-earth blackmail . . . feasible . . . Some small, very simple thing would be enough, some photographs for example, maybe a bit risqué for a certain provincial mentality. Just look how some of these British politicians topple . . . A mere nothing, *una cazzata*, isn't that what you say?"

"Oh, sexual blackmail is so vulgar, so parochial. No, it won't do. Besides, Lometto is invulnerable."

"Why? Blackmail is blackmail, so long as it works."

"I don't agree. By continuing to be successful with sexual blackmail people will continue to think that sexuality *can* be blackmailed, too lazy to convince themselves of the contrary. This style does not suit me. I exclude it for ideological reasons."

"But it's classic! An adultery, a little passing infatuation, just for the pleasure of getting a taste of it . . . You traveled together so much and, as they say, he who runs with the wolves learns to howl."

"Jasmine, you're incorrigible, too romantic. It's quite clear that you do not know either Lometto or his wife, South or no South, she would certainly be proud of it," Angelo says, putting Belart completely off track. Edda, on the contrary, would not forgive him at all, would be quite capable of acting like Medea, setting house and annexed Den to fire and flame. Or like a woman of the South finish off the little holier-than-thou troublemaker from the South, or bump off with blows of the rubber stamp the postal official who forced him to play the male partner . . . Or . . . And yet Lometto lying back on the hood of the car with his shorts pulled down and his T-shirt held between the teeth above his Buddhaesque tits, someone prone on him at the height of his crotch . . . an obedient servant, or a she-dwarf from the workshop . . . an unfortunate, a defenseless, indifferent person . . . repeated flashbulb bursts . . . his face with eyes wide open in surprise, Boeotian eyes, the open mouth of a foredoomed victim, the suddenly limp ears, with the repentance of a person too good to fall for it . . . Black on white, color isn't necessary. After all, Lometto, when he makes little old ladies scurry back to the sidewalk by driving through the red light, always says that he's color-blind, not that he's in a hurry. Also when he drenches with black mud the gray pedestrians at the side of the road. Also when he addresses waiters—white jacket and black pants—with the familiar *tu*, also when he leaves a light blue five-hundred-lire bill as a tip for three hours of service during a business dinner and then swears that he left five thousand. His ravenlike villainies, his candid tyrannies. Or like the time when Angelo could have sworn that Lometto was aiming his wheels at that little clump in the middle of the road, the tiny gray muzzle stunned by the headlights, immobile, a porcupine, and he had yelled "Watch out, turn the wheel!" and Lometto had run over it and one felt the slight feathery bump below and Angelo was terrorized by the delighted laughing brutality at his side. Oh, a blackmail without style would serve him right, hashed and rehashed, the documentation of a blow job given him by a transvestite, for example, or a filthy old hag, or while he is buggering a meat-hound found by chance, gratis, on an escarpment, something like that, and Angelo shouldn't have to rack his brains just because he has given the formal promise he would never use the tape and has forgotten to put in conditions in regard to Giorgina Washington's possible death, and is evaluating all other possibilities, knowing very well that a photo-reportage in a parking area along the Sun Highway would mean a bull's-eye right off, quickly, one hundred percent in the center—that is, the old-fashioned way.

From the floor below or alongside the music of *Lied* furtively reappears. Angelo has a shiver of dismay, he is as afraid of encores as Adam of snakes. Judas's kisses are three.

"They've been playing this blessed record since seven o'clock this morning. I can't stop myself from listening to it carefully every time, but it makes me so sad. Do you know it? It's Schubert. And as if on purpose: look at those linden trees toward the shore, all the leaves dripping down." Angelo in his thoughts enumerates and rephotographs: first of all, two gins in two tall glasses, but the waiter—a hand of his, a sleeve of his jacket—has emptied the tonic bottles for them and then kept them on the tray. This must have been the first photograph snapped by the man who appeared in the hall downstairs, halted on the runner, and lit a cigarette with Belart's gold lighter. An ashtray. And she: a ruby, an oval diamond, a small emerald on her left hand; small diamonds in a platinum crescent, a garnet-colored stone, a wedding band or security band of dull gold on the right hand, and the horrible ring with the skull and the tiny, very green eyes. No more ivory. Earrings like those of a shooting-gallery carny. The platinum brooch on her left lapel; the necklace like a thick snake with many charms that sway in and out of the neckline, over it the string of pearls, a strange juxtaposition. A second and a third cigarette on the stairs and then at the door—as if the cigarette had been badly lit or he were playing with the lighter between his fingers walking away down the hallway. His hairstyle. The sixteenth-century shoes. It was vital not to overlook even one particular of this particular day. A photograph of her and Angelo alone here at the hotel, and Lometto would never believe that this was the first time that Angelo was seeing Jasmine

Belart after the business in Vipiteno and not, let us say, a year ago or even two as this sort of madwoman might claim in order to corner the unsuspecting Angelo in a false but irrefutable, *true* premeditation as regards the imminent, unspecified crime. Ah, all one has to do is have one's head shaved at summer's end one year and lose one's hair the next for lack of love.

> *Am Brunnen vor dem Tore*
> *Da steht ein Lindenbaum;*
> *Ich träumt' in seinem Schatten*
> *So manchen süssen Traum.**

Says the *Lied*; rhymes apart, the verses could have been written by any Italian poet of the 1980s desirous of becoming a senator for life.

"What do you say, ten percent for me? Thirty million? Twenty of which right away, *on the nail*?" Angelo says, brimming with entrepreneurial impudence; but when all is said and done, as much as he trusts Belart, he would even be satisfied with seven percent.

"You're a tough customer, Dr. Bazarovi."

"So are you, Signora Belart & Ghosts, Inc. Let us say that I betray Lometto, for his own good of course . . . and for that of the first of his designated and 'innocent' sons . . ." he says childishly, as if he were telling a fable exceeding his real capacity for wonder ". . . and that I am so clever as to supply you with the key to open the lock or safe or sepulcher of the three hundred million . . . Three hundred are quite a few and to me it seems impossible to pry them loose from him, I repeat, with all the investments that man makes at the drop of a hat, thirty million for me, because I don't even know whether you have any, let us say, *moral* right, *objective* legitimacy to get them, thirty million for me isn't very much after all. And, Signora Belart, what if this were only a swindle to get money out of Lometto thanks to my ingenuity or because you have to have certain information concerning an altogether different business, but you do not know what use to make of it and think that I will decide to do it for you? What if there was no potato starch to stir with your ladle? You see how many ifs I could come up with . . ."

"But thirty million . . . and it *is* potato starch! And you know

* *At the fountain before the gate / there stands a linden tree; / I dreamed in its shadow / so many a sweet dream.*

many things about Lometto, very many, it'll be child's play, I feel it."

"Now, really, what do you take me for? You come down the Alps after two years and more, you call me, and I, just like that, point-blank, am supposed to help you get two hundred and seventy million by providing you with an effective blackmail and furthermore carry it out myself. But this is slapstick! Do you realize how many Jasmine Belarts would be ready to do business if they all knew that I'm so capricious with other people's secrets which I happen to know? And you've even snapped photos, but I don't worry too much about them: you could have called me, I might have even posed for you and then left disgusted by your proposals. A witty but hopeless expression. That's not damaging evidence."

"I'll discuss it. We'll see. The photos . . . I . . ."

"Are you looking for justifications now? Does Lometto know that you're here?"

"Precisely here in this hotel, no. But he knows all the rest, of course."

"Have you already communicated to him your 'or else'?"

"Yes. A complete failure."

"Perhaps your 'or else' wasn't well translated. You need the proper intonation. What was his reaction?"

"Oh, him! He says he's got nothing to do with it, how could he know about it, he wasn't there cooking the Coptafuk, etc. Stuff like that, enough to make your hair stand on end. Like an irresponsible child. And he drops the names of a party secretary, a pharmacopoeia, a printshop and its straw men. Damnit, Lometto actually betrays everyone the minute he smells smoke. And you instead have all these scruples. He's a buck-passing rabbit. And, commercially speaking, amoral, and he always thinks he knows more than anyone else. A pig who would look fine with his throat cut. Does he want a gang war? He'll get it. But this is exactly what I would like to avoid."

But Lometto and Belart are already two gangs by themselves.

"And my little girls. I assure you, they are well protected, they don't even have my name. Only I know where they are, and my first ex-husband. Not like his kids, who ride their bicycles to school."

Angelo sees two very proper daughters, pretty, pedantic, who study city planning or journalism or communications in some American university, play tennis, are majorettes in support of their beloved football team, dress in "Made in Italy" clothes, and regularly receive checks from their slutty mom, slightly dirty checks which they never talk about. They see their mother once a year and are a bit ashamed of it. And again Angelo thinks in capital letters: "JASMINE," and the echo pushes him toward her, who now has all the signs of an emotional and bank-tellerish weariness under her deeply bruised eyes.

The window onto the balcony is opened again, it has stopped raining, and a quatrain frosted by the breeze slips inside.

Bin gewohnt das Irregehen
's führt ja jeder Weg zum Ziel:
Uns're Freuden, uns're Wehen,
*Alles eines Irrlichts Spiel!**

"Do you hear that? do you hear? One must leave, always leave. And make others leave. In every season, not only in the winter."

And they move as one from the anteroom–living room into the next room: the beds are two, separate, a raincoat like his and a man's hat on the clothes rack. She is alone, and totally unpreoccupied about erasing the traces of a companion now momentarily strolling, smoking, and photographing the bougainvillea in the garden.

"Would you like some champagne?" Jasmine asks, loosening her hair but flinging it behind her shoulder and retrieving the wild face of her best moments, a wildness which is no longer "artistic," as when she did her belly dance.

"I hate to keep my clothes on when I'm indoors" and she takes off her dressing gown and she's completely naked underneath. Her sparkling beauty spots seem bursting with private inks, pleasing capsules that one can open at will, lethal. But the triangular arrangement is food for thought. He could swear that the last time he saw them, all three were perpendicular one above the other. There's always this hokum about real champagne when the adulterators of water and living vines believe they must operate in certain spheres and not in others.

"Sure" Angelo says, standing immobile, *listening*.

"In the other room, in the mini-bar, go and get them."

And Jasmine lights a cigarette, perfectly at ease, with a pillow on her belly and her head resting against the headrest of the twin bed.

"Let's make it fifteen million now and fifteen million upon com-

* *I'm weary of wandering / every path leads to the same goal: / our joys, our sorrows / all a will-o'-the-wisp game.*

pletion of the operation. Felicitous completion" she says, smiling at him in an unequivocal manner. "If, however, you could get your hands on the Mantegna . . ."

"You have my word that the operation will be felicitously completed so far as my money is concerned: if I fail I will return all of it to you. Therefore it is just as well if you give me twenty now and ten afterwards. On my word. With me you run no risks. At most I will keep this million for general expenses. As for the Mantegna . . . that would be quite an achievement. I ought to increase my demands. Do you know how big it is?"

"One meter eighty by one meter twenty."

"Exactly, even I know someone who would pay you a billion lire for it on the nail."

The cork pops with very little brio, the fluted glasses are filled. This is the usual ritual of adolescent romances, his fifth heterosexual erection over a span of thirty-five years which makes its way through a jungle of half realities and half quasi-erotic fantasies, the realm of the possible that becomes concrete, turgid, only if it is frazzled by the exhausted mists of a siege of oneself.

"And what plan do you have, what's your idea?" she asks, unbuttoning his jacket, loosening the knot of his tie, slipping a hand inside his T-shirt, smoothing his hairs and pinching a nipple with two fingernail tips.

Angelo moves his mouth to her earring and, inhaling the acrid smell of her hair and neck, amorously whispers to her:

"First the money, do you mind?"

Now, while Belart's breasts full of health press against his chest, he thinks: volume two, let us say page forty-eight, chapter entitled "Climacteric." And he begins. He frenetically devours several pages, skips others, only to go back to them, zigzagging immediately afterwards, this woman's parchment is precious and fresh, turning the pages there is the smack of a finger inside other lips, to turn a further, very long page made up of rather tedious descriptions of the world's wickedness and of how to manage when one is a young and pretty girl. The vocal harmony of sighs in Osmanli, the throat used little or not at all to articulate. Smyrna? Ankara? Troy? but this definitely belongs to the first volume and he wants to be not curious but omnivorous. And then that moan of hers, of unprecedented geographicality: "Yes, yes, also the Dardanelles!" which makes him arch and forget the alchemy of that recurrent dream: he's making love to a woman and in the dream he draws a blank. He wakes up and realizes that he has to take a leak.

Increasing the rhythm, he concentrates his mind on a single word, which keeps at bay all extraneous and nefarious reflection. He repeats it for good luck or, more precisely, it is the word itself that now comes and goes, accelerates and grunts, and in its repetition sweeps the pneumatic void of the brain in the act of fucking. We have all had an important lover in our youth. And Angelo can no longer hold back the probably fetish-onomatopoeia of the young girl sold in the marketplace, who after a quick tour of duty in dance and belly, embraces high-ranking odalisqueship in order to attain as soon as possible the gates of Vienna, where, alas, she discovers that she is by now too experienced to make a new life for herself!

"A-ta-türk! Ah!" and Belart empties out in a crystalline laugh and definitively digs her nails into the clipped shoulder blades of Angelo, who turns his head with a jerk and thinks: who knows whether the sleuth hasn't lit a cigarette behind my back. And then: what an incredible charmer!

"What a silly boy! I'm Syrian!" Belart exclaims, without a hint at wanting to change position and situation, raising the fluted glass to the large halo of sucked lipstick, lighting another cigarette with Angelo under her. "You and I will make billions together, you know?"

"Oh, I'm sure of that. But thirty million are already more than enough for me."

"What will you do with them?" Belart asks with an air of superiority, revealing one of her secret thoughts: that psychologically Angelo is, let us say, a retarded graduate left behind by life and with a few naïve projects ahead of him.

"Oh, just put them next to the others, like Lometto, since I told you that I haven't got a lira."

"What a liar! At the least you're thinking about an island or a trip around the world. You're so young! Everything will be for the best."

Are we starting all over again with the Suzannas?*

"You can certainly say that, Signora Belart. I am madly in love with a young Bolivian whom I would like to move to Italy, but the Rothschilds are against me. He works as a maître for them in Paris."

"Oh, this is a good one!" and Jasmine laughs, incredulous, amused,

* *Aldo Busi,* Seminar on Youth *(Milan: Adelphi, 1984), p.* 75.

shaking the mass of her chestnut-colored hair and propping herself up on an elbow. "Don't you want to know anything about the man who's with me?" she adds, a trifle disappointed, nodding at the hat and raincoat.

"No. He appears to be even slightly younger than Hans, and more tender."

"Yes, appearances. A con, a little angel-face capable of anything, of stabbing you in the back. *You* are tender, Dr. Bazarovi, nobody's as tender as you, I have two very beautiful daughters, a son-in-law like you . . ."

"I prefer you, Jasmine, I do not like old young women."

Belart laughs full-throatedly, holds out her hand for him to pleonastically help her to get up, he kisses it full of gratitude, she pecks him on the forehead.

"You are priceless," she adds, moving toward the bathroom dragging her dressing gown behind her.

"Not literally, I hope," Angelo remarks, putting on his shorts and silently complimenting himself between the legs.

"Tomorrow morning you will have fifteen million in cash, all right?" she says, throwing cold water on her face and immediately closing the door. The noise of other waters. She reopens the door, already in her suit and with bare feet. She begins the operation of making up her face, dusts it, delineates it, puts on the finishing touches.

"Splendid. But not in cash. A cashier's check, if you don't mind, so I don't even have to go to the trouble of counting them. Between us . . ."

"And immediately after you'll explain to me what you intend to do."

"What I already have done in all probability. Nobody must make contact with Lometto until I say so. And give Penzana a wide berth. One must strike with the unexpectedness of a lightning bolt. Tomorrow at what time?" Angelo asks, without the shadow of a plan in his head.

"Eleven."

"No, let's make it twelve. But not here. Have you already visited the Vittoriale? In the small piazza. And do me a favor, let's not complicate matters: no rabid smokers, agreed? No photos à la James Bond."

"Agreed. No Hans Two. That one isn't happy unless he's causing some sort of trouble."

"Then, later . . . we could come back here . . ." Angelo suggests, thinking about himself standing next to the elevator door wearing the pillbox hat of circus ushers.

She continues making up, flattered. Angelo takes a step toward her, remains respectfully on the threshold, touches her shoulder lightly with one hand.

"And what will you do with all that loot?"

"What do you mean, what will I do with it? It isn't all mine."

"Who knows! But if you have engineered all this by yourself, Jasmine, my compliments. I don't care whether you do or don't have an organization behind you. I will adopt this theory to the extent that it can work, even though knowing that Lometto in any case knows all there is to know—about you, and the rest. Except, precisely, what I know."

"Excellent. Thanks. But don't consider me a charity case. My two girls, with what they cost, are an organization apart, believe me. And the smoking photographer and the gentlemen who make the phone calls . . . Men are expensive, the less they're worth, the more demanding they are. Do not underestimate me by overestimating me, Dr. Bazarovi. I wish it were so!"

"You make me feel so important, Jasmine. All this attention for a fellow with a degree in foreign languages. I think you're pulling my leg. Also as a lover I must not be . . ."

"You're the graduate of yourself, Dr. Bazarovi" Belart cuts in with severity, offering him lips and tongue before applying the definitive layer of lipstick.

Angelo kisses very well and by instinct he knows that with women one must always dig the tongue out of their mouth and suck it inside one's own and then leave them the initiative of digging you out. Going with a woman one loves, and this is just a way of speaking, where intensity is concerned, is like going with a man you don't care for.

Walking down the staircase—Belart never even rings for the elevator—she leads. The bellboy slips by swiftly inside his cage with its load of saturnine blue and black gazes. Nobody in the lobby. Jasmine is resplendent next to the glass-paned door framed in gilded chromium plating. It certainly won't be easy to repeat or pick up all this exactly if the sleuth has continued, unseen, to snap photos, even if he forced her to do everything all over again exactly like this tomorrow or the day after tomorrow, when Lometto will be summoned here, and it would certainly seem that they were snapped in the *now* of the imminent future. Angelo knows that he can no longer get off this story when he wants to, and that he does not want to. Even if every time he were able to get rid of Lometto for a few moments so that the photos snapped would seem contemporary with those in the *now of later*, thousands are the details of the present which would elude past and future, even if Belart agreed to dress exactly as she is dressed now.

In the photos taken a short while ago their eyes must have a charge of unrepeatable energy, this detail by itself would already be enough to show to the world and to the least attentive person that those-these photos were snapped in that precise instant which does not resemble any other instant, not *this*, not that, but simply a time before the meeting with three participants that Angelo foresees as necessary. In some way he does not want to have met Jasmine Belart *forever*, this encounter which has so *been* and reproduced, so usable. Angelo makes a very simple decision: "All right, Signora Belart, you will now go to Hans Two and make me a gift of your cigarette lighter, loaded. I will keep it as a souvenir."

Jasmine makes a sudden gesture of rebellion and irritation, then she does an about-face. Angelo's most amiable smile does not brook objections. Belart returns with a clenched fist which she opens, giving him her hand and burdening his with a light weight. She looks at him without trust, without melancholy, as though at a station in which she no longer can get her bearings. And proudly offended and grateful. Belart is just as he feared: one of those women who if you do not take something *material* away from them do not feel taken into the proper account and lose all respect for you. They were formed in the hard school of dictatorships.

"Jasmine, don't look at me like that. So, tomorrow at noon up there."

"Will you come?"

"Yes. If the roll inside is really today's, yes."

Going out onto the gravel-covered drive and heading for the back of the hotel, Angelo smiles at the thought of his bravura and recklessness. The crow is still there, a phosphorescent black as if it had been waiting for him, to accompany him outside. Belart remarks on the weather, she knows she has completely exposed herself, that she has declared her loneliness to its depths, her soloist being and acting. Or it is another little kiss, the small performance of a great artist. No matter which: applause.

"Till tomorrow" Angelo says, squeezing her wrist. He through the car window, she standing outside. Their attention is captured by the record's finale:

Wunderlicher Alter,
soll ich mit dir geh'n?
Willst du zu meinen Liedern
*deine Leier dreh'n?**

Angelo smiles and looks at Jasmine: wondrous a-menstruate woman! The crow takes off in flight from the pilaster, croaks a little farewell. The car starts at the first try.

Will he be able together with this goddess in the machine to set in motion the Organ of the Present? Driving home under the clouds and the sudden tattered glimpses of lovely weather, Angelo is pervaded by the sensation that what comes next is a thousand times more simple than betraying a woman, letting her know about it, and leaving her satisfied—about herself and yourself. There will be no difficulties in getting Lometto to hand over three hundred million lire, and without Angelo having to go back on his promise not to have recourse to the reel or the business of Giorgina Washington—not her directly. Already on other occasions he formulated for himself the concept that it is success which produces talent, not the other way around. Jasmine Belart is goading his loins to get him to produce talent for himself. Oh yes, to make all the same mistakes over again with her, pick up and take a trip around the world. Angelo cannot disappoint Belart with a lack of success. He must elaborate it, wresting it from the well-settled laziness of his disillusioned cells. He must force them to move about and collide at random, and at a much higher speed than they have attained until now. It will never be an open weapon that will deliver the blow to Lometto's heart—that is, his wallet—in the sense desired by Belart, but a way for him to uncover it; not the obvious consequences which will allow him to calculate immediately the gash on the basis of the wound, but rather the suggestive power of the devastating epilogues neither imagined nor unimaginable. Angelo senses that this talent is about to arrive with widespread wings. He will always be able

* *Wondrous old man / should I go with you? / Will you turn your barrel organ to accompany my songs?*

to tell him you're the one who dragged me into this business, it's your fault that Belart dares to threaten me. And he would blast him with a well-programmed look.

It is incredibly late, how fast the hours go by when you force yourself in a disciplined manner to be the partner of foolish time, which is performing a belly dance for you. At five o'clock, perhaps because of the storm which has been threatening since morning, there is an ugly, false, leaden twilight all around.

"A man came, a southerner, as soon as you went out this morning, he left an envelope" his mother says.

"Where is it?" there! a sign of success masterfully laid at his feet.

"In your room. Pick up some books from the floor. I'll end by killing myself. This time I didn't have to pay any postage due, he wasn't a mailman," she says, reminding him of something she's concerned about.

"Do you want a million, Signora Bonaventura? Here it is!" and he hands her the envelope.

Remaining completely dressed, he feels he has dressed up more for this occasion than to meet Belart; he opens the envelope, slowly shifts the three photographs from one hand to the other, goes over them again, goes *blub blub blub* with two fingers on his lips, as when he wanted to make little Giuditta smile.

She's not your ordinary street waif, it is unquestionably she: Fortunata Tartaglione. And all by herself she would be worth thirty million lire. Now also Edda Napaglia's imploded revenge is explained. And he gets back into his car.

The country around Mantua is the strangest region that exists because of the fog and fumes which are exhaled from the very first days of September at the end of August. While elsewhere, a few kilometers away, the sun shines even at street level, here, at the same hour, a curtain of fog lifts which prevents at least Angelo from going into high gear. He feels inside him an orderly tornado, ready by now to fit completely into a small bottle of after-shave lotion: to let it evaporate and set the bottle on the shelf together with other emptied and empty glassware. This is the revenge that Edda was hatching inside and did not want to let out, recorded there, on the tape, never again listened to, that one must hope one will not be forced to listen to again so as to have it listened to in its entirety, by her separately or, if it were not possible to extract from her anything close to three hundred million, by husband and wife together, by the two married principals. "O Ilario, O Belisario, O Berengario" this is what Edda had said, as she was quite simply proceeding by elimination. Either one or the other or the other yet. Giorgina Washington, daughter of a multiple incest. A revenge that Edda has hatched for years, instant after instant, for not having been able to force Santina Tartaglione to have an abortion, and perhaps also Lometto had butted in to make sure she did *not* have an abortion. And here it is now, in the envelope in his pocket, the loose end that will lead to several hypothetical skeins. And their prickly little problems.

Fortunata has the same blond hair, the same flapping ears, and is thin as a rail. And her eyes: unmistakable, light blue. Daughters take after their fathers if, as Lometto's mother had said, sons take after their mothers. And Fortunata is as similar to Lometto as a drop of water. Santina Tartaglione, what a poor deluded creature! She certainly must have had her vain dreams to give such a ridiculous name to a child of no one, a super-nobody.

And now this reserved but in fact blocked adoption. Typical of Lometto: she can't be his, she won't be anyone else's. His false love which kills and extinguishes little by little all the blood that isn't his or is his and cannot become so officially, capitalistically, because its other half is morganatic or adulterated. To embalm life: after such a long time, Angelo again smells that odor of phenol in his nostrils.

And also over the phone he had asked the Naples policeman, "Couldn't you try and see whether in the same institution a newborn mongoloid made its appearance and disappearance?" "Oh, but nobody would want to have her, and besides, disappeared how, what do you mean?" "Well, I'll explain: if I needed a mongoloid two or three weeks old let's say to shoot a film for that famous scene where you see a razor blade cutting into an eye . . ." an eye? black or blue? Angelo asks himself, interrupting the reconstruction of the phone call: Dr. Perpetua ought to know. ". . . Do you think I could come South, find a mongoloid, pay, blind it, get rid of it, and get away with it?" and Galeazzo answered with that depressing, fatalistic sentence, "Everything is possible." Since Angelo, even though recognizing that he's naturally inclined to all forms of fantastic ratiocination, still cannot come to terms with the fact that, at a distance of so many months from her death and the end of the construction work in the chapel, Aurora Lometto still has not been laid to rest in the place to which she is entitled, at Toigo. It is days and days—since he showed up with the marble angel for Aurora's grave in Penzana—that Angelo has begun to disentangle the simplest thought, and the one best supported by his experience on the subject of "blood of one's own blood." Lometto is stubborn about one thing, about Fortunata's bastard state, and so is Edda: the blood to which each of them is directly entitled. Which could even be coagulated and unfortunate and mongoloid and incestuous blood from head to foot but, once it has escaped the anonymity of a transoceanic euthanasia, *their* blood *and* alive *and* dead, officially, publicly, religiously *theirs*, and thus worthy of every sepulchral consideration just as much as an aesthetically *normal* blood of theirs. If Giorgina Washington persists in not setting foot in the chapel and will never do so, it must be because, ultimately, something must have slipped out of the hands of Lometto, always so busy, perhaps even somewhat insistently busy and absent-minded about their three children. Those three pairs of pellucid black eyes fixed on the taxidermic offering of that extraordinary little daughter-sister . . . A unique opportunity. And off to the Tower. Edda and Lometto would be capable, cornered by the sartorial art of Ilario, Belisario, and Berengario and confronted by the fait accompli of having bought a small mongoloid girl with an active case of meningitis, of letting her die immediately upon arrival and then showing her to a few intimates, with the blessing of the priest and the local medic, who would be able to tergiversate in a thousand ways, invent a thousand explanations, while not giving any. Or, actually, not know anything about it. By Don Galetta's own admission the little girl with the fulminating meningitis had slowly been fulminated in Penzana, with his most tacit general acquiescence. And then the Lomettos, who call the veterinarian to "close her eyes"—which did not want to close and kept reopening. As if they were made of glass . . . But Dr. Perpetua would have realized at least this, or should one not trust a Catholic veterinarian too much? capable of mistaking a hippogriff for a turtle dove. But both she and the priest arrived in extremis: the *perpetua* saw Aurora only after she was dead. No, Giorgina Washington's stuffed corpse cannot be the one displayed in the coffin during the exequies, nor even the one buried in Penzana, because otherwise, if Aurora were Aurora, she would be in the cemetery at Toigo. The eyes closed and opened again were the real eyes of a real corpse. But then who is in the coffin in the small, would-be Anglo-Saxon cemetery? And who knows whether the wonder women from the ex-basement were present, mirroring themselves in the little yellow dress of the small corpse which in death was as beautiful as they would never be in life. If only the *perpetua* would answer a simple question! "What color were the eyes of Aurora Lometto in her coffin?" If they were black he is screwed with all his suppositions, but if they are any other color . . .

Arrived in the center of Penzana he parks near the town's only bar and asks to use the phone. There are already people at seven o'clock eating tripe in their white bowls and a good smell of garlicky salami.

"Hello? Don Nocciolini, how are you?" Angelo asks without hostility in his voice.

"Have you decided to come for confession? You always get the time wrong, my dear fellow" Don Galetta answers, quietly laughing. "Still poking your nose into things around here?"

"No, I'm not around here. And I no longer need to confess. I only wanted to speak a moment with Signorina Marta. An affective matter, that's all."

"You may speak to me . . . Affective!" he exclaims in a mocking tone.

"Your assistant, I'm sure, will be able to answer me without making fun of me . . ."

"She isn't here, she's in the sacristy ironing and there's no extension."

"Oh, it's not important, I'll call some other time. How is your market for religious antiques doing?"

"Bastard and blasphemer!" and Don Galetta slams down the receiver. Angelo hastily pours down his throat the glass of red wine he has ordered, goes outside, and heads for the church. It has begun to rain again and the fog blends with the flare of distant lightning. He starts to run, he only has a few minutes before the small gate is locked again. He flings open the door and there is the Lord's veterinarian, the usual cigarette between her lacquered fingers, the usual caftan down to her heels. She too is startled.

"Good evening, signorina. Please excuse me, I'm here only for a sentimental matter."

"What do you want now?"

"You know, I had grown very attached to Aurora Lometto. Now I've become obsessed by the loss of a memory. Her eyes. I no longer remember what color they were" Angelo says, delving again into the magnetic black of Giorgina Washington's pupils when they removed the green bandage from her forehead.

"Is that all? they were . . . hard, yes, and that's why they continued to open up."

"Hard? as if of glass?"

"I mean hard. As if . . . a hard film or . . . She had suffered a lot from her eyes, they said. Hard and yellow, frightening."

"Yellow?" how strange.

"A bit of jaundice, perhaps. She had all the misfortunes" she says, edging with her iron around an embroidery on a stole. "Oh, Don Nocciolini!"

The priest looks at Angelo, furious.

"Excuse me" Angelo says and rushes toward the small door that opens on the cemetery. He pulls back the inside bolt with all his strength, he is already outside under a torrential rain. Excited voices behind him. Angelo hears the crunch of gravel under running feet. It is the agitated sound of people demanding a return of justice, something from below, very much under his steps, tells him that his marble angel was never placed over the right corpse.

"Whoever you may be under here, forgive me, but this wasn't for you. I'll make you another one just as pretty as soon as I can" he says loudly, so those two over there, at the door, kept back by the rain, can hear. And as he picks up the white angel with both hands a close-up lightning flash gives him a glimpse of a sparkle right there alongside: the small perfume bottle with the gilded atomizer! It is the one Professor Witzleben used to perfume the pittosporum hedges! Dawn is under here instead of Aurora! With her eyes humanized by yellow contact lenses.

"But are you really sure that it was a newborn girl?" Angelo asks out of breath, shaking the rain from his hair. The two look at him pityingly.

"And what was she supposed to be, a dog?" Don Galetta says, suspended *a divinis* in a contemptuous impatience.

"They're all crazy. Today that little man with the yellow Vandyke brings a small bottle here with a spray that seems piss, and now this one comes to take back his little statue . . . all crazy, crazy." The veterinarian sighs, pushing home the bolt. Angelo stops to stare at them, grateful for all these confirmations they are giving him without meaning to: that the devout are not accomplices. In the name of the

Lord they act or *omit* truly in good faith for the good of a humanity in bad faith. Then under the stunned eyes of the priest and his *perpetua* he goes out through the semicircular corridor, looks around in the church, stares at the empty altar where the *Crucifixion* used to be, and dashes out through the portal, down the five steps with his retrieved angel. Who knows whether Giorgina Washington came out well and if she was really placed with all honor in a crystal casket like a sleeping princess, vertically, or horizontally, in her trough-crib. Or, if a botch, thrown away with the other carrion that are growing maggots over there, behind the stable in the common grave. And who knows whether now, dissensions placated and difficulties set to rest, and the little rascals properly scolded for this new prank, everything goes ahead in the best of ways with the "Bolero" in the background. And Professor Witzleben has finally found the right style in which to sacrifice his many times patched-up virgin and make her ascend to the human rank par excellence: death . . . Dog hairs! "Some thick hair!" Lometto's skill in passing off an ugly bitch as an acceptable hairy mongoloid! and nobody who, officially, dared express doubt on the matter of the ersatz-flesh funeral service! Her little paws and her little paw-hands inside tiny gloves and knitted woolen booties, a funeral, a mass, a benediction: from a TWA container to a consecration, though not very Jewish, nevertheless still within the ambit of the divine.

A turn into Private Road, in the direction of the underground-farmhouse–manor of Lometto & Co.'s mysteries. There will be absolutely no need to have recourse to the reel, to threaten Edda with doing so, revealing her interesting condition with her sons. There must be so many other corpses and crimes scattered through the wounded astonishment of any middling entrepreneur, it will be enough to go to the trouble of wanting to open one's eyes and dig in one's heels about the fact that glowworms aren't lanterns and vice versa. And if every background, despite or thanks to the fact of his wanting to see through it, will vanish into thin air, Angelo will be able artfully to invent another that will descend, dragging down with it Lometto or Edda or both, in the living flesh.

Some lights of the Mikado of horrors are lit, it must be dinnertime. There isn't even one of the typical watchdogs, what brazenness: they feel safe, they take no precautions, they think that no one with less than servile intentions would dare approach. Now they must have heard the car door slam more than necessary, Don Galetta will as usual have phoned. He rings the bell.

"Who is it this late?" says the voice of a Lometto, Jr.

"Who could it be?" Angelo points out.

The silence of a grave inside, a silence which denotes many presences immobilized in themselves and about what to do next. After a long moment the light goes on in the hallway. The door opens. Lometto steps out shielding the door, alongside of him the profile of a black polyester hip, behind him from the kitchen come first Ilario, then Belisario, then Berengario.

"I brought you this" Angelo says, entering preceded by the marble angel, held aloft with both hands like a tabernacle. "You know better than I do where to set it up in front of Aurora, the true Aurora."

The small fledgling fathers lower their heads shamefacedly and pull back frightened, but with a feigned fright, simulated to gain time. Perhaps they are already preparing one of their exploits, on how to stuff a spoilsport, and if he's an interpreter, everything considered, wouldn't it be best to empty him out by extracting his tongue first or hang him up by a hook in the neck, like a rag doll on a yucca plant.

Now Angelo and Celestino stare at each other fixedly.

"By the way, Lometto, I received a phone call from your Belart" Angelo says; Lometto holds his breath, spellbound by the whiteness of the statue which is reflected on the angel's exterminating expression. Nobody wants to accept the statue, also Edda still stands there with her arms behind her back. Lometto has gotten even fatter, there are no signs of particular discomfort in his exposed eyes, it is no longer the same face that uncovers its glasses as if it still had a soul it wanted to bare. He finally seems to have understood that he does not dispose of any soul to which he can have recourse, not with Angelo. It is the impartial face of a man who for a rare time in his life has been cornered and rallies all his histrionic professionalism to appear truthful. And now what will Lometto do? Angelo reads something that constantly slides from his thoughts to that of his antagonist. He sees hazy things in the nebulous atmosphere: there are stairs to descend or ascend, then a sudden change of temperature, like a humidified room, an armored door, a flaming lamp which emanates an eternal light and the mummy of Giorgina Washington upon a catafalque and above her a large painting, a solitary figure with its arms spread wide against the background of a calvary at dawn. Lometto whispers to Angelo "It's a print . . ."

". . . and an invitation to lunch with the usual *or else* . . . main dish very rare meat and no side dish, this time . . ." Angelo adds.

It is Edda who tightens her hand on the automatic door handle and shuts it with superfluous energy. Lometto is wetting his lips. Now in her other hand has appeared a key which she turns one two three times in the lock, the sons show one after the other their hands, which come out from behind their backs each holding something tightly: a thick needle, a thread of raffia, a tiny scalpel and a handful of hemp. Edda pulls out the key and clutches it in her fist. Angelo stares at Lometto and smiles at Edda and the bloodthirsty giants and shakes his head.

Lometto opens his hand under Edda's fist, stares at her. Now the key leaps into the open palm, is slipped back into the lock, goes back over the same route, under fading vulpine eyes.

"Four months. And not a phone call, not even a postcard . . . Hey, Nana, there's a short trip coming up."

"A trip from the Tower?"

"No, to The Hague, by car."

Oh, the thorn of that last word . . .

Monday.